Also by Anthony O'Neill

Scheherazade

The Lamplighter

A NOVEL

Anthony O'Neill

✠ ✠ ✠

SCRIBNER

NEW YORK   LONDON   TORONTO   SYDNEY   SINGAPORE

SCRIBNER
1230 Avenue of the Americas
New York, NY 10020

SCRIBNER and design are trademarks of Macmillan Library Reference USA, Inc.,
used under license by Simon & Schuster, the publisher of this work.

For information about special discounts for bulk purchases,
please contact Simon & Schuster Special Sales:
1-800-456-6798 or business@simonandschuster.com

DESIGNED BY ERICH HOBBING

Text set in Garamond No. 3

Manufactured in the United States of America

1   3   5   7   9   10   8   6   4   2

Library of Congress Cataloging-in-Publication Data
O'Neill, Anthony.
The Lamplighter : a novel / Anthony O'Neill.
p. cm.
1. Philosophy teachers—Fiction. 2. Edinburgh (Scotland)—Fiction.
3. Serial murders—Fiction. I. Title.
PR9619.4.O54 L36 2003
813'.6—dc21   2002036453

ISBN 978-1-4165-7532-0   ISBN 1-4165-7532-4

Photographs for chapters IV, V, and XX © Peter Stubbs, Edinburgh—www.edinphoto.org.uk;
for chapters II and XVII © SCRAN, Edinburgh; for chapters I, VIII, XXII, and XXIII © GWW
Archive, University of Aberdeen; for Prologue and chapter XII courtesy of Peter Stubbs;
for chapters VII, IX, X, XI, XIII, XVI, XVIII, XIX, and Epilogue from *Victorian
and Edwardian Edinburgh from Old Photographs* by C. S. Minto (Anchor Press, 1971).

The Lamplighter

✠ ✠ ✠

There is a dreadful Hell
    And everlasting pains;
There sinners must with devils dwell
    In darkness, fire and chains.
        ISAAC WATTS,
        Divine Songs for Children

If God has thought proper to paint "thief," "robber," or "murderer" on
certain brows, it isn't for nothing; nay it is for something—that the like
of me should read the marks, and try to save the good and virtuous.
        JAMES MCLEVY,
        Edinburgh police detective, 1861

Prologue—1860s

THERE WERE NEARLY sixty of them in Edinburgh and they swarmed out of their crevices at dusk and swept through the city in a systematic raid on the streets, closes, wynds, and parks. Beginning as always with the ornamental lamps outside the Lord Provost's home, they clambered quickly to the heights of Calton Hill, coursed down the gilded esplanade of Princes Street, curled through the courteous crescents of the New Town, and sallied into the sooty recesses of the Old Town labyrinth, regulating themselves by the church bells and shirking only those darker tendrils of the Cowgate from which even the light recoiled. In less than two hours they knitted together a jeweled chain of lights that on clear evenings resembled an inverted cosmos of sparkling stars and on nights of dense fog—when sea mist merged with chimney smoke, locomotive steam, and the noxious emissions from over-crowded graves—helped enclose the city in an enormous glowing lampshade. They were the "leeries"—the lamplighters—and they were rarely seen in the sun.

✠

Evelyn lived in the Fountainbridge Institute for Destitute Girls, in a district of gasworks and foundries where the lamps were few. She was not the youngest (six) and far from the oldest (sixteen) of almost a hundred orphans. The building itself was an erstwhile slaughterhouse, the dormitory a tilted killing floor, and the past still lingered in the bloody sawdust that had infiltrated the cracks and powdered the rafters and even now, on the trigger of a significant thunderclap, would sprinkle across the startled girls like a benediction.

But these were not unhappy times. Broth and buttermilk were moderated with fresh meat and greens, typhus was unheard of, tuberculosis and scarlet fever rare, and only respiratory complaints and toothaches kept the girls spluttering and moaning through the night. As well, the orphanage governor's vibrant young wife indulged the girls as her "bairns," and took a special fancy to young Evelyn, who with her raven hair, blue Highland eyes, and boundless imagination was like herself reborn. She offered the girls toffee drops, shared books from her considerable library (she was the daughter of a respected advocate), and promised that she would one day escort them on a trip to the Pentland Hills, where they would see the same farm animals which to that point they knew only from their squeals (the slaughterhouse had been relocated to larger premises across the street). The woman's enthusiasm was so infectious that it even managed to mollify the Calvinistic extremes of her husband, Mr. Lindsay. But then her visits to the orphanage became less frequent, for she was imminently to give birth to a bairn of her own. And when she expired in a manner that was eminently mysterious—for her constitution was as resilient as Evelyn's—a pall settled over the Fountainbridge Institute for Destitute Girls that had about it the stench of martyrs' blood, tormented souls, and a shame as old as Deuteronomy.

✠

Mr. Lindsay withdrew all sugar from their diet, rationed the meat, replaced *Robinson Crusoe* with *The Redeemer's Tears*, Jonathan Swift with John Knox, tore the woodcuts from *The Pilgrim's Progress*, stepped up the Scripture readings, and tossed away the punitive tawse in favor of a knotted birch cane. Unsettled by the new severity, the nurses assured the monitors that it was a natural grieving process that inevitably would pass. But it did not pass.

On the dormitory ceiling above the rafters there was a flamboyant mural of indeterminate age—"The Signs of the Zodiak"—beneath which innumerable livestock had unceremoniously been hammered between the eyes. Invested with life by the pulsing glow of the streetlamp outside the window, it had become the prism through which Evelyn, clamped by sheets in her iron-frame bed, would nightly unleash her fever-ish imagination. Weaving astrological deities with the stories of Mrs. Lindsay and her own rudimentary knowledge of history and geography, she would mesmerize the other girls with flights of fancy and slide into sleep on paths already slippery with dreams.

When Mr. Lindsay had the ceiling painted black, shortly after his wife's demise, her imagination found compensation in the streetlamp itself, which in summer drew moths, in winter flurries of snow, and each evening its own Prometheus—the leerie—who himself began to assume properties of great mysticism. In a silence undisturbed by so much as the rustle of bed linen she would follow his cheerful whistle and crisscross-ing advance up the street to their very own lamp, hear the snap of his lad-der clamping onto the crossbar, the tread of his ascent, the uncapping of the glass lid and even—if she strained hard enough—the hiss of running gas and the pop of ignition. She never saw more of him than his billowing shadow (like the moths blown to fantastic proportions), but in her sto-ries she was able to contrive for him not only a precise appearance but a host of progressively more ambitious itineraries, so that from his beat in Fountainbridge he had soon progressed to the docks of Leith, then across the waters to the boulevards of Paris, and before long was draw-ing his fire map from the bazaars of Constantinople to the quarters of Cal-cutta and the temples of celestial Peking. The monitors warned her that this was no time for nocturnal storytelling, but Evelyn was stubborn by nature and nurture, and responded to subjugation with only rebellion. Inevitably she was ushered to the office of Mr. Lindsay.

"It gives me no pleasure to see you here, child." He was a figure cut from boilerplates, with hair of steel grey and pouches of rust beneath his eyes. "But you are thick-sown with ideas that serve you ill, and it is my righteous duty to turn you into a worthwhile servant of the Lord."

In the absence of his own daughter he saw his charges not as surrogates but as beings that feasted greedily on God's grace at the expense of his own, and he despised them in a way that for him was indistinguishable from love.

"I should not have to tell you that life is rarely sweet, child. That a fiery imagination scorches all before it, and the independent will needs to be crushed to prevent later grief. You should remember that life is but a way station to the greater realms beyond, and if you turn your mind to anything it should be the rewards that await you there. Though I doubt," he added somberly, "that you are meant for paradise, child, and I tell you this without joy. The righteous are destined for the palace of heaven, but for reprobates there is only a room with no doors and windows, for beyond it there is only darkness."

"Then I shall dream as I like," said Evelyn boldly, "for no harm can be done by it."

At which point Mr. Lindsay caned her legs so righteously that she limped for a fortnight.

✠

While she healed, the visits of the lamplighter were succeeded by no stories, but in time she could not restrain herself, and the furtively whispered adventures of Leerie enthralled the others with the added varnish of wickedness. The monitors were appalled, fearing that they themselves would be censured. But it was another incident entirely that returned Evelyn to the governor's notice.

Colored inks were strictly forbidden in the Institute and the girls had been divested of all drawing implements but for the slate pencils that were returned dutifully at the end of each lesson. But one winter's day during noon recess a fantastic chalk apparition materialized on the blackened courtyard wall: a majestic dragon, part Babylonian and part *Beowulf,* and rendered with exemplary style. When Mr. Lindsay discovered it, however, he saw only a demon, and he ordered the girls lined up in the dormitory.

The matron was instructed to search the girls for the incriminating utensil. But when she came to Evelyn she found the young one refusing to open a tightly clenched right fist.

"Pinion her," Lindsay ordered, and, lodging his cane under one arm, he forcibly raised her hand and uncurled her fingers.

A blunted stick of white chalk fell to the floor and rolled to the tips of his gleaming boots.

He stared at it for endless seconds and eventually raised his eyes.

"They have a saying where I come from, child. 'If you draw the devil on a wall, you invite him to appear.'"

"I drew not the devil," Evelyn insisted.

"By God, you will hold your tongue, child!" Lindsay was spluttering with rage. "The devil speaks as much through your insolence as he does through your fantasies. And aye, if he responds only to the birch then so it must be. I ask not for forgiveness, because I act only in the name of greater mercy, but be assured the responsibility hangs about me like Matthew's millstone. So step into my office, child, and let it be done with haste. No amount of imagination will shield you from God's displeasure."

She uttered not a bleat through the caning, but from across the street came the transitional cry of a calf turned to veal.

✠

There had never been enough consistency in the orphanage for anyone to be surprised by a change of heart, so when Evelyn was called again into the governor's office some weeks later, directed to a corner desk, provided with several blank sheets of paper, pens, and inks, and instructed to draw, she did not question why, though she suspected that no good would come of it. Her abstinence had by that time become so wearying that she could not resist, in any case, and she filled sheet after sheet with vivid images. Mr. Lindsay inspected them as he would an unfavorable testament, but he did not punish her for them, simply locked them in a drawer and ordered her to return the following day.

At the end of two weeks she was introduced to a handsomely attired man with a star-shaped scar under his right eye. Bright-eyed and energetic, with thick black hair shiny with macassar oil, he dropped to his knee and smiled affectionately. He was holding a china doll.

"Hullo, Evelyn," he said. "Or do you mind if I call you Eve?"

"This is your father, child," Mr. Lindsay informed her. "Mr. James Ainslie, the Laird of Millenhall."

Evelyn was puzzled. The matron had told her she had been dumped on the orphanage steps when she was barely the size of a turnip, and as far as she knew her surname was Todd, not Ainslie. And while she had often dreamed of her mother, she never thought it possible that she might have a father.

"I have only recently learned of your existence, Eve," Ainslie said.

"And in truth I thought you had not survived. But now I have come to claim you from the Institute. I know it will be difficult for you to leave, but I assure you that you will not regret it. You must not resist, Eve. I urge you not to resist."

Evelyn looked into his hopeful eyes, smelled his sweet soap and lotions, and glanced over his shoulder to a governor staring down his nose like some city chambers statue.

"I will not resist," she assured Mr. Ainslie, who at once hugged her with conspicuous relief, as though she truly had a choice.

✠

The transfer was effected with unusual haste, as though Mr. Lindsay were eager to be divested of her. She was not given time to say farewell to her friends, but the disappointment was quickly suffused by a mounting excitement. She was escorted to a waiting brougham and deposited onto one of the plush seats, the first time she had been in a carriage. When they swept around the corner it was impossible not to feel that she had begun a great adventure.

"Millenhall is a wee distance from here," Ainslie told her brightly. "You'll love it dearly, Eve. But I'd very much like it to be a surprise for you."

He produced a tartan scarf and secured it around her eyes, chuckling like a game player. But even the blindfold could not contain her imagination.

"We enter a country road," she declared excitedly as the carriage wheels trundled onto a dirt track. "Tree branches overhead. Sycamores—I smell the sap."

Ainslie laughed.

"Chestnuts. Whin-bushes with a honey fragrance."

"Your imagination serves you splendidly, Eve."

She heard wood warblers, song thrushes, and other strange birds. She felt the shadowy caress of swaying branches, and inhaled air tainted by wood smoke and the tang of paper mills. She was intoxicated.

The brougham drew up, a gate creaked open, and they wheeled around a substantial forecourt. She was led across flagstones, through a poorly oiled door, and carried up stairs to a chamber smelling of freshly disturbed dust. Here Ainslie lowered her to the floor and closed the door behind them. He unfastened the blindfold.

She found herself in a bedroom, furnished with only a washstand, a chair, and a freshly quilted bed. The shutters were tight, the only light entering through a frosted gable window. But she thought it worthy of a princess.

"Do you like it, Eve?"

She nodded vigorously. She could barely contemplate such luxury.

"It's important that you settle in very quickly," Ainslie said. "And when the time comes we shall go places. On boats, on fox hunts, and we shall travel on trains. Would you like that, Eve?"

She thought there could be no greater pleasure.

"Later," he promised, smiling. "When your mother recovers."

He locked the door behind her, leaving Evelyn thrilled by the prospect of at last being embraced by the woman who had dumped her like a turnip on the cold orphanage steps.

✠

But for a long time she saw nothing other than the paneled walls of her bedroom. Twice a day she was brought warm water and hot meals by Ainslie, who spellbound her with recollections of his travels and military service. He had lived much of his life in London, he said, and journeyed as a merchant seaman to Bombay and Java, caught shrapnel in the face in Sevastopol, and been stationed with the Royal Rifle Corps at the Gold Coast of West Africa, where he had played the pipes to the monkeys like the Pied Piper.

He produced watercolors and inks and encouraged her to paint, and as she had nothing else to do her output was prolific. Ainslie inspected each picture with enthusiasm, and seemed especially approving of those featuring an avuncular gentleman dressed in a peaked cap, blue fustian jacket, and grey scarf.

"Who is he, Eve?"

She told him it was Leerie.

"A man you know?"

"A man I have never seen," she replied. Her picture was in fact a composite of appealing features: the pointed beard of the old doctor who visited the orphanage, the emerald eyes of the maintenance man, the attire of the coalman.

Ainslie considered the matter. "And this Leerie . . . do you imagine that he might walk in those fantastic cities you draw?"

"There is no place he cannot go."

Ainslie encouraged her to show the lamplighter in all manner of exotic locales and situations: in storybook castles, in fabulous forests, soaring over waterfalls on winged steeds. The pictures were carried off at the end of each day, and she saw them again only when she was asked to refine a select few, as though they were being prepared for exhibition before the Queen.

✠

Her incarceration, such as it was, was nothing new, and the bed was soft and capacious, the food plentiful, she had pretty new petticoats, and in health she flourished. She discovered one of the shutter leaves was ajar, and occasionally was able to see out to a neighboring graveyard overgrown with thistle and weed, and to the forecourt, where carts would frequently pull up laden with articles of furniture. The lodge was being hastily fitted out, it seemed, and into her own room Ainslie introduced a looking glass, a wardrobe, and a painting of the Zoological Gardens.

"Your mother will arrive shortly," he assured her. "And soon we shall go for a long trip—to some of those same exotic cities you draw for Leerie."

That very afternoon she saw a trap pull up and a sandy-haired woman alight at the door. The woman, most agreeable in appearance, was greeted by Ainslie with an intimate smile and a whisper, and Evelyn, turning from the window, paced restlessly around her room, excited by the possibility that she had for the first time set eyes on her mother.

But when Ainslie came up that night he wore a funereal expression.

"I want you to come downstairs with me, Eve," he whispered, "and I want you to be very quiet and respectful. Your mother is very ill, as I have said, and may not recognize you."

It was the same person she had seen from the window—she was sure of it—and yet when Evelyn approached she found her mother unnaturally white, pale-lipped, and creased with dark lines. The woman trembled as she enclosed Evelyn in spidery arms, and smelled of powder and wax.

"Let me look at you, Eve," she croaked, and tilted her daughter's face to examine her with ill-focused eyes. "Can you ever forgive me?" she implored. "Do you think you might be capable?"

And though Evelyn was poorly acquainted with remorse and was reluctant to admit any measure of disappointment, she sensed no real love in her mother's voice, no genuine grief, and when she withdrew it was with confusion in her heart.

Later Ainslie discovered the loose shutter and had her windows painted over from the outside.

✠

More furniture was shifted into position. She heard new voices, edgy murmurs, and once a woman's voice raised in indignation. Ainslie appeared one evening with an apologetic look.

"I regret that I've not been able to attend to you, Eve, but there has been much absorbing my attention. Soon, I promise, we will travel far. But in the meantime it is very important to me that you feel at home. I want you to think of this as the house where you have always resided. Do you think you could do that? Forget the Institute entirely?"

She suggested that it would be no disagreeable task.

He smiled. "Then if anyone asks, you will not challenge the notion that we have always been a family?"

It was a curious request, but she felt disinclined to resist.

"I fear your mother has worsened, Eve. I've had to call on a special doctor I know from my days in Africa—a tribesman of the Ashanti. If you see him I do not want you to be alarmed. He could well be our salvation."

He left without locking the door.

When she ventured out some time later she heard a visitor being conducted around the lower floor like a prospective buyer. She waited at the top of the stairs and eventually Ainslie appeared with the strangest man she had ever seen.

He was exceedingly tall, as black as Crusoe's Friday, with a gleaming oversized head ringed with hieroglyphs. He wore flowing saffron robes and carried a scepter of interlocking bones. Chewing continuously and humming without melody, he made a sweeping survey of the hall, his eyes lingering on the Turkey carpets, wicker baskets, mounted stag's head, and other articles Evelyn had not previously seen, as well as on the cornices, the architraves, the paneling, the pilasters . . . on every distinguishing feature in the hall, in fact, as though making a concerted effort to emboss the images onto his memory.

When his head rotated toward the upper level, his eyes settled on Evelyn and his humming abruptly ceased. She felt pinned in place, violated by his scrutiny, but his broad lips quickly peeled back in a smile. Ainslie indicated that she should come down the stairs.

In the visitor's proximity she smelled herbs and ash. The man stroked her head and caressed her face with velvety fingertips, and in this simple gesture she perceived more tenderness than anything she had felt from her own parents. He examined her with his cloudy eyes, traced the contours of her neck and shoulders, and eventually resumed his tuneless humming.

He was taken on a tour of all the upstairs rooms, spending well over an hour in Evelyn's bedchamber alone, as outside Ainslie assured Evelyn that all was proceeding well and that shortly they would go on their great journey.

✠

Her door was never locked from that point, but she was discouraged from moving from her bedroom, and even when she did she saw little but closed doors, covered windows, and incongruous furnishings. Her mother was still present and recuperating, Ainslie assured her, though she was too ill to be seen. Water and food continued to be brought up to her with prisonlike regularity, a long-case clock marked the passage of several days with its wheezy chimes, and Ainslie paced around with a bearing of increasing impatience, or perhaps apprehension.

✠

One night the house timbers groaned as though squeezed by some supernatural force. A storm pounded the roof and lightning sprayed through the gable window, expanding and contracting her little room like bellows. A trembling Ainslie entered briefly and lit a candle by her bed, promising that it would soon subside. But the lightning was alarmingly close. The paneling appeared to undulate. An unpleasant odor invaded the room and the air rapidly chilled. Evelyn, with the blankets bunched up around her, watched her breath condense in clouds until she was convinced a spectral shape was sewing together in the air above the bed. And when the candle flame flared and hurled a very human shadow onto her wardrobe she could no longer bear it.

She bolted for the stairs, but halfway down Ainslie gathered her up and attempted to soothe her.

"Eve? What's wrong?" But he himself was shaking.

She told him a man had got inside her room.

"A man?" He exuded fear like a musk.

"In my room!"

"Well . . . who do you think he might be, Eve?"

She could not answer.

Ainslie forced a laugh. "Then we should find out, eh?"

He braced himself and started carrying her back up the stairs, his heart hammering against her like a fist on a door. Rain was spilling from the eaves and trickling in the pipes. As they inched stiffly down the hallway it was evident from the very quality of light that the room was not empty.

A yard from the door Ainslie crouched down and forced Evelyn to the floor. With stony features he prodded her back toward the room as though offering a lamb to some beast of prey.

Evelyn stared at his averted eyes, inhaled his sickly perspiration, and suddenly saw with great clarity that, whatever this man called himself, he was not her father. That he represented no security. And she understood very clearly, too, that the powdery woman had not been her mother. There would never be any journey, or any freedom.

She was alone, as she always had been, and stepping back with revulsion she was simultaneously drawn to the bedroom as though to a great fatality.

She turned and froze with disbelief when she saw the man, standing on the far side of the bed, his face gilded by the candlelight.

He had a pointed beard, a peaked cap, a blue fustian jacket, and a grey scarf, and his emerald eyes seemed to shine with all the lamps of Edinburgh.

She gasped in astonishment, and his face creased with genuine compassion.

"It's me, Eve," he affirmed.

His whisper was as light as gossamer, and the sincerity of his affection was manifest.

"It's Leerie . . ."

He beckoned her forward and she moved trancelike into the room. Ainslie shut the door behind them and twenty years later the streets were red with blood.

December 1886
Chapter I

Thomas McKnight, Professor of Logic and Metaphysics at the University of Edinburgh, had certainly noticed the young lady busily taking notes in one of the rear benches, but he did not stop to contemplate the incongruity, the implications, or indeed to give it much thought at all. He went on lecturing as though in a dream.

"Gentlemen, I want you to look at me now and ask yourselves if I exist. I want you to consider the possibility that I might be no more than a shadow, or something else of completely immaterial value. Not, I hasten to add, because I regard myself as a ghost, or indeed a shadow. In fact, I would be recognized as human in any number of venerable faculties. In Law they would certainly admit into evidence that I am a man, of average height and unremarkable appearance, silver-haired, green-eyed, and spade-bearded. The Faculty of Medicine, were I to surrender my body to its examinations, would certainly attest that my heart pumps blood, that my lungs inflate with air, and that I give every indication of being a living human being. In Science they would draw samples of my blood, dissolve specimens of my flesh in jars, examine them under microscopes, and ascertain that I am a bipedal composition of carbon and water, of the *Homo* genus, and of an age defying calculation. And the Faculty of Divinity might see nothing godly in me, or even saintly, but it would have little difficulty accepting me as a temporal manifestation in which there is nothing fundamentally miraculous."

His speech was a clockwork mechanism unwinding with great precision and little enthusiasm. Each word, each inflection, and every flash of humor had been so calculated, and delivered with such little variation, that were he to lapse into an unexpected silence or be forced into a hasty departure, a student of a previous year, consulting old notes, might be able to complete his every sentence—the entire lecture.

"No, gentlemen, if I ask you to look upon me as a shadow it is because in this chamber it is our duty to peel away all existing layers of prejudice, strip back all preconceived notions, divest ourselves of all resistance, and cast the withering eye of skepticism on the fact that I exist at all. That the chair in the corner exists. That the room exists. That anything beyond the room exists. And to emerge with the possibility that everything we have established and agreed upon may in fact be a collusion in ignorance."

There would come a day, no doubt, when he would not need to be present at all. When he would be spared the ordeal of pacing around the room puffing clouds of pipe smoke into the frigid air—the University's gas pipes had clotted, leaving the halls without light or heat—and be replaced by a tin conch projecting his voice with coils and vibrating filaments. When he would not, as today, have cause to envy Professor Egan of Botany, who had repaired to the Tropical Palm House of the Royal Botanic Garden, there to lecture his students amid the misted glass and sweating ferns.

"Now in the front row the gentleman with the red hair has little doubt that I exist: he has fixed me in place with his eyes, my voice resonates in his ears, and I exude a certain warmth without which the room might be fractionally colder. And in the middle row the lad in the velvet jacket, being of a more poetical persuasion, has already ascribed to me certain human qualities. Charming? Indubitably. Wise? Without question.

Generous? To a fault, gentlemen, though I urge you not to test it. Even tempered? Of course, but only because my placid nature is balanced so precisely with eruptions of unexpected violence."

But where once he had filled the chamber with laughing throngs, his tone was now too hollow to elicit anything but a token chuckle. He had not even bothered to familiarize himself with the student roll, so that where once his lecture was interpolated with interchangeable names—Aldridge/Devlin/McLaren/Raithby/Scott—he now relied on his weakening eyes and the bridge of his imagination (it did not really matter if that jacket was really velvet). He did not despise his students, but he felt of no use to them. They wanted to see him as an inspiration, a target beyond the travails of confusion and hunger. They were greedy for enlightenment—or at least cap and gown—and all he could offer was despair.

"Now of those two appraisals," he continued, turning cheerlessly at the end of the platform, "it would be safe to suggest that the one offered by our sentimental, velvet-jacketed friend is a process of induction based on unreliable criteria. Perhaps in appearance I remind him of his favorite uncle. Or perhaps his least favorite uncle. Perhaps my voice evokes memories of another lecturer, or a tradesman, or a doctor, with whom he is already well acquainted. In all instances we can agree that he might well be the victim of a misapprehension based on subjective interpretation. But it is our duty in this chamber to apply the same flame of doubt to the assumptions of his redheaded classmate, gentlemen, and conclude that there is nothing that the senses can perceive objectively, and no object upon which we do not subjectively impose a reality."

The students, clustered in the benches closest to the door, and itching to spring to freedom as soon as the bell rang, needed no uncanny instincts to sense his disillusionment. In the latest edition of *The Student* they had already registered their bemusement:

> *What ails Professor McKnight,*
> *He seems in a spot of blight,*
> *There's no Logic to a humour seldom sighted,*
> *His Philosophy entombed,*
> *It might need to be exHumed,*
> *Or good Lord, the Prof will never be McKnighted!*

McKnight could barely remember it now, but upon first arriving at the University he had felt as though appointed to the Sacred College of Cardinals. They were reorganizing the library at the time, and when asked how much space should be relegated to the works of philosophy he had responded, with the confidence of an astronomer mapping the stars, "One bay for the works already written and sixteen for those yet to come." But now, an eternity later, he had come to accept that his was a faculty with no exhilarating triumphs, no sacred cities, and no achievable destination.

"Plato introduced the demon of doubt . . . René Descartes labeled him . . . Spinoza and Leibniz toyed with him . . . Hume and Reid with their formidable Scots steel refused to be ruled by him . . ."

He had reached the meat and bones of the lecture now, a litany of names as endless and exacting as any Genesis genealogy.

"Kant urged us to look beyond logic and knowledge . . . Malebranche linked belief in the real world to supernatural revelation . . . Bishop Berkeley suggested that the pillars of existence have become dangerously fragile . . ."

Hearing the odd fragment echo off the flat walls and curved benches, he raised his eyes to make a perfunctory sweep of the class—it was important at least to pretend he was aware of his students' existence—and noticed, without much interest, that the young lady had shifted forward a few rows and was no longer taking notes.

"Hamilton saw God in the Unknown . . . the Scots championed the doctrine of the dual existence of mind and matter . . . the temporal devil . . ."

It was not unknown for women to attend university lectures, though officially they were tutored only extra-academically, and the voluntary nature of their presence meant that he himself saw few. This one—an ethereal creature, her paleness offset by clothes of clerical black—seemed to have lost interest in his lecture entirely, not that he could blame her, and was staring fixedly out the window.

"The devil of nature . . . of metaphor . . . of time . . ."

He followed her gaze, almost against his will, and noticed some police officers striding across the quadrangle, escorted by an unusually grave-looking Rector. He might have been disturbed, or just plain curious, but he had forced even the most pressing realities into the abstract and found it hard to summon a flicker of concern. And when he turned back he could not even see the young lady herself. She had moved again, or sunk behind another student, or disappeared like an apparition. It did not seem to matter.

"Locke compared the mind to blank paper, which the senses help furnish with words. Hume extended the metaphor with the notion of impressions, in which ideas become like type on a printing press. But it is left to questing temperaments like ours, gentlemen, to wonder how much of that book is autobiographical, how much societal, and how much set and inked by cosmic forces beyond our understanding . . ."

And how much is simply financial ledgers, medical reports, and documents of title; and how many pages should be squandered on anything less pressing and basic.

"We study no scrolls, we shatter no rocks, we disinter no bodies and plunge into no volcanoes"—he raised his voice irritably because some loudmouth in the corridor was calling for the Chancellor—"and yet we are the greatest adventurers in these halls. We burst through barriers without fear of what monsters might lurk behind. We bring light to the hideous and we digest the unpalatable. And we do all this because we cannot live without the truth. Because we alone, gentlemen, are intrepid enough to unlock the gates of the Unknowable, and courageous enough to allow the stream thus released to carry us to regions that time alone will reveal. And he whose heart quails at the prospect still has the option of returning to the comfortable bosom of illusions."

And to the bosom of purpose. And contentment. And altruism. Gazing one last time upon the emburdened heads of his students—struggling to work out if the lecture had really ended—he wondered if his adversaries in Divinity were right, and the only victim of delusions was the philosopher who foraged fruitlessly through the Realms of God, seeking something minuscule enough to bring nourishment to his miserable existence below.

"Though it must be admitted, gentlemen . . ." he added, in a spontaneous coda, "that I find it difficult to question the subjective nature of the cold when my very tongue freezes to the side of my mouth . . ."

He sighed wearily and, sensing that his students were still unsure if they were dismissed—where once the finality of his tone would have been clear—he added curtly, "Be off with you, then."

The students rose as one, with a conspicuous relief, and piled around the door.

"And one other thing . . ." McKnight said resentfully. "One other thing. If I hear any more sniffing in my classes"—he glared at them—"I will personally wrap my scarf so tightly around the offender's head that I might well obstruct the circulation to his brain. . . ."

Almost immediately he chastened himself—it was the sort of impulsive rebuke that had gone well beyond his control—and retreated guiltily to the antechamber to collect his books and empty his pipe. Emerging a few moments later he again registered the presence of the mysterious young lady, lingering behind to speak to him, to ask him an urgent question (something about the devil; it was as though he could read her mind), and though he actually paused for a second, and almost stopped to accommodate her, he quickly thought the better of it. He avoided eye contact, nodded evasively, and escaped into the corridor without a second glance.

He was threading his way through milling students to his cluttered crow's nest of an office, there to lunch on week-old bread and insipid black coffee, when he was approached by the somber-looking Rector.

"Tom . . ." the man said, still managing to use his Christian name with some hint of endearment. "Have you heard?"

"Heard?" Moving from place to place McKnight had developed a sort of irresistible momentum, unable to be pinned down or intimately examined.

"About Professor Smeaton? Of Ecclesiastical Law?"

"Smeaton?" McKnight, who had barely slowed, rarely welcomed the name: Smeaton had frequently attacked him at the meetings of the Senatus Academicus for his reported "devout atheism," for his heretical teachings, and for his indulgence in abstractions no more productive than a child's desecration. "His objection to the Barlow Endowment? Aye, but I expected nothing—"

"No, no, Tom. I mean what happened this morning, at dawn."

"I heard nothing."

The Rector swallowed. "He's *dead*, Tom."

McKnight actually stopped in his tracks and stared incredulously. "Smeaton?" he asked. "Dead?"

"Torn open. As if by wild beasts."

McKnight frowned. "Where?"

"The body was found in the New Town, by a milkmaid."

"In which street?"

"In *several* streets, Tom."

McKnight's frown deepened. "Murdered?"

"Aye. By someone. Some *thing*. The body has already been identified and removed to the mortuary in the Cowgate. The police are with the Chancellor now."

McKnight set the pipe stem between his teeth.

"There'll be an investigation, Tom. You might be called in for questioning. Formal procedure, you know. For motive, and the like."

"Of course . . ." said McKnight, and the Rector, clearly uncomfortable in his presence, set off to inform the others.

Resuming his way up the corridor, McKnight approximated a familiar look of consternation, so that any onlooker would have little doubt that he was troubled by the news. But inwardly, and with an unsettling laceration of guilt, he thought that the murder was the most logical thing he had heard in many years.

Chapter II

Carus Groves, acting Chief Inspector of the Edinburgh City Police, had been imagining this moment all day. Indeed, for all the horror he had encountered since sunrise, all the demands of investigation, the interviews, the confrontations and speculations, it could be reasonably calculated that most of his mental energy had been engaged in projecting him forward to the moment when, squeezed into his desk in the corner of his Leith Walk bedroom, illuminated by a paraffin lamp, he dipped his pen into an inkwell, raised the nib over a blank page, and lovingly inscribed, in a headlinelike script:

THE MURDERER FROM THE MEWS

Then he settled back to watch the glistening ink dissolve into the paper with the authority of God's inscriptions on the Sinai tablets.

It was not the first title he had considered. "The New Town Murder" had given way to "The Murder of the Great Professor," which in turn was superseded by "Murder by the Good Book," and—penultimately and most ambitiously—"Murder Most Dark & Sinister." He had settled with delight on "The Murderer from the Mews," not for its accuracy—there was in fact little evidence that the killer had been hiding in the mews lane—but for its alliterative quality, which even to his policeman's ears, attuned more to whistle blasts than poetry, carried a sonorous ring.

He returned to the text promptly, for his little schoolroom desk was not conducive to lounging (and indeed had been purchased, from the defaulters' furniture market opposite Craig's Close, for that very reason), and applied his loving pen to the page.

This was the most brutal example of attack this detective has had the misfortune to set his eyes upon, he began, and this was no exaggeration: Professor Smeaton's body had been scattered across the intersection of Belgrave Crescent, Queensferry Road, and Dean Bridge in three ragged chunks, a nauseating spectacle for Groves, who had seen smothered children ("The Lothian Street Horror") and maggot-infested corpses ("The Body in Dean Village"), but on the whole had been spared involvement with the city's most gruesome investigations. And this was the reason "The Murderer from the Mews" carried such enormous personal significance.

Groves had been at the forefront of nearly three thousand cases in over twenty years, but in all that time he had toiled in the consuming shadow of Chief Inspector Stuart Smith, a man famed throughout the kingdom for a near-perfect correlation between investigation and conviction. By virtue of his authority and experience Smith secured nearly all the cases involving capital offenses and the sensitive realms of Society, leaving Groves to concentrate on hucksters, thimblers, drunks, Jezebels, shoplifters, and other pests—a thankless task he performed with inordinate pride. Singular in the force for his literal interpretation of the first oath—"He must devote all his time & attention to the service"— there was nary a petty criminal in Edinburgh who was not familiar with his overhanging brow and frostbitten dome, and had not seen him at some stage stalking the wynds, patrolling the streets, and nabbing suspects with a brusque clap on the shoulder and a stern pronouncement in the ear: *"You cannot escape the hand of Groves."*

But Chief Inspector Smith was currently in London supervising the installation of his likeness in Madame Tussaud's Wax Museum, in a Chamber of Horrors tableau celebrating his arrest of "Silly" Sally Crombie, the Canongate poisoner hanged in Calton Jail ten years previously. The *Evening News* had dubbed him "Edinburgh's First Man in Wax," and later—when it was pointed out that Sir Walter Scott and David Hume, not to mention Burke and Hare, were already residents of the famous museum—simply "the Wax Man," noting that it was a status he shared with Napoleon, Lord Nelson, and Henry VIII.

Groves, on the other hand, had invested his hopes for immortality entirely in the completion of his memoirs, begun some thirteen years earlier and augmented every evening with detailed notes relating to fresh cases. When each investigation was complete he would critically examine his ledger-book notes, embellish those details not verifiable, add a moralizing flourish, and only then decide if it was worthy of transcription into his gilt-edged casebook entitled *The Fearsome Knock of Inspector Groves; or, The Reminiscences of a Detective in the Modern Athens.*

The book would of course not be complete until he had officially retired, and to this point had been perused by only one acquaintance: the late Piper McNab ("The Philosopher on the Corner"), the fully kilted bagpipes player whose accessible fund of gossip and wisdom—the man had been more a fixture of the streets than any patrolman—had earned him, in Groves's view, the honor of being the first to run eyes across his much-considered words. McNab had registered admiration for the work but had observed, in the friendliest manner possible, that to ensure success the book would need to be "seasoned and garnished" with more of the "salacious and sensational" incidents without which the contemporary reader's "lamentable attention span wanes and his voracious appetite for scandal goes unsated." In effect what he was saying—and Groves was not so conceited that he could not see it—was that a record of shopliftings, forgeries, snowdroppings, and petty larcenies did not constitute the makings of a publishing milestone. "Blood lust," the sage Piper offered, "is as much in the nostrils of the curate's wife as it is in the muzzle of the Cowgate cur."

I had arrived as usual at Central Office in the High Street when I was informed of this most grisly tragedy, he wrote. He had in fact been relishing the idea of performing an unsolicited tidy-up of the Wax Man's appalling paperwork when a breathless constable had bolted in with the news: the Reverend Alexander Smeaton, Professor of Ecclesiastical Law at the University of Edinburgh, had been viciously murdered. A shiver

immediately ran through Groves like a lightning strike. A leading figure of the city's intellectual and theological communities cut down. No
witnesses. No culprit apprehended. And now it was upon his rounded
shoulders to apprehend the demon responsible. This was no longer the
sort of case that he observed from the periphery; this was his very own
investigation, and it was his duty to be decisive—he was aware the
others were looking at him expectantly.

"I want a photographer," he said. "Four constables to roam the area.
A sheet, of course, and the hand ambulance. Notify Dr. Holland. And
where the devil is Pringle?"

Dick Pringle was the Wax Man's indefatigable young assistant,
assigned to Groves for the duration of the Chief Inspector's absence. It was
a sensible yet in practice curious arrangement: Pringle was in awe of
seniority, and Groves, for his part, was assiduously guarding his mystique
for fear that the slightest flaw might unveil his vulnerability.

"Smeaton, sir, did you know him?" Pringle was sitting beside
Groves in a racing cab, four constables clinging to the outside.

"There are few in the city I do not know," Groves replied, though in
fact he had little reason to associate with a divinity professor.

"He was none too popular at the University, they say."

"They say the same about many at that institution," Groves remarked,
making a mental note to launch his investigation at the University as
soon as possible.

They arrived in the New Town shortly after nine, minus one of the
constables, who had fallen off swinging around the Mound, to find the
murder scene closed off by local patrolmen.

*No one had ever seen a body like it, and my first instruction once the photog-
rapher had attended to his duties, was to have it covered by a sheet, to protect the
delicate sensibilities of the ladies in the district.*

Belgrave Crescent was in an area of perfectly aligned terrace houses,
strictly regulated shrubs, and mirrorlike gold plaques—home to famous
surgeons, advocates, academy presidents, and "more knights than there
were in Camelot." Groves had always disliked the New Town for its self-
reliant discipline and secretly enjoyed the idea that its immaculate
streets had been soiled with blood.

*The Professor was a man of habit, every morning he cut across Dean Bridge
on his way to the morning office at St. Giles, the murderer was waiting for him*

at the end of the Crescent, lurking there in the mews opposite the Holy Trinity Chapel.

It seemed an eminently feasible speculation. But Groves's search of the immediate area, as the professor's body was shoveled into three oil-skin sacks, turned up little: cart tracks in a shoulder of mud, loose straw, some hoofprints. The milkmaid who had discovered the corpse, drained by the various manifestations of shock, was interviewed and her details recorded. A deacon was interrogated as he scrubbed blood from the church facade with a soapy brush. The constables swept through the district to question residents. Groves and Pringle themselves headed off to face the family with a palpable sense of purpose. In nearly all the cases involving violence with which Groves had been associated (including "The Hawker's Surprise," "The Grief of the Bereaved," and "Not Seen in the Stars") the perpetrators were of the victim's kin. He had even dared to pronounce as much to Pringle while raising the brass knocker to administer his fearsome knock: "Watch closely when I prod," he said under his breath. "There's likely some wound I'll make bleed."

RAT-TATTA-TATTA-TAT.

But Mrs. Smeaton was an inconsolable mess. Further, she had already been informed of the death—had identified the body, in fact, at the request of an enterprising constable ("Get the cove's name" was all Groves said)—thwarting a proper assault. There were two children, one in Cornwall, the other on the Continent. The servants were accounted for. There were no other close relatives in Edinburgh, and the widow could not conceive of possible motives.

"You must know that your husband was not popular at the University?"

"Who . . . who said such a thing?" she asked indignantly, a handkerchief clasped to her face.

"It . . . has been said."

"Lies!" she insisted, and the handkerchief bellied like a sail. "My husband was the most respected man in Edinburgh!" And she launched into such a sustained burst of sobbing that Groves saw no option but to retreat.

Once a Minister in the parish of Corstorphine, he lectured in Bible history and other church matters. Smeaton had written books on Agnosticism, Theism, and the history of the Holy Land to the time of Constantine. His class at the University was over a hundred strong, made up of budding ministers of the Scottish kirks, native and foreign, along with some older types—retired soldiers and advocates, mainly—who in their declining years had assumed an interest in matters theological. And to Groves every one of them was a suspect.

"He was intimidating in many respects, and marked with a corresponding appearance," the Chancellor of the University admitted later in his gloomy office. "You've seen his face, of course?"

Groves did not want to admit that the face was in no state to be appraised for its characteristics. But he had certainly examined a portrait in the Smeaton home. "A man to be reckoned with," he agreed suggestively.

"A man of strong views and little hesitation. A challenging man, yes, but I would not say threatening."

"Ah?" Groves offered a grin that might have been a smirk. "These lines are delicate, are they not?"

"I think you will find, Inspector," the Chancellor said, "that most of his colleagues were stimulated by his manner. Provoked, yes, but these are men of intellect who secretly relish a sport, no matter how much they might deny it. I can certainly think of no one who might inflict physical damage upon him."

"And yet his body now lies on a slab in the morgue."

The Chancellor ignored the insinuation. "You've heard of Professor Whitty in Forensic Medicine, of course? The finest in his field. I suggest you allow him to examine the body closely."

"You suggest that, do you? And how can I be certain that this man is trustworthy?"

The Chancellor frowned. "Whitty? Trustworthy? Clearly you don't know the man."

It was true, Groves knew Whitty only through his close association with the Wax Man, though in this alone he found sufficient reason for resentment. And the thought of the man now solving the mystery with one brilliant forensic flourish, and thus robbing Groves of his rightful glory, was decidedly unappealing. So he hastened on. "What of Smeaton's students, then? Young men are prone to grudges and rash temperaments."

"I think you might find these lads more devoted to prayer and reflection. They may not have loved Smeaton, or even liked him, but they respected him enormously, which you'll see for yourself when you meet them."

"And you?" Groves asked of the Chancellor pointedly as the two men departed the room. "What did you make of the man?"

The Chancellor paused to consider. "I think the University will be the poorer for his passing," he managed, closing the door behind him.

The divinity students looked ashen when informed of the news. Groves asked each of them a few terse questions and Pringle took a list of names and addresses. The professors were called one by one to a vacant storeroom beside the Chancellor's office, and—fortified by his contempt for such lettered eccentrics, who knew nothing of the real world— Groves passed much of the afternoon conducting curt interviews and meaningfully jotting notes.

There were a couple of these learned gentlemen, rivals no doubt, whose attitudes I did not like, they tried to look upset, but I knew Smeaton was not popular, and I could read on their brows the word "deceit."

"Any ideas, Inspector?" Pringle asked later.

"Nothing I am willing to admit at this stage."

The professor of forensic medicine—"Whitty by name and nature"— accompanied them in a carriage to the mortuary. "A body in three pieces . . ." he mused, shaking his head. "A case, it would appear, in which the body is as much a puzzle as the murder."

Groves frowned at the inappropriate mood. "A grand thing, sir, that you look upon this business in such a way. I assure you that this is no game."

"I can only pray," said the good professor, "that the culprit shares that sentiment."

The preliminary death certificate had been signed by the police doctor, subject to amendment, the manner of death listed simply as "decapitation by means unknown." An unusual "expression of feeling" had been appended to the bottom of the sheet: "Most Curious."

"That barely begins to describe it," said Professor Whitty, once he had peeled back the sheet and examined the pieced-together corpse under hissing gaslight. He pointed at the compressed head. "Observe the

mandible . . . the way it's been all but forced through the upper jaw
. . . the collapse of the septum . . . and the ragged character of the tears
to the throat. It's difficult to conceive of this as having been perpetrated
by a normal man."

"How so?" Groves asked through a tightened throat. There was the
penetrating odor of carbolic disinfectant in the air.

"It's as if the body were some sort of doll, made of rags and ceramic,
picked up by a spiteful child, squeezed around the arms, bitten around
the head . . . and torn simultaneously in three directions."

"You're not suggesting this was done by a child, sir?"

"*Cum grano salis,* Inspector. But still . . . the enormous power it
would take . . ." Whitty tapped a pencil against his chin. "And acts of
unusual strength are invariably linked to passions of exceptional magnitude . . ."

"A madman?"

"I'm not certain," Whitty admitted. "The intensity of this hatred . . .
I find it difficult to attribute this to a human being."

"You're saying it could have been an animal, then?"

"Did you find any evidence of an animal in the vicinity?"

"Only hoofprints."

Whitty pursed his lips. "I was thinking more of a saber-toothed
tiger."

But Groves could not quite read his tone. "You can't make any conclusions, is that it?"

"Not on a superficial examination, no, and to go further I'd need a warrant from the Fiscal. Though it seems to remind me of another recent
case." He glanced at Pringle. "You remember that man brought in last
month?"

Pringle nodded. "The lighthouse keeper?"

"Aye. The way his face had been gouged from his skull?"

Groves interjected. "What man was this?"

"A case of Chief Inspector Smith's," Pringle told him. "You must
remember, sir. The man walking his dog by Duddingston Loch?"

"He was a lighthouse keeper?"

"Retired."

"A murder of profound savagery," Whitty explained. "And like this
requiring a formidable strength. As if a pitchfork had been inserted into

the man's head and the face wrenched free. A most curious business indeed."

Later, returning to the High Street Central Office, Groves quizzed Pringle for further details. "I thought that particular investigation was closed."

"For all intents and purposes it was," Pringle agreed uneasily, "but it could be reopened at any moment."

"So there was no perpetrator found?"

"Chief Inspector Smith called it a robbery-based homicide committed by persons unknown."

"And was the victim in fact robbed?"

"There were no valuables on him."

Groves thought about it. "He was a retired lighthouse keeper. Walking his dog. What sort of valuables would you expect to be on him?"

Pringle looked sheepish about his peripheral involvement. "There seemed no better explanation at the time, sir."

Inwardly, Groves felt exhilarated. Not only had the exasperating Professor Whitty failed to discover anything with his postmortem examination, but now the mystery had deepened with a possible connection to a failed murder investigation conducted by his illustrious comrade Chief Inspector Smith. It was widely known that the Wax Man was unorthodox and self-serving—that he would do anything to preserve his sterling record and was far more interested in grieving widows than murdered men—but official disapproval was mitigated by his frequent glories. Now Groves had a chance not only to emulate the man but to embarrass him by revisiting a case prematurely retired.

In the Central Office he felt the eyes fixed on him—the expectation, the aspect of deference—and in response he seemed to grow a foot taller. When he was approached by Douglas Macleod of the *Evening Dispatch* he was generous with the details. The *Dispatch* was already running off a special edition with several news columns headed "Respected Professor Killed in New Town." Ideally the case would provide headlines for a further week and culminate in the triumphant "Respected Inspector Arrests Killer." But there was still, Groves admitted to himself, a lot of work to be done.

He filed an initial report for Sheriff Fleming, checked the student and teacher rolls against criminal reports, fielded a variety of unsolicited theories and offers for assistance (there was a woman who claimed to have dreamed the murder in precise detail; he told Pringle to send her away), and before he left for the evening he was summoned to the office of the pumpkin-faced Chief Constable. "A sinister business, Carus."

"Aye."

"A man of God struck down in one of our finest streets. The Fiscal will be keen for answers. Do you think you can handle it with no assistance?"

"I have Pringle."

"Aye, I mean Chief Inspector Smith, though. He returns from London in a day or two."

Groves bristled. "I think there might be other matters occupying our Wax Man."

"That's so," the Chief Constable admitted. "I don't believe Smith would wish to get involved in an investigation already begun."

"If," Groves said meaningfully, "the investigation did not really begin a month ago."

But if the Chief Constable understood he gave no hint. "I wish you all the luck you are not able to make for yourself, then," he finished, dispatching the Inspector with a rare expression of sympathy.

At the end of the day, Groves wrote presently, *it became clear that The Murderer from the Mews was a mystery daunting the finest minds in the city, and I alone had the strength to commit myself wholly to its solution.*

He withdrew his pen, blotted the ink, folded the ledger book, and slid it away under the desk lid, retrieving as he did the gilt-edged "official" casebook, holding it lovingly in his hands and wondering how soon he might enter the complete episode in its sacred pages. Groves came from a particularly large family—his father, a godless Aberdeen whaler, had spent just enough time ashore harpooning his mother to produce a formidable litter—but he was certainly the first of the brood to attempt such an ambitious chronicle, and in this he felt an almost paternal responsibility. He had no children of his own. He could not foresee any progeny. He lived with two of his seven sisters and was married more devotedly to his vocation than a Jesuit missionary.

He flipped to the opening page and read with pride his carefully worded dedication.

THIS BOOK IS DEDICATED
TO THE CLERGY OF CRIME FIGHTING
THE DETECTIVES EXCELSIOR
THE ADMINISTRATORS OF JUSTICE
WITHOUT THESE MEN THERE WOULD BE
BARBARITY!!

How long he had agonized over the phrasing! The simple analogy to the clergy! And the word *excelsior* (the exact meaning of which still eluded him)! And how perfectly noble it now seemed!

He sighed with satisfaction, put the book away, pried himself from the tiny desk, and worked the numbness out of his limbs. He made his toilet, changed into his nightshirt, laid out his braided inspector's tunic for the morning, loosed the curtain cords, and, to the sound of his sisters snoring musically in the adjoining room, slipped into his narrow bed with the excitement of a child awaiting Christmas.

In the darkness, sea mist kissed his windows and swept through the city like an Egyptian plague. Warm and tightly bound in his multitude of sheets and blankets, Groves was the victim of a roiled imagination, unable to rest for the feeling that the whole city was laid out before him waiting to be seized. He actually resented sleep, that it would disengage his conscious mind from more active service. And indeed, for all his overconfidence and childish excitement, he was about to venture down darker and more perplexing paths than any he had previously imagined.

Chapter III

A STROLL had become a march. McKnight had no pipe in his mouth, his cane was barely touching the ground, and his customary waxen pallor had surrendered to a ruddy tint. His blood was clearly pumping, his mind swarming with ideas, and he was moving with unusual zeal, as though impatient to be home. It was an incongruity that Joseph Canavan, to whom the harmony of their stride was as natural as breathing, could not fail to notice.

"You've heard by now, of course?" the Professor asked as soon as he encountered his walking companion at their nightly rendezvous point outside the Free Church on St. Leonard's Street.

"Smeaton?" Canavan nodded somberly, already struggling to keep pace. "An odd business."

"What do you know?" McKnight asked. Canavan came from among the Irish of the Old Town, where tongues printed news more efficiently than any press.

"Probably not much more than yourself. It happened in the New Town somewhere—"

"Belgrave Crescent. At the junction with Dean Bridge."

"—and it was extremely brutal. The body torn apart like a ginger-bread man."

"Aye—a colorful description."

"How old was he?" Canavan asked. "Sixty-five? A terrible, terrible thing. But at least, by God's mercy, it was swift."

"Swift, certainly." McKnight knew that Canavan spoke sincerely, when others of his kind might be toasting the man's demise: Smeaton had had little tolerance for the Irish. "Savage, undoubtedly. But was it really a premeditated murder? Or just an arbitrary killing?"

"Has anyone suggested it was arbitrary?"

"There was no indication of theft, or of any identifiable weapon being employed. And the attack was positively bestial."

"An animal hunting for prey," Canavan mused. "Giving no thought to identity. Is that what you're saying?"

"Not quite. There were no signs of postmortem predation. A hungry beast would be inclined to take home some dinner, wouldn't you think?"

"Perhaps the beast was disturbed."

"Of course. But still I wonder how many savage beasts there are loose on the streets of Edinburgh."

"Those you would not regard as human, in any case."

McKnight smiled. "Were I to include bipedals," he said, "the field would be too vast to contemplate."

The Professor's unusual humor, to Canavan, was as appreciable as his pace. It was not that McKnight was ever openly morose, or even self-pitying, but after two years of walking together the two men were capa-ble of recognizing in each other the most minor fluctuations. This when ostensibly they had little in common. The Irishman was half the Profes-sor's age and hewn by hard labor and emotional scarring. He was brawny and tall. He had never stepped inside a university. He was keenly reli-gious and a sentimentalist. He was naturally poor—he had never known anything else—whereas the Professor had lost his inherited wealth through financial mismanagement in the wake of his wife's death.

"The search will begin for suspects, then."

"The search has already commenced," McKnight corrected. "At the University this very morning. And I'd be profoundly surprised if I have not already been considered as one of the suspects."

"You?" Canavan snorted.

"Why not?" McKnight said, and made a show of glancing around, as though for pursuing detectives. "Consider the facts. Smeaton was an acknowledged nemesis. He was vocally disapproving of my teachings. He objected to all my proposals and tried to obstruct my funding. I had every reason to hate him."

"But not to kill him. You couldn't."

"Maybe so, but that doesn't mean I cannot be a suspect, if a motive is seen to exist."

"And it doesn't mean you should enjoy the idea, either," Canavan observed, "because it offers you some sense of urgency."

McKnight chuckled guiltily. "Well . . ." he admitted, accepting that there was little he could hide from his friend.

Canavan was a night watchman at a crumbling cemetery three miles from central Edinburgh. McKnight lived in a sequestered cottage nearby, not far past Craigmillar Castle on the Old Dalkeith Road. Some years earlier he had first noticed the longhaired Irishman striding home ahead of him as he himself set off for the University. Depending on the season he would frequently see him again on his own way home, the younger man now carrying a small bag of victuals in preparation for the night ahead. But in those days, despite the fact that they moved at a pace so identical they might have been marching in formation, they never spoke, or even acknowledged each other's proximity. The morning walk, for McKnight, was a precious opportunity to marshal his thoughts, to take solace in the bracing air and stirring bird life, and arrive at the University, if not bursting with enthusiasm, then at least in a mood that was not acrimonious. On his journeys home, feasting vicariously on the waft of savory dinners, he found refuge from the need to orate, to reason and listen: a relief too precious to be invaded by company. He consistently spurned offers of transport from market gardeners and coal carters, even the occasional affluent student in a plush carriage. Besides, as much as he could not afford cabs, he equally could not afford to be seen as one deprived of them. He cultivated the air of one who favored a challenging constitutional, and it quickly became true.

But there was one week when his debt became so tyrannical that he could barely afford to eat at all. He was not even past Craigmillar Castle Road when a chilly sweat seized him, his vision filled with pinpricks of light, his chest constricted, and his cane slipped from beneath him; the next thing he knew he was on the ground, delirious, his nostrils filled with musty earth, and his stomach heaving but without anything significant enough to eject.

He might have resisted any offers of help, but before he could object he had been hoisted from the ground, slung like a lamb across some great wood-hewing shoulders, and carried, with no say in the matter, back toward his cottage. The indignity was heartbreaking. He tried to mumble a protest but his Good Samaritan was not listening. And inevitably he became aware that his savior was in fact the Irishman, his younger shadow, the very same man he had ignored so often on his walks—a man who surely would have little to say anyway, and clearly nothing worth hearing. But now, if he allowed this to go on, he would be indebted to the man permanently. He wished he were dead.

McKnight was not to know that such gratification was the farthest thing from Canavan's mind. Finding himself taken home by a circuitous series of back paths and then deposited gently on his comfortless bed, the Professor inexplicably lapsed into colloquialism—"You won't be hailing a sawbones now, lad?"—but apart from a token nod the Irishman was entirely unresponsive, as though refusing even to acknowledge his own presence. The younger man left the cottage for a while—impossible for McKnight to gauge how long, for he lapsed into unconsciousness—and returned with bacon rashers, a bread loaf, and a few sips of whisky. He administered these more or less forcibly to his patient, made sure he was well provided with blankets, and departed without a further word. Two days later, when he resumed his walks to the University, McKnight nodded gratefully in the man's direction and found a reciprocating nod so unassuming that he was suddenly convinced—he knew it instinctively—that the episode had been recounted to no one. It might never have happened. Canavan had gone out of his way to preserve a stranger's idiosyncratic sense of dignity. It was impossible not to feel trusting of such a man.

"You've read Smeaton's treatises, of course?" McKnight asked presently. They were passing the modern villas of Newington, where lamplight winked and flared in the freshly installed windows.

"A few of them. He was a passionate man."

"Even passion must be disciplined, or it is prone to develop into zealotry."

"It would be wrong, I think, to call Smeaton a zealot."

"Dogmatic, then."

"Dogmatic, perhaps," Canavan agreed, "but not a madman. Even if you did not always agree with him."

McKnight smiled, never tiring of the Irishman's magnanimity. "Not mad, or not entirely. But Smeaton was by nature a fighter, as you know. He challenged all sorts of reforms. To politics. To worship. To the very idea of hymnals and the installation of church organs. To the increasing prevalence of science in our educational institutions. Naturally he was disdainful of the geologists, the biologists, and most especially of Mr. Darwin. Everywhere he looked he saw a threat, and every threat drove him even deeper behind the barricades."

"These are challenging times for theologists," Canavan admitted, "and the strength of Smeaton's response shouldn't be unexpected."

"Of course. When one's beliefs come under siege, the modest man questions his convictions and the stubborn one dons the breastplate of righteousness."

"*Breastplate* is a little strong. Smeaton was a clergyman, not a centurion."

"I use the phrase pointedly. 'The Breastplate of Righteousness' is the title of one of his own published tracts."

"Well . . ."

"Smeaton's opinions were as fixed as railway tracks," McKnight insisted, "and the catechism as clear to him as gravity. He had cast himself as a prophet and was incessantly warning others of damnation. He wanted to redeem people. He needed it as a vocation. And such men almost actively generate enemies—for the very challenge of the fight."

Canavan thought about it. "I think I can vouch for the Irish," he said. "And I'm not aware of any other community where the hate might be murderous. I can offer no obvious suspect."

"Nor do I believe that there will ever be an obvious suspect. And you know, for all the indignation Smeaton might have incited through his ideologies, for some unaccountable reason I suspect his death is unrelated."

"It's not like you to be intuitive."

McKnight grunted. "Admittedly I have no sound reasons. But the manner of the man's death is such that I cannot reconcile it with any regular grievance. A very bold statement was made, it seems to me, and I sense that is connected to some profound transgression."

"Of what possible variety?"

"I'm not sure. Not at this stage."

"At this stage?"

"I don't know," McKnight protested uncomfortably. "We are truly in the streets of confusion."

They crossed Peffermill Road into a lampless area of darkling meadows and windblown trees, the branches foiling and parrying overhead, and here McKnight decided to let the matter rest, embarrassed to admit that he had been truly confounded by hunches and irrational convictions. That he felt uniquely challenged by the mystery. That those same capacities of logic and reason—which only hours previously had seemed as empty as his bank accounts—had suddenly taken on the aspect of invaluable resources. But then Smeaton's death represented a beginning, he was strangely sure of it. He felt the tremors like an approaching thunderstorm, and it was only a matter of time before he would be specifically summoned.

Forging into the inky darkness in a pensive silence, both men now simultaneously discerned a spot of light ahead like a clouded lamp on an advancing carriage. But as they came closer they perceived that it was in fact a person's face perched atop garments of implacable blackness. And when they were near enough to distinguish features it became clear that the figure was an unaccompanied woman, staring dazedly ahead as though having returned from the scene of some tragedy. Gliding wraithlike up to the two men without seeming to register their presence, she breezed past on their left with the fluency of a black cat, and only when she was gone was McKnight struck by the strange conviction that it was the same ethereal lass he had glimpsed earlier that day in the lecture hall. But when he turned to verify this suspicion, she had already disappeared, swallowed by the night as though by the sea. Noticing that Canavan had also turned, similarly unsettled, he shook off an eerie presentiment, and a strange sense of self-consciousness, and quickly sought a digression.

"And how goes that lady friend of yours?" he asked. "That—what's her name—Evelyn?"

"Emily," Canavan corrected stiffly. "Emily Harkins."

"Emily, that's right. How is the lass?" Neither man was by nature inquisitive about the other's private life, but for a while Canavan's enthusiasm about a certain Welsh shop assistant had become uncontainable. She was an angel, he claimed, a vision of peerless beauty.

"I no longer see her," Canavan admitted.

"Whatever happened?"

The Irishman seemed reticent. "We . . . parted."

And then it struck McKnight in a flash, and he cursed his poor memory for such matters, and his compounding insensitivity. Because in fact he had heard of this same Miss Emily Harkins through the University grapevine: the comely miner's daughter who inadvertently had stolen the heart of the thrice-married Francis Purves, President of the Mercantile Insurance Company and benefactor of the Faculty of Law. The wealthy laird—an eminently disagreeable fellow—had squired the lass, beguiled her with gifts and blandishments, and quickly had her galloping through the lilies of his estate on his prize steeds, his partner in matrimony and stepmother to his impressive brood. It had certainly crossed McKnight's mind that this was the same lass who had been the object of his friend's infatuation, but he had simply not spared sufficient time to ponder the full consequences. Love, to him, was a foolish affliction bringing nourishment only to poets, narcissists, and the irremediably self-destructive.

"Were there any indications?" he asked uncomfortably. He seemed to remember that Canavan had been on the verge of proposing.

"There were warnings, I suppose."

"How did she explain herself?"

Canavan seemed unwilling to elaborate. "I think she had lived long enough without security," he said, generous enough to make excuses for her.

But McKnight suddenly saw with great clarity that the lass had rejected Canavan simply for the condition of his cuffs. And though the Irishman might publicly disavow any disappointment—and might indeed still harbor an abiding affection—McKnight was sure that, for an idealist, such an act of cynicism would have been a bitter blow.

"When I married my own Meg," he now found himself saying, not sure how it would help, "the two of us had no savings and few prospects, but we had each other, and by God that was enough. And those early years were tough, let me tell you, but we fought through it, and I believe we were never happier." And for a moment he was lost in a delightful nostalgia for those sunny days prior to the onset of his wife's pneumonia, when it seemed they might live forever on the strength of the one's philosophies and the other's practicality.

"Truly, I envy you . . ." Canavan managed, but at the same time he was dismayed by his own insincerity. For he had seen an old calotype portrait of the married couple against a backdrop of St. Giles, and no amount of charity could suppress the notion that the much-mourned Mrs. McKnight, for all her exemplary qualities, had a face that would not have looked out of place glowering from one of the cathedral cornices.

Which left both men wondering, as they continued into the cutting breeze, why it was so often the case that an angel could have the heart of a demon and a gargoyle could have the heart of a saint.

Chapter IV

DEEP INTO the following night a clinging haar swept off the firth with the east wind and crept like a tide of floodwater across the fields between Craigmillar and Liberton, piling up against the barbed walls of Drumgate Cemetery and, eventually surmounting them, drifting in threads and knots around the tangled sycamores and lichen-blotted headstones. Well after midnight Canavan heard a groan and an unearthly creak, like that of a crypt being opened, and saw a whorl of disturbed mist rise up and dissipate in the southeast corner. He picked up his feeble lamp and headed out to investigate, though in truth he was not concerned.

Ominous noises were familiar to Drumgate. Dating to the days of James IV, the old cemetery was set on an acre of sloping earth and bramble between the ruins of a chapel and a burned-out hunting lodge, the resting place of everyone from lords advocate and Covenanters to consumptive peasants and Gilmerton coal miners. Before it was finally closed by the Chief Medical Officer in 1870, it had become the cheapest available burial ground for the city's poor and destitute, and opportunistic superintendents, seeing to it that not an inch of earth was left unturned, had shoehorned tinderbox caskets and canvas-wrapped cholera victims into graves often scandalously close to the surface. The crowding of this subterranean population, together with a legacy of subsurface cavities from the body-snatching days (the cemetery's isolation made it an easy target), meant that, years after its official closure, it was still prone to belated settlings and unexpected tremors, its air still polluted with the occasional eruption of some long-brewed putrescence. As well, though there were no cats in the cemetery (unlike at central Greyfriars, where they ran in swarms) and no foxes, badgers, or even birds, a sizable colony of long-eared bats had taken residence in a decayed ash tree close to the center of the yard, and, squeaking and flapping, they would regularly wheel out on some nocturnal expedition. All of which meant only that there was no shortage of explanations for any sound, disturbance, or apparition emerging from the ruptured earth, and no real reason for Canavan to investigate other than an ingrained sense of duty and a simple need for purpose.

Rumors that the place was haunted—a malevolent demon, they said, or a specter of supernatural terror—most likely had been cultivated by insecure sextons hoping to ward off the medical inspectors in the 1860s. But the reports of desecration ultimately had become so frequent, and so inexplicable, that the Town Council had gone to the lengths of appointing a nominal superintendent and a night watchman: families of historical renown were buried here and, notwithstanding the cemetery's official closure, there was still the odd addition to a family tomb. But though not ill-disposed to the belief in miracles or any other permutation of the supernatural, Canavan himself had in four years of solitary nights encountered nothing that raised even a mild shudder. And certainly he had seen no demon.

With the lantern held at shoulder height he now picked his way diligently down the curling paths. He knew every headstone, plinth, and cracked entablature, every rock, thorn, drooping branch and berry of cotoneaster. Where possible he avoided crossing the graves themselves, but many of the paths were so narrow and uncertain that quite often he had no option but to pick his steps over the consecrated plots and hold his breath respectfully. In the southeast corner, where the sound had seemed to issue, he turned in a circle, holding the lamp high above the mist, trying to find an anomaly.

There was nothing immediately apparent. He dropped to his haunches and made a sweep of the earth. He prodded around amid the rotting leaves. He angled the light at the gravestones, the table monuments, the sarcophagi, the bowed trees, and looked pensively at the domain of stars. The mist gathered at his side and oozed around him. He glanced back across the jumble of crosses, fractured obelisks, and fluted columns to the superintendent's cottage and the two-story cylindrical guardhouse, his second home, which in the light of the gibbous moon stood out like a castle turret in a sea of fog. He inhaled the frosty air, satisfied that there was nothing amiss but unable to reconcile a curious sense of disappointment.

It was ostensibly a miserable job, of indeterminate duration, offering no prospects and paying a pittance. When not performing his perfunctory rounds he spent the entire night in the tower with a rug draped over his legs, nibbling at his meager rations and reading academic texts provided most graciously by Professor McKnight. In lieu of a university education, the expenses of which were far beyond him, he now studied every subject from biology and astronomy to rhetoric and metaphysics, so that, while physically confined to a watchtower in a dour Edinburgh graveyard, his mind capered from primeval slush pools to the cusp of the very heavens. He was currently alternating among Brown's *Lectures on the Human Mind,* Thoreau's *Walden,* a tattered Douai Catholic Bible (a frequent companion; he was a self-educated student of Bible translations), and the numerous books of moral philosophy to which inclination made him most partial.

Canavan came from a family of ill-fated Galway coopers and from the start seemed destined for physical labor—quarryman, coalman, maltman—and the sort of menial tasks which were in truth far beneath his capabilities but to which his altruism inevitably directed him for fear of depriving some stranger of a more glamorous vocation. He was particularly sensitive to the brutality of comparison, and shirked any public exhibition of contentment that might throw another life into unfavorable relief. He was prepared to be uncompetitive—even in love, withdrawing from the pursuit of Emily's affections upon learning of a rival suitor—but only, paradoxically, because he felt so powerful: capable of wearing defeat with equanimity and simultaneously sparing the weaker and more volatile.

He felt most comfortable with McKnight, but in fact, for all his owlish hours and meager income, he maintained a wide field of acquaintances and was never less than adaptable, generously adjusting his manner and concerns among the Irish of the Cowgate, his festive companions in the shebeens, and the prostitutes of Happy Land. His association with the last might to a stranger have seemed the most puzzling—all the more so because he consistently rejected their sympathetic advances—but he was drawn to such fallen women by a powerful need to provide them with a male presence that was not carnal, parasitic, or admonishing (he had little interest in lecturing them). Hardy and tragic, with shoulder-length hair, doleful eyes, thickset arms, and a chest of considerable girth, he might well have caused many a female heart to flutter, but in intimacy he was hindered by a tremendous flush of impermanence—the implacable conviction that his life would be truncated without the realization of those things generally associated with happiness: marriage, progeny, a steady accumulation of years culminating in a peaceful surrender. But the profundity of this belief, which could be distinguished sharply from self-pity, afforded him a sort of transcendence: the ability to be unfettered by selfish and materialistic concerns, and the gift of savoring each new day, and each new friend, as an inexhaustible well.

Presently he released a despondent sigh and pushed himself to his feet. Satisfied that there had been no intrusion, but with his feelings still unresolved, he began sauntering in a circuit back to the guardhouse, flashing his lamp left and right at the graves like a loving matron in a dormitory. He favored the ornate stones of the southern wall, as always, where among the bunched scrolls, cherubs, drapery, and carved roses were the epitaphs that so invariably moved him.

I have finished the work
which Thou gavest me to do.

And the sun went down while it was still day.

And, most affecting of all, a comparatively recent epitaph that bespoke an intolerable tragedy: twenty-six-year-old Veronica, dead on December 25, 1865, and buried with her daughter, Phoebe, born and died on the very same day:

Sweet hallowed ground,
I'll long revere thee,
I'll cease to love thee but with life,
In thee my truest friend is laid,
My young, my dear beloved wife.

It was a terrible and exquisite thing, to have a heart that was not a muscle but a wound. McKnight, for one, would have found no logic in squandering pity on the unknown dead, but in sentiment the Professor only saw vulnerability, while in his own Canavan found a home.

He suddenly heard a noise—a thud—from the guardhouse, and a stir of activity: the musical clatter of his pencil. He narrowed his eyes, staring, but from a distance, with the tower unlit and the lamp in his hand, it was difficult to detect anything out of order. A knot of moonlit mist had temporarily enveloped the guardhouse in any case, and when it passed on, trailing its torn pennants, there was no indication of any presence. Clearly something had fallen, he decided—a book left in a precarious position—and after a few cautious moments, listening intently, he set off on a more direct return course.

When he arrived in the proximity of the tower, however, with the lamp creaking in its brace, he perceived further activity and saw what looked like a great inky shadow detaching from the window and soaring through shreds of mist.

For a moment he was frozen, unsure what he had witnessed and unwilling to trust his senses. But then he heard the great beating of leathery wings and, turning, discerned a squadron of squealing bats returning to the bowl of the ash tree.

He breathed out, satisfied with the corollary, and stepped into the tower to find that the Bible had indeed fallen to the floor with his notebook and pencil. Setting his lamp in place and resuming his seat, he drew the rug over his legs, huddled against the cold, and sat watching the breakers of mist swell and crash across the old cemetery and the last of the agitated bats file one by one into their nest.

He hoped that the solitude was not playing tricks on his imagination. It was part of his unforgiving fate that, as much as he felt at home in the presence of others, the majority of his time was spent alone. And there was always the possibility in such circumstances that a man might hunger for company of even the darkest and most inexplicable kind. So he now made a firm resolve to resist such inclinations, no matter how attractive, with all the power of his common sense.

It was only when he returned to the Bible—he had been studying the Gospel According to St. John—that he noticed that a single page had been torn raggedly from the binding.

He could find no explanation in reason or intuition.

Chapter V

By THE TIME the mist had reached the garden cemetery at Warriston, on the other side of Edinburgh, it had developed into a fog *as thick as the broth my dear mother once cooked* (Groves would later write), *though not half as warm.* The Inspector, wrapped tight in his uniform greatcoat, looked down at the ravaged grave at his feet and was given cause to remember the note the police doctor had appended to Smeaton's death certificate: "Most Curious." He sighed and snapped open his pocket watch. It was not yet noon.

Much larger and newer than Drumgate, Warriston Cemetery was arranged in a curvilinear network of pathways and graves ranked as precisely as New Town villas: Gothic shrines, neat Romanesque vaults, Ionic pillars, and Grecian urns in exacting and reverent order. In a triangle of the cemetery beside the gurgling Water of Leith, cut off from the rest of the yard by an embankment of the Edinburgh and Leith Railway, Groves now stood with Pringle, a couple of constables from the Stockbridge substation, a frustrated photographer, and an apprehensive cemetery superintendent, staring down at the brutally exhumed body of Colonel Horace Munnoch, "A Christian and a Soldier."

The Colonel's wizened remains, attired in the scarlet doublet, withered feather bonnet, and tartan of the Seaforth Highlanders, and with an impressive array of medals and clasps at his breast, had been dragged from the casket and dumped on the ground with his head bent grotesquely and the eyeless sockets staring past Groves's boots to the lines of wide-flung dirt. The chest had long collapsed, the uniform was discolored, and the legs were still dangling into the hastily dug pit. Blackbirds were waiting patiently on nearby branches to raid the disturbed earth.

Pringle was typically informative. "He saw action in the Kaffir Wars and the Crimea, I think, sir. He owned a lot of land—he was the fifteenth Laird of Strathrae in succession, something like that. He lived in Moray Place but spent most of his time in the clubs. He gave a lot of his money to Church interests. To the Magdalen Hospital. To orphanages." Some years earlier Pringle had been an "Educated Boy," one of the well-spoken youths paid to visit the city's clubs and read aloud selections from *The Scotsman* for those with inadequate eyesight, and he still spoke in a declarative tone.

"Aye," Groves said. "Episcopalian, was he not?"

"That's right, sir. Very strict, I believe. He did not sing, or drink, or even smoke. He was peculiarly spartan—you can tell that, if I may suggest, from his grave." The stone had only a name, a date, and a prosaic epitaph. "He did not care much for his estates. He had a mansion he barely visited and a couple of lodges. He divided his time between Edinburgh and Colinton. I think he owned an island somewhere."

Groves sniffed. He was well aware that the Colonel had been one of the city's most eminent citizens—he would not have been here otherwise—and he disliked being upstaged by Pringle, who had the advantage of a prodigious memory and years of reading obituaries to acquaintances of the deceased. But he had already embarrassed himself, upon first inspecting the corpse some minutes earlier, and he had little desire to seem petulant by issuing a gratuitous reprimand.

"Do we have any idea how long the man has been buried?" he had asked the superintendent. "Are there records available on site? Or can we determine something from the state of decay?"

"I think," the superintendent answered, a trifle nervously, "that the headstone will do as good a job as any." And he gestured to the dates: 1802–1872.

Groves immediately seized up with humiliation, and it took him a painfully long time to manufacture a particularly feeble obfuscation.

"Aye . . ." he said. "But I've heard they sometimes rearrange the plots at these cemeteries. Dig up the coffins and lay them elsewhere. I thought perhaps the wrong grave had been visited, and the wrong body brought up."

"We do no rearranging here at Warriston," the superintendent assured him.

"Aye, that's grand. Then we can agree that there has been no mistake." And he immediately performed a few laps of the grave, peering in from various angles with a frown of consternation, as though troubled by his examinations.

"What is it, sir?" Pringle asked.

"Most curious," Groves intoned, clicking his tongue, but he scrupulously chose not to explain.

He was tired, that was the truth of it. He had barely slept in two nights, giddy with responsibility and excitement, and exceptionally aware of the personal interest of higher authorities—the Lord Provost himself was said to be taking a more than mayoral interest—as well as the imminent return of the Wax Man. He felt a formidable weight on his every movement, order, and decision, all the more so because he had never been saddled with a case of such gravity. But, as unflagging and determined as he had been, his investigation into Professor Smeaton's singular demise was yet to yield any answers. The previous morning the Chief Constable had again elected to impress upon him the intolerable nature of the crime, and—with a trace of embarrassment, as though reciting a speech written by higher authorities—had stressed Edinburgh's sensitivity to such atrocities and historical intolerance for bloodshed. This when the city was practically marinated in the effluence of violence and death: in witch burnings, body snatching, public hangings, plague, pestilence, and the carnage of war. The blood had congealed between the cobbles and, dampened with rain, was still prone to infiltrating the nostrils and disinterring memories buried far deeper than personal experience.

Kindled by the exhortation, in any event, Groves had immediately headed back to the University, still at this stage filled with an adventurous spirit, and captivated by three things mentioned by Professor Whitty in his cursory examination of Smeaton's body. That the killer would need to be a man of extraordinary strength. Or a beast. Or a combination of the two.

He deliberately had singled out for questioning those associated with Smeaton who were of formidable size and manifest power or those whom, through some uncanny perspicacity, he regarded as having a close association with the animal kingdom. In particular he had been plagued by visions of one particular student he had glimpsed on his initial visit, a boy as black as coal tar and improbably attired in a Highland kilt. In fact, Groves congratulated himself for not underestimating the intelligence of the Negro races and could not bring himself to dislike them, when so many others could not see past the vile rumors. Indeed, reading the reports of the troubles in Zululand, where the natives had almost overcome the superbly armed British forces, he would frequently doff an imaginary hat in admiration. So when he tracked down the ebony divinity student—Morgan Forsyth, absurdly, from the West Indies—he let the boy know promptly, through his unflinching gaze, repeated sniffing, and the slapping of his notebook against his thigh, that he was wise to his capabilities and had little doubt that, were the idea to take hold of him, the boy would have no trouble summoning his reserves of brutish strength to rip his tutor to pieces, bolt for cover like a cheetah, or indeed orchestrate his revenge through some secret communion with the clawed and fanged beasts of the earth, such as whatever fauna it was exactly that populated the environs of darkest Jamaica.

Frustratingly, however, Forsyth was unfailingly eloquent and polite, seemingly unruffled by Groves's insinuations, and in possession of a most sterling alibi: he was in fact a lodger in the house of Professor Calderwood of Moral Philosophy, who could attest to his presence on the night of the murder. Groves shut his notebook and narrowed his eyes.

"I shall be speaking again to Professor Calderwood," he said, as though he suspected some collusion between the two, or even that, with Smeaton out of the way, the young black might now turn his sights on his own sponsor.

He conducted the remainder of his interviews in a state of distraction and headed off with a sense of relief to visit Professor Moir of Natural History in his laboratory of taxidermized zoology. Here he discovered just what he had suspected: the saber-toothed tiger was in fact extinct, so that in naming it as a possible culprit Professor Whitty had been speaking facetiously, or even through ignorance. "But there are no end of cats in this town," Moir added. "I should not have to tell you that, poor creatures."

"I prefer the noble dog," Groves said, thinking of his lamented police mastiff. (At one stage it had been customary for policemen to patrol with hounds.)

"I was referring to wild cats," Moir explained. "Predatory cats." And when Groves still looked perplexed: "Lions and tigers, if you will."

"If you mean the Zoological Gardens, sir, they have been closed for many years."

"I mean circuses, good chap." Moir studied the Inspector with frank curiosity. "Dear Lord, are you really telling me you've never been to one?"

Groves felt taken aback. Certainly he was aware of the city's circuses— in recent years there had been a proliferation—but since his days on the beat he had felt no inclination to venture inside, thinking them the domain of conjurors and acrobats, and other entertainments best left for the likes of children.

"I wouldn't be far wrong in saying there are more species of wild beast in Edinburgh than there are left in some Indian jungles," Professor Moir said with a disdainful snort. "And I doubt whether some of them have set foot on ground so cold since the days of the woolly mammoth. I'm often called upon to attend to them, you know. And it's not just circuses. You remember Wombell's Menagerie, of course?"

"Of course."

"They sold off their animals at Waverley Market some years ago. Everything. Lynxes, jackals, llamas, even a Tasmanian devil. A retired bank manager bought a black panther and walked it each evening like a trained beagle, until it ate his neighbor's whippets. There are likely a few of those lamentable beasts still in Edinburgh, chained in coops and stables somewhere. I suppose one of them might be capable of the savagery you mention, assuming it got loose. But you'll need more than good luck if you're meaning to track them all down."

Groves recalled a biblical verse that Piper McNab had been wont to quote: "Be sober, be vigilant, because your adversary the devil, as a roaring lion, walketh about, seeking whom he may devour." The sage piper had been drawing a connection to Arthur's Seat, the volcanic plug that dominated the city's eastern skyline and from certain angles looked uncannily like a great lion ready to pounce. Which only meant, according to the good piper's philosophy, that the inhabitants of fair Edinburgh should be uniquely aware that evil lurked in the most unlikely places and should be especially alert lest they be snatched in a moment of inattentiveness.

Groves decided he had no option but to take seriously the insinuations of Professors Whitty and Moir, and indeed of Piper McNab, and pursue such lines of investigation vigorously. He went first to Newsome's Hippodrome on Nicolson Street, but here found only tightrope walkers, trained Arabian steeds, laughing mirrors, and twirlie pokes. A similar story at Cooke's Circus, set in a substantial brick palace in Fountainbridge. But at Moss's Second Year Carnival at Waverley Market, in an inferno of flaring greaselamps and colored smoke, he discovered Count Batavia's Colossal Den of Performing Lions, being a couple of scrawny beasts in a cage stuffed with moldering straw. The Count himself seemed openly amused by the suggestion that his "bastards" might have broken loose or been trained for some nefarious purpose, and encouraged Groves to venture his hand through the bars and tickle their ears. But Groves had no intention of doing any such thing, thinking it might be some rash plan to have him eaten before he could manufacture more nettlesome questions. So the Count squeezed into the cage with his cats and slapped them, tugged at their tails, sat on their backs, and smothered them with kisses, and the beasts did little more than blink and rumble disconsolately. They were sedated with measured doses of whisky, he explained, even while performing, so that one would be in more danger from an organ grinder's monkey. And despite the man's crude mouth and Cockney accent, Groves felt inclined to believe him. He watched one of the somnolent lions as its lips curled back on glistening enamel fangs, feeling curiously aroused.

In a tormented state of half-sleep that night, however, he wondered if he had been unduly narrow in his focus, and was haunted by some of the freaks he had glimpsed in the course of the day, many of whom, like Chang the Mongolian giant, were of fearsome size and obvious mental instability. And in a state of semi-delirium he remembered the clown elephants of Moss's Carnival and had a startling vision of a rogue pachyderm

goring Professor Smeaton to death, recalling also that the 78th Highlanders had years earlier shipped home a teary-eyed Ceylonese specimen
that marched at the head of the regiment as a ceremonial mascot. He
knew the beasts had sizable memories, too, and he thought it entirely feasible that Professor Smeaton might have inflicted some indignity upon
it, many years ago, for which he had been hunted through the lanes and
crescents of the New Town before being speared through the face with
a well-directed tusk.

In the light of dawn, feeble and misty as it was, such whimsies
appeared unlikely even to Groves, and he decided that in this entire angle
of investigation he had wasted invaluable time. He cursed his inexperience, doubting that he had yet produced anything that he would be able
to record with distinction in his memoirs, and wondering if Professors
Whitty and Moir had been deliberately misleading in their suggestions,
or speaking in some cryptic code of academic sarcasm. He suddenly
loathed them and wished that they, too, were lying dead and faceless in
the Cowgate mortuary.

At Central Office he was again told of a mad Irishwoman who was
claiming to have dreamed major revelations. And Pringle, failing to read
his sudden exasperation and wishing to be as helpful as possible,
informed him of a recent trip he had made from Carlisle in which the
train had stopped to allow a broken-down Gypsy circus to board. He
had shared his own carriage, he said, with the infamous Pink-Faced
Lady, who he discovered was actually a shaved bear. The lady now
resided with other Lawnmarket Gypsies and frequently shuffled through
the streets in their company. Was it possible, he suggested brightly, that
she had reverted to her original bestial state and killed Smeaton indis-
criminately before being hauled off and spirited away?

Rather than answering, however, Groves was wondering just how
Pringle had become apprised of this particular aspect of his investigation,
when it had been his intention to be as secretive as possible about anything that had the potential to embarrass him. He was indeed painfully
sensitive to his inadequacies, fearful of committing error, and counter-
ing such insecurities with manufactured surges of confidence that
recoiled at the slightest hurdle, only to regroup later and build up into
even greater and more reckless forces.

He had been saved by a summons to the office of the Procurator

Fiscal—the chief prosecutor—where he was informed of the new scandal, the brutal exhumation of Colonel Munnoch. On the surface there seemed no definite link to the murder of Professor Smeaton—or indeed to that of the lighthouse keeper, which Groves had to restrain himself from mentioning—but it was rumored that in life the two men had been acquaintances, despite age and denominational differences, and, more to the point, both had connections with Henry Bolan, the current Lord Provost. So the coincidence was striking, and the pressure steadily mounting.

"We are currently treating Smeaton's death as a willful murder committed by person or persons unknown," the Fiscal informed him.

"It's the right thing, at this stage," Groves said, as though asked for approval.

"Have you made any progress that might alleviate us of this verdict?"

"The investigation," Groves said steadily, "is progressing according to plan."

The Fiscal seemed unconvinced. "You could do a lot worse than to settle this matter promptly, Carus. This is no time for the circus."

Startled by the last mysterious comment, Groves set off distractedly for Warriston Cemetery, where Pringle had already arrived with the Stockbridge constables. And here they were now, wondering what to make of it all, as the blackbirds hopped onto closer branches so as not to lose sight of them in the thickening fog.

"You say you have no idea when the crime took place?" Groves asked the grizzled superintendent.

"None, sir, and that's the truth."

"When did you discover it?"

"Just after dawn, sir, on my rounds."

"And before that, when was the last time you saw the grave?"

The man was working his cap around his hands and looked bleary eyed and evasive. "I think it were last night, roughly midnight, but I canna rightly say."

Groves sniffed. "Have you no schedule, man, to which you apply yourself?"

The superintendent shook his head. "None, sir. It always seems best not to work to a timetable."

"And why would that be?"

"So that the ghouls canna plot their activities around ye."

Groves frowned. The man seemed almost old enough to have been around in the resurrectionist days, but was he really suggesting the body had been dug up for the purposes of theft?

"You think they might have aimed to sell the body for medical research, is that it?"

The superintendent took a puzzled glance at the decomposed corpse. "Not in its current state, no, sir."

"Then what is this talk of ghouls?"

"I only mean the standard troublemakers, sir. Larking young 'uns and the like. This part of the yard, with the railway embankment, is 'specially popular with such types."

Groves sighed with disgust. He did not trust the superintendent, who smelled of gin and incompetence, but he relished the feeling of intimidating the man, a precious moment of mastery in the midst of all the confusion. "All the more reason, I would have thought," he said, "to make this the area of more frequent patrols."

The superintendent gulped, genuinely fearful for his job.

"Never mind, man. You heard nothing, in any event?"

"The embankment . . ." the superintendent said feebly.

"Makes it difficult to hear, all right. How long do you calculate it might have taken to dig, then?" He looked at the roughly gouged pit. The top half of the casket had been pried from the earth just enough to allow the lid to be smashed open—wood lay in shards and splinters—and the body dragged out by its shoulders.

"With a pick and a shovel," the superintendent said, "and a man or two . . ."

"How long?"

The superintendent did not answer directly. "It's more the way the pit's been dug, sir. It don't look like a shovel's been used, or any other form of implement."

"What do you mean?"

"I mean . . . a man'd be more likely to dig a roughly square hole, separating the grave boards and turning the earth on either side of the plot."

Groves looked behind him at the disturbed earth, sprayed out in a great fan. "Are you trying to say this pit was dug by hand?"

The superintendent looked reticent. "Seems . . . seems something like that, sir."

"By a beast?"

The superintendent shrugged. "A beast would have no interest in meat as rotten as this, sir, with all respects to the deceased."

"Then it's a man?"

"A man wouldn't punch open a lid like that, but use a lever."

"So which is it—man or beast?"

But the superintendent could not answer.

Again the specter of bestial strength had been raised, leaving Groves to wonder if his tour of the city's circuses had been so foolish after all. A man and a beast—or a number of beasts—in combination. He remembered the hoofprints in Belgrave Crescent and scanned the area around the grave for more clues, but whereas most of Warriston Cemetery had been planted with evergreens—cedars and cypresses artfully distributed—here in the lost corner there was an abundance of deciduous varieties, so that the ground was carpeted with decaying leaves and no prints or tracks were apparent.

He watched the photographer curse and splutter at his apparatus, unable to get a clear shot through the fog. Pringle spoke up. "Should we take the body back to the mortuary, sir? I'm not sure if we'd need a warrant, what with the body already exhumed."

But Groves disliked the prospect of Professor Whitty or his ilk poking around again and making equivocal observations. "There's nothing this body can tell us," he decided. "And it's against the law to exhume a body after ten years."

"Twenty years, sir."

"Aye." Groves felt flustered. "That's very well, but all we can do now is return the Colonel to his box and seal him up as best we can. If the family wants a new casket they can make their own arrangements."

But as Pringle and the others bent over to gingerly raise the corpse it became apparent that the head had fallen loose. Pringle stood at the edge of the pit and held the jawless skull up, Hamlet-like, looking into the face and frowning.

Groves took the opportunity to chastise him. "This is no time for morbid gestures, laddie."

"There's something here, sir," Pringle explained. "In the eye socket."

Groves frowned. "What is it?"

Pringle pincered his fingers, inserted them into the cavity, and withdrew a crumpled ball of paper, which he handed across.

Groves unfurled it distastefully. It was a page torn raggedly from a Bible, "ST. JOHN CHAP. VIII" printed across the top. He flipped it over. And saw that a particular phrase of Verse 44 had been crudely underlined in pencil.

"'He was a murderer from the beginning,'" he recited blankly, then looked up from the page, gathering his senses. "Is that all there is?"

Pringle took another look inside the skull. "That's all, sir."

Groves turned to the superintendent, holding up the page. "Could this have been buried with the body?"

The superintendent looked uneasy. "I don't believe it common for the dead to have pages stuffed in their heads, sir."

"I ask not for your opinion. I merely asked if it was possible."

Pringle interjected: "If the page were inside the body for fourteen years, sir, it surely would be more brittle."

"Fourteen years?"

"The length the Colonel has been buried, sir."

Groves nodded. "So it's a message, then?"

"Seems that way, sir."

A *message*. And, notwithstanding the bodies themselves, their first tangible lead. Somebody human, with or without the aid of beasts, had worked Colonel Munnoch's body to the surface for perhaps the sole purpose of inserting this sinister libel in the dead man's skull.

He was a murderer from the beginning.

Groves looked from the decapitated body to the head still poised in Pringle's hands, wondering what secrets the illustrious Colonel could possibly harbor to warrant such a belated accusation. His eyes wandered to the spartan stone and the man's epitaph—"A Christian and a Soldier"—and he had a brief, Godlike vision of his place in the scheme of this mystery, the simple whaler's son flung into the cauldron of Scotland's capital and, at the end of his worthy career, sent to do battle with unimaginable forces. He felt the palpable presence of evil, too, its very sanguine taste, like nothing he had previously experienced, and he looked again at the page of Gospel in his hand as though it might actually spell out what his heart already knew—he was on a divine errand.

Then, lurching out of these thoughts, he became aware of the others staring at him expectantly, and he frowned at them crossly.

"Just get that body put together and laid to rest," he snapped. "We'll need to prowl the area for more evidence."

Then he turned, as the others repeatedly tried to restore the Colonel's head to his body, and, looking into the rolling fog, became aware of a peculiar tension in the air, the song of shuddering steel, and a monstrous panting sound, building in force and proximity. And he stiffened, momentarily wondering if the murderer might be returning expressly to rip him apart—the others had paused, too, with the corpse still in their hands, and the blackbirds had launched into the air—before, with great explosive puffs of steam and smoke, a red and black loco-motive of the Edinburgh and Leith Railway surged out of the fog and thundered along the embankment in front of them, hauling behind it a string of first-class carriages, at the windows of which, staring through the mist at the grotesque tableau, sat a line of bonneted society ladies on their way to a Newhaven seaside banquet.

Chapter VI

McKnight examined the plundered Bible in the golden glow of the firelight, fingering the ragged remnant of page still clinging to the binding. "Remarkable . . ." he breathed, and when he looked up his emerald eyes were sparkling. "A beating sound, you say, like the wings of a demon?"

Canavan crossed his legs. "It was surely the bats I heard."

"But bats don't tear pages from Bibles."

"No . . ."

"And you saw no signs of human intrusion? The gates are locked, are they not?"

"They are."

"The fences are barbed?"

"Aye."

"Then to tear a page from a book and escape without leaving a trace, a man would have to be unnaturally—dare I say supernaturally—adroit?"

"The mist was unnaturally—dare I say supernaturally—thick. He could easily have hid behind a gravestone and escaped at his own pace."

59

McKnight chortled. "And then there is the destination of the page itself," he said, for the full details of Colonel Munnoch's exhumation, and the deposit in his eye socket, had already been disseminated through the city's press. "How might you explain that little mystery?"

"It could have been from any Bible."

"Naturally," McKnight said with a wry smile, and he examined the book as though the missing page were still present. "'He was a murderer from the beginning,'" he quoted, and looked up at his friend quizzically. "Can you recall the King James Version?"

"'He was a murderer from the beginning,'" Canavan replied.

"The English Revised Version?"

"The same. The King James, the Douai, the Challoner revision—all the translations offer no variation in that particular line. And knowing it's a page of a Douai translation wouldn't prove, in any case, that it came from your particular Bible."

"True, but it would add a pinch of coincidence to an already significant mound, you'll admit that?" And when the Irishman still looked reticent: "Come now, is the devil's advocate in you so unwilling to accept a miracle?"

"It's not the miracle that bothers me," Canavan said, "but the fact that you seem so hungry for a personal invitation."

"The invitation has already been delivered," McKnight corrected, with barely concealed relish. "And it's now just a matter of composing the acceptance."

Canavan scoffed. The paradox of their current debate—that he had somehow assumed the role of skeptic—did not strike him as anomalous, for both men often arbitrarily adopted extremes as a means of establishing the parameters and locating the quickest path to the truth. What troubled him was that on his way home from Drumgate that morning he had for the first time in many months not encountered McKnight, and indeed, passing the man's huddled little cottage—a place that seemed moored to the earth by a spidery net of ivy, and like its owner permanently wreathed in mist—he had discerned a thick line of smoke issuing from the chimney; this when the Professor had come to apply logs to his hearth with the same thrift with which he applied beef to his tongue. So, as eager as he was to return the ravaged Bible and to apologize for its condition, Canavan had elected to pass on by, convinced that his friend was not ill but—even more worrisome—was simply filching a day from the University's calendar to apply his mind to his own burgeoning interest: the mystery of Professor Smeaton's murder.

Canavan was aware that as a lecturer McKnight had grown distracted, even irascible, and that his increasing failure as a teacher only exacerbated his financial insecurity. Pending annual salaries, the professors were paid by the students themselves at the opening of each seasonal session, meaning that, in the manner of a popularity contest, it was those most charismatic and accommodating who consulted the finest timepieces and were swept home in the swiftest broughams. The choleric were rewarded with classes small and inherently self-punishing, and the distracted—such as Professor Piazzi Smyth of Astronomy, who had developed an inordinate fascination with the Great Pyramid of Cheops—were incrementally ostracized and ushered in the direction of premature retirement.

But if McKnight was now troubled by the implication, or even perceived it, he gave little indication. From a leather pouch he produced what appeared to be genuine shag tobacco and filled the bowl of his pipe, tamping it without a trace of self-consciousness. He leaned into the fire to light a match and chuckled when he singed his fingers. He ignited the tobacco with a flourish and, employing some previously hidden skill, blew out a flawless smoke ring. And all with such a gleam in his eye, and such an electricity in his spirit, that Canavan wondered idly if God might accept the current mayhem as an acceptable trade for the revival of a worthy man's enthusiasm.

"But let us first examine the story so far," McKnight went on. "Beginning with the lighthouse keeper."

"The lighthouse keeper?" Canavan frowned.

"You must have heard of it?" McKnight settled back into his armchair. "A month or so ago, before the current dramas, a retired lighthouse keeper was savaged to death while walking his dog."

"I remember the murder. But I wasn't aware of the man's former profession."

"I did some research," the Professor admitted. "The similarities to the two more recent incidents, take my word, are more than simply striking."

"And you claim it's the work of the same murderer?"

"I claim nothing. I observe, examine, and try to prevent further tragedy."

"I think," Canavan submitted, "that this is most certainly a task for the police."

"The police, as fine as they are, sometimes need assistance, don't you think?"

"They certainly don't need meddlers."

"I have no intention of meddling. The police are welcome to their legwork. The investigation I propose—for both of us—will be conducted on a separate but equally arduous plane. That of logical and spiritual deduction."

"Aye?" Canavan smirked. "And what makes us suited to the task?"

"A talent. A vocation." McKnight puffed out an aromatic cloud. "In my case, a predilection for unraveling layers, which I fear to this point has been unhappily squandered. In your case, assuming you're willing to join me, an enslaving propensity for good deeds."

Canavan snorted his amusement but did not commit himself, for it was part of a foil's duty not to be too accommodating. "Let me first hear those supposed similarities," he said, with a strange feeling he would regret it.

McKnight did not hesitate. "Three men," he said, "not one younger than sixty. Two dispatched with inhuman force. One disinterred with, from all accounts, a similar force—and surely the only reason Colonel Munnoch was not himself killed was the rather inconvenient fact that he was already dead. No apparent motive. No mutilation of the bodies apart from the initial injuries. No attempt to conceal them or deposit them in a place where there might be more certainty of their being discovered. Unless the police are hiding something, and at this point I have no reason to believe that they are, the appointed investigators are most likely exasperated."

"And since you seem to have given it a fair deal of thought," Canavan noted, "what might you be able to tell them?"

"At this stage, what they should already know. The motive is almost certainly revenge, and for some injury that in some way extends back farther than fourteen years."

"How so?"

"Colonel Munnoch was buried in 1872."

"A long time to hold a grudge."

"The injury is no doubt fitting."

"But why now? And not any other time in the past fourteen years?"

McKnight smiled enigmatically. "Take a look at this fire," he said, and he gestured to the hearth. "So vaporous and yet so powerful. The fundamental stuff of the universe, Heraclitus called it. And yet, as elemental and powerful as it may be . . . and as quickly as it can burn flesh . . . fire still takes time to forge steel."

Canavan was confused. "You think the killer is a kettle that has just come to the boil, is that it?"

McKnight chuckled. "Only that he might have spent the intervening years changing his very mettle. Building to a point where he can kill like a lion, soar like a bat, and vanish like an apparition."

Canavan was about to protest—this seemed more madness than metaphysics—but at just that moment a fierce wind buffeted the cottage, whistled down the chimney, and harassed the flames into fleeing spirits and serpents. He shot a glance at the stammering window and for one unsettling moment thought he saw a woman's face staring in at them, before deciding it was just a distorted reflection of the fire.

"And the message?" he asked, to distract himself. "The biblical verse?"

"Curious and invaluable. For what reason would Munnoch be labeled a murderer?"

"Munnoch was a soldier," Canavan said. "Perhaps the revenge has a political bent?"

"No, I have an indefinable feeling about this. I'm convinced—I see it as if written in stone—that these men were intimately embroiled in some unspeakable crime prior to 1872."

"Involving murder?"

"The biblical verse certainly implies it. And it could well be the case that they have just been identified by the killer—accounting for the delay."

"A professor of ecclesiastical law, a distinguished colonel, and a lighthouse keeper." Canavan shook his head. "There seems no obvious link."

"If seeking a connection, one should think of them as they were fourteen years ago."

"And how was that?"

"Smeaton had just been appointed to the University. Prior to that he had been minister in the parish of Corstorphine. The lighthouse keeper had retired five years previously. I checked the records today at the Northern Lighthouse Board in Queen Street."

"Very thorough," Canavan said, vaguely disturbed that his friend, for all his insistence that their investigation would be a strictly cerebral one, had gone to such practical lengths.

"For Colonel Munnoch I did not have to travel quite so far. His memoir was published in 1864. At six hundred pages it's what might be called a rather meticulous chronicle."

"You have a copy?" Canavan asked, unsurprised.

"Naturally." McKnight nodded. "A very illuminating text. Would you permit me to read you a passage?"

"I have just enough time," the Irishman said, for he was due shortly at Drumgate.

McKnight clamped his pipe between his teeth and reached down beside his chair for the volume, which he had already retrieved from his redoubtable library.

Through the direst financial straits, McKnight had never been able to part with his books. He had stripped the cottage bare of just about everything else—every article of disposable furniture, from his pianoforte to his shaving mirror—and now slept on a monastic pallet, bathed in a laundry tub, and grilled his food in the fireplace beside Canavan's crossed legs. But of his magnificent library, which contained many of his most financially valuable items, he could not select even a single fragment for sacrifice. He had started assembling the titles almost as soon as he could read (using money, in some cases, intended for the church plate), and before he graduated from university he was actually evicted from his student lodgings, because the landlord feared the weight of his collection might threaten the foundations. And he still had every one of them, squeezed into cheap shelves that groaned and creaked like ship timbers in a mysteriously sizable cavern in the cellar of his cottage, the strangely elastic walls of which seemed to expand and contract in direct response to the rarity of the text being hunted. It was a surreal chamber, dark and cobwebbed, where McKnight would lead the way bearing only a slush lamp filled with train oil, and the disorientated visitor was forever bumping his head against haphazard projections or stumbling over orphaned piles of manuscripts.

"*A Christian and a Soldier, Volume One,*" McKnight announced, hold-ing up a thick book bound in green morocco leather. "I refer to page two hundred and forty." He had already donned his rather severe spectacles, the lenses of which Canavan suspected were well past sufficiency, and he now opened the volume at a bookmarked leaf.

"'There was the islet of Inchcaid,'" he read, "'a frowning reef of phonolitic rock past Bell Rock north of the firth. A dreich place, where Covenanters were once imprisoned and smugglers roamed, and which was now given over to razorbills and seals. I had no inclination to visit it, believing it to be real estate of no particular value, but it was drawn to my attention that sailing ships had a propensity for imperiling them-selves on its serrated edges, and was informed that a lighthouse would need to be constructed on the easternmost shelf. To this I gave my per-mission without a second thought, and upon its completion in 1846, I felt my interest sufficiently prevailed upon to make a visit, in the com-pany of the proud engineers, and I found here a grand Pharos, a pillar of dovetailed granite slabs pounded by foaming waters. I spent a day meeting the obliging keepers, inspecting their quarters and storerooms, and examining the immense polished lenses and angled prisms of the great lamp itself, and from the heights surveying the ungodly huddle of rock, dusted with hardy gulls, that my family had acquired through some convoluted transaction or ancient gambling debt.'"

McKnight folded the volume and set it aside. "That is all Munnoch has to say about the lighthouse itself. He has scant regard, in truth, for much else but his military campaigns. But for our purposes it provides a direct link to one Colin Shanks, a keeper at the lighthouse from 1846, when Munnoch visited, to his sudden retirement in 1867, aged forty-six."

"Shanks being the man slaughtered last month while walking his dog?"

McKnight nodded. "No reason is given in the lighthouse board's records for his premature retirement. But I noted that a fellow keeper at the lighthouse also departed the board's services the same year 'in tragic circumstances.'"

Canavan frowned. "Murdered?"

"An accident, according to what I was later able to find in the files of *The Scotsman*. During a violent storm the man was swept into the sea. It gives no indication how—just that his identifying cap was washed ashore two days later."

"Any suggestion Mr. Shanks was involved?"

"It may indeed be entirely unrelated, though I'm prepared to add it to the list of mounting coincidences, and attempt to account for it only when I have gathered more comprehensive information. But for the moment I'll settle for the link to Colonel Munnoch."

Canavan shrugged. "And Professor Smeaton? Anything in the book that links him to the Colonel?"

"Nothing readily apparent. But the rest of the autobiography is rife with combat and expressions of seemingly divine righteousness. Munnoch fought in Java, Persia, and the Crimea, and marched on Lucknow and Tientsin. He battled Mussulmen, Hindus, Chinamen, and godless savages, and his book practically drips with colored flesh and unbaptized blood. He has a peculiar eye for the exotic and sensational, and nary a page passes without a majestic Oriental palace or a great tempest."

Canavan could not see the point. "He should have been a novelist, perhaps?"

"I merely ask you to imagine such a man pumped full of shrapnel and sent home to waddle around fair Edinburgh for the remainder of his days. Naturally he feels inhibited. Of course he hurls himself into his memoirs. And it's not unreasonable to imagine him turning thoroughly eccentric. He spurns, in any case, the pleasures of self-indulgence available to him through his wealth and hungrily seeks some righteous cause into which to channel his considerable resources. Or a friend, at the very least, who shares his combative temperament."

"Professor Smeaton being a man of many righteous causes . . ."

"A man, you'll recall, who adorned himself in the very breastplate of righteousness." McKnight reached for the second volume of the Colonel's memoir. "May I draw your attention to the final paragraph?"

"It's not for me to stop you."

McKnight flipped through to the last page and readjusted his spectacles. "'Unless you are fighting, you are not a soldier. Unless you are struggling, you are not a Christian. Unless you are armored in *the breastplate of righteousness*'"—he leaned on the phrase—"'and sharpening your swords for the fields of Armageddon, you have no place in the Kingdom of God.'"

Canavan shifted. "Tenuous, perhaps," he said, "but I concede there might be a connection."

"And you'll assist me in finding it?"

"I'll agree to think about it."

McKnight smiled and removed his spectacles. "Then we have most certainly made progress after all."

Departing into a wintry breeze a few minutes later, Canavan noticed a squadron of bats winging frantically across the waning moon. But he was too preoccupied to pay much attention, still trying to determine if he should welcome his friend's newfound vitality with enthusiasm or regard it warily, as something innately volatile and potentially dangerous.

In recent times McKnight's whole punishing philosophy, his crisis about the very nature of the self—what Kant had called "the transcendental thread"—had radiated from self-doubt into the realms of misanthropy and self-hatred. Was there anyone, he had mused recently, who had the right to be called an individual? Was there a man anywhere who had not acquired his "thread"—his whole gossamer-thin identity—from family and historical precedents? Did he himself have the right to claim a "personality," when his entire character seemed a composite of more famous Scottish identities? From Boswell, he argued, he had plagiarized his abiding fondness for the underdog; from Carlyle the icy disaffection of his devoutly Calvinist parents; from David Hume the very architecture of his philosophies; and from Sir Walter Scott his impatience with pecuniary matters and his heroic dedication to paying off his debt. But now even this counterfeit identity seemed to be deserting him, his recollections fading in the mist, and his past like a trail of ignited gunpowder sputtering after him and threatening to blow him apart.

Such men, riven with self-doubt, were of course vulnerable to fantastic theories and fabulous missions, and equally at risk of driving deeper into self-destruction. But Canavan now assured himself that he could never let that happen. He would sacrifice himself for McKnight as quickly as he would sacrifice himself for the world. But if the Professor continued with this investigation and, as an understandable consequence, was suspended from the University, then there would be alarming practicalities to face. Canavan barely earned enough to feed himself, let alone McKnight, and what was left over he shared with acquaintances and used to purchase offal for the city's stray dogs. Struggling

with the complexities of dividing his meager income, or even reminding the Professor of his responsibilities in a way that did not sound con-
descending or reproving, he came upon the gates of Drumgate to find
himself alleviated of the problem in a most brutal way.

In response to the desecration at Warriston, the Lord Provost had
recommissioned officers of the Parks Constabulary to guard those cemeteries regarded as underprotected or significantly historical. At Drumgate at least two uniformed sentries were visible through the thorned
gates, patrolling the grounds with leashed mastiffs.

Canavan no longer had a job.

Chapter VII

BELL'S TEAROOMS on Princes Street had a glazed veranda at street level offering sweeping views of the Castle and the smoking Old Town. Chief Inspector Smith, the "Wax Man," freshly returned from London and mysteriously attired in a royal-blue doublet and dappled cravat, had secured a seat facing the gloriously sunlit promenade so that he might secretly admire the parade of sauntering ladies in their foulards, clinging gowns, and velvet ribbons, and speculate as to the texture and color of their undergarments. He had been absent for a fortnight and was keen to capitalize on his transborder notoriety.

"Quilted satin drawers," he said authoritatively. "That's the new fashion in London, you know. Damnable nuisance getting the things untied, though. There's more loops and strings than you'd find on a cardinal's corset."

"Is that so?" asked a discomfited Groves. He had his back to the street and was prodding distractedly at some kippered herrings on a small saucer.

"Cleopatra," the Wax Man said, recalling the Egyptian Room at

69

Madame Tussaud's. "Now there was a wench who knew how to impress a man."

Groves glanced warily at the well-to-do ladies of the neighboring table, but in truth the Wax Man's superbly trained words had not ventured beyond their private space. "I've always thought," he returned tightly, awkward with such banter, but keen to contribute in some way, "that with all the bustle around today, it's difficult to tell the Jezebel from the common housemaid."

But the Wax Man, with his gaze absently tracking something on the street, did not seem to be listening. "Of course they don't know precisely what she looked like. I think they modeled her after a Greek seamstress or something. With the likes of my figure, though, you could rightly walk in and think you were staring at the real article. They spent a week just perfecting the eyes. The lass said she'd never seen such eyes on a man, like spring lavender. Spent another week on the skin tone, they did, and cut my hair from a Clydesdale's tail. Rarely seen locks so virile, or skin so robust, she said, in a man of my vintage."

With nary a hair on his head since his twenties and already feeling adequately inferior—in fame, rank, experience, venereal achievements, and even bodily travails—Groves understood that he was meant to be impressed. "Do they preserve the mannequin in such a state?" he asked. "Or will you be required to return, now and then, so that they might update your features?"

"Oh, I doubt there'll be much updating going on," the Wax Man chortled—not, as it turned out, with any sort of hubris. "No," he said. "Unless the figure is as popular as Cleopatra and remains that way, these things are designed to be melted down and remodeled in some other guise, according to fashion."

His own mannequin, he explained, had been molded out of the drippings of Socrates, the King of Siam, and William Penn, the founder of Pennsylvania. In fact, it was Penn's suit he now wore—a direct exchange for his regular serge jacket, which he had donated to the museum in the interests of authenticity. "If I last five years in that Chamber of Horrors I'll be happy," he said. "And if I outlive the dummy, I'll be even happier."

This cheerful disregard for the mortality of wax, let alone flesh, left Groves privately nonplussed. He had just spent another night agonizing over the wording of his latest diary entries, and yet here he was sitting with a man who seemed to live exclusively in the present and had no real interest in his own legacy. A man whose memoirs, were he to invest enough time in compiling them, would all but obliterate Groves's in sheer contrast.

"You don't look the best, Carus," the Wax Man said frankly, sparing the time to examine his colleague directly. "You should rest, man. Are you finding enough sleep?"

"It's . . . it's this case," Groves explained. "Murder and the like. I won't be at ease until I have the culprit on the gallows."

"But you must get your kip, Carus. An inspector's essential faculties are impaired otherwise. Doesn't matter if Genghis Khan himself is loose in the High Street, a policeman needs to regulate himself in all things."

"Aye," Groves agreed, though inwardly he bristled, for he knew he was the most disciplined man on the force.

"I've heard about the case, naturally."

"In London?" Groves had secretly been hoping that the news would have reached the British capital and had made a point of checking the papers as soon as they arrived by coach.

"When I returned last evening. I had a meeting with the Chief Constable and the Fiscal. They wanted me to assume control, of course."

"Of course." Groves tightened, determined not to betray his alarm, though the Wax Man did not even seem to be looking at him but at some point beyond his shoulder.

"I told them Groves is a capable man. Like a good hound who always finds the bone. It's not for me to take over now, I said. Leave Pringle at his side, and Groves'll fetch a conviction."

"That is certainly my intention," Groves said, but inwardly could not decide if he was relieved or disturbed. He had arrived at the tearooms fearing that the Wax Man had summoned him to announce that the case officially was being taken out of his hands, the tea being a way of breaking the news gently. But now there was the daunting prospect that the crafty Chief Inspector had shirked the case exactly because he had deemed it too challenging, or even unsolvable. This returned Groves to the prematurely retired investigation into the murder of the lighthouse keeper Colin Shanks: a scandal he was poised to thrust into the conversation like a saber at the choicest moment. Inexperienced with such tactics, however, he was not convinced he would even recognize such a moment when it presented itself.

"I knew neither of them," the Wax Man admitted. "Smeaton or the Colonel. Of course, they did not move in circles such as mine." Like Groves he had a way of making such an observation sound like an insult. "But I knew of them. Birds of a feather and whatnot. Have you found any connections?"

"Connections?"

"Aye, you know . . ."

"If you mean a certain lighthouse—"

"Family," the Wax Man clarified. "Of the victims. Were the families able to provide you with anything?"

Groves adjusted. "Not Smeaton's family. And the Colonel's wife is long dead."

"Pity."

"It's the extreme force that really binds the incidents. The monstrous strength needed to murder one and dig up the other."

"Aye," the Wax Man said. "The classic madman is troglodytal. Have you heard of Dr. Stellmach? I'll give you his address. Done all sorts of studies into such things. University of Berlin or something."

Groves had indeed heard of Stellmach, who had assisted the Wax Man with aspects relating to psychological traits, and did not want to appear less informed. "I've always said there are two types of criminal," he declared. "Those who have been turned that way by necessity and those that are steered that way by their blood, without any say in the matter. And it is my firm belief that it is the latter which in number now prevails." He nodded, pleased with this little morsel of philosophy, which he had already recorded in his casebook.

But again the Wax Man seemed to be exercising an alarming capacity to sweep his eyes from one side of Groves to the other without even noticing him. "Oh, quite . . ." he said, returning as though from some illicit reverie.

Groves sipped at his tea. "I'm compiling a list," he said.

"Hmm? A list?"

"Of the suspects to this point."

The Wax Man looked disapproving. "Lists are one thing, Carus," he said, "but it's boot leather that gets answers, not ink."

"Of course," Groves agreed, vaguely irritated.

"There's a woman involved," the Wax Man decided. "It's rare that there's not, but with crimes of this sort of passion, there always is. Mark my words—there's a woman at the soul of this case."

"Professor Smeaton was not killed by a woman," Groves assured him.

"No, but by someone working on the woman's behalf. A possessive lover. A solicitous avenger. Did you not think of that, Carus? The power a woman can work on a man's mind is greater than any witch's potion."

"Of course I've considered it," Groves managed, and briefly entertained the captivating notion that the Wax Man himself was responsible. "But the biblical verse suggests a different motive than lust."

"'He was a murderer, and always was'?" the Wax Man misquoted. "I wouldn't pay too much attention to that. It could easily be a ruse. And it still doesn't rule out a woman. Munnoch served in India, did he not?"

"Aye, I questioned some of the men in his regiment. They agree he was eccentric, but certainly not mad. He shot some Hindus and black men in his time, but not one of his fellow soldiers, not even accidentally, so there is no evidence of hostility from the military."

"Any involvement with the women of the Subcontinent, though? Those Indian whores can turn you inside out."

Groves flinched. "From all accounts he was devoted wholly to his wife."

"Or so he told her."

"My investigation has not been helped by the fact that not a soul seems to have witnessed the crimes."

"Regrettable."

Groves now eyed the Chief Inspector steadily, resolving at last to make his move. "What do you do," he ventured, "when there are no witnesses? No leads? Nothing to assist you with an investigation?"

"Hmm?" The Wax Man looked at him directly.

"If there's nothing pointing in any direction," Groves went on, "what are you likely to do with a case?"

"I'm not sure what you mean."

"What do you do," Groves found himself prodding helplessly at his herring again, "when the mystery offers no answers?"

The Wax Man sustained his stare for a further second, then sniffed and looked away. "There's always answers, Carus, if you know where to look."

But Groves detected a vulnerable tone to his response and finally saw his chance. "I ask because I have reason to suspect . . . that the current crimes are linked to one that occurred last month . . . one that fell under your jurisdiction."

The Wax Man looked back at him again.

Groves cleared his throat. "The lighthouse keeper . . ." he said huskily.

And when the Wax Man still looked puzzled:

"At Duddingston Loch . . ."

No response.

"Walking his dog . . ."

And then, quite abruptly, the Wax Man unleashed a volley of laughter. "Oh, the *dog*," he said, as though misreading Groves entirely. "The dog—aye." He laughed. "A regular Greyfriars Bobby, that cur. Saw its master done for, let loose a trail of keech half a mile long—we found it strung out alongside the loch—and bolted home, scratched open the door, and threw a fit. Why, were you thinking of questioning it?"

Groves was speechless.

"Had to be finished off, poor thing. A wolfhound, too. Usually a sound dog."

Groves struggled for words. "I mean the—the—"

"Ah, you think there might be a connection?" the Wax Man said innocently. "I see your point. The man was certainly torn open in an unusual way. Aye." He nodded, considering the matter. "But on the other hand he had gambling debts, and a history in the brothels. Such men draw targets on themselves, and no one really misses them. His son, too, was very keen that I conclude the matter without upsetting the widow. It was the least I could do. But if you're saying you want to reopen the investigation . . . ?"

Groves shook his head helplessly.

"If it has to be done," the Wax Man went on, "then there's no avoiding it. I'll offer all my assistance, of course, but one thing you should know. The lighthouse keeper was the bastard brother of the former Chief

Constable." And he winked conspiratorially. "Best not to dig up too many such truffles if you can, Carus. Might get your snout bitten."

"Of . . . of course," Groves said, but inwardly he was astounded. In a matter of seconds the Wax Man had converted a stain of expediency into a banner of strength.

"Look at you, Carus," the Wax Man said, leaning back in his seat and smiling victoriously. "Look at your face. Clearly you don't appreciate the mantle that's been bestowed upon you. Chief Inspector in a famous homicide case, sniffing around amid murder and mystery. The ladies will be onto you like flies to a carcass. Blood is like French perfume to the Edinburgh hussy, Carus. Any offers of assistance so far?"

"Assistance?"

"There's always a lass who comes forward in such murder cases, claiming to know a thing or two."

"There's been no lasses."

"Know nothing, most of them. Just looking for attention. For a good seeing-to. You wait—some lickerish little psychic will step out of her burrow."

Groves remembered. "There has been one lady," he said, "who claims to have dreamed the crimes."

"There you are. What does she look like?"

"I've not met her. An Irishwoman."

"Irish?" The Wax Man frowned. "I don't recall any Irish psychics. What did you do with her?"

"I sent her away."

"Shouldn't do that, Carus. Never know what she might have to offer, if you get my meaning."

Groves felt unsettled.

"That fetching assistant at Tussaud's," the Wax Man chuckled, suddenly remembering. "I asked her what she'd do with my wax mannequin once it ran out of favor. Know what she replied?" He dabbed his lips. "She said she'd like as not take it home, put it in her room, and plant a wick in it. And do you know what I said in response?" He leaned forward, tightening the reins on his voice again.

Groves shook his head feebly.

"I said if she took me home right away I'd happily return the favor!"

The Wax Man exploded into laughter and Groves forced a chuckle also, though in truth he did not quite follow.

"Silly tart," the Wax Man added, settling back again. "Didn't have the brains to understand."

Groves worked his chuckle up a couple of notches, just to be sure, and stuffed his cheeks with herring.

✠

Before he crossed it out a few days later—and still later tore out and disposed of the entire page—Groves introduced the Irishwoman into his provisional notes with the following words: *I have a keen eye for character, it has served me well for many years, and as soon as I saw the lass I could see she was up to no good, she knew nothing that could help, but in the way of such wastrels was looking for attention, in this she was fortunate she had found a man patient enough to hear her out without locking her up, even though I had much more pressing matters to consider.*

In fact she was not really a girl, though it was difficult to ascertain her precise age: anything from nineteen to thirty. Her black hair was cut brutally short, as though by glass, and she was dressed in a wrinkled crepe frock of funereal black: a pitiable creature, pale and hollow, as though every ounce of moisture had been drained from her body through her tear ducts. Her accent was enigmatic, sometimes faltering from the prevailing singsong Irish to a more brusque Scots and even, most mysteriously, an almost Continental trill. She was an odd package, certainly not voluptuous, and Groves enjoyed his scorn.

"—don't want to be intrusive," she was saying, wringing her hands. "I have no doubt you are exceedingly busy, and I would not interrupt if I did not think I could contribute."

Groves had not risen. In a sort of petulant response to the Wax Man's pronouncement about the futility of ink he had returned immediately to his desk in the Squad Room to construct an elaborate map of Edinburgh, linking the crime scenes to the residences of the victims and the suspects. He was not sure what it would achieve, but he was defiant in his resolve to find something. When Pringle informed him of the return of the insistent Irishwoman, however, he welcomed the diversion and ordered her in. They were now alone but for the sound, from the neighboring prison cells, of a drunk trying to prove his sobriety to the presiding constables with a particularly challenging tongue twister.

"Never mind that, lass." Groves sat back in his chair and pressed his foot against the desk. She was standing in front of him like a remorseful student, unable to pry her eyes from the floor, and he enjoyed the idea that his gaze was so searing, so masterly, that she could not bear to look at him. "My assistant, Pringle, tells me you claim to have had some dreams."

"That's correct, sir. Dreams of a most vivid nature, which seem of significance. And when I heard of the events of the past few days . . ."

"You claim to have dreamed of Colonel Munnoch's exhumation, is that right?"

"I did."

"What did you see in your dream?"

"I . . . I dreamed of a cemetery. I recognized it as Warriston."

"You have been to Warriston before?"

She nodded sheepishly. "A few times."

"You have family there?"

"No . . ."

Groves was about to query her further on this matter, but was distracted by the voice of the drunk from next door—"*The sweep shook the shooty . . .*"—and a round of derisive laughter. He blinked and looked back at her. "Go on."

She continued with effort. "It . . . it was night, in my dream, and there was a thick fog. It was very hard to see, but I heard much activity. Showers of earth and the like. I thought it must be the keeper but then the fog cleared for a moment and I saw that it . . . it was not the keeper."

Groves shifted. "A beast?"

"I'm not sure, sir."

"A large man?"

"I could not rightly tell."

"*The sweep shook the sooty shweet . . .*"

Groves sniffed. "This is conveniently vague, lass." But inwardly he was relieved, having briefly feared that history might record that the identity of the criminal—the whole solution to the mystery—had been furnished by a mad Irishwoman.

"I saw a body being dragged from the ground," she hastened on, as though determined to get it out before she was dismissed. "And a note shoved in the eye socket—a page of Scripture."

"This much is general knowledge."

"Then I woke up, and that was all." She glanced up at Groves apologetically. "It was a nightmare, sir, and I could stand it no longer."

For just a moment Groves thought he had detected something in her—sincerity, perhaps—before deciding it was just an illusion.

"The sweep shook the shooty sheet . . ."

"So you saw all this," he asked, "and yet you failed to notice who was actually doing it all, is that it?"

"Fragments of my dream . . ."

"What?"

She squeezed her fingers. "Fragments of my dream return unbidden, sir. I have not yet been able to identify the figure, that is true . . ."

"A grand thing."

"But I feel that it will come to me—I cannot escape it. I feel that I *know* him. I have seen him before. He is someone who has traveled far . . ."

"Do you know many men who have traveled far?"

She looked uneasy. "No . . ."

"Then where have you seen him before? In the street?"

"In my dreams, sir. I have seen him before in my dreams."

"A dream figure." Groves delighted in his scorn.

"It was the same figure that I saw k-kill Professor Smeaton, sir."

"Aye, that's right—the Professor's murder. You saw that, too?"

"I did, sir."

"You could not identify the murderer, though?"

Her brow furrowed. "It was dark and terrible, sir. I saw Professor Smeaton attacked . . . I cannot describe it . . . a terrible force, a whirlwind . . . I woke up screaming."

"The sweep shook the city . . . shook the sooty . . ."

Groves sighed. "All this is again common knowledge, lass. I can see no reason for you to be here."

"There was a message, sir . . ."

"The Bible page. You've mentioned that. Again, this is—"

"No—an earlier message. A message was left beside Professor Smeaton, just as there was with the Colonel."

Groves stared at her. "There was no message."

"I had a clear image of a message."

"There was nothing," Groves said defiantly, not liking the suggestion that he had missed something.

"Accusing w-words. I saw them clearly."

"On a page, were they?"

"I'm not certain, sir."

"And yet you say you saw them clearly?"

"I know it is difficult to explain . . ."

Groves examined the wee creature framed against the water-stained walls. She looked wounded and afraid. As though sent under instruction to do something for which she had no real appetite.

"The shweep sook the sooty . . ."

"I'm a busy man," Groves sighed eventually. "As you yourself have observed. And this is a case of the greatest urgency. So I can only ask that you and any other psychic you know should have the good manners to look elsewhere for attention before you distract me from my proper duties." He returned pointedly to his map.

"I . . . I'm not a psychic, sir."

"Eh?" He looked up.

"The dreams . . ." She gulped, fearing she had not made herself clear. "They're not prophetic. I dream of the events exactly as they unfold."

"As they unfold."

"Exactly as they occur, sir. It's as if . . . as if I am there."

"Without being able to tell me anything I do not already know?"

"Fragments, sir. The dreams return in fragments."

"Fragments." For some reason Groves thought of the pieces of herring he had left on the tearoom saucer.

"It could be that his identity comes to me soon, that my dreams reveal him to me . . . but . . ." she faltered, "of that . . . I cannot be sure."

"The sweep shook the sooty street . . ."

Groves exhaled expressively, having had more than enough. "Pringle will show you to the street, lass," he said. "And get some sleep. A woman should regulate herself in all things."

Before she retreated she shot him another glance with her watery blue eyes that he would long remember: doleful, even defeated, but also possessed of a rare spark (he would later decide it was demonic, though at the time he mistook it for simple guile). It sent a curious, disconcerting signal to his loins, in any event, and impulsively he decided to pin her in place with a final question.

"That accent of yours," he said. "You came from Ireland, did you not? As a child?"

"I *went* to Ireland as a child," she replied, her hand on the door. "I returned to Edinburgh just recently."

"What part of Ireland? I don't recognize the brogue."

"County Monaghan, sir. I went to Sparks Lake Boarding School and was educated by the Sisters of St. Louis. They're French, sir."

"Ah," said Groves, as though he had suspected just as much.

"The sweep . . . shook the sheet . . . shook the sooty sheet . . ."

"And what's your name, lass?"

She hesitated, her eyes still lowered. "Evelyn," she admitted finally, and might have blushed. "Evelyn Todd." She waited, as though expecting further questions upon that revelation, or even a rebuke, but, hearing nothing, she bowed her head and went out guiltily, easing the door closed behind her.

"The sweep shook the sooty street . . . shook the street in the sheet . . . shook the . . . ah, to blazes with the lot of you."

Chapter VIII

EMERGING INTO the morning sunshine from a back door that was not his own—a pastime he had pursued with some enthusiasm—James Ainslie, entrepreneur, philanderer, gentleman thief, took a lungful of the bracing air and marched briskly down Clyde Lane in the direction of St. Andrew Square, his guilt successfully masked by his distinguished bearing, his immaculate attire, his perfectly waxed mustaches, and most especially by his vaguely militaristic gait—a legacy, like his scars, from his days in the Royal Rifle Corps.

It was not, let it be said, that Ainslie was a man on whom guilt fed with any nourishment. In his childhood he had armored his heart through the torture of small animals; in his adolescence he had graduated to the mental persecution of pretty young ladies; as a soldier he had murdered with the exoneration of war; and as a businessman he had stripped investors bare with the impunity of personal necessity. It was an insincere and precarious lifestyle, founded largely on guile and the misplaced trust of strangers—and in no small part on the lupine instincts that had always enabled him to elude pursuing creditors—but it was also

81

a life crammed so tightly with incident, danger, and the pressing need to survive on sharpened wits that he could conceive of no other existence. Even when, as now, he had been reduced yet again to petty larceny and groveling to impressionable fools.

The wind shrieked around him and flapped the tails of his topcoat, but he was as impervious to meteorological conditions as he was to remorse. Gaily whistling a martial tune of the sort he had once bellowed from the pipes, he cut across Waverley Bridge and climbed Cockburn Street past the opulent apartment at which he rarely awoke, and at the junction with the High Street he paused to appraise himself in the gilded mirror of an antique dealer's window. Here he fastidiously adjusted his necktie and plucked a single speck of soot from his lapel, determined to look his most dashing for his imminent meeting at the Caledonian Loan and Mercantile Association, where he intended to exert all his sparkling charm on the stammering finance director—a man he suspected was secretly in love with him.

This was no misplaced conceit. Ainslie's confidence, his devil-may-care philosophies, his taste for peril, and his seeming imperviousness to punishment—all had helped him accumulate innumerable admirers of all ages, sexes, and social strata. There were times, indeed, when simply strutting down the street he would be stared at like some parading zoo creature, some magnificent upright fox. Even now he caught a glimpse, in the shop mirror, of a lady in a Quakerish dress—a young creature who could easily have been his daughter—studying his movements fixedly from the opposite corner. But in a typically lightning assessment he dismissed her as too tightly laced to be worth even passing attention, and, resuming his grip on his cane, he took off again at a clip.

As he crossed Hunter Square he victoriously patted the pocket holding the real prize of the previous evening's conquest: a ruby-embedded bracelet of considerable quality, liberated from a velvet-coated case at the bottom of a poorly fastened hatbox. For close to three hours he had hunted diligently through wardrobes and bureaux for just such an item as his vanquished lover snored and groaned through a whisky-soaked haze—scotch being one poison against which Ainslie had inoculated himself with a lifetime of systematic and patriotic consumption.

The conquest herself was the exceedingly plain wife of an India rubber merchant whose frequent absences had frayed her endearment. She was stroking her ring finger in a corner booth of the Crypt of the Poets—a sunken public house in West Port renowned for its darkness and ambiguity—when a prowling Ainslie had immediately identified her as a woman flirting with the very notion of infidelity. "Madam," he had said, leaning forward with a feigned expression of earnestness, "might you have seen a lady with dark red hair approach this table? Hazel eyes, rather round face? I'm meant to meet her here, you see, at this very table. Would you mind so much if I sat beside you to wait?"

But when the wait inevitably became rather prolonged, it proved most conveniently mitigated with conversation and increasingly frequent glasses of liquor. And by the time it became clear that the chubby-cheeked redhead most certainly was not going to appear, Ainslie had little need to feign disappointment. "What charming company you've been!" he exclaimed, artfully tapping his newfound companion on the knee. "One would think we'd known each other for years!"

But alas, midnight was approaching unsympathetically. "I fear they will shortly be closing," he observed, with no mere hint of regret, "and we'll be dispelled forcibly if we try to stay. But might I make it my duty to escort you to your door? Our city's streets are rarely safe at night, after all, but most especially with the strange goings-on of recent days."

And further, once they drew up outside her terrace house: "I knew both the victims, you know: Professor Smeaton—the one that was killed—and also the Colonel that was dug up. You laugh! But I'm quite serious—I had some business with them some years ago. Queer fellows, the two of them. Would you care to hear more?"

And when, a few taxing hours later, he was confident she was completely insensible, he had gone to work, strategically ignoring some of the more conspicuous valuables and searching, as was his habit, for buried treasure. In the morning, triumphant, he methodically loosened the sash and broke the latch of a back window, to cloud the issue of culpability, and deposited a disingenuous sovereign on the pillow beside his dozing Bathsheba, before heading off to his prearranged meeting, sprinkled lightly with the wife's rosewater and fortified heavily with the husband's snuff.

Presently weaving between traffic on the South Bridge he happened to catch another glimpse of the Quakerish young lady, still behind him, still watching him, though when he looked at her directly she lowered her eyes with a sort of fearful deference. He turned into Infirmary Street and glanced back with curiosity. Again she swiftly rounded the corner, as though tracing his path—purposely following him, he was sure of it.

But he was in truth more intrigued than alarmed, finding in her persistence something peculiarly arousing. And he was in high spirits, after all, and certainly he had been followed by adventurous young women before. So with the inclinations of a seasoned game player he decided to make a sport of it. He ducked down a lane beside the Public Baths and soon heard the young lady's footfall behind him. He turned into Drummond Place, and she followed him again. He curled into Nicolson Street past the Railways Parcel-Receiving Office, and once more she matched his urgency.

He smiled inwardly, thinking that he was like some magnet that drew particles by some immutable force, some phenomenon not strictly within his control. And reverting to his military training, as he so often did, he decided it was high time for an ambush, a manly confrontation. Swinging into Hill Place, then, he turned immediately, arms folded, and set himself up beside a corner pillar-box. And when the startled young lady appeared seconds later he was ready for her.

"Hullo there," he said with a grin.

She almost collided with him in her haste. "Forgive me, sir! I was—"

"Following me, I take it?"

"No, sir!" she protested, drawing back. "No, sir!"

"I believe you were."

"Not at all, sir—I am simply on my way to work!"

He smirked. "And you work around here, I suppose?"

"Aye, sir, I do!" She had not raised her eyes above his collar.

"And where might that be, then?"

"Where—?"

"Where do you work?"

"I work there, sir," she said, gesturing timidly across the road to a bookstore, where two old men were rummaging through the outside stalls.

Ainslie looked back at her doubtfully. "And you followed me around the Baths because you lost your way, I suppose?"

"Because I needed to post a letter, sir—at the pillar-box near the hospital!"

"And this one here would not suffice?"

"That one is very popular with students, sir, and prone to overfilling!"

Ainslie grunted skeptically, recognizing as he did something disconcertingly familiar in her manner, her exaggerated air of innocence. "I've seen you somewhere before," he decided.

"No, sir!" she insisted, surprisingly vigorous, and moved to pass him.

"I believe so," he reiterated, stepping out to block her. "Yes," he said, squinting. "You were at the Crypt of the Poets yesterday evening . . . under the portrait. "

"I was not there!"

"Or outside my lodgings, then—I've seen you in Cockburn Street."

"It was not me!" She shook her head emphatically.

"But I'm convinced I've seen you before," Ainslie said, scrutinizing her pale features, the delicate lines of her face, and unable to reconcile a feeling pitched somewhere between curiosity and unease. "I'm convinced of it," he said again, strangely haunted.

"I've no idea what you mean, sir," she stated, and moved to pass him again, and this time he did not impede her, for in truth she was not quite pretty enough to warrant his torture.

"Then what might be your name?" he called out after her. "Can you tell me that?"

She stopped halfway across Hill Place and looked at him directly for the first time. Her head was lit up by a probing shaft of sunlight, and her brilliant blue eyes shone like pharmacy lamps.

And now it was an altogether different face that Ainslie saw: a timeless expression of defiance, resentment, even accusation. But the young lady did not identify herself, nor did she need to.

"Evelyn!" called one of the old men from the bookstore. "Evelyn!"

She continued staring at Ainslie.

"Evelyn," the old man cried again.

She tore her eyes away and turned to face her employer.

"Can you help us here, Evelyn?" the old man called. "There's a book we need to find."

Evelyn.

She shook herself and darted over to provide assistance, all other concerns swiftly buried, and standing stock still by the pillar-box Ainslie felt the blood drain from his face like water from a sink.

Evelyn.

Or do you mind if I call you Eve?

His tongue curled and recoiled, as though touched by some caustic liquid. The skin felt flattened against his face. He stared, not breathing, at the jittery little thing, so much older than when he had held her against his hammering chest, until he was sure there was no mistake.

They had assured him she was dead.

But she was alive, she was back in Edinburgh, and a whole series of terrible associations now whirled and coalesced in his head, unable to be denied. And suddenly his appointment, the bracelet, all his plans for the rest of his life—all became irrelevant. And when he finally found himself able to move he wrenched himself around and headed without delay for his apartment, already trying to decide what he should pack and what he should leave behind.

Chapter IX

EDINBURGH IS A CITY of angles and abysses, its Old Town a medieval warren of steep, winding streets, plunging stairways, and tenements clinging to sheer slopes. It is also, by virtue of its singular construction, a city of subterranean vaults, secret tunnels, and sealed-over streets. The showpiece Princes Street Gardens themselves lie in the ravine of the emptied Nor' Loch, a once putrid cesspool of decomposing waste and floating corpses, from which luminous gases frequently issued. And at the eastern end of the old lake, buried in a gap between the markets, pavilions, circuses, and its mammoth railway hotels, lies Waverley Station, down the carriage ramp of which, on Friday night at eleven o'clock, Inspector Groves descended past the police cordon and into the realms of nightmare.

He was immediately assailed by the stench of panic, sweat, soot, vomit, horse dung, and death. The station was not crowded, fortunately, populated only by staff, railway policemen, cabmen, and some wide-eyed onlookers who had lingered to feast on the horror. Pringle stood at the base of the ramp with an East Coast Railways representative, ready to direct the Inspector to the narrow London platform. Down the line, under a catwalk bridge, a chestnut horse had plunged headfirst onto the tracks with a cab twisted behind it. The cabstand was still in disarray and portmanteaux and carpetbags were strewn everywhere. Crompton arc lamps, suspended from the crisscrossing rafters above, blazed starkly across a single human figure, splendidly attired in a blue-beaver topcoat and dislodged hat, lying spread-eagled across the platform in a pool of glistening blood.

"What's the man's name?" Groves asked tightly. He had been hauled from bed just as his head sank into the pillow after another dogged and fruitless day.

"James Ainslie," Pringle answered. "According to the cabman who brought him here."

"Ainslie . . ." The name sounded familiar. "The showman?"

"That's right, sir. An entrepreneur. A wee bit shady, or so I believe."

"Aye." Groves nodded vaguely, seeming to recall that the man had assisted him once or twice with a case of theft, though he had never liked him. "Has a doctor seen to him?"

"Dead as Julius Caesar, he said, and much quicker."

"No one apprehended?"

"No one, sir."

There was no certainty that this death was related to the others under investigation, but the sheer gruesomeness was immediately familiar. The victim's neck had been opened as though by a scythe, the tongue was lolling from a gaping rictus, and the eyes were unusually protuberant; clearly not the sort of murder that any normal man could effect, in such a public space, and escape without being caught. Groves consequently might have delighted in another potential key to the mystery, but the body also reintroduced the real fear that, despite the Wax Man's renunciation of responsibility, the case was expanding far beyond his control. And so, in lieu of an appropriate emotion, he settled on a churning stomach.

"What in God's name is the matter with his face?" he asked, having moved in for a closer inspection. He was referring not to the injuries but to the unnaturally whitened skin, darkened eyebrows, and some wispy facial hair that seemed pasted on with spirit gum.

"Seems like he made himself up, sir."

"Like an actor?"

"He was a fixture of the theater community, sir. Seth Hogarth was one of his friends."

Groves grimaced. "So he was trying to disguise himself? From his assailant?"

"Can't say, sir. Seems it didn't work too well, in any case."

Groves looked around at the frowning railway constables and gawping onlookers. A couple of enterprising urchins had gained a vantage point on the catwalk bridge. "Get those imps down from there," he snapped. "And cover the body. This is no . . . wax museum." By dawn the news would engulf the city and knit the air with whispers. His potential fame would expand in direct proportion, but containing all the details in some manageable form suddenly seemed as futile as catching a cloud in a jar.

"You're the cabman?" he asked a white-capped figure standing nearby.

"I'm the . . . aye." The man had a graze on his head and seemed dazed.

"Where did you bring the victim from?"

"Mr. Ainslie . . . ?"

"Where did you pick him up from?"

"From . . . from Cockburn Street."

"Cockburn Street?" It was connected with Waverley Bridge, well within walking distance. "He lives there?"

"Aye."

"And he took a cab?"

"Mr. Ainslie . . ." the cabman managed, "paid very well. He was keen on privacy."

"Privacy?" Groves blinked. "What do you mean?"

The cabman seemed short of breath. "A footman hailed me . . . and directed me right up to the door of Mr. Ainslie's building . . . and Mr. Ainslie dived into the cab like he did not care to be seen."

Pringle interjected with the details. "He had a one-way ticket on the second-class carriage to London, sir. The ten o'clock train."

"The ticket," added the Railways representative, "was purchased by a footman earlier today."

Groves glanced at the empty track. "The train has departed?"

"That's correct, sir."

Groves frowned angrily. "Who allowed such a thing? There might have been witnesses aboard."

"It was already pulling out when the murder occurred, sir," Pringle explained. "Apparently Mr. Ainslie had paid to sit in his cab until the very last moment, sir. His trunk was already in the luggage van, but he had an idea he could personally transfer to the train after the last whistle had sounded."

Groves looked at the cabman for verification. The man nodded, gulping. "Had . . . had the blinds down," he said. "He was boxed up, out of sight, just waiting . . . for that whistle."

"Are you telling me he could have stepped out of the cab at any time, but he chose to remain inside until the train was actually pulling out?"

"Seems he was really trying to avoid detection, sir," Pringle offered. "The painted face was just the beginning. He did not want to be seen in public. He did not want to be stopped."

"Avoiding detection . . ." Groves mused, chilled. As though fully aware that he might be hunted down and killed, even in a railway station. As though he had seen what had happened to the others, knew that he might be next, and had panicked. But even with all the precautions could not avoid his bloody fate. Groves looked at a rivulet of blood leaking across the platform from under the concealing sheet. "Did you see the one who did it?" he asked the cabman.

"No . . . sir." The cabman was swallowing dryly.

"You did not see the killer make off?"

"The horse bolted."

Groves looked down the line to the dead chestnut. "That's the horse?"

The cabman nodded, gulped, and seemed about to sob, or vomit, or both.

Pringle explained, "The cabman jumped free before the horse left the platform, sir. But he saw nothing. The horse apparently did."

Groves was put in mind of the lighthouse keeper's wolfhound, for the horse too had left behind a trail of ordure.

"Did no one else see anything?" Groves asked.

"A few were in the vicinity, sir, but it was very late." Pringle directed him to a small group waiting nearby: a stationmaster, a few bystanders, a couple more cabmen, and a man Groves knew as a noted pickpocket ("The Nimble Fingers of Jem").

"Mr. Carroll," he said, selecting the last. "Plying your trade among the travelers again?"

"I like watching trains." Jem Carroll sniffed. He had served much prison time and was little intimidated by the law.

"You have sharp eyes, Carroll."

"That's the truth."

"What did you see?"

"Hard to say, Inspector." His tone was typically defensive. "One minute the train's all steaming and pulling out. Next there's a sound like ripping fabric and a man's flung like a rag-and-bone sack across the platform."

"You saw the killer?"

"From the corner of my eye."

"And?"

Carroll struggled. "Hard to say. A huge shape, that's all. Wearing a cape, maybe. One moment he's there, plain as a full moon, the next he's nowhere to be seen."

"You're not telling me he disappeared into thin air?" Groves said, though it was entirely in keeping with what he knew of the killer's capacities.

"I swear, Inspector."

In the end Groves did not trust the pickpocket sufficiently—the man was conceivably even a conspirator—and turned to the others. "Did no one see the killer clearly?"

There was a tremulous shaking of heads.

"Are you telling me," Groves said, finding strength in incredulity, "that a man was struck down on a platform of the city's major railway station and no one saw a thing?"

"The train was moving," the stationmaster protested. "And there were great drafts of steam and smoke. And it was hot."

"Hot?" The night had in fact acquired a significant chill.

"Hot." The stationmaster acknowledged the incongruity, thought about it, and nodded. "Aye . . ."

"The air was twisting," one of the cabmen offered. "Like over a stove."

Groves's head was hurting. "Let me understand this." He looked at all of them impatiently. "The train was pulling out, and there was much steam and smoke. There was a great heat. And no one saw the man killed?"

"There was a . . . shape," the stationmaster offered. "Black . . ."

"Black?"

"Wearing black. A great force."

"Where did it come from, then? It must have been waiting somewhere on the platform."

No one answered.

"And where did it go once it had killed the man?"

Silence again.

"The heat," the stationmaster protested. "And the smoke. It was all over in a blink."

Groves looked around him, wondering if there were some hole or trap through which the killer might have disappeared. One of the railway tunnels, possibly? For years the disused Scotland Street tunnel had been used for nothing but mushroom culture—could the killer be lurking there? Or in any other of the uncharted apertures, underground passages, sweatshops, or old oyster cellars in this godforsaken city? Did this explain the supernatural ease with which he appeared and disappeared? And the extraordinary efforts to which Ainslie went to conceal himself? Groves's eyes wandered up to the station ceiling, vaulted and ribbed like that of a cathedral, and again he had cause to wonder about the forces arrayed against him.

"There was a page fluttering about, sir," Pringle said. He unfolded a sheet not dissimilar to one of Groves's own ledger pages. "One of the transport police picked it up, sir. The first one at the scene."

"Where was it?"

"On the platform a wee distance from the body."

"A message? From the killer?"

Pringle handed the page across. "Seems likely, sir."

Groves looked at the crude black-ink message:

CE GRAND
TROMPEUR

He nodded sagely. "It's French," he decided.

"I know a wee bit of French, sir," Pringle offered.

"Aye? What's your translation?"

"'This great cheat.' 'This great swindler.' Something like that."

Groves squinted at the words. "Seems about right." He glanced at the covered body. "Was Mr. Ainslie from France?"

"No, sir. But there's no reason to say that the murderer might not be."

"So the murderer writes the accusation in his native tongue?"

"It's possible, sir."

Ce Grand Trompeur. For some reason Groves thought of Evelyn Todd, the delicate Irish lass with her sheepish claims. She had mentioned something about a second message, hadn't she? *Accusing words.* Could this be a third one? And what had she said of the killer? *A man who has traveled far.* A man who might be familiar with Scripture and the languages of the Continent. Who might have business with professors, philanthropists, and entrepreneurs. And who might somewhere in his wanderings have encountered the sorcerous ability to move like a shadow, surround himself with smoke and twisted air, and make off like a rat or a blast of steam. And who could kill like a bear or a saber-toothed tiger.

Groves recalled the look Evelyn had given him before departing his office. The mysterious gleam which, in combination with the Wax Man's assurance that a woman was at the heart of the case, had haunted him ever since. Indeed, the whole image of the mysterious waif—her tortured eyes, bloodless skin, and raven attire—had been circling him like a wasp all day. He wanted to wave it away but at the same time he was stimulated by its proximity, the suggestion of a sting. He looked again at the newfound message and wondered if he had in his very hands a way of establishing the veracity of her assertions. For if what she claimed about her powers was true, then it was fair to expect that she had dreamed of Ainslie's murder also. But he would need to be swift if he was to catch her unguarded. Already he could see Douglas Macleod of the *Dispatch* approaching with an open notepad.

"Have the body removed to the mortuary," he told Pringle. "Have Professor Whitty hauled away from his gizzards and see if he might find something useful this time. And that lass—the Irish psychic."

Pringle looked surprised.

"Do you know her address?"

"Aye, sir. On Candlemaker Row."

"Give me the exact number, lad. I'll meet you later at Central Office."

And without a word of explanation he folded the message, slipped it

into a pocket, and headed purposefully up the ramp, out of the nightmare and into the night.

✠

*She did not respond to my knock, as much as I tried, and then another door in
that squalid floor of sub divided rooms opened up, and a slattern looked out at me
and told me to look for her in the wash house, for which I tipped my hat and went
downstairs, and so I came upon the wash house, it was a place of much heat and
steam, and I was very much put in mind of what the witnesses had said about the
shape of the dark force, the one that had slayed the entrezpinoir Ainslie.*

"Evening," he said, in a sharp tone deliberately calculated to startle her
delicate nerves. But Evelyn, with her back to him and scrubbing what
looked like socks or mitts against a washboard with a foaming bar of
black soap, did not jolt, or even shudder. She glanced around, to verify
the presence of the visitor, but that was all. So he coughed command-
ingly. "I was passing," he lied, "and thought I might clear up a thing or
two." He was determined to appear nonchalant but was painfully aware
that it was a characteristic he was ill accustomed to manufacturing.

"Clear up a thing or two?" she echoed. She had barely interrupted her
washing. A boiler was gurgling in the corner.

"Aye. Something you said yesterday, at Central Office."

She continued scrubbing. Her cheeks were flushed. She was dressed
in a boyish jacket and loose-fitting trousers, and with her cropped hair
looked strangely like a message boy.

"Something you said," he went on, "about not being a psychic."

"A psychic . . . ?" she said eventually. Her bony shoulders rose and
fell with the rhythm of her scrubbing.

"You said something about seeing the murders exactly as they happened."

She continued as though oblivious to him. Foam was spilling onto
the oilcloth floor. The room was festooned with candles—in dishes and
the necks of bottles along the windowsill—and the bubbles glistened in
the fluttering light.

"I said there was—"

"I heard you."

He frowned. The heat in the room was stifling.

"Then what," he said, "did you mean by it?"

"I said everything I wanted to say," she said, and soapy water sluiced between her fingers.

He swallowed. "Are you denying it now?"

"I'm not denying it." She examined her washing as though it were far more interesting than anything he could possibly say. "You were there, and you have ears."

He straightened. "What do you mean by that?"

"You heard me."

He had simply not expected such a disrespectful tone—it was impossible to reconcile with the timorous doe that had appeared in the Squad Room—and through his disorientation he struggled for an expression of displeasure. "I do not like this, woman," he managed eventually.

"Like what?" When she finally turned, the candle flames made embers of her eyes. "You heard me yesterday and you hear me now."

"I do not like this tone of yours," he said, as assertively as possible.

She kept her eyes trained on him for a few challenging seconds, then returned to her washing. "You clearly had no time for me. And every word I said was true. Why should I believe that anything has changed?"

He watched as she put aside the washboard and rinsed the mitts in a sink of water. The boiler lid was stammering nearby.

"I was short with you," he heard himself admitting. "But I do not have to offer reasons."

She squeezed and swirled.

"And I have since had time to give the matter thought." He forcibly had to remind himself of his purpose in being there. "I was wondering if you have had any more dreams."

She sniffed but did not answer.

"More dreams of murder."

She did not even acknowledge him.

"I have asked a question, woman."

She shrugged her scrawny frame. "And I have not answered."

He drew air through his teeth. "So you have had no dreams, is that it?"

"I can't remember."

"You can't remember." She seemed determinedly evasive, but he could not bring himself to force the issue. He recalled the French words of the message and tried instead to establish a link. "Well, what of the second message, then—the one you spoke of?"

"What of it?"

"You said some details returned to you in fragments."

"I did."

He shifted. "Well, might you have recalled the language of that message?"

"Why should I have done so?"

"You said the words were strange. And you said the killer had traveled far. Have you seen any further messages like it?"

She frowned and abruptly turned. "Why?" she asked. "Have you found a third message?"

He could not help it, his eyes fell away—and only with great effort did he force them back up. "I have found no message," he lied. But like the Wax Man she seemed to have some talent for gazing through his skull and leaving him vacant with her indifference. And when she turned back to the sink, drawing the plug so that the water drained through the cloth, he almost gasped with relief. "I believe, in any event," he managed, "that you called the killer a dark force."

"I suppose I did."

"Do you have anything to add to that?"

"Why should I?"

"It is too vague a description."

"As you have already told me."

Groves cleared his throat. "Did you happen to see a cloak?"

"A cloak?"

"When you saw the killer. Was he wearing a cloak?"

She seemed on the verge of frowning. "He might have worn a cloak. It was dark, as I said to you."

"Aye." He sniffed. On one hand her new attitude seemed to confirm that her previous demeanor had been a fraud, and she genuinely had nothing to offer. On the other there was something decidedly curious about her, and he could not overcome the notion that, rather than undermining her credibility, her petulance only gave it weight. He watched as she moved for the boiler. "You are an odd one, aren't you," he tried.

No answer.

"What do you—" he began to ask, but she removed the lid and steam abruptly swept through the washhouse, swatting at the candle flames and stinging his face. He blinked as the room flooded with mist, and for a few chilling moments, not seeing her, he sensed only a bestial presence, heard a guttural gurgle, and his skin prickled fearfully. But then the steam dissipated and he finally located her, leaning over the bubbling cauldron with a wooden pole.

"What do you do?" he asked, straightening. "During the day?"

She shrugged. "I work."

"Where?"

"For Arthur Stark."

"The bookseller?" Groves knew of him, an old eccentric with radical political views and a crowded store near the University.

Evelyn did not answer. She had inserted the pole deep into the water and was stirring around for her garments.

Groves wet his lips. "And can you explain why you are here," he demanded, "at this ungodly hour?"

"Why do you ask? Is it against the law?"

He was about to reply, but he saw her bending into the boiler, fishing deep, and he had the rogue, illicit hope that he might catch a glimpse of her floating undergarments. He almost teetered over, in fact, making sure he saw the items when they came to the surface. But it was only bed linen—pillowcases and a sheet. She transferred them to the sink in preparation for the wringer and he settled back on his heels.

"It's past midnight now," he insisted, frustrated. "When . . . when do you sleep?"

She returned the lid to the boiler. "When I'm tired."

"That's not a proper answer. Do I need to remind you who I am?"

She wiped her brow with the back of an arm. "I slept before," she said. "It was enough."

He thought about it. "You slept through the evening?"

"I suppose I did."

"And when did you awaken?"

"When I was no longer tired."

"You would be well advised not to be bold with me, woman."

She sighed. "Half an hour ago."

"So you were asleep through ten o'clock, in any event?"

Silence.

"And you are able to report no dreams? Not even fragments?"

"Nothing."

"Might you have heard of a certain Mr. Ainslie?"

"Never." She blinked, as though something had just occurred to her, and turned to stare at him with her cobalt eyes gleaming. "Why do you ask?"

He felt a most perplexing current bolt through him. "I . . . I have no further questions," he said in a forced sneer, and clapped his hat to his head. "Good evening to you, then." And, loosening himself with effort from her spell, he turned and marched off into the night with a face wet with steam and sweat.

Visions of the dead Ainslie returned to me again and again through the night, and for this reason I slept hardly at all, he wrote in his journal, but it was a lie. For it was in fact images of Evelyn Todd that plagued his slumber: the inexplicable contrast in her bearing, her hostile eyes, her unconvincing denial of any significant dream or knowledge of Ainslie. And then there was *Ce Grand Trompeur,* too, the mysterious message left behind by the killer. He had forgotten it at the time, but she had all but admitted in the Squad Room that she knew French (how could it have slipped his mind?). And so by dawn the little darkly dressed creature in the washhouse, for all her evident frailty, seemed eminently capable, in his delirious mind, at least, of transforming into a homicidal force wrapped in heat and steam, and with every rattle of his frost-coated windowpanes he shuddered under his quilts, recalling the Wax Man's prescient words—*"the power a woman can work on a man's mind is greater than any witch's potion"*—and terrified that at any moment she might pounce out of the darkness, wrap her bony limbs around him, and clamp her talons on his thumping heart.

Chapter X

CANAVAN SLEPT in a cubbyhole at the very top of a corkscrew stair in a twelve-story pinnacle of a tenement overhanging Waverley Station, his fitful slumber interpolated with departure whistles and the hiss of gathering steam. On Sunday mornings it was his habit to put on his faded morning coat and a carpet tie and attend an Old Town church of no particular preference—he was of mixed parentage, and believed the Apostles themselves had no denomination—and afterward roam the back alleys distributing morsels of food to Edinburgh's homeless dogs (this because the city's ash buckets, the primary source of the strays' sustenance, were not put out for collection on Saturday nights, and the Sabbath for the dogs was a bewildering day of hunger and despair).

On this particular Sunday, however, the Third of Advent, he dressed in an irregular coat and duck trousers and headed with particular haste across the city to the majestic St. Mary's Episcopal Cathedral in Palmerston Place, the New Town. It was significantly out of his way, but he knew that in front of his more commonly attended churches the dogs would already be gathering expectantly, and, with no money to buy them food and a heart as heavy as a church bell, he could not bear to face them or to present them even fleetingly with a promise he could not fulfill. Nor could he bring himself, during the service, to accept the consecrated Host, for fear that he might be tempted to hold it on his tongue and later distribute it among his own starving congregation.

It was an unusually solemn service, the week's horrors of a type that could not be denied with the most devoutly muttered prayers. Even in the pews the parishioners clustered in protective numbers and shot reflexive glances at the slightest shuffle or creak. The bishop, who had many years earlier presided over the funeral of Colonel Munnoch, saw fit to remind them that evil gains strength through fear, but in fact quails at the contest, so that no one should think for a minute that any male-factor is incurable, or greater than a true Christian's resistance. Canavan slipped out during the offertory hymn:

> My heart is pained, nor can it be
> At rest, till it finds rest in Thee.

He was relieved to find no dogs waiting outside the main doors, but equally surprised to spot a familiar figure, dressed in a Norfolk jacket and Sunday bowler, sitting patiently on a bench nearby. Since he had not informed anyone where he would be—or even that he was no longer employed—he suspected that the Professor had followed him, or even divined his whereabouts with some newly discovered intuition.

"You know," McKnight said, removing his pipe and getting to his feet, "I mentioned your practice—your dog-feeding practice—in a lecture some weeks ago. I hope you don't mind."

"Always happy to assist the cause of education," Canavan said, privately disconcerted that his concerns had been read so plainly.

"I did not mention you by name, of course, but I said I knew a certain illogical fellow who persists in feeding the homeless dogs of the city, thus ensuring that they are sufficiently nourished to beget even larger generations of strays, compounding the problem—and the hunger, and the suffering—indefinitely."

"It's always been my belief," Canavan countered, "that kind gestures themselves beget generations of kind gestures, so that whatever the

number of the strays, there will always be an equal number of those willing to provide."

"Perhaps," McKnight conceded. "But that does not change the
immutable law. With very minor fluctuations, the percentage of starving strays in any city will always remain the same."

Canavan was resilient. "If God can provide for the sparrows of the
world, I believe there's certainly enough room for me to look after the
stray dogs of Edinburgh."

McKnight chuckled. "Very well put," he said, seemingly happy to
concede defeat, and he gestured across the church grounds. "Have you
time for a walk?"

"I suppose so," Canavan agreed, not wanting to give the indication
that he had time for almost anything. "But to where?"

"Call it a perambulation. Where distance and discussion lead to a
mysterious destination."

"I hope I won't regret it."

"Nonsense," McKnight said. "You were veritably born for it."

The two men took off at once past the cathedral scaffolding and the
foundations of the chapter house, and without further ado the Professor
introduced his more pressing interest. "You've heard of the carnage at
Waverley Station, of course?"

"It's been difficult to avoid," Canavan agreed somberly. "What have
you learned of the victim?"

"Very little," McKnight admitted. "The man has published no literature and has had no literature published about him."

"From what I know of him, the man wouldn't have enjoyed any
commitment, even that of ink."

"You've discovered some details?"

"Almost accidentally." Having spent much of the previous day in the
shady district of Happy Land, in fact, Canavan had been exposed to a
great deal of gossip about the man, and had listened with a strange sense
of duty.

"Go on."

"Well . . ." Canavan shrugged. "The victim was well known to
numerous fallen ladies."

"That much could be speculated."

"A dealer in indecent prints. Recently involved in the Mammoth Diorama at Albert Hall—those huge pictures of the Afghan and Kenyan wars. Staged a few performances by some French ventriloquists. Was based in Edinburgh, but moved freely through the country, and to other shores."

"And in less recent times?" McKnight asked. "Prior to the death of Colonel Munnoch, for example?"

"I think he might have lived in London for some time. He'd been a soldier at some stage. He was always displaying his scars to the ladies. Had a particularly noticeable one under his eye."

"Did he serve in Munnoch's regiment?"

"I don't think so, but that part of his life seems deliberately veiled. He had some experience with the Ashanti, and liked boasting about his time on the Gold Coast. But he was a renowned liar, from all accounts, so it all could be fantasy. Thus, I suppose, the note—*Ce Grand Trompeur*. Did you hear of that?"

"It was in the newspapers."

"Any idea what it means? Some connection with his occasional visits to France?"

But McKnight was curiously evasive. "Look at these houses," he said, pausing at the corner of Manor Place and with a sweep of his cane indicating the splendid uniformity of the Coates Crescent villas. "David Hume was one of the first residents of the New Town, you know. The great empiricist in this little quarter of reason and efficiency. Houses of infinite harmony, gardens of perfect precision, streets of glorious symmetry. Everything measured, tagged, compartmentalized, and assigned an identity. A triumph in greystone over the ungodly disorder of nature and all things beyond human control."

Canavan admired the sunlit street. "You seem to be suggesting there's blasphemy here, while others might see God in the very desire to be clean and disciplined."

"Blasphemy is an incongruous concept in the New Town. *Blasphemy* is a word that will soon be redefined in man's own image, when God Himself is pushed to the margins."

"I am speaking to Thomas McKnight the Atheist?" Canavan asked, puzzled.

The Professor smiled. "This way," he said, gesturing again, and they crossed a largely deserted Maitland Street. "And back through the mists of time."

They were moving directly from modern Edinburgh to its dark medieval heart, and Canavan now became alarmed. If they were to venture into the Old Town they would come within range of the hungry strays. The dogs would approach him imploringly and the pain of his inadequacy would be exacerbated. He buried his hands in his pockets.

"There's a lass, is there not," McKnight asked, "who claims to have dreamed of the crimes in unusual detail?"

Canavan nodded, surprised that the Professor had heard of her, for this had been printed in no newspaper. "It's what they say."

"What have you heard of her?"

"She lives off Candlemaker Row in a tiny room of paper-thin walls." A neighbor, Canavan could have added, to a makeshift brothel, the denizens of which could not decide if she was angelic or deranged. "A private woman, who lives alone. I've been told there is something genuinely strange about her. She is," he added, "from Ireland. Or claims to be."

"And there are so many impostors around." McKnight smiled, before going on, "But do you believe her claims?"

"I've never met her. Though I've no reason to doubt her."

"Then how might you explain her powers?"

"I've not given it any thought. It's likely just a coincidence. Why? Do you think it really has some relevance?"

But McKnight again became frustratingly enigmatic. "You know," he said, "there are African tribes that believe the soul leaves the body in dreams, and the dreamer is directly responsible for all the actions there committed."

Canavan could not quite see the point, but was not slow to take up the challenge. "The Church, on the other hand, has decided that man is not guilty for acts committed in his dreams."

"Aye," McKnight agreed cynically as they began climbing King's Stable Road along the skirts of the Castle. "The Church spent centuries building up its defenses against all sorts of pernicious thoughts, and yet felt particularly vulnerable in sleep. Hence the notion, from Augustine and Jerome among others, that dreams come from Satan."

"In their dreams," Canavan conceded, "the saints were the victims of ungodly desires. To call dreams the work of the devil, then, is a largely innocent reaction—a mistake."

McKnight chuckled. "Oh, I did not say it was a mistake. The truth is that we are rarely more set upon than we are in dreams. Terrors, conflict, ungovernable impulses, the loss of all reason and logic—dreams are the showcase for unconscious fears and desires, and it is not for us to say that they might not be the work of some malignant force. The *genius aliquis malignus* of Descartes's dream, perhaps. The devil in all of us."

"That's the philosophical devil, not the biblical one."

McKnight pursed his lips. "The only difference, as I see it, is that philosophy is yet to decide if the devil represents truth or lies. The Bible is less ambiguous. That verse underlined and left with Colonel Munnoch, for instance. From the page removed from our very own Bible."

"A theory yet to be proved."

"John 8:44, in any case." They passed under the King's Bridge. "Could you recite the entire verse, and not just the underlined phrase?"

Canavan had been examining the verse, in fact, just the previous day, and was able to recite it practically verbatim. "'Ye are of your father the devil, and the lusts of your father ye will do. He was a murderer from the beginning, and he abodes not in the truth, because there is no truth in him. When he speaketh a lie, he speaketh of his own: for he is a liar, and the father of it.'"

"The father of lies . . ." McKnight said, savoring the words. "A phrase that returns us, does it not, to *Ce Grand Trompeur*—the Great Deceiver."

They drifted into the Grassmarket, former site of hangings and witch burnings, and now crowded with banks, coffeehouses, and hotels.

"I'm still not sure I see your point," Canavan said edgily. He had spotted his first stray, a particularly pitiable-looking terrier wandering across the street ahead.

"How so?"

"You seem to be drawing repeated connections between philosophy and the Church."

"Well . . ." McKnight shrugged. "Both institutions have always been essentially fearful of the prodigious powers of the imagination, and the enormous amount of time we spend enslaved by it."

"The imagination is only a tool, and can be used at will." The terrier was looking their way, without seeming to notice them.

"No one uses it entirely at will," McKnight insisted. "Have you ever stopped to consider how much time even the most unimaginative man each day spends, neither willingly nor unwillingly, in the world of his imagination? In aspects of thought that involve speculation or alternative history? Why, a simple train journey will set off a spontaneous chain of fantasies—everything from the locomotive jumping the rails to the weather upon arrival to the possibility of an unplanned romance. Anything that offers a range of possibilities will have the mind rummaging crazily through the realms of fantasy to locate the most appealing prospect or the worst possible outcome. So it could be said that the imagination never rests—it is indefatigable and voracious. It cannot be shut down even in sleep, when all but the most essential functions of life are subdued, but ceaselessly seeks stimulation, and it may even go farther—for it is not for us to attest—beyond the moment of death. It could well be the case that the last thing a man sees is not that which his eyes settle upon, but that which his imagination furnishes for him. Which might indeed be heaven, if he is lucky, and of course it might be hell. It could be argued quite reasonably, in any case, that this imagination is what really constitutes a man's soul."

Canavan snorted. "So you call the soul a voracious predator now?"

"Harboring a malignant demon."

The terrier had slunk away through a sunless wynd, but Canavan knew it would not be the last. "Leaving aside original sin," he managed, "I have trouble accepting the place of a demon in the soul."

"I think we know instinctively that our imaginations—and our souls—are ravenous," McKnight argued, as they approached St. Giles. "And the Church's whole mission might be seen as establishing barriers to regulate that appetite."

"Comforting to know your anti-ecclesiastical ideologies haven't deserted you completely."

"Oh, I don't seek to indict the Church in particular. It's in our nature to establish boundaries and restrictions. We consciously impose limits on our own thoughts and settle into an expedient system of simplifications and archetypes. We willingly stamp archetypes even upon ourselves, to fall into the world we have constructed out of easy recognitions and the disinclination for complexity. The unconscious, however, remains unsated and frequently rebellious."

"Finding expression in dreams."

"To the extent that it is able," McKnight said. "For it is possible we have imposed boundaries even here." They were well into the Old

Town now, with its chaos of tilting tenements and hidden howffs, but the streets were eerily deserted and silent even by Sunday standards: no jingle of horse-drawn trams or clatter of carriage wheels, no coalmen or hawkers; even the combative Sabbath bells were unusually subdued. People gathered, where they gathered at all, in cautious groups, sparing wary glances to the left and right, as though fearing they might be attacked at any moment, and there was even, Canavan noted, a surprising dearth of strays, as though the canine world itself had recoiled. They turned onto the empty North Bridge.

"The parameters become visible in the spatial metaphors we use in reference to the mind," McKnight continued. "'Out of his head,' 'buried deep in memory,' 'put to the back of the mind.' But in truth the mind in its purest form has no spatial dimensions. Even our conviction that the mind is unable to interact directly with the physical world is a self-imposed restriction. Let me give an example. A destitute young girl owns a doll she adores. The doll is her only pleasure in life: her mother is dead and her father is a violent brute. A neighborhood bully, responding to the very affection she exhibits for the doll, seizes it, tears it apart, and distributes it all over the street. The girl is distraught and weeps for days. How would you describe such a story?"

"Heartbreaking."

"Aye. The girl in her innocence has projected a personality onto something that is mere rags and ceramic. And certainly any competent doctor would be able to prove that the doll never had a pulse, that it was matter without mind, never a living creature and never a dead one. And yet the devastating emotions the girl experiences cannot be dismissed as entirely immaterial. In fact, we know instinctively that they are not, and the proof is in the metaphor you yourself have used—'heartbreaking.'"

Canavan thought about it. "The same competent doctor who performed the doll's postmortem should also be able to prove no real damage was done to the girl's heart, or to my own, for that matter. Beyond a fluttering of the pulse, I'm sure."

"Oh, I would argue much more than that. There are intense disturbances we are as yet unable to accurately gauge. I would argue, in fact, that the girl has been cut by a blade that, no matter how imaginary, is no less powerful than a butcher's knife, and inflicts wounds that might be even deeper."

"This is the arena of psychology."

"It might be if the girl were real," McKnight said. "But in fact she is completely fictitious. A metaphysical figment of my imagination. Whose story, by your admission, had a physical effect on you. Now multiply that effect many times over and project it into reality. Apply it to some more sinister grievance and try to imagine the intensity of that anger. If the loss of a doll can cut through a girl like a knife, imagine the blades a fully developed adult might unsheathe."

And now, piecing together all the Professor's previous words—about accountability for dreams, the dimensions of the mind, and the devil of the unconscious—Canavan at last thought he perceived a point. "You're not trying to suggest," he said incredulously, "that three men were killed by an angry impulse?"

He expected a laugh, but McKnight was alarmingly silent.

"My God," Canavan said, thinking about it. "It's the Irish lass, isn't it? The dreamer?"

No answer.

"You really suspect she's involved somehow?"

"Oh, I'm almost certain she's involved. It's just a matter of degree."

"You're not serious?"

McKnight smiled. "I'm most decidedly serious."

"But how?" Canavan asked, already oddly defensive. "How can you say this based on what little we know?"

But again McKnight chose not to answer directly. They were crossing over bloodstained Waverley Station, where Sunday train service had recently been introduced, but even the platforms were abnormally silent. "The world seems so solid and absolute. Stubbornly and intractably real. Yet I ask you to consider how much of reality is constructed exclusively in our imaginations."

Canavan sensed he was being guided down another long and twisting path, and he decided to stand fast behind an indisputable statement. "No man can walk on water," he said, "even if he doesn't recognize it as water."

"Aye," McKnight agreed, and snorted. "But only because he is bound inextricably to recognizing himself as a man."

They turned past the General Post Office and headed into Waterloo Place. Having left the Old Town without having encountered another stray, Canavan now regarded himself as out of danger. But he was too distracted to dwell on his guilt, or even his pity.

"Care for a little climb?" McKnight asked, and without waiting for a reply digressed to the rock stairs of Calton Hill. They ascended swiftly and nimbly and soon were at the top amid the jumble of Gothic and Grecian monuments.

"Plato said that in all of us there is a lawless wild beast that peers out in sleep," the Professor observed, looking at the Doric columns of the National Monument, the city's unfinished Parthenon. "And that the bridge between the worlds of mind and matter is the soul."

"Which you've already equated with the imagination."

"You know," McKnight said, and paused to relight his pipe, "all my life I've wanted to find this bridge. I've wanted to believe in an imagination so powerful that it can break free of all the shackles and hurdle all barriers. It has always seemed like a profoundly beautiful thing, invested with all the power of God. But I remember the wild beast and now I wonder . . ."

They stood for a minute watching a devil's-head cloud yawn briefly across the sun before fragmenting and dissolving.

"Care for another climb?" McKnight asked.

Canavan looked pointedly at the vacant air. "To heaven?"

But McKnight was already heading down the stairway, and Canavan tried to conceal his dismay. If the Professor had some purpose in this stroll, it was still eluding him.

They rounded Holyrood Palace with its pacing sentries and gold-crowned streetlamps and set off across the empty Queen's Park. "The Salisbury Crags," McKnight said, gesturing to their final destination. "The birthplace of geology."

They spared a bracing glance at the forbidding cliffs—where James Hutton had first formulated his theory that igneous rock had a volcanic origin far older than any biblical calendar—and it finally occurred to Canavan that the Professor had led him on a calculated course through the history of the human mind, from the mask of modernity through the Middle Ages and Ancient Greece to the naked face of prehistory, in possibly the only city in the world where such was achievable in a Sunday stroll. They ascended the rocky path known as Radical Road.

"For all the layers of the mind we peel back," McKnight said, fighting for breath, "we find more layers concealing the primeval soul. We search for God in our purest instincts, but in truth we are terrified we will discover only the devil."

They stopped high above the sprawl of the city with their backs to the corrugated crags, and McKnight handed his bowler to Canavan so that he might mop his brow. But the Irishman's grip on the hat was tenuous, and as he passed it back to the Professor a fierce gust of wind blew up and wrenched it from his hand. The bowler took off like a bird.

Startled, Canavan made to scramble down the path in order to retrieve it at ground level. But McKnight clapped a restraining hand on his forearm.

"It's only a hat," he said. "If God means us to find it, then we surely will."

Canavan settled back, puzzled. "God again . . . ?"

"Or the devil," McKnight admitted ruefully, and they watched the hat, carried on a furious updraft, gallop far across the sea of Old Town church spires and chimney stacks and vanish into a drifting veil of mist. "The primeval mind . . . the philosophy of the Greeks . . . the discipline of the Church . . . the revolutions of modern philosophy . . . all this, and it still returns to God and the devil." His voice had dropped to a marveling whisper. "I set out to discover the nature of good and evil . . . and in the fog I found them indistinguishable. I aspired to be a great philosopher . . . only to see my philosophies devouring themselves. I came to Edinburgh to separate reality from fantasy . . . only to discover that there is no city on earth more conducive to dreams."

Cloud shadows sprang and dipped across the fields of turrets and crowstepped gables.

"If we're to succeed in this investigation," he added, repocketing his handkerchief, "I warn you we must prepare ourselves for anything. We must look in the cracks of the unconscious, in the gaps under metaphors, in the dark spaces where imagination has pasted over inexperience. Where everything is questionable and all accepted laws are suspended."

Canavan noted the implication that he had already been deputized. "Is it this you've been leading to all along?" he asked, vaguely disappointed. "A call to arms?"

"A call to arms, aye," McKnight said approvingly. "For I cannot face these terrors alone."

They discerned the discordant bellows of a practicing piper in the park below, and from a more distant quarter the flowering skirls of a more seasoned performer. The younger piper paused a minute and then, after a few stuttering attempts, tried to emulate the master with his own wavering pibroch. And in turn the more senior piper hesitated, considered, and then resumed his playing with a few encouraging bars, halting generously so that his unseen apprentice might duplicate his performance. And soon the younger piper had fallen dutifully into place, grateful for the assistance, and quickly, hoisted beyond his station in the urge to succeed, he was weaving sonorous threads around his tutor's promptings, the two of them defying age, experience, distance, and the wind to merge in splendid harmony. The Castle time-gun blew one o'clock with a thumping report and the filaments of mist slowly dispersed.

"You needn't worry about your dogs," McKnight promised. "I'll find some scraps. The finest money can buy."

Canavan was alarmed. "I'm . . . I'm not sure what you mean . . ."

McKnight had not raised his eyes from the smoking city. "I ventured up to Drumgate. I heard of your dismissal."

Canavan sighed and looked away guiltily. "I did not want to tell you."

"Nonsense, lad," McKnight said, and added in a meaningful undertone: "Now neither of us has an excuse."

When the full implication dawned on Canavan his face immediately slackened. He looked down upon the distant dome of the University, as though for confirmation, then back at McKnight, who nodded resignedly.

"Summarily suspended by the University Court," he said. "'Conspicuous lapse of commitment,' the good men judged."

Canavan was dismayed. "For . . . for how long?"

"The council suggests that I might be able to resume duties in the summer. But I anticipate a somewhat longer penance."

Canavan took a moment to measure his own despair.

"Fear not," McKnight assured him, with a mirthless laugh. "I had a small bank account, which I liquidated. And I dispensed with a few unnecessary volumes."

"You sold some of your books?"

McKnight waved away any gesture of protest. "It's more important, at this stage, that we are not distracted by anything frivolous, and certainly not concern for some hungry strays. There is much mental energy to be expended."

But the Professor saw from Canavan's troubled expression that his friend was not convinced, and so he slapped him affectionately on the shoulder.

"Descartes had his famous dream in 1619," he said with a mysterious gleam in his eye. "Twenty-two years later he identified the malignant demon in the publication *Meditationes de prima philosophia.* In 1647 this volume was translated from scholarly Latin into his native French. In it he speaks of some force, very powerful and cunning, that has tried to persuade him that there is no heaven and no earth, no colors, no matter, no minds—that he does not even exist. He called the force "this great deceiver.' *Ce grand trompeur*."

He smiled victoriously.

"So you see? We have been personally summoned, you and I. First through the Bible in your possession, and now through the very language of philosophy. We have been invited purposely, and perhaps even maliciously, deep into the heart of the mystery."

Canavan, without a proper protest, seemed dazed.

McKnight shook his head in wonder at it all. "Would you happen to know exactly where this Evelyn lass lives?"

"I . . . I suppose so . . ."

"Then we must arrange a meeting as soon as possible. I believe she might have some very significant things to tell us."

They picked their way down the rocky path, Canavan's mind too agitated to engage in meaningful conversation. Could the Professor be right? Was the killer deliberately baiting them? What special powers could they possibly possess, to make them the subject of such a challenge? Was the Irish lass really at the heart of it all?

And how, for that matter, had the Professor learned her name?

It made no sense at all.

But when he returned to his sky-high garret and found McKnight's wind-borne bowler sitting neatly on his only chair, he was suddenly convinced logic had flown out the window as surely as the hat had flown in.

Chapter XI

IT WAS THE FIRST DAY I heard of the lamplighter, and the first time I got wind of some conspiracy, Groves later recorded in his memoirs. *It was another day of mounting mystery, with Professor Smeaton now put to rest, and nothing to do but to forge on through the confusion that hung on the city like a blanket, and the fear that hung on it like a sheet. Ainslie's footman was of little help, but again he mentioned his employer's links to the theatre, and to be thorough I could not avoid a visit to "the realms of fantasy," to which I had not been since my days as a wean.*

The Royal Lyceum was a newly erected theater on Grindlay Street with an audience capacity of two thousand people. On the boards outside were pasted newspaper reviews of the latest sensation, the great Scottish tragedian Mr. Seth Hogarth, direct from the London stage, in the title role of *Othello,* with Miss Lindsay Grimes as Desdemona. "Mr. Hogarth," trumpeted the *Review,* "informs his every word with electric passion, and now threatens Tommaso Salvini in his claim to the definitive Moor." During the day, at popular prices, Hogarth was also appearing in *Seven of His*

Most Popular Shakespearean Interpretations, performing selected soliloquies in the character of everyone from Benedick in *Much Ado About Nothing* to Macbeth in the Scottish Play. He was supported by the Brothers Gonzales and Their Eccentric Donkey.

Groves picked his way through the backstage ropes and pulleys and rapped on the indicated dressing room door.

"Come forth," a voice boomed expectantly. "The door is unlatched."

The Inspector entered a tiny windowless room to find the famed actor standing imperiously before a vacant chair, his fists lodged on his hips. Hogarth, he had already been informed, habitually concluded his matinee performances as a fully made-up Moor and remained in character until the final curtain of the evening performance. He was currently costumed in an amber robe with a jeweled collar, burnt-cork makeup, frazzled crepe wig, and gold earrings.

"'Tis Groves?" he asked in his imposing voice.

"It is," replied Groves, vaguely unsettled.

"Five thousand welcomes," Hogarth boomed. "Pray, take a seat."

Groves perceived an imperative tone and ordinarily might have resisted on principle. But he was uneasy enough in the environment, and now on top of that disconcerted by Hogarth's manner, and so he found himself settling almost against his will into the provided chair. It was not the first time he had set eyes on the actor—he had arrived late in the performance and endured the final "interpretation" impatiently, privately rueing the fact that he had missed the donkey—but he found the man even more fearsome in person than he had appeared onstage.

"Have you visited the theater before, Inspector?" the actor inquired. He had not offered his hand, but his eyes blazed with warmth.

"This is the first time I've been," Groves admitted. "But it has not been open too long, in any event."

"I mean any theater. Theater, the father of dreams. Have you never slipped into a play to ease the pain of a torturing hour?"

"I went as a young 'un. And got a headache from the houselights."

"We use electric filaments in glass globes now," Hogarth said proudly. "Only the backup footlights are gas. The naked flame is truly the theater's nemesis." He did not have to mention the Theatre Royal in Broughton Street, which had a nasty habit of burning down every ten years.

"A policeman has little time for such trifles," Groves observed. "Though I caught you before in the guise of the Negro."

Hogarth, as though on cue, affected a theatrical flourish. "'By heaven, thou echoest me . . . as if there were some monster in my thought . . . too hideous to be shown . . . !'" He projected his gilded voice to some imaginary audience and let the words hang in the air and dissipate, his hands still curled, and Groves got the impression that he was meant to applaud, or express some manner of approval. But he only grunted.

"You've heard of the murder at Waverley Station, sir?" he asked, eager to waste no time.

"Unsavory news," said Hogarth, lowering his head, "which truly has turned my countenance."

"What do you know of it?"

"Murder most foul, strange, and unnatural. People's hearts are brimful of fear, and Edinburgh is spoken as a term of terror."

Groves was baffled by the actor's grandiloquence, but he had always suspected that actors were mad. "It is said by more than one that you were a close friend of the deceased, Mr. James Ainslie."

"Pish," Hogarth snorted. "A small acquaintance, hollow friends at best."

"So he was not a friend, you claim?"

"He was a close friend of no one, Inspector. Disgrace knocked often at his door, and I always suspected wrath or craft would get him in the end. Still, to give the devil his due, he could play the gentleman well enough, with those requisites that green minds look after."

Groves decided to register his impatience. "This is a most serious investigation, sir. You would do well to cooperate."

"It is my duty, Inspector, and I hold my duty as I hold my soul."

Groves sniffed. "I would like to know how you met him."

Hogarth again dispensed with his histrionics, if only briefly. "I was appearing as Richelieu at the Royal, coming off my great success as Mr. Tollaway in *My Black Eye*. Perhaps you've heard of it, Inspector?"

Groves shook his head.

"An aching farce. *Punch* called it better than *Who Speaks First?* But you weary of my tedious prattle, I see. Let me rouse my tired memory. Ah, yes—it was twenty years ago or more. Mr. Ainslie was introduced to me as a most worldly financier."

"Had he been to France?"

"There was little Gaul in him, but a great stain of the soldier. Yes, that was it—he had in uniform seen the world. Though more of his soldiership I know not."

This much Groves had already established: a dishonorable discharge from the Royal Rifle Corps and a swift retreat to his city of birth. "Did he speak of his service?"

"Of most disastrous chances, hairbreadth escapes, and insolent foes. But he was an infinite and endless liar, and his heart was clearly set on some future mischief."

"Yet you mixed with him?"

Hogarth sighed heartily. "Limelight brings forth the adder, Inspector. I associate with such serpents, and seek to dodge their fangs when they strike."

"What was his business, then?"

"In the theater?" Hogarth shifted posture. "I believe at first it was simply a bounteous madam by the name of Annabelle, who was appearing with me in *Richelieu,* but had most successfully played the Royal in Manchester in *The Belle's Strategem.* I was Doricourt."

"A harlot?" Groves had little regard for actresses.

"A shallow, changing woman, whom I once considered my own, but who was drawn away by Mr. Ainslie's revels. The man played many a strumpet in his bed, Inspector, though at the time I believe he had commissioned her for something more. There was some evil plan he had hatched, and she was to play a prominent role."

Groves stiffened. "What sort of evil plan?"

"I remember a mist of things, but nothing distinct. There was some orphan involved—some unfathered fruit. And he seemed to be visiting the churches."

"The churches?" Groves thought of Professor Smeaton. "Did you ask why?"

"I did not. But he appeared one day shivering and looking pale, almost beside himself with fear. I took it that he had dared damnation, and elected not to pry."

"He did not tell you anything?"

"Nothing."

"He was tight-lipped, then?"

"I was tight-eared."

"Had you spoken to him recently? This is important."

"Not in many a season," Hogarth said, "though of course he orbited the theater like a wandering moon."

Groves now began to wonder about the actor himself. There was no question he was a cultured man, after all, of the sort identified by Evelyn. And certainly he had traveled far . . .

"The company was dining late that night," Hogarth suddenly offered, as though reading his mind, "a fruitful meal at the lodgings of Oliphant Bentley, the tea merchant, when some caddy did arrive with the news. We all did pale, and lamented Mr. Ainslie's passing like Christians. A rascal he may have been, but at heart we're all bastards. Disguised, was he not, in some odd semblance?"

Groves nodded, making a note to verify the alibi later. "A rough job," he said, "done without expertise." He glanced pointedly at Hogarth's sponges and blending powders. "You've not heard of him, perhaps, prowling around for brushes and pastes?"

"Alas, no, but it would not be unlike the man to improvise. Lead paint, perhaps, which causes the eyes to swell and the skin to shrivel."

"Can you think of any reason for such a mask?"

"Well, as I say, Mr. Ainslie had kept an evil diet long, and might have known his hour of reckoning was nigh. Is there as yet any clue to the identity of the beast responsible?"

Groves shifted. "I am closing in on the killer."

"I warrant that the beast now shivers, knowing such a man has his scent. I pray that when his cue is called, he says the proper lines, and goes to his maker with humility."

"Aye," Groves agreed, though he still was not certain if the man was mocking him.

"Some tea cake, Inspector?" the actor asked, gesturing with a flourish to an ornate tin. "'Tis as luscious as locusts."

But Groves decided that he had already had enough of trying to comprehend Hogarth's ornate jargon. "Kind of you," he said, pushing himself to his feet, "but I fear I have too much to do."

"Pish!" Hogarth exclaimed. "We have scarce begun! I beseech you for more of the theatrical expedition of your sapling years! Which play did you enjoy, and who did perform that day?"

Groves smoothed the brim of his hat. "I don't rightly remember who performed," he said, "though I remember the play well enough." In fact, his dear mother had taken them in the interests of patriotism, and if he recalled it so vividly now it was only because of the sacrifices she had made to do so.

Hogarth's eyes sparkled. "A tragedy? A comedy? A tragicomedy? A history, pastoral, comical-pastoral?"

"A depressing piece," Groves said. "*Macbeth*."

The actor grimaced visibly, but swiftly collected himself. "And did you enjoy it," he asked, swallowing, "for all your tender age?"

The man must surely have had some poor review in the role of Macbeth, for every time I mentioned the play he blanched and spluttered, and in the end, for all his noises of hospitality, he wanted to evict me like a heckler, and I would have protested had I not myself wished to be free of the place, the theatre I say again being no place for the man of practical mind.

"Soft you, a word or two before you go," said a pained Hogarth, seizing Groves's arm at the door. "I have done the state some service, and you know it." Beads of perspiration had materialized on his blackened forehead and he was panting like a heated dog. "No more of that. I pray you, in your letter, speak of me as I am. Nothing extenuate, or set down aught in malice. Speak of me as one who loved not wisely, of one not easily jealous, of one whose hand threw a pearl away, and one who dropped tears as fast as Arabian trees their medicinable gum! I dispatch you to your mystery!"

And he released a confounded Groves and shut the door with an audible gasp.

I have here attempted to record his words with some exactitude, but I fear they are of a brand that one does not easily recall, and speak of one whose salad days are well behind him, and one who has sunk to the level of a blinking idiot.

✠

Absurd though Hogarth was, Groves nevertheless came away deeply impressed by his physical command of the enclosed space, which had him briefly starved of air, and so when Pringle entered the Squad Room late in the afternoon to inform him that Evelyn Todd had returned and most earnestly desired to speak to him, he immediately resolved to make the most of the lesson. He repaired to the neighboring room, the claustrophobic office of the Chief Constable, and quickly set up a chair to face him, dimmed the gaslight, inflated his chest, and stood to his full height, so that he might subjugate her in the style of the Moor.

He cleared his throat gravely. "Fetch her," he said to Pringle, tightening his muscles. "And then set yourself in the hall outside. If you hear me raise the alarm, run in at once with truncheon ready."

Leaving the Royal Lyceum with Hogarth's mention of an orphan fresh in his mind, Groves had made a visit to the New Register House to locate the birth certificate of one Evelyn Todd, specifying the years 1856–65. The search had yielded no immediate results, but the curator reminded him that prior to 1855 all civil registration was in the domain of parish ministers and session clerks; was it possible the woman he sought was of an older vintage? Groves paused to recall Evelyn's delicate features and agreed that, for all her maidenly aspects, it was just possible that she was in the region of her early thirties. But the curator warned him that, without further details, it would take time—hours, at least—to track down the right entry, for the parochial registers were many and voluminous. Groves told him to issue a message when he had succeeded, and returned to Central Office with oddly magisterial steps.

"Enter," he now said when there was a light knock on the door. He was standing in front of the narrow window, his arms folded imperiously and lamplight from Fishmarket Close forming a blazing aureole around him.

Evelyn oozed in like a mist. She was wearing mourning black again, and with a high, faintly clerical collar she looked eerily nunlike.

"Be seated," Groves intoned, nodding at the seat, but she did not even seem to hear him. She slid into his shadow and gripped the back of the chair.

"I beg your forgiveness," she said hoarsely. "I know I was rude, uncommonly rude, but . . . I cannot explain it . . . I have these episodes . . . you must not hold it against me!"

Her face had twisted into creases of long-carved anguish, and she looked every minute of a woman in her thirties. Groves might have been relieved at this rediscovery of her submissive aspect—and indeed his muscles loosened of their own accord—but he was still not certain what to make of it: the contrast was again inexplicable. "Calm yourself, woman," he said loudly, so that his words might be overheard by Pringle, "and make good your account."

"You will not believe me . . . I cannot blame you if you think the less of me, that I am some vile creature, some duplicitous thing. But I ask you to consider that what I say must have some merit, for I would not dare to show my face before you if it were not so! And in truth I am not a liar, and I leave it to my conviction to prove it to you!"

Groves narrowed his eyes. "What are you talking about, woman?"

She looked at him directly for one galvanizing second. "The murder at Waverley Station," she said, and gulped and gasped. "I dreamed it all in great detail . . . exactly as it happened . . . and I saw the message—*Ce Grand Trompeur*!"

This was a feeble boast, for the message was well known, and Groves now wondered if he was witnessing a performance as contrived as that of Seth Hogarth. "Take a seat," he commanded again, but she only gripped the back of the chair more tightly.

"I saw it!" she insisted. "I saw it as I slept! The murder! The note!"

"You might have read about it. Or heard about it, for it is no secret now."

"No, no—" She shook her head vigorously. "The train departing, the man leaving his cab, the great shape striking him down—I saw it all in my dream, and the message also, in rough black ink splashed across a page—'This Great Deceiver.'"

There had been no details in the newspapers about the precise form of the message—the "rough black ink"—but then again it would be easy enough to guess. Groves tightened his arms and stared down his nose.

"What else do you claim to have seen?"

"Just what I have mentioned—but most clearly! I might have been there, it was so clear!"

"Perhaps you were there."

"I was asleep—the nightmare woke me!"

"At what point?"

"As soon as the man was cut down."

"But again you did not see the killer, I suppose?"

"Only steam, and a dark shape. I swear it's true, in God's name!"

Groves grunted. "In the washhouse you told me you had been sleeping until just before I arrived."

"I was not entirely truthful," she admitted, "but you must believe me now!"

For a moment Groves was almost swayed by her performance—and certainly her contrition made him feel deliciously powerful—but ultimately he rejected it all with an unsympathetic sigh. "This is all very grand," he said, unfolding his arms and clasping his hands behind his back. "One moment the shallow strumpet with nary a thing to say, the next calling upon God and whiter than snow. Which is it to be, woman? Settle on your true face so that I can be sure of you."

Evelyn shook her head. "I was dismayed that you did not believe me earlier, that is the truth of it. When it had pained me so much to come to your office and lay myself bare."

He snorted. "Pain? Why should it be painful to tell the truth?"

"It hurts to look back," she said.

"Into your dreams?"

"Into anything."

Groves shifted sideways and a shaft of lamplight struck her like a blade. She winced and drew back into the security of his shadow.

"When were you born, woman?" he asked, remembering his failure at Register House.

"I don't remember."

"You must have been told."

"That part of my life is . . . not clear."

"Who was your father? Your mother?"

She struggled. "I don't remember. But——"

"Where does the name Todd come from?"

"Someone . . . someone told me that was my name. But please——"

"Who?"

She shook her head. "Someone," she managed, "at the orphanage."

The orphanage. Groves felt his muscles tighten again. "You came from an orphanage?"

She looked disconcerted. "I . . . I believe so."

Groves retained his composure. "Which one?"

"A place in F-Fountainbridge. But please, this is not——"

"The Fountainbridge Institute for Destitute Girls?" Groves knew of the place from his days on the beat, an ugly black building mysteriously incinerated sometime in the late 1860s.

"Aye. But——"

"When did you leave there?"

She was visibly uneasy. "My . . . my family claimed me."

"What family? You said you were an orphan."

"My *family*."

He detected some manner of evasiveness, or dishonesty, and he rose several inches on his feet before settling back. "Do you never tell the truth, woman?"

"I am not a liar," she said.

"When did you return to Edinburgh?"

"Two years ago."

"Why?"

"It seemed I should."

"Why?"

She was growing increasingly uncomfortable. "It's my home."

"What did you do when you returned?"

"I was a match dipper. I washed dishes at the Bell and Candle. But—"

"Anything else?"

"I did needlework. Then Arthur Stark gave me work and—"

"What about Professor Smeaton? Did you ever work for him?"

"No—"

"What about Colonel Munnoch?"

"No, no—"

"Do you know of a lighthouse keeper called—"

"*No!*" she cried. Suddenly the washhouse witch had returned in force, and she seemed ready to snap the chair with her hands. "I know of no lighthouse keepers!" she said through gritted teeth. "And that is not why I am here!"

For a long time the only sound was the tick of the Chief Constable's eight-day clock.

By degrees Evelyn seemed to acknowledge her inappropriate temper and wavered like a reed, shaking her head apologetically. "I have seen another message . . ." she whispered, balancing herself on the back of the chair.

"Aye?" Groves took the opportunity to refold his arms defensively. "Which message is this?"

"The other message . . ."

"The French message? We have spoken—"

"No, no—the earlier message I spoke about. I strained hard and the vision returned to me."

Groves was silent a moment, and in the silence heard a creak outside and realized that in the wake of Evelyn's outburst both their voices had hushed notably, so undoubtedly Pringle would be concerned. "The message you said had accompanied the murder of Professor Smeaton?" he asked, almost yelling.

She nodded. "I saw the words scratched on a wall."

"Which wall?"

"A wall near the body."

"I inspected the area nearby. There were no words."

"Still I say," Evelyn insisted, "that I saw a message."

"And what was the form of this message?"

"I could not properly make it out, but I know it was in Latin."

Groves decided to risk scorn. "Pish," he said. "You might have inscribed it yourself!"

"I did no such thing," Evelyn said, and glanced up at him with her shining eyes. "And that is not all," she added quickly, guiltily. "For I think I now have an idea as to the killer's identity."

Groves hesitated. "Oh?" he asked, still not sure he wanted the great mystery revealed to him by a madwoman.

"I cannot say I recognized him exactly, but I am now certain I have seen him before."

Groves denied the possibility. "You make no sense, woman."

"He is the lamplighter," she announced.

Groves blinked. "The what?"

She released the chair. "The lamplighter, I am sure of it."

"The lamplighter?"

She nodded.

Groves judged it safe to prod. "Which lamplighter?"

She could not answer.

"There are many lamplighters in this city," he noted, "lest it not have occurred to you."

"I do not know why I am certain of this," she admitted, and briefly shook as though nauseated.

"It's a feeling, is that it?"

"A certainty."

"Yet you cannot describe this particular lamplighter?"

"No."

"Nothing about him at all?"

"No."

"Not his name? His face? His beat?"

"Nothing," she admitted, and looked up, her gaze lost momentarily on some point over his shoulder.

Turning, Groves became aware that she was staring at the lamp in Fishmarket Close, and suddenly he was convinced—he took hold of the whole idea with enthusiasm—that this new revelation was just a spontaneous invention. She was toying with him again, and for reasons that still eluded him.

"Aye," he said angrily, "you must learn to cooperate, woman."

"I am cooperating."

"I can have you put on the flogging bench yet. Or sent to the gallows, if you fit the crime."

But once more Evelyn momentarily seemed unable to contain her emotion. She glared at him like a willful dog before tearing her eyes away again, biting her lip in self-rebuke.

He gulped, unable to recognize his own feelings. "Is that all?" he heard himself say.

Defeated, she still did not respond, and abruptly looked on the verge of tears.

"Be . . . be on your way, then, woman."

She headed for the door, head bowed.

But now, encouraged by her blushing retreat, Groves decided that he had not been sufficiently intimidating, and impulsively he circled the desk, feeling a strange urge to touch her skin. "A word before you go."

She stopped, her hand on the knob.

"I have rarely met the likes of you," he told her truthfully, withholding his own hand at the last moment only because he feared she might turn on him like a riled cat, "and I am not yet convinced that you do not belong in the madhouse. But keep in mind that I am not easily fooled. If you are tied up in these foul murders, and if you conceal something from me, then I will set myself on you like a brace of hounds, and upon my life I will not stop until you are brought to bay."

She nodded meekly, her cheeks burning, and muttered something unintelligible.

"What . . . what did you say?" he asked.

"' . . . *for they know not what they do . . .*'" she finished mysteriously, and opened the door to depart.

In her wake he stood breathing heavily, disconcerted by a range of dizzying emotions. His heart still galloping furiously, he turned and contemplated the hellish glow of the outside lamp, and buried under generations of family abstinence he felt a yearning for a dram of whisky to quell his combustible nerves.

✠

Both Groves and Pringle were equipped with bull's-eye lanterns brimming with paraffin. They had already examined the walls of the houses on the corner of Belgrave Crescent without success, and now they turned their attention to the northern side of Holy Trinity Chapel. It was almost midnight, exceedingly dark, and the air bustled about them with all the harbingers of a punishing storm.

Pringle found it eventually, two rows of neatly scratched letters in the ashlar wall under the stained-glass angels.

MVITNECONNI
ROTVCESREP

"This might be it, sir," he said. "But I don't rightly recognize the language."

"It's Latin," Groves said authoritatively.

Pringle examined the words doubtfully in the pool of light. "What does it say?"

"That I don't know. It's not a language for a mere inspector." Groves lowered his lantern and started jotting the message in his notebook.

"What do you think it all means, sir?"

"It could mean anything. The woman might have planted it here in the last day or two, with the intention of misleading us."

"I'm not so sure, sir," Pringle said, adjusting his own light. "I cannot say this with certainty, but I have an idea these letters were here when we found Professor Smeaton's body."

"You saw them?"

"I thought they were something to do with the church, sir. And they made no sense."

"Aye," Groves sniffed with finality. "They're Latin." He glanced down Belgrave Crescent, where agitated leaves were advancing like a swarm of locusts. "We'll need them translated fully."

"A clergyman?"

"I don't wish to involve the church."

"Professor Whitty, sir? He lives in Lynedoch Place, not far from here."

"Speaks Latin, does he?"

"After the Ainslie postmortem he bade me good night in Latin, sir. All such medical men are trained in its use."

For a few moments Groves again entertained the delightful notion that Whitty himself was involved somehow, before coming to his senses. He looked up at the fulminating rain clouds and closed his notebook protectively. "Then let us see if the man can be of some use after all," he said, picking his lantern from the ground.

A few minutes later, in the study of his handsome villa, a silk-gowned and tousle-haired Professor Whitty, roused from slumber along with his forbearing wife, lit a lamp over his rolltop desk and settled into his chair to examine the message more closely.

"It's Latin," Groves told him, because the man seemed to be having trouble deciphering it. "Something biblical, it looks to me."

Whitty squinted, turned the page to and fro, and eventually seemed to arrive at an understanding. "It's Latin, certainly."

Groves grunted.

"Reverse Latin."

Groves blinked. "Aye?"

Whitty took out a pencil and wrote the message back to front. "'Innocentium Persecutor,'" he said, and he held the notebook up. "'Persecutor of Innocence.'"

Groves felt his throat clench. "Reverse writing . . . ?" he whispered.

"A riddle," Whitty suggested. "A game. Demon worshippers sometimes use it."

Groves contained a shudder. *Persecutor of Innocence.* He thought of Evelyn, her frail aspect, her victimized attitude and muttered words, and for a moment felt personally accused. He remembered her venomous eyes, used sparingly, like precious weapons, and in such a way that he could not decide if she was challenging him or seducing him, or indeed if there was any difference. Then, snapping out of his reverie and feeling distinctly inadequate in this lettered man's study, he felt the overpowering need for fresh air.

"No doubt they do," he said, and, leaning over, quickly retrieved his notebook and slipped it into his pocket. He nodded to Pringle. "Come along, lad, we have much work to do."

Whitty got to his feet and escorted them dutifully down the hall. "May I ask where you found the message?"

"Why?"

"The location could be significant."

Groves felt vexed. "I don't feel ready to avail you of such information," he said curtly, and donned his hat. "Though of course I thank you again for all your assistance."

Whitty shrugged and held open the door. *"Bene agendo nunquam defessus,"* he muttered sardonically as his guests stepped out into a cascade of leaves and raindrops.

"And good night to you also," Groves said, getting into the cab with Pringle at his side.

Chapter XII

BOTH MEN had reason to feel at home. Her lodging—smaller, even, than Canavan's—was an erstwhile milliner's storeroom squeezed tightly under the gables at the top of twelve flights of dogleg stairs. There was a narrow bed, a tiny stove, a couple of calico lines on which to hang her washing, and a sheet of yellow muslin fastened over a windowpane (her only view, she said, was of Greyfriars Cemetery, and she had little inclination to look down on graves). The walls were of thin lath, there was the scamper of rats in the ceiling and some bestial moans from the neighboring rooms, but everything in her own dominion was meticulously dusted and clean. In lieu of more expensive lighting she employed a slush lamp and tallow candles, but for all her obvious constraints she had rows upon rows of neatly ordered books, occupying almost an entire wall, so that in all the room resembled a miniature version of McKnight's own stygian and sparsely furnished cottage.

"Mr. Stark allows me to take them home," she explained when she noticed McKnight examining the book spines. "Only those titles which are not in demand, of course, and I must return them unsoiled when I've finished. I wear gloves when I read."

She was wearing gloves now—a spotless cotton pair—and kept tugging nervously at the cuffs.

"I know Arthur Stark," McKnight said. "He publishes some worthy academic titles in that basement of his."

Evelyn nodded eagerly. "And I assist him there. I do some of the quarter binding, and I'm working through a sewing apprenticeship."

"You assist with the printing, too?"

"Aye."

"And your fingers get blackened by the inking rollers?"

"Aye." Evelyn looked impressed. "But how did you know . . . ?"

McKnight smiled. "The reason you wear the gloves, is it not, is so that you do not smudge the book pages with ink?"

Evelyn glanced at Canavan, as though to register wonder at his companion's deductive skills. Canavan simply nodded, to assure her that the Professor was in fact real.

"Mr. Stark," she said, "calls it 'the black art.'"

McKnight grunted. "You might want to find a more innocuous term for it," he suggested, "if discussing your trade with the authorities."

She smiled self-consciously and McKnight finally settled into a chair, placing his illogical bowler in his lap and asking if he might light his pipe. Canavan elected to stand by the table and its guttering candle. Evelyn herself took to the edge of her perfectly turned-down bed and apologized again for her poor hospitality, for she had prepared no refreshments.

"That's quite all right, Evelyn," the Irishman assured her. "We're not here for a picnic." Then, becoming aware of his presumption in calling her by name, "I'm sorry—may I call you Evelyn?"

"As long," she replied, "as you do not call me Eve."

"We are here," McKnight said, discharging his first cloud of smoke, "at the request of no one, and we are naturally very grateful that you have seen fit to admit us. Both of us have been following this ghastly business with some interest, and cannot help but feel we are in possession of certain talents that might prove invaluable in application. In case you're not aware, Evelyn, I have been known to wear the title of Professor of Logic and Metaphysics at the University of Edinburgh."

"I know who you are," Evelyn said.

"Oh?"

"I've sat in on lectures at the University," she explained, "including some of your own."

For the first time it occurred to McKnight that this might be the same lass he had seen in the lecture hall—and, for that matter, the same figure he had passed on the Old Dalkeith Road—and he shot a glance at Canavan, who seemed to be in the throes of a similar suspicion. But he did not pursue it directly.

"Excellent," he said, intrigued. "Then you are not unfamiliar with my particular domain?"

"Mr. Stark has printed many lectures on philosophical subjects."

"I imagine he has. And those of the late Professor Smeaton?"

Evelyn seemed uneasy and looked at Canavan as though for assistance. "I don't believe Mr. Stark has sufficient interest," she said self-consciously, "in such things."

"In ecclesiastical matters?"

Evelyn nodded and tugged at her cuffs.

"And yourself, Evelyn," McKnight asked, "may I be so bold as to ask if you are a believer?"

"I believe in the purity of faith," she managed, "but as to whether I can claim to be a believer as such . . . that I can no longer say."

It seemed a painful admission, and Canavan was understanding. "It's a challenge, always," he said, "to maintain faith in the face of adversity."

But Evelyn looked uncomfortably silent, as though wanting to add something, but not wishing to offend him.

McKnight said, "It is common for one of your age, immersing yourself in the waters of philosophy, to question the nature of your beliefs. May I ask if you were born in Ireland, Evelyn?"

"No—in Edinburgh."

"Ah. Do you have any memories of this city as a child?"

"Only of the orphanage. We were not permitted to leave its confines."

"And of the orphanage? What do you think of when I mention it now?"

She considered. "I think of a parcel tightly bound."

"A parcel? Not a cage?"

"Cages," Evelyn said, "have air."

McKnight took in a draft of smoke, contemplating her. She was in a spotless flannel dress, of the type she might have worn to work, her hair short and tousled; a not-unattractive lass, he decided, but for the conspicuous semicircles under her eyes, so deeply impressed they were practically scars. She was swallowing repeatedly.

Canavan registered her discomfort and again felt obliged to interject. "You don't have to answer any of these questions," he assured her. "Just remember that in the eyes of the law we have no authority, and this is certainly no court. We only want to assist, and you may put us out at any time."

She looked at the Irishman gratefully. "But I am happy to answer your questions. I know you are here to help. And it is a relief to unburden myself in such a way, when others, I think, are disinclined to believe me."

"The police?" McKnight queried.

She nodded.

"Have they suggested that you have had some personal involvement in the murders?"

"I'm . . . not sure," she said truthfully, and shuddered.

"I fear, in any case, that it is only a matter of time."

But Evelyn was clearly alarmed by the last comment, and moved impulsively to a sort of declaration. "But I have already advised them . . . I have already told them who the killer is."

McKnight was genuinely surprised. "Oh?"

Her lips trembled and then, as she had with Inspector Groves, she forced the revelation over an imaginary hurdle. "He is the lamplighter."

McKnight glanced at Canavan.

"The lamplighter," she affirmed, fearing that the Professor had not comprehended. "The figure I have seen in my dreams—the lamplighter."

"The lamplighter," McKnight repeated, looking at her blankly for a few moments. "A man?" he asked. "Or a metaphor?"

But before she could reply there was a fresh eruption of moaning from the neighboring rooms, and in pausing to acknowledge it Evelyn might even have blushed. "My walls," she apologized, "are made of veils."

"And your answers, perhaps?" McKnight said, releasing another nimbus of smoke. "Are they also made of veils?"

She blinked, unable to understand his meaning, and indeed it seemed to Canavan that the Professor had spoken with surprising discourtesy.

"I apologize—" she began.

"There is no need for that," McKnight said, and smiled wanly. "But tell me . . . how long have you had these sorts of dreams?"

"My nightmares?"

"If that is what they are. Dreams in which you have witnessed people murdered."

"Only . . . only recently."

"You remember none previously?"

"I'm not sure. Perhaps. I was in Ireland . . ."

"Go on."

"I saw . . . a priest. I saw him murdered outside a cathedral in Dublin."

"And did you subsequently learn of any priest slain in such circumstances?"

"No, but I had little access to such news. Any news."

"You were in another orphanage?"

"I lived on an egg and poultry farm with my family."

"Your adoptive family?"

"My family," she agreed, as though not understanding the qualification.

"You went direct from the Edinburgh orphanage to the egg and poultry farm?"

"I believe so."

"So your family came to the orphanage to claim you?"

She struggled and went pale. "I don't remember."

Canavan again found McKnight's questions uncomfortably close to an interrogation, and could not resist a further intrusion. "The murder of this priest, Evelyn," he asked, in a more sensitive tone. "Was the lamplighter responsible too?"

She looked at him helplessly. "I honestly cannot say. These memories . . ."

"Return in fragments?"

She nodded appreciatively.

Spirited groans from the next room now. She raised her voice as though to distract them. "It is difficult to explain," she said, "and leads the police to think I am inventing my dreams. But I am *not* inventing them." She looked at Canavan for support. "Do you believe me? Do you at least believe me?"

"We believe you," Canavan assured her.

She was visibly relieved. "I've been terrified of sleeping for fear of what I might see next. I feel . . . ripped apart. Responsible, in some way."

"You should not feel responsible," Canavan said. "They are only dreams."

She looked at McKnight for confirmation, but his face was blank. "The relation of the unconscious to the conscious mind," he mused, "is somewhat like that of a cat to a house. During the day the cat is content to remain indoors, fully recognizing its boundaries, but unleashed at night, in dreams, it frequently travels beyond its owner's jurisdiction. To places its owner might not recognize in the midday sun. To perform indecencies and indiscretions of which the owner might be ashamed."

There was a climactic sigh from next door.

McKnight shrugged his eyebrows. "And of course we should never forget that there are many species of feline, from the humblest house-trained cat to the growling jungle tiger. And from the outside of the house it is not always possible to determine which sort of creature resides within."

Evelyn found his exact meaning still unclear, but there was allusion to the early theories relating to Smeaton's murder—that he had been torn apart by a wild beast—and she was not sure how to respond. "I hope," she managed eventually, "that I do not house a tiger."

"There would be no shame in doing so," Canavan told her. "We do not blame a stomach, after all, for its appetite." But he was aware of the expedience of the comment, which he doubted was theologically sound.

"In these nightmares," McKnight went on, "did you happen to see the killer—this lamplighter—prior to the killings?"

"No—and I was torn from sleep as soon as the men were struck down."

"And in the case of Colonel Munnoch?"

"As soon as . . . as soon as I saw the corpse. And heard a crack, like twisted bones."

McKnight nodded grimly and whispered an aside to Canavan as though to an assisting surgeon. "Here we witness the suicidal impulse inherent in the nightmare. Most dreams bind the dreamer tightly within the sleep state, even conspiring with outside elements such as intrusive noises. But the nightmare is hopelessly self-destructive. Such is the strength of its disdain for the unconscious, for its host, and even for itself." He turned back to Evelyn. "May I ask what format the dreams assumed prior to the actual killings? Were they nightmares, do you recall?"

"They were not nightmares. They were . . . nothing."

"There was some sort of a story involved?"

"Nothing."

"May I ask what you were doing in them?"

She seemed puzzled by the question. "Oh, I was not present in these dreams."

McKnight frowned. "I beg your pardon, Evelyn? Did you say you were not present? In your own dreams?"

She nodded.

McKnight paused to consider. "So in your dream you were not actually in the New Town when you saw Professor Smeaton struck down? And you were not at Waverley Station when Mr. Ainslie was savaged?"

"I wasn't there."

"Not even implicitly? As an observer?"

"I observed it all, but not with my own eyes."

"With God's eyes?"

She seemed embarrassed by the notion.

"Forgive me, Evelyn, but I must understand this clearly. In your dreams you see things without participating, is that it?"

She nodded.

"So at the station, for example, you only saw people talking? Purchasing tickets? Moving for carriages? But you were not part of it yourself?"

"Is . . . is that unusual?" she asked, as though genuinely perplexed.

McKnight let the pipe smolder in his hand.

Canavan again sought to assist. "Such a dream would only make the explosion of violence, when it came, all the more shocking."

"Shocking," she agreed.

"Do you never," McKnight asked her, "make an appearance in your own dreams?"

"I do sometimes."

"Ah? And what do you do in such dreams? Walk the streets?"

"Aye."

"Imaginary streets?"

"The streets of Edinburgh."

"You see the city through your own eyes?"

"I see myself as I walk the streets."

"Like a separate observer? You see yourself as others might see you?"

"Aye."

"And you speak to men like us, as we are speaking now?"

"Exactly as we are speaking now."

"But do you never have imaginary dreams? Vivid dreams?"

"My dreams are always vivid," she insisted. "At Waverley Station, for instance, I saw everything with great precision. The streaks of soot on the walls, the nipped cigarettes on the platform, the cracks in the station clock . . . everything. And in other dreams I dare say I have more profound conversations, and more elaborate processes of thought, than I do in real life."

"But what about fantasy elements? You'll agree that in dreams anything is possible and all reason suspended?"

"I am past that age," Evelyn said with a hint of disdain.

"Oh?" McKnight frowned. "You think fantastical dreams are the domain of childhood whimsies?"

She agreed.

"And flights of the imagination? Works of fiction? Something of which one should be ashamed?"

"One can become irreversibly lost in, and corrupted by, the . . . the imag— the imagination," she replied.

McKnight was curious. "May I ask where you learned that?"

But Evelyn seemed almost offended by the notion that she had acquired this belief, rather than formulated it herself.

"Have you never read Swift?" McKnight went on. "The fanciful stories of Poe or the adventures of Dumas? Your shelves are rather dry of such titles."

"I am familiar with Monsieur Dumas," she admitted. "I was a postulant at the Convent of the Sisters of St. Louis. Some of the Sisters were from France, and the library was stocked with French texts."

"And your opinion of such writing?"

Her lips twisted. "Nonsense," she said.

Canavan interjected again, intrigued. "A postulant, Evelyn? You didn't make it to the novitiate?"

"I was not worthy."

"But your family were religious people? To send you to a convent?"

"They did not send me there. I sent myself."

"And you must have been deeply religious yourself until recently?"

She nodded. "After returning to Edinburgh I continued attending Mass for a while. At St. Patrick's."

Canavan nodded, thinking that he might have seen her there, though as a memory it was appropriately dreamy.

"Did the nuns," McKnight asked, "discipline your imagination in any way?"

"It is the nature of women to be unnatural," she said carefully, as though quoting some influential figure, "and it is in their own interests that their desires are monitored and where necessary trimmed."

McKnight snorted. "Did the nuns tell you that?"

"Not the nuns."

"Who?"

She did not answer.

"Might you recall the day you were actually removed from the orphanage?" McKnight asked. "Your family coming to claim you?"

"I have told you that . . . I do not remember this," Evelyn said, tensing noticeably, and Canavan was disturbed that the Professor seemed to be returning to a sensitive region with calculated ruthlessness.

"May I ask if you were mistreated at the orphanage in any way?"

She shook her head evasively.

"Did you become aware of any exploitation?"

"I'm . . . not sure what you mean."

"Children hired out for chimney sweep duties? To the cotton mills, or to clear drains? Nothing like that?"

"No."

"Did you know of any lamplighter back then?"

"No." But her fingers had clenched.

"Would you agree that there is a gap in your memory between the orphanage and your arrival in Ireland?"

"There are gaps in everyone's memories," she replied, and for the first time she stared at McKnight challengingly. "Are there no gaps in yours?"

"Well . . ." McKnight said, but, as though stung by the accuracy of the comment, he was momentarily silenced.

Beside him, Canavan spoke up.

"No one can remember everything, Evelyn," he said. "And we're not here to bring you any pain. But when we learned of your visions we simply had to speak to you. There are parts of this business that seem strangely relevant, and seem to have dared us to trace them to their source."

"*Ce Grand Trompeur?*" she prompted, looking at him.

McKnight's ears pricked up. "Aye—are you familiar with this term, Evelyn?"

"The Sisters had French texts, as I have said."

"And they carried Descartes's *Meditations* in their library?"

"I . . . I suppose they did."

McKnight drew on his pipe. "Are you familiar with John 8:44?"

"It was left with Colonel Munnoch."

"You did not see it inserted in his skull?"

"It was dark and misty."

"And you were, after all, dreaming."

"That's so." She raised her eyes fractionally, as though preparing for another attack.

"Is there any reason you can think of why he might have been exhumed?"

"No."

"Any reason why he might have been called a murderer?"

"No."

"Or any reason Ainslie might have been labeled the Great Deceiver?"

"*No,*" she snapped. "And nor do I know why Professor Smeaton was called the Persecutor of Innocence. You ask too much if you expect such answers from me."

A silence ensued, so tight that McKnight's eyebrows could almost be heard rising. "'Persecutor of Innocence,' Evelyn?" he asked. "We did not know of this."

She looked away, embarrassed. "It . . . it was written in Latin on the church beside Smeaton's body. I've already informed the police."

"'*Innocentium Persecutor,*'" McKnight whispered, and registered Evelyn's barely concealed flinch. "It means nothing to you, naturally?"

"Nothing," she agreed hastily.

"And if it did, you would no doubt have told us by now."

"I would have no reason to lie to you."

McKnight stared at her and ultimately seemed to decide that he could be correspondingly churlish. "Very well," he sighed, and started rising. "Then I fear we already have taken too much advantage of your hospitality. But you have given us much to think about, that is certain, and hopefully from your information we will soon derive some manner of a direction for a further inquiry."

Abruptly Evelyn's whole bearing changed, as though a curtain had been torn from her face. "You're not . . . leaving?" she asked hoarsely.

"Unless you can think of a reason we should stay?"

"But . . . your . . . your questions." She had pushed herself to her feet, and the stricken look on her face was heartbreaking. "There must be more. . . ."

"There is little more we can ask at this stage."

"But you will be coming back?"

"If we can be of assistance, then there will be no avoiding it." The Professor smiled faintly. "Provided you feel in the mood to accommodate us, of course."

"But . . . but I have been helpful, haven't I?"

"Of course."

"And there is a good chance you will achieve progress?"

"We certainly hope that is the case."

"And you will inform me of anything that you discover?"

"As you will inform us?"

"As I . . . aye, of course."

But she looked so wretched that Canavan could barely bring himself to leave, wanting to linger in the room, to communicate a sense of assurance or a flash of understanding—anything. But her eyes were fixed stubbornly on McKnight, and she looked too distressed even to notice him.

"Your toy, Evelyn?" the Professor asked. He had taken a parting glance at her shelves and discovered between the books an incongruous rag doll.

"Not . . . not mine," she said, as though accused of some indiscretion. "There is a family downstairs for whom I sometimes make toys."

"It's quite a skill." The doll was of shop standard.

"I make all sorts of things," she added hastily. "Tea cozies, kettle holders, and needlework. It is a duty to be industrious and always occupied."

"Very practical. But is it not perhaps also corrupting?"

She looked genuinely alarmed. "What do you mean?"

"Might not a child be inclined to invest the doll with a life of its own?"

"I . . . I would hope not."

"But it is so very lifelike."

"It is nothing but rags," she said firmly.

"Alas, and it will never be more," McKnight agreed, as the two men left.

✠

"I must express my disapproval," Canavan said as they stepped onto the rain-slickened cobbles.

"An admonishment?" McKnight suggested, with what seemed to Canavan a maddening attitude of contentment.

"I thought you were unnecessarily harsh with her."

"I agree I was harsh."

"Then I must add my disappointment that you do not in any way seem ashamed."

"Nonsense, lad," McKnight said, relighting his pipe. "Did you notice the look of dismay on her face when I announced we were leaving?"

"A natural reaction, I would've thought. After all the questions, there still were no answers."

McKnight shook the match out. "No," he said. "The truth is she wants us to be brusque and uncompromising. She needs us to flay her, if that's what it takes, to induce the revelation that is destroying her from inside."

Canavan snorted. "It's as if you believe she's really admitted to a role in the murders."

"Oh, I have no doubt of it."

"Aye? And what exactly did she say to incriminate herself?"

"Everything."

"*Everything.*"

"You heard her."

But the Irishman, exasperated, could not bring himself to ask for the details. "So what's your aim, then? To lead a lamb to slaughter?"

"To lead her to the truth, and let her do the rest."

"She's vulnerable, I ask you to remember that."

"Volatile," McKnight agreed. "Did you notice the way she repeatedly tugged her gloves up her wrists? I suspect she was attempting to conceal the scars of a suicide attempt."

Canavan felt a flush of anger. "Then why twist a knife in the wound?" he asked, and a passerby turned, surprised by the outburst. They were halfway up Candlemaker Row.

McKnight stopped and looked at his friend patiently. "We are here to cauterize the wound and drain its poisons. I certainly have no interest in inflicting further damage. It is our task, indeed, to shield her from those who in their haste might seize her prematurely, and do more harm than they could ever imagine. If I did not consider myself a sort of guardian angel"—and here he reached into his jacket—"I would not have taken this."

He produced a black-bound book.

"A Bible," Canavan said, taking it with a frown.

"A Douai Bible. Remarkably similar to my own."

"You lifted it from her shelf?"

"When she was not looking. Before others discovered it."

Canavan was puzzled.

"Check it, if you wish," McKnight said. "John 8:44: 'He was a murderer from the beginning.' The entire page is missing."

Canavan moved to the corner, where gas lamps swept down the street like a line of votive candles. In the fluttering light he leafed through to the final Gospel and discovered that the page had indeed been torn out, leaving nothing but another serrated edge clinging to the binding.

"But this . . . doesn't incriminate her," he protested. "Any more than it incriminates us."

"Truly, I would prefer to believe you."

Canavan drew a breath. "And then there's the lamplighter," he noted. "The figure she has already identified as the killer."

"Ah, yes, the lamplighter . . ." McKnight said skeptically as the midnight omnibus rattled past.

"What, you don't believe even that, I suppose?"

"Oh, I think her conviction is certainly real. But of the lamplighter himself . . . I believe he has always been a convenient scapegoat."

"So you know who he is, too?"

"You could say I have a fair idea."

Canavan briefly considered a further expression of doubt, but ultimately could not contain his curiosity. *"Who?"* he asked tightly.

But McKnight only narrowed his eyes at him reprovingly. "Good Lord," he said as the streetlamps flickered and faded eerily, "I would have thought that to you, of all people, that would have been fundamentally obvious."

Chapter XIII

THE CORSTORPHINE CHURCH of St. Andrew was a crusted, crocketed little brig with mullioned windows, built on a hill by retired mariners in the seventeenth century. The headstones of its graveyard, where Professor Smeaton himself now rested, were surmounted by sailing ships, anchors, compasses, and sextants, its single spire by a sort of crow's nest, and the crow's nest in turn by a golden weathervane in the shape of a fully rigged schooner. The last was squeaking and sailing in the stiff wind when Groves made his way through the drifts of dead leaves and entered the little church close to ten o'clock, finding a memorial service in progress for the dead of the *Ben Nevis,* wrecked off Berwick some thirty years previously at the expense of half her crew.

He took to the comfortless rear pew, exuding impatience. Though he was not yet prepared to elaborate on his mounting suspicions about Evelyn to his superiors, the pressure for a solution was all the time building steam and might have been enough to push him beyond the bounds of prudence but for two reasons: the Sheriff's own investigation had failed to yield any results (the Procurator Fiscal himself had noted that it was a mystery "unlike anything seen in this city since the days of the warlock Major Weir"), and the Wax Man still was eschewing any involvement and loudly proclaiming confidence in his colleague's abilities. Groves tried telling himself it was an opportunity more than a burden, and again reminded himself of the wisdom of Piper McNab. "The thing about poison chalices," the old sage once said, "is that they can sometimes turn out to be Holy Grails."

Presently Groves shifted and the whole pew creaked like a crypt door. The congregation was a mixture of sea-scored survivors and briny widows, muttering their prayers dutifully as the fat, warble-voiced minister went through the motions of an interminable service. Groves's eyes wandered restlessly to the arched ceiling and alighted on an unusually flamboyant mural of seething seas and swirling clouds, through which a giant hand marked "Jehovah" dragged the imperiled boats clear of a huge black dragon labeled "Persecutio."

Persecutio. Already Groves had constables at Central Office rummaging through both Bibles and Catholic missals in search of a context for the words *innocentium persecutor* (it was the Papists who still employed the Roman language in their liturgies, and Evelyn was of their ilk), and now he wondered if it might be more than just a coincidence that Professor Smeaton had once been the minister of this little parish with its terrible dragon. Could it mean that the murderer had visited this little church? Had been a parishioner? And sat in this very pew?

These were waters Groves had never dreamed of navigating. As much as he was becoming increasingly convinced of Evelyn's involvement, he still could not reconcile the ferocity of the attacks with such a frail member of the weaker sex. In fact, he had never been able to settle on a firm impression about women: on one hand he viewed them as sort of holy sepulchers, whose strength lay in their very delicacy; on the other he had encountered too much cunning and depravity in their ranks ("The Lavender Tassels," "The Blossoms of Elm Row," "Merry Molly Shows Her Colours") to be surprised at their capabilities. "The sly little creatures come from Adam's rib," Piper McNab once reminded him, "and when they strike a man it's most likely in the place where that very rib is missing." And it was moreover all too easy for Groves to conceive of Evelyn as a construction of ribs, because she seemed made of little else.

But a dragon? A savage beast? Groves still was trying to establish a *taint.* If he could see that in her—a record of prostitution, or petty theft—then, combined with the look of primeval indignation she had employed once or twice in his presence, he would begin to find her capable of anything. But word from the Register House was still pending. He had assigned Pringle to shadow her all day and had constables poring over the police records. And at the North Bridge Telegraph Office he had cabled a message to Ireland to verify details of her education under the Sisters of St. Louis.

He ached for decisive progress, for a divine hand to drag him clear of his own persecuting dragons. Again and again he pictured the discovery of the final incriminating article of evidence—located through his sheer persistence, his preternatural attention to detail—and the glorious moment of righteousness, when he clamped a hand on her quivering shoulder, declared her under arrest, and hauled her off to some soulless cell and a more comprehensive punishment. Anything standing in the way of this moment was now an obstacle to be disdained, and as he surveyed the grizzled old heads lined up atop the pews like melons, he wondered what it might be like to crack them open with his truncheon.

Finally the minister rose to offer a solemn blessing and the precentor exhorted the congregation into hymn. When Groves slipped out of the church in anticipation of following the minister to his manse, the mourners had submerged grief in a stirring celebration of a mariner's defiance:

> Purge the deck, lads, unlock the brig!
> Cast down evil to its realm,
> For sharp reefs the ship is bound,
> With the devil at the helm!

✠

The minister, still in his collar, was a strange one to my mind, a ruddy faced gent with a fondness for buttered scones, his lady wife was forever offering them to me like they were God's own, but I was not there for the pleasures of the stomach. He seemed eager to please, too easy to my mind, like he had some secret bottled up inside, and he had his grand children wailing and kicking up a ruckus in the surrounding rooms, the little imps seemed lacking in discipline to me, but that is the days we now occupy, when even a man of the cloth can no longer control his charges.

"Are you certain I can't offer you a scone?"

"I thank you, Reverend, but no."

"They really are splendid scones."

Groves coughed. "You were saying about Professor Smeaton, I believe."

"Well . . . yes," the minister agreed, a little disappointed. "Yes . . . he really was a man of his own convictions, as I say. But you'll appreciate that it is difficult for me to speak poorly of an esteemed predecessor, and most especially in the week following the unfortunate man's demise."

He looked at Groves, who stared back unsympathetically.

"But he was an archconservative, let me say that," the minister managed, "and of a type that, while always admired for its resolve, is nevertheless . . . a trifle anachronistic, if you understand my meaning."

Groves nodded, though in truth he was not sure he followed. "A persecutor of innocence, perhaps?"

"It would be a wee bit extreme, I think, to call him that. Professor Smeaton was a man who believed hard men are needed for hard times. He had lived through the Disruption, you see, and was trying to come to terms with all sorts of scientific discoveries. His beliefs were under siege, everything he held dear, and it's not difficult to see how he developed certain . . . orthodoxies."

"So you don't share those beliefs, is that what you're saying?"

"Well . . ." The minister chuckled lightly. "It's been a century now since the Enlightenment."

Groves stared at him.

"And . . . and the Church has embraced concepts that no longer make certain theologies viable. It's impossible to believe, for instance, that people are born into the world incurably wicked. That is repugnant to reason. But all the same, you can see how it is possible to disapprove of such flawed philosophies, and yet admire a man like Smeaton at the same time. For his very inflexibility."

He seemed to be saying that he had little respect for the late professor, but in such an unmanly way that I found myself wishing that I was speaking to the maligned deceased, who from every account was not one to shirk a harsh word.

"Have you ever heard of a certain lamplighter?" Groves asked.

"A lamplighter?"

"Or of Smeaton's association with a man of this trade?"

"I don't believe so," the minister said. "But my dealings with Professor Smeaton were minimal, you understand, and only go as far as the transitional days when I assumed control from him, and our occasional exchanges thereafter."

One of the minister's grandsons now darted into the room and ran around giggling and slapping the walls. "Not the spyglass, Billy!" the minister cried, fearing the fate of a shining brass telescope perched on a nearby sideboard. "Not the spyglass—not the—that's it, boy, that's it!" The child departed the room, gurgling and squealing, and the minister settled back, laughing with seeming admiration. "Such energy . . ." he marveled. "Truly astounding." He looked at Groves apologetically. "But the spyglass, you see, it belonged to Sir Francis Drake . . ." And he chuckled again self-consciously, inviting the smallest hint of understanding.

But Groves merely grunted. "Did you know of Smeaton's association," he asked, "with the others who have recently perished?"

The minister thought about it. "Well, not exactly. But Professor Smeaton . . . yes, I suppose he certainly had some important connections."

"Aye? What sort?"

"Perhaps you've heard of the Mirror Society, Inspector?"

Groves paused, wondering if this was general knowledge. "A mercantile association?"

"Not quite. It was a small group of men, from all walks of life, who met every month or so, in secrecy."

"For what purpose?"

"To understand that, you would need to know the story that inspired its name," the minister explained. "Have you heard, by any chance, of a certain Enoch Rutherford, a minister from Selkirk?"

"I have not."

"He was a man who suffered a crisis of faith after looking in a mirror, would you believe."

The minister laughed uneasily, but seeing Groves's expectant look, and realizing he had more or less committed himself to further explanation, he steepled his hands and forced himself on, with as much conviction as possible.

"Each morning, you see, the man would shave in front of a small mirror in his bedroom and then repair to his kitchen for breakfast. But one day it occurred to him to wonder if his reflection was simultaneously enjoying breakfast. The reflection that he could no longer see, that is, the reflection in his mirror. Further, when he set off on his rounds he wondered if his mirror image was also doing the same thing somewhere in the labyrinth of the mirror world. And when he took to the pulpit that morning he became distracted, insensible even, fascinated with the idea that somewhere in the realms behind the mirror his reflection was also sermonizing."

Groves frowned incredulously, and the minister elected to chuckle.

"It's a peculiar story, no doubt. But the man was vulnerable, you see, having recently been exposed to the works of certain philosophers and scientists. He was beginning to doubt his own claim to identity . . . he was losing faith in himself . . . and it seemed to him that the mirror universe had as much claim to existence as the world in which he imagined he lived. For why is it, he actually asked his congregation, that we believe an unseen reflection does not exist? If that is the case, do we ourselves exist when unseen? And since we perceive objects in the mirror of our own eyes, can a mirror not also be said to perceive . . . ?"

Here the minister paused, disconcerted by Groves's deepening frown, and again he had to force himself on, hoping he was not driving the Inspector deeper into confusion.

"And when one looks in one's own reflection, does one see what one's own eyes see or what the mirror sees? And who can say that he is not in fact a reflection or the reflection is not in fact real? And who can say that a reflection does not have its own reflected thoughts and feelings? Or that a reflection does not doubt its own existence, and in its own way wonder about the world on the other side of the mirror . . . the world Enoch Rutherford no longer had the presumption to call reality?"

"He was mad," Groves said tersely.

"That is one interpretation." The minister chuckled, relieved for any reaction. "But, you see, this doubt—which threatened to shatter his faith, his entire sanity—this doubt could be said to have been sown by the boundless skepticism of the Enlightenment. And because of it he had become incoherent and muddled in his convictions. This doubt was a demon, you see, and it had to be overcome, and it all came back to what he saw in a mirror. So do you know how he dealt with this? How, in the end, he confronted and overcame the crisis, and defeated the demon?"

"He plucked out his eyes?"

"More simple than that." The minister smiled. "He smashed the mirror."

This was the first I had heard of the Mirror Society, and the first hint I had of its activities. It was a peculiar story, and as such was exactly in line with the whole case, so that I could not help but sense a connection, and swoop on it like a hawk.

"Who were the members of this Mirror Society?"

"It was more or less a secret gathering, as I say. Though I believe they met in a room in Atholl Crescent Lane."

Groves knew the area well, having once been posted at the nearby West Port Station. "And what did they discuss there?"

The minister seemed uncomfortable. "Again, Inspector, it would be presumptuous of me to be critical, but I believe they were united in their opposition to the new philosophies, and the trends in science and theology, which they thought were potentially dangerous and even destructive."

"Is it possible that Colonel Munnoch was a member?"

"Based on what I know of the Colonel, I would agree that is entirely possible."

"And theatrical types? Lighthouse keepers?"

"Less likely, I would think."

"Other clergymen, then?"

"Possibly, but Professor Smeaton was not—how can I phrase this?— not the most tolerant of clerics. Although . . . now that I think of it . . ." The minister's face contorted as he battled to retrieve a memory.

"Aye?"

"Yes," the minister said. "I think I do recall him saying . . . and this was many years ago, mind, so you'll appreciate that my memory of the exchange is hazy . . ."

"Aye . . ."

"I do remember him saying he had been meeting with a Roman Catholic monsignor. And this of course surprised me, because he was not that fond of Papists, as he called them."

"And this monsignor was part of the Mirror Society?"

"Possibly . . ." The minister shrugged, remembering how strange it had all seemed. "I simply recall Professor Smeaton availing me of this information for no apparent purpose. It was as if he simply felt uneasy, or even guilty, about the association and needed to unburden himself. He certainly had not been in the brightest of moods, and when he revealed this . . . I'm not sure, but I had the distinct impression that he was fighting the urge to say more."

Groves thought about it. A secret society. Covert meetings in Atholl Crescent Lane. A strange association between usually antagonistic clergymen. *There was no certainty that it was all related to the current crimes,* he later wrote, *but I sniffed it like a bloodhound.*

"I believe I can smell some more scones on the way," the minister said. "Are you quite certain I can't offer you one?"

"Aye—I mean, no," Groves said distractedly. "But one more question before I take my leave. And I ask you this as a simple policeman to a man of God."

"Of course," the minister said, with appropriate solemnity.

"With the nature of these murders in mind—the way in which the men were killed, and the way in which the murderer has so far escaped justice—with all this in its proper place, do you think it possible that some dark force has been employed?"

It was suddenly the minister's turn to frown. "Dark force?"

And now it was Groves who had to force himself on. "I mean some manner of power . . . beyond that which is normally at the disposal of man . . ."

"You mean," the minister said steadily, "the art of witches and warlocks?"

Groves cleared his throat. "In a manner of speaking, aye."

The minister thought about it, decided the Inspector was not entirely serious, and judged it not improper to chuckle. "Well," he said, "I would not like to see us venture down such paths again."

But then, seeing from Groves's expression that he had little inkling what he was talking about: "The days are long past, Inspector, when one could judge a woman a witch, bundle her up in a sack, and hurl her into the Nor' Loch. . . ."

Groves contemplated the idea, it seemed to the minister, with a conspicuous aura of disappointment.

"Which is not to say it is beyond the realms of possibility," the minister now added expediently, to his everlasting shame. "I mean . . . if there is one area where even the most orthodox clergyman will find himself in accord with the most modern philosopher, it is in the acknowledgment that what we know about our powers is but a microscopic fraction of what is yet to be discovered."

He laughed feebly, cursing his own weakness, and ultimately was saved by his grandchildren, who now ran in and swarmed about him, staring at Groves with disapproving abandon.

I might have pressed on and inquired what he meant by these mysterious words, only his imps had come bundling in again, and I did not want to sting their minds with frightening notions, though if truth be told they seemed willful little rascals, with more than enough demon in them already, and little inclination to fear.

☒

Their number had swelled to just on seventy, and the lamps themselves to more than ten thousand. Now employed by the Town Council at three shillings a day, they formerly had fallen under the direct jurisdiction of the police and were still prone to being hauled out of bed by officious patrolmen to replace panes of glass or reignite extinguished flames, the brightness of the streets being in direct relation to the propensity for mayhem. In his days as a night watchman Groves had been especially officious, recording any dereliction of duty in his notebook with great assiduity, and thus he was not fondly remembered by the lamplighters, for whom he in turn accorded little respect: they were a clannish lot, clearly without the aptitude to hold down a job of any responsibility, and to him they always seemed a wee bit vacant of mind, which he attributed to the inhaling of so much effluvium from the lamps themselves.

Lean and hollow-cheeked, and on their feet for hours (lighting the lamps through the evening, extinguishing them partly at midnight, partly at dawn, and repairing them through the day), they now filed into the Central Office Muster Room (where they reported every day and were fined severely if late), and Groves watched them sag onto benches and slouch against walls, grateful for any opportunity to rest. He recognized Angus Norton, the ancient and unofficial chief of the tribe; Pat Kemplay, who sang arias on his beat with the authority of a celebrated tenor; and even Herbert Cieslak, the little Polish lamplighter who once had helped him apprehend a thief ("The Courtesan's Music Box"). With the others he was less familiar, though he recognized some of them by appearance and sensed that they had stiffened defensively under his gaze. Raggedly dressed in sooty overalls, holland jackets, waterproof capes, and thread-bare trousers and caps, and pale to a man, they possessed, for all their lowly status, a curious tribal dignity, which they brandished like an impenetrable shield. These were men practically unblemished by scandal, for all their noctambulations; men who cherished their work, for all its miseries; men who were in temperament seemingly incapable of rash anger, for all their sleepless nights; and men who were almost universally regarded with affection, especially by the children, who hugged at their heels trilling, "Leerie, Leerie, light the lamps, long legs and crooked shanks!"

As such Groves found it difficult to believe they might be guilty of murder, or indeed much of anything sinister. Physically they did not seem powerful enough to inflict bestial blows, and in intellect they lacked the facility to escape with preternatural guile. On the other hand, he had been in little direct contact with them for many years, and certainly he had been informed of a stewing tension in their ranks. These were, after all, increasingly uncertain times for leeries. The evil electric light—which already blazed through the boulevards of Paris and the theater districts of London—was incrementally creeping north. In Birmingham factory workers toiled through the night under suspended arc lamps. In Sheffield a sporting club had conducted a football match in its horrendous glare. At the Edinburgh International Exhibition some months earlier a display of Jablochkoff candles had the ladies unfurling parasols to shield their eyes. There were seventeen electric lights already suspended over the plat-forms of Waverley Station, and Princes Street itself—where gaslamps were spaced in such proximity that a man could read a newspaper as he strolled—had been strung, for a three-month trial in 1881, with electric lamps so radiant that Edinburgh had been proclaimed "the land of the midnight sun." The advantages of such light, as those of a "progressive bent" were apt to point out, were manifest: it was more powerful, more reliable, cheaper, and less polluting. The gasworks required to feed the old lamps were themselves considered dangerous, with suggestions in alarmist newspaper editorials that a single explosion in Holyrood might level the entire city like some latter-day Pompeii. In the hunger for change, for some sort of perceived advance, no one seemed to acknowl-edge that the new light, even shaded in alabaster globes and mounted on gallowslike brackets, was severe to the point of offensive and offered no hint of the fluttering flame that had warmed the heart of man since the days of the Neanderthals. And now, in its annihilating glare, the cheerfully whistling leerie, patroling his well-worn paths with aplomb, for the first time was forced to contemplate his own extinction.

Groves watched Leonard Claypole, the Town Council's formally dressed Inspector of Lighting, call the assembly to order and solicit reports on breakages and the installation of new lamps. One of the leeries reported troublemaking near the iron foundry on Salisbury Street, the panes smashed with well-targeted stones. Another suggested the gas supply in the vicinity of the Royal Horse Bazaar was becoming dangerously unreliable, and with the winter now hardening, and with it an inclination to heavy frost, the pipes might require cleaning or even replacing. There was a general grumbling about the new move, advanced by some of the papers, to have the residences of all the city's Knights of the Realm signposted with ornamental lamps, as already existed outside the residences of the Lord Provost, the bailies and police judges (ornamental lamps were more delicate, difficult to clean, and a magnet for vandals). And there was much pugnacious chatter about the inequitable designation of beats since the introduction of the newer, diamond-headed lamps, serviced with a smoldering pole, in which the younger leeries had taken to specializing, without acknowledging that they took altogether far less time to light than the whale-oil globes that had been around since the dawn of streetlamps. With these lamp types frequently intersecting, and the beats accordingly, it had been openly recognized by the Town Council, forever seeking to cut expenses, that the younger leeries were more efficient in their duties, and this provocative acknowledgment had in turn raised the hackles of the more senior lamplighters. The speed of lighting patrols had always been regulated by a tacit consensus, and it was considered insurgent to execute one's duties with a swiftness that threw the rest of the tribe into unflattering contrast. But now, with the specter of electricity bringing with it the prospect of a dwindling population, some of the more cavalier leeries seemed to be going out of their way to impress the lighting inspector with their productivity.

Ornamental lamps, the threat of electricity, and the inevitable emergence of self-interest: these were what constituted seething tensions in the tribe of lamplighters. But were they enough to turn one of them into a brutal murderer of professors, colonels, lighthouse keepers, and entrepreneurs? Groves had no idea why Evelyn might indict one of their trade, but he suspected some manner of hoodwinkery, generated for reasons best known to the waif herself.

When Leonard Claypole turned the floor over to him he stepped forward to a ripple of murmurs. "Good day to you, gentlemen," he said, standing before a large ordinance survey map with beats marked in loops and circles. "I have no intention of detaining you as I see it is already darkening outside"—near the winter solstice, streetlamps were lit as early as two-thirty—"but it has often been the case that your type has proved helpful in assisting the forces of justice in their duties, and you must have heard of the terror that has blighted this city in recent days. I ask you now to consider if you have seen any person or beast roaming the night streets who in some way might have raised your suspicions?"

He narrowed his pale eyes and conducted a sweeping gaze of the room.

"Nothing at all?" he asked.

Not even a blink.

"No mysterious figures? Stealthy types in capes?"

"There's always those," offered Billy Nichol.

"I mean figures of a peculiar size," Groves said, and could not resist the description used by the Waverley Station witnesses. "A dark force?"

Silence.

"No savage beasts? Wild animals?"

"Saw a couple of Americans th'other night," someone piped up, and there was a swift volley of guffaws, promptly stifled by Leonard Claypole with a stern warning.

But the amusement lingered in the form of grim satisfaction: it was the Americans of the Brush Electric Light Company who had erected the arc lights in Princes Street with the intention of decisively establishing the superiority of electricity over gas. Failing to account for the virility of Edinburgh's breezes, however, their delicate carbon contacts had dislodged on the night of the very first demonstration, resulting in a humiliating blackout and hasty summoning of the lamplighters: a moment toasted long into the night in the leeries' favorite howff. Famously persistent, however, the Americans had struggled on through a largely unsuccessful three-month demonstration and still had not the good grace to depart, their engineers continuing to toil away in some steam-driven plant in Market Street, fully confident of eventual success.

"Aye," Groves acknowledged, as though sharing their amusement. "What about a young lass, then, with clipped dark hair—a slip of a thing, usually dressed in black? Anyone fitting this description you might have deemed unusual?"

The men shrugged.

"She might have been in the company of another. One who was doing her bidding."

Nothing.

"And none of you have any regular association with such a lass? None of you has had cause to give her grief, or earn her spite?"

Not a word.

Groves sniffed. "Surely, though, you have read of the victims so far. Has any of you had cause to dislike any of them? To wish them ill? Or to inflict some harm upon them with dark powers?"

There was a collective creasing of brows as the leeries belatedly realized that they themselves had not escaped suspicion, though they were unsure what to make of it.

"Then that is all I can now ask of you," Groves concluded. "But you should prepare yourself for more questions before this nasty business is through. I ask you to be especially sober, and look about you with clear focus, because you never know what your eyes might chance across. And you cannot discount the possibility that you yourself could be savaged one night and carted to the mortuary, think of that. These are dark days, gentlemen, and you would be advised to be wary. And if you are hiding some secret, concealing it under your hats, then be assured that Inspector Groves will find it in you like a tick in a dog and cut it out with a blunted knife."

He lacerated them all with another slitted glare, but most of them were staring at the floor with their customary dim-witted expressions, as though they tolerated such rebukes every single day. Which, considering the reputation of the choleric Claypole, was highly probable.

It was much as I thought, they were of no help to me, nor could I see in any of them animal malice. Pringle reported that none of them seemed shaken or pale as I spoke, neither were any of them angry, and I left convinced that the lamplighters had no reason to be slandered by the Evelyn woman, they knew nothing of the murders, and the only demon they knew was the Yankee.

Chapter XIV

CANAVAN PLUNGED into the Old Town after an exhausting night of debate in front of McKnight's crackling fire. The Professor's newly stated theories were convoluted and riddled with gaps—the Professor himself was happy to concede as much—and so bizarre that he dared not broadcast them beyond the ears of close friends. But as McKnight himself had observed in his own defense, there are crucial points in history when events and extrapolations coalesce in such a tempest that theories once deemed incredible suddenly burst into the form of revelations, and men once dismissed as insane take on the aura of prophets. Not, he hastened to add, that he had assumed any transcendent mantle. It was reality that would bear him out, he said, if indeed there was any reality left to do so.

They had parted friends, as always, but Canavan was still troubled by the enthusiasm with which the Professor had seized upon his explosive theories, like a reckless boy stumbling across a keg of gunpowder in an abandoned fort. Nor was he convinced that the man, for all his repeated assurances, really had the welfare of Evelyn as his primary concern.

There were times, indeed, when she seemed little more than a hideously deformed patient, to be analyzed, sampled, and exhibited with the same sort of procedural insensitivity exercised by the lecturing doctors of the Royal Infirmary.

"Never forget we're talking about a young woman, not a crocodile," Canavan said sternly at one stage.

"Evelyn? A woman impossible to dislike," McKnight agreed. "And I have never said she is guilty of anything."

"But your theory is based completely around her guilt."

"My theory transcends such traditional notions."

"Aye, but you must accept we haven't yet reached a stage when such theories can be used in any court, no matter how profound and admirable they might be." Canavan had actually clenched his fists, he was so earnest, and he hoped the Professor had not noticed.

His knuckles were still white now, his muscles still tight, and for all the heavy chill and the hoary hour he could not bring himself to rest, returning home by the most circuitous of routes and all the time warding off the cold with the one phrase he had retrieved from the evening to warm the chambers of his heart: *a woman impossible to dislike.*

He had been captivated by her immediately, of course. From the moment he stepped into her room with a strange rush of familiarity, to the way she repeatedly glanced at him, hunting for security, he had been at the mercy of forces more powerful than rationality. It was not romantic love, exactly, or not in the guise in which a man might usually recognize it. This woman was no unearthly beauty—no Emily Harkins—and his feelings were untainted by the madness of lust. Rather, it was the overpowering sense of understanding, and a deep conviction of tragedy, along with a corresponding desire to comfort and defend her, which in Canavan was a drive infinitely more powerful than carnal desire. He was staggered by the force of such emotions, as always, but also fearful of his inability to match them with any sort of security beyond his considerable physical strength. And that he was destined to protect her was practically incontestable: it was a vision as clear to his heart as anything he had seen with his eyes. And if his first task in its sovereignty was to clash sabers with his good friend Professor McKnight, in order to protect her against a most astonishing assault . . . then so be it.

"She hides something," McKnight had declared, pacing restlessly in front of the glowing hearth. "You must surely have noticed the transparency of her answers concerning her departure from the orphanage. You might say she was ostentatiously evasive. As if she were peeling away a bandage and practically inviting us to attend to the wound. And it's this wound, I advance, that is the key to unlocking the code of her unconscious."

"Some atrocity, I suppose you believe."

"Do you not find it conceivable?"

Canavan paused. "What I find inconceivable," he said, "is the ability of a young lady to perform a revenge of such brutality, even in her imagination."

"But she has openly admitted to just that—it's common knowledge."

"She's admitted to nightmares, which are not the same thing."

"Ah, indeed," McKnight said happily, as though arriving exactly at his destination, and he turned to his friend with a mischievous gleam. "Would you care for a deductive argument?" he asked, for all the world as though he were offering a cup of tea.

Canavan felt a curious sense of dread. "I'm always ready for a deductive argument," he said stiffly.

McKnight smiled. "Very well, then," he said, and inhaled, as though to snare inspiration from the air. "The major premise: Dreams are entirely subjective, since by their nature they can be perceived by one person alone. The minor premise: Nothing that cannot be perceived objectively—that is, by more than one consciousness—is real. And the conclusion: Dreams are not real. How does that strike you?"

"Very solid," Canavan conceded. "Though I fear you've set it up specifically to be demolished."

"Wise fellow. For I now ask you: Is the minor premise really valid? Evelyn, you'll recall, has insisted that when she dreams she is no more than a God's-eye observer. She dreams what others might see awake, at precisely the same time that she is dreaming. Her only part is to reimagine streets with the utmost vividness and accuracy. Waverley Station, for example, was reconstructed from the highest rafter to the deepest speck of soot. So perhaps in Evelyn we have discovered one who does not dream subjectively but objectively." McKnight shrugged. "And if this is so, then the argument is unsound. Because either dreams are *not* entirely subjective or Evelyn's dreams are not dreams at all."

Canavan frowned. "So what's your conclusion, then?"

"Well," McKnight said, "I find it impossible to believe that anyone, let alone Evelyn Todd, has no dreams. Nor do I believe that any traditional dream can affect objective reality. But then Evelyn's dreams, as we've already observed, are not at all traditional. There is practically no appreciable difference between them and reality. And this acknowledgment allows me to draw my conclusion in one particularly challenging logical deduction."

"I wait breathlessly."

"The major premise," McKnight said, "is simply this: *Evelyn's dreams are no different from reality*. You can argue degrees if you like, but I ask you to accept it here on the balance of evidence. For the minor premise, on the other hand, I will accept no challenge: *Evelyn's imagination is able to distort her dreams*. This, of course, is an understatement, and is as true of anyone as it is of Evelyn Todd." He smiled. "And the ultimate conclusion? The point to which logic has led us irreversibly?"

Canavan had a fair idea but did not feel moved to contribute.

"Evelyn's imagination is also able to distort reality," McKnight finished victoriously, and Canavan could only scoff.

"Aye," said the Professor with an acknowledging chortle. "An outlandish statement in any other circumstances, I'll admit that. But I would not say it were I not convinced of her exceptional imagination and the exceptional suppression of the same."

"You have no evidence that she ever had a great imagination."

"My evidence is in the very stoutness of her denial. In her discomfort at the very invocation of the word *imagination*. And in bookshelves that are laboring under the weight of so many academic texts that they are almost ready to collapse. These are the signs of one who has endured a serious punishment, or has been deeply branded with dogma and corrective measures, and has engineered traps and barbs to repel all accusations of weakness and depravity."

"Your own bookcases strain under the weight of academic texts."

"Naturally. I am a musty old professor, long lost to hope."

"So you think it's improper for a young lady to take an interest in the reality of the world, is that it?"

"On the contrary, I find it most admirable. But for one of her age to impose such a severe discipline that even her dreams are drained of any threatening color or emotion . . . I certainly find that indicative of some unnatural repression."

"But you cannot say her dreams haven't threatened her. They've done nothing but torment her."

"Aye, but only as a completely aloof observer. And this is the very point: she is so ashamed of her own dreams that she can only bear to appear in them as an objective figure, a person whose movements she observes as she might yours or mine. Further, the reality she has constructed for herself, outside her dreams, is a being so bland that it is incapable of any sort of inspiration beyond sewing dolls for children. And this is an image she guards like a candle flame in a tempest, presenting to the world this upright, pitiable character untainted by a single corruptive notion."

"Her immense imagination again."

McKnight ignored the skepticism. "I believe the fortress containing it was formally constructed at about the time of her departure from the orphanage—the 'parcel tightly bound.' Perhaps the foundations had been laid prior to this, and I certainly suspect she was reprimanded severely in those days, but then, at some crucial point, a dungeon was built to entomb her imagination so deeply, and under such force, that it has now inevitably protested, slipped through the bars of its cell, and driven violently into the open air, where to Evelyn's horror and shame it cannot be restrained, and has become manifest as the demon that terrorizes the streets of Edinburgh."

"This is absurd," Canavan said.

"*Ce Grand Trompeur,*" McKnight went on, undaunted. "A euphemism for the destructive demon of the mind. 'A murderer from the beginning'—a biblical reference to Satan. Don't you see? The killer is not identifying his victims. He's identifying *himself*. In a language that can only be understood through the likes of us. In a language that is inviting us to hunt him down."

Canavan struggled to protest. "And 'Persecutor of Innocence'? There are no such references in the Bible."

"Not precisely. But *persecutor* and *innocence* appear independently in practically every book from Genesis to the Apocrypha. And I hardly think it presumptuous to assume that, when we eventually find it, it will prove to be another reference to the devil. All the shameful and undisciplined imaginative inclinations Evelyn has buried, you see, are challenging us to apply to them their proper collective name. And there are so many names to choose from, are there not?" McKnight smiled mysteriously. "Tell me—what do you know of the name Lucifer?"

Canavan was flustered. "I need to know, before anything else, if we're meant to be dealing with an innocent woman or the devil himself."

"We are dealing with a human being called Evelyn, and a devil inherent in all of us. A primeval instinct, a fundamental component of evolution. Breathing the atmosphere of an imagination so fertile, and so violently repressed, that it has developed into an incarnation of hate."

"Absurd," Canavan insisted. "I say it again."

McKnight was patient. "And I say again, what do you know of the name Lucifer?"

Canavan sighed. "Lucifer," he managed, failing to see the point, "is one of the many names given to the devil."

"I'm sure a good theologian can do better than that."

"First used by the early Christians," the Irishman offered wearily, "and later popularized by Saint Jerome. A name generally used to designate the devil as he was before his fall from heaven."

"Aye—the magnificent Seraph, God's most brilliant and industrious courtier before the schism: the very icon of unchecked ambition. But you still haven't defined the name itself."

"Lucifer appears but once in Scripture, in Isaiah—a translation of *heilel,* Hebrew for 'spreading brightness.'"

McKnight nodded approvingly. "And in Latin?"

"It means 'the bearer of light.'"

"Aye. The bearer of light. The carrier of fire. Spreading the fundamental stuff of the universe." McKnight raised his eyebrows suggestively. "And so I ask you: Has not Evelyn all but given him his rightful name?"

The lamplighter. Canavan froze with the realization.

He was speechless for full seconds, struggling for an objection and fighting in vain against the implications.

"But . . ."

But later he would not even remember how he had protested. He vaguely registered McKnight continuing along some tangled meta-physical line, but in truth he found it exceptionally difficult to concentrate. Because for all the current assimilation of philosophy and theology there was still an essential difference between the Professor's Lucifer—the corrupted instinct—and his own—the Prince of Darkness. Repeatedly the image of Evelyn's tortured and innocent features returned to him, and again and again he tried to find it absurd to think that this face, which he had already gilded in his memory, might shield some unspeakable evil. But ultimately he was too awed by the revelation to be an effective advocate for the defense, and too staggered by the knowledge that he was no longer denying the possibility of her involvement, and it was indeed just a matter of degree.

"I know what this must seem like," the Professor admitted generously at one stage. "A wizened old man frayed by cynicism and disillusionment latching on to fantastical theories with the enthusiasm of a doctor testing revolutionary antidotes. But I stand by the logic of my conclusions. It is not my intention to become famous by this announcement, but I will make it cautiously anyway: in the young lady Evelyn Todd I believe we have found a being who is not just another thread in the weave of reality, *but one who is able to knit her imagination into its very fabric.*"

And it was this last audacious remark that continued to reverberate wildly in Canavan's mind as he wandered up Chambers Street past the Phrenological Museum, trying to come to terms with its full meaning. Because if Evelyn were truly capable of what McKnight was suggesting, then it made her something more than simply human. This truly was the power of the devil. And the possibility terrified him.

Pausing now at the intersection of Merchant Street and Candlemaker Row, he looked pensively at Evelyn's darkened garret—not a hint of a glow at its shaded window—and wondered if she now slept and dreamed. Or if both he and McKnight, having introduced themselves into her universe, were now players on her stage and thus subject to her displeasure, and consequently capable of being killed. Would Evelyn herself desire that, even in her darkest realms? What did she make of him? The imploring looks she gave him—the sense of shared communication—surely that was not a figment of his own inadequate imagination?

Standing there, filled with anguish, he suddenly discerned a man lounging against the gates of Greyfriars Cemetery, rubbing his hands for warmth and glancing alternately at Evelyn's window and the building entrance. That he was a detective, plainclothed like a "beggar hunter," Canavan did not doubt for a moment. Clearly the police themselves suspected Evelyn of an involvement more substantial than dreams, but without the aid of radical philosophy they were no doubt confused, battling to establish means and motive. The detective's presence was evidence enough of their intentions, and the man was surely under instruction to follow Evelyn closely were she to strike out on some potentially sinister mission.

Retreating to a dark alcove of his own, Canavan wondered if he had a duty to warn Evelyn or if he had the right to interfere. If McKnight's theory was fundamentally true then she was guilty at most of harboring an advanced form of original sin, and was no more accountable than Canavan, or the detective lurking in the shadows, or the judge who might send her to the gallows. It was the sort of repudiation of personal responsibility that in the past had always troubled him: the reduction of man to bestial cravings and instincts rather than the celebration of his altruism and integrity. It offered Evelyn the possibility of a moral acquittal—as well, perhaps, as a practical alibi—but in this Canavan found as much dismay as relief. Further, it did not admit the possibility that the devil was an external force, and the corresponding notion that the murders had been committed by a truly separate entity. For why could it not be that the lamplighter was in fact real and that even her unconscious was innocent?

The chimes of the High Street kirks were bruising the midnight air when he noticed a hunched little chimney sweep worm out of the building and shuffle purposefully down the street. Neither he nor the detective paid much notice at first, and it was only when the figure had almost curled around the bend that Canavan was jolted out of his distraction with an unaccountable suspicion. He shot a glance at the still-lounging detective, who remained staring at the building, and then launched from his own hiding place and took off before the sweep was lost to sight.

Rounding the corner into Bristo Place his quarry straightened and darted nimbly across the road, heading rapidly up Lothian Street behind the imposing sandstone bulk of the University. Canavan kept a discreet distance at first, but was soon emboldened when it became clear that the sweep had no intention of looking back or doing anything but moving at a progressively faster clip. When they came into the vicinity of the City Hospital, however, the figure folded into a stoop and resumed its ungainly shuffle past an ambulance wagon, only to unfurl again when they moved into the more desolate region of breweries and glassworks.

Now Canavan was certain that the figure was Evelyn. But he could not imagine her reasons or guess where she might be heading. And his heart was seized with fear.

But if indeed she had a destination at all, she gave little indication. Hunching into her guise only when she passed another figure or a row of residential windows, she performed a swift circuit of the belching gas plant in New Street, cut through the district of foundries and pickle factories, and stopped just twice: near White Horse Close, the departure point for London stagecoaches, and in the proximity of Queensberry House, where she took some time to examine the neighboring buildings and look up at the dim outline of the Salisbury Crags. Then she set off again, without any logic to her progression, taking unexpected detours, crossing the street only to cross back again, and sometimes inexplicably cutting through wynds before doubling back and retracing her steps—this last especially difficult for Canavan, who nevertheless resisted detection. But at the same time she seemed uniquely alert, absorbing the environment with all her senses, and except when shuffling she was as silent as a silverfish.

Turning from St. Mary's Street into the Cowgate, however, it suddenly became clear that she intended to pierce the slum at its befouled heart, and Canavan was further alarmed. The infamous chasm under the George IV and South Bridges was a magnet for thieves, hawkers, housebreakers, magsmen, cinderwomen, beggar prostitutes, and consumptive, barefoot children. Only the police and terminally bored aristocrats ventured here in darkness, and even then with trepidation. Canavan himself, for all his affinity with the destitute, walked here most infrequently. And yet frail Evelyn now surged west into the squalor without a moment's hesitation, as though soliciting a secret challenge or willing upon herself some assault, and behind her Canavan primed himself to defend her physically, dreading a confrontation that seemed inevitable.

The street was infinitely squalid, thick with coal dust, rag fibers, gin vomit, and expectoration, its population bunched around sputtering fires, blowing steam off soup and haranguing one another from windows. Yet Evelyn glided through it all with dreamlike ease, summoning not a single sneer or a flicker of acrimony. She raised her head a few times—seemingly to embrace the sight of the jostling tenements and frowning bridges—but otherwise moved so unobtrusively that she might have been a shadow, and with such deftness around obstacles that it was clear this was a journey she had made a thousand times. She traveled to the very end of the street without being assaulted, accosted, or even glanced at suspiciously, and when she at last climbed out of the ungodly pit and made her way back toward Candlemaker Row, Canavan actually sighed with relief.

But, to his renewed surprise, she did not immediately head home. She shuffled again past her building, once more under the eyes of the unsuspecting policeman, and proceeded back up the street to the altarlike parapet of the George IV Bridge. And here she stopped to look down, perhaps reflectively, into the inferno through which she had safely passed.

Canavan watched her from a distance—a sorrowful figure under the reddish lamps, she was moving not an inch, as though transfixed—and quickly the combination of her salient vulnerability, her previous recklessness, and her ultimately angelic passage—not to mention his own deeply stirred protective instincts—combined to intoxicate him, and he could not resist the urge to edge across the road to join her. He hesitated a few yards distant, however, and almost turned away, thinking that he had no right to disturb her private respite, before deciding that, on the contrary, it was important at least to offer her the suggestion of company, the notion of a kindred spirit.

He crept up to the parapet, and when he eventually spoke it was in a whisper of both admiration and gentle rebuke. "There are many reasons for you to be careful."

She gave no indication of responding at first, so that for a second he doubted he had made himself heard. But just as he was about to repeat himself she snarled a simple "Why?"—as though aware of his proximity from the very start.

He swallowed his unease. She had soiled her face and ruffled her hair, and her voice had affected a surly quality that was even more pronounced, and more incongruous, than when she had turned on McKnight.

"For a start," he managed, hearing himself as though from afar, "it's surely unsafe to walk the streets at night."

"I always walk the streets at night," she said flatly. Her eyes reflected the Cowgate's greaselamp glow.

"May I ask why?"

"It's what he wants."

He could not force himself to ask why, or who. "There are other matters—"

"I care not for danger."

He coughed. "Men are watching you."

"Men are always watching me."

"Aye." Canavan was perplexed by the bitterness of her tone. It was such a contrast to that of the frail being he had met previously that he could not fathom from where his attraction had come, and wondered if she was even the same person. "I can protect you," he heard himself declare heedlessly, to deny his loss of faith.

But she only smirked and for the first time rotated her head to pierce him with a gaze.

"What makes you think that I will not protect *you*?" she said, and he felt the words seep like chilled water into his heart.

He had tried to offer her a tender gesture, but she no longer required comfort. He had tried to warn her, but she was beyond the need for protection. He had yearned to console her, but she resisted pity. She was an entirely different being . . . and yet he still could not bring himself to abandon her. He believed in her resolutely, with instincts more powerful than doubt.

He turned to face her again but found that she was staring fixedly into the underworld.

"Oh, look," she whispered, with an inscrutable smile. "It's Leerie . . ."

Trying to interpret her expression, he only belatedly became aware of her actual words. Startled, he followed her gaze into the hushed depths of the Cowgate, and with horror glimpsed what could only have been a huge dragonlike creature slithering into a dark narrow wynd, trailed by a snaking diamond-tipped tail.

Chapter XV

AS WELL AS A MAN whose counsel Groves regarded as far more reliable than that of any richly paid advocate, the venerable Piper McNab had been a devoted Scripture reader and had once suggested to the Inspector that his memoirs might be afforded a veneer of authority were he to number each sentence like a biblical verse. Initially Groves had regarded the idea as extreme, even profane, but the good piper had reminded him that it would scarcely be audacious if the subject itself was weighty enough, and now, well past midnight, hunched over his journal, fighting valiantly to ensnare the words cascading from his mind, Groves began wondering if that which had once seemed a sacrilege might soon constitute a fitting imprimatur.

He had long been aware that the Lord Provost had been taking a more than common interest in the investigation: canceling engagements, making daily inquiries, and at one stage even visiting Central Office to make sure the best resources were available. This when, between his duties on the Town Council, his role as head of the Boards of Sanitation and Kirk Restoration, his honorary status as Admiral of the Firth, and his predilection for unveiling statues of Robert Burns, it was a wonder the man had found time for a single arched eyebrow. But the leeries' passing reference to his streetlamps, earlier that day, had put Groves in mind of his intention to make a personal approach to the man to assure him that the investigation was proceeding well—as swiftly as could be expected—and the city's reputation was in sure hands. He had been daunted, however, by the presumptuous nature of such a move, along with the Lord Provost's redoubtable reputation—he was said to be an impossibly fussy man, particularly sensitive to any potential obstruction to his knighthood—as well as his long-standing acquaintanceship with the Wax Man.

All these concerns were hurdles he would need to overcome before he could make his move with confidence, but returning to the Squad Room he was availed of news that at last established the *taint* for which he had so long been searching. Courtesy of the Register House curator, this was the discovery that Evelyn had been base-born to one Isabella Todd in Fountainbridge Parish in 1854 (the curator had appended a note explaining that when the father was unknown it was common for the child to adopt the mother's surname). The district, the year of birth, and the name of the mother now pricked in Groves a dormant memory, which he confirmed through a chance meeting with the Wax Man in the Central Office corridors: Isabella Todd had been a noted prostitute at the Cloak and Sash near the Cattle Market before expiring in one of the cholera epidemics of the 1850s. "Ticklish Todd? 'Course I remember her, Carus. Hammered her half a dozen times myself back in those days, when I had a taste for trollop. She had a daughter some claimed was mine, you know. Same spark, they said, but I never gave it much stock—they said the same to half the men in Edinburgh. She was looked after by the ladies of the Sash for a while, and they doted on her like their own before figuring she was better handed over to an orphanage. Young enough, the wee lass was, to have formed no memories, and they decided they'd tell her nothing of her past. Why, Carus, you old rogue? Is this some nymph that's now come forward to help you?"

Without offering a word of explanation, however, Groves had walked away brimming with vindication. Evelyn was a whore's progeny. And by his own admission possibly sired by the Wax Man. It said everything.

An hour later, crossing Charlotte Square to the Lord Provost's impressive abode, he took a lingering glance at the twin streetlamps—green-painted, gold-capped, and freshly polished—with a curious sense of providence. Rapping confidently on the front door with a lion-headed knocker, he was greeted by a cadaverous servant and ushered through lavishly appointed halls to a sitting room where the Lord Provost, the Right Honorable Henry Bolan, M.D., J.P. (the first physician to ascend to the post), was sitting, with an impressive bearing, as the celebrated painter George Reid applied the finishing touches to an official mayoral portrait. Bolan was fully attired in his scarlet and ermine robes, with gold medals, chains, and buttons gleaming, civic mace across his knees, sword at his side, and a deerhound snoring contentedly at his feet. It was the latter that first acknowledged Groves's arrival, snapping awake long enough to raise its head and sniff the air in a vain attempt to identify the Inspector's smug and apprehensive musk, before dropping its head between its paws and resuming its slumber.

The servant glided across the floor to announce Groves's arrival in his master's ear. Bolan, his chin raised imperiously, at first seemed irritated by the intrusion, but at the mention of Groves's name he paled visibly, shot a glance in the Inspector's direction, immediately shook off his pose, thrust the mace into the servant's hand, stood inadvertently on the dog's tail, and swept across to direct Groves into a private room thick with vinous red curtains and brocade, to the muffled chagrin of the painter Reid.

"You have discovered something?" Bolan asked earnestly. He was an immense and florid man, which only served to make his urgency all the more pronounced.

"I merely wish to inform My Lord Provost," Groves said, "that I am closing in on a certain suspect and feel close to putting an end to this grim chapter."

Bolan seemed unsure what to make of him. "You have the murderer in your sights, is that it?"

"The one I have in mind might not have landed the fatal blows, but is surely tied up in the gruesome business and will doubtless lead me to a conviction."

Bolan drew air through his teeth. "Who? Who is this person?"

But Groves had already committed himself to circumspection, and even fatigued and intimidated was still able to exercise caution. "It would be best if I do not make any accusations until I am ready to procure an arrest warrant."

Bolan regarded him for several seconds and finally nodded, as though he had no other option. "Very . . . very good." He fondled the hilt of his sword. "You must surely know," he added, thrusting out his chin, "how I feel personally affronted by these crimes?"

"I understand how this must be so."

"Nothing like this has ever happened in my city."

Groves enjoyed hearing the idea given official endorsement. "That is certainly the case."

"I never knew Mr. Ainslie," Bolan said. "But Professor Smeaton was close to my family at one point. And Colonel Munnoch, too; I served in the army with him, and I removed shot from his foot in the Crimea. So I had dealings, in short, with both men."

"It has been said to me, and I share your grief."

"Grief . . . yes." Pronouncing the word with a hint of disapproval, Bolan now examined Groves some more, as though debating how much he should reveal. "You have been on the detective force for some time now, Inspector," he stated, as though to reassure himself.

"Twenty years and three weeks, My Lord Provost."

"And Chief Inspector Smith tells me you are a tenacious investigator."

"I would like to think so."

"As reliable as a donkey, he says."

"He said that, did he?"

Bolan, still fidgeting with his sword, pressed on uneasily. "May I . . . may I share something with you in confidence, then, Inspector?"

"Of course, My Lord Provost."

"Something I want to go no farther than these walls."

"Of course." Groves felt honored.

Bolan lowered his voice. "Both those men—Smeaton and Munnoch— I associated with them some time ago, certainly, and I can never deny this. But I was a friend of neither man."

Groves nodded. "I understand, My Lord Provost."

"Not a friend—an adversary," Bolan insisted, and, staring at Groves, decided to go even farther. "They were God-fearing men, both of them, but they had what I regarded as extreme values."

Groves nodded.

"Extreme values," Bolan said again. "Ideals I did not share and of which I could not approve. Some years ago—so long ago I barely remember it all now—they solicited my membership in some club or cabal they were forming."

"The Mirror Society?" Groves asked.

"The what Society?"

"The Mirror Society."

"The Mirror—?" Bolan shook his head. "No, I've not heard of that. But I know they were seeking the assistance of a qualified physician, for reasons that were unclear."

"They never hinted at anything?" Groves asked.

"The club was steeped in secrecy, of a brand that frankly I found threatening."

"They threatened you?"

"Nothing like that, Inspector, but I fear . . . I fear that our disagreements were of a pronounced nature. And I fear that if such a long-standing animosity were ever made public . . . then I wonder if I myself might be considered a suspect in this terrible case. . . ."

Groves found the idea absurd. "I assure you that is not so, My Lord Provost."

"Or . . . or even worse," Bolan went on, "I fear that my association with such men, if indeed they were involved in something untoward—I fear that such a connection, as tenuous as it is, might be fodder for scandalmongers."

Groves nodded sympathetically. "I understand, certainly."

"And if any of this were made public, you see, it could prove most damaging to my reputation. To what I have achieved in the past and my aspirations for the future. This is why I have been so eager for a solution and have made my interest plain. I cannot afford to have my good name discolored by rumors."

"That would be most unfair."

"I have my family to think of," Bolan said. "And if they were to suffer because of some distant association . . . it would be unjust."

"Unjust," Groves agreed.

Bolan swallowed, uneasy with the plaintive tone. "Then I hope we have understood each other."

"I would be happy to think so."

"And you will certainly mention this meeting to no one?"

"You may rely on me, My Lord Provost."

The Lord of the Burgh looked at me as a trusted brother, but I had the sense he was not telling all he knew, there were secrets about the deceased he did not want to reveal, he did not want to dis-colour their names any more than he had, or dis-colour his own name in doing so.

"Very well," Bolan said again. "Then you will see fit to inform me when you feel in a position to make an arrest?"

"I am confident that will be very soon," Groves agreed.

"It . . . it is as I wish it," Bolan said, and finished on an appropriate note of civil solemnity. "It is a dastardly business, Inspector. A truly evil business that brings good to no one, and I can only pray our streets are not further blemished with blood."

"I pray also," Groves said.

Bolan released him to the care of his deathly servant and returned to the sitting room to resume his pose with the deerhound at his feet, and when Groves departed he noticed George Reid adding to the painting, with a couple of deft strokes, a sheen on the man's brow that might well have been sweat.

⌖

Slamming a door on his way out of Central Office that evening, Groves was so consternated that he barely noticed a dislodged fragment of masonry bouncing off his head. He donned his hat and wandered aimlessly through the streets, thrilled and dismayed in equal parts by the curious encounter with the Lord Provost. It was unquestionably a significant conversation, of the type he would lovingly record in his casebook, but he was also vaguely disappointed with his failure to pursue all the apparent avenues of interrogation. He wondered if he had been too accommodating of Bolan's desire for secrecy, as understandable as it was, and he speculated as to what arts of diplomacy the Wax Man might have employed in a similar situation, if indeed the Wax Man would have asked any questions at all.

Absently watching his shadow bloom and recede under the street-lamps, he suddenly became aware of some distant choir in an improbably festive refrain, and he found himself inexplicably drawn to its source, being the ugly Cowgate church of St. Patrick's, the principal Roman Catholic worship house in the Old Town. Like Smeaton, Groves had an ingrained distrust of Papists—they stank of incense and performed rituals that were flamboyantly arcane—but, recalling Evelyn's background, as well as the words of the Corstorphine minister, he recognized a serendipitous opportunity to reclaim his authority with some intimidating questions. So he digressed to the friary and met Father Withers at the door, addressing him with curled nostrils and stiff cadences.

"You take services here, do you not?"

"Every day," the priest assured him as the choirboys trilled.

"Do you know all your parishioners?"

"That would be difficult," Withers admitted. "But are you sure you won't come in? I have some logs on the fire."

"I'm quite comfortable here, thank you. Would you happen to recall an Irish lass if I described her?"

"I can certainly try."

Groves furnished him with a well-worn description, now appended with the adjectives *sly* and *two-faced*.

"And you would be well advised to be honest in your answers, Padre," he added. "Which I say in the best interests of the lass, as well as yourself."

"Oh, but I have an idea to whom you refer," the priest said, with no intention of being secretive. "A most mysterious girl, invariably attired in black, as you suggest."

Groves narrowed his eyes. "What do you know of her?"

"She no longer frequents our church. Though she might well attend Mass elsewhere."

"When did she leave?"

"You would need to ask her, Inspector. I know only that she was given to . . . odd behavior."

"What type of odd behavior?"

But at this point Withers became distracted. "Are . . . are you certain you won't come in?" he asked, squinting at Groves's forehead. "There seems to be a line of blood above your left eye, Inspector . . . coming from under your hat."

Puzzled, Groves put a hand to his brow and, drawing it away, examined his fingertips.

"Are you sure you're all right?" the priest asked.

For a moment, looking at the blood, Groves wondered if he had done so much thinking recently that his skull had exploded. But then he recalled the sting of the falling masonry and wiped his forehead with a pocket handkerchief.

"I'm perfectly well, thank you," he said irritably. "But the lass," he went on, determined not to be distracted. "What type of odd behavior?"

"Well, the girl . . . the young lady . . ."

"Aye . . ."

"She seemed attentive most of the time . . . you might say angelic."

"Go on."

"But on occasion she seemed to take exception, most inexplicably, to parts of the liturgy."

"What do you mean by 'exception'?"

"She would rise in the pew, and spit out some sort of imprecation, and storm off."

"Imprecation?"

"Not blasphemy, exactly . . . just something expressing disapproval."

"She did not like what you were saying, is that it?"

"It seemed so. It was unpleasant, certainly, but not without precedent. I tried to tolerate it, but it reached the stage where an approach was necessary, and I was on the verge of confronting her when I noticed that she was no longer attending. I hope no ill has come of her?"

Groves belatedly realized it was a question, but he did not deign to answer. "Which part of the service provoked the outbursts, do you recall?"

"There was one time during the Offertory of the Victim," Withers admitted, "when she seemed especially put out. She rose and snarled something—I think it was in Latin, as indeed the prayer was—and fled as if possessed."

"And what is this Offertory of the Victim?"

The priest smiled indulgently. "It follows the Consecration of the Wine. The congregation offers the Victim—the body and blood of Christ—to the Lord God as sacrifice."

"A sacrifice," Groves echoed, pondering it. "Anything else?"

"It's difficult to remember every incident, though I think she flinched, as if stung, whenever the name of the Agnus Dei was invoked."

"The . . . ?"

"The Lamb of God. Who takes away the sins of the world."

"Aye," Groves said, feeling that the taint was becoming clearer now, for far from the bleating doe she had appeared at their first meeting it was obvious that the woman was prone to vicious, even violent, turns of character. It was not enough to arrest her—not yet—but his nostrils flared with anticipation and excitement. "Have you ever heard of a certain Mirror Society?" he asked.

He examined the priest closely, but saw no evidence of evasiveness behind his answer. "The Mirror Society? Why, no . . ."

"Did you know Professor Smeaton?"

"He was a man I tipped my hat to," the priest answered carefully, "and I mourn his death. But I was not a companion of his."

"He had no association with your church, then?"

"I would regard that as most unlikely."

"This might have been twenty years ago, or more."

The priest shrugged. "I was very young then—a novice."

"Did you ever hear of Smeaton contacting a certain monsignor?"

The priest considered. "I don't recall any monsignors based in Edinburgh at that time. There were a few, I suppose, who passed through."

"Any of these you recall in particular?"

"There was Monsignor Dell'Aquila, of course," the priest said, and in the background the hymns abruptly faded. "From the Vatican. He arrived here in a cloud of great secrecy, as if on an urgent mission. Yes, I remember that most clearly."

"And who was he, to have traveled from such parts?"

"A famed demonologist, Inspector—an exorcist. The most experienced in all the Church."

"A sorcerer?"

"A priest who casts out spells and devils. A small, uniquely somber man. He looked very much as though he had been to hell and back. Which is," Withers added, "to be expected, I suppose."

"Is it possible he was summoned by Smeaton?"

"Well, Inspector, of that I can't say. As far as I'm aware, Monsignor Dell'Aquila never uttered a word about his purpose in the whole time he was here. Though when he left, as I recall, there was certainly hanging about him an atmosphere of defeat."

"Defeat?"

"He looked at least ten years older, and he had shed a considerable amount of weight."

"And where is this monsignor now, Padre? Where can he be contacted?"

"Oh, I regret that's no longer possible."

"He won't speak to me?"

"It's not that he *won't* speak, Inspector," the priest said grimly. "It's that he *can't* speak."

Groves read the implication with dismay. "He's dead?"

Withers nodded. "On a visit to Dublin," he explained as the choirboys resumed with some sprightly new noel. "He was cut down one evening in front of St. Mary's Cathedral and ripped to pieces as if by wolves. It was most uncommon, as I recall."

Chapter XVI

ARTHUR STARK, book dealer and publisher since 1855, had personally printed pamphlets by Marx, Engels, and the newly founded Fabian Society and was exceedingly sensitive to the notion that private enterprise had a way of inhibiting knowledge and exploiting desperation. He sometimes tried to convince himself that his was a vocation of civil—if not divine—good, and to assuage his conscience he frequently supplied books free of charge to charities and educational institutions. And he had once been a penniless university student himself, surviving on stony bread, re-strained tea leaves, and the vaporous dreams of some future prosperity. So he was hardly unsympathetic to the gaunt and sallow young man who now stood hopefully on the other side of the counter.

But just the previous night he had been examining his accounts, a distasteful procedure in his trade, and he was acutely aware that if he was to keep his business afloat he would need to revive and exercise some ruthless trader's instincts. Without them he might not last another two years. He had little saved for any contingency. Barely enough to maintain his beloved presses. And almost nothing to continue rewarding his assistant for exceptional performance, as he so liked to do.

"Let me see . . ." he muttered, shuffling the old books in his hands and squeezing them like market oranges.

"The condition's fair, I hope?" the student asked.

"Not unacceptable, not unacceptable, but . . . but these are not what you might call sought-after items, lad, I hope you understand that."

The student nodded. "Yes . . . I appreciate that."

"And, er . . ." Stark faltered, "and I cannot offer you much, you know, I cannot offer you much."

"I understand."

"Then let me see . . . let me have another look."

In fact, he was doing everything possible not to betray his excitement. Because—while three of the volumes were dry academic texts, of little value to any but those studying natural history—the last book was an exquisitely decorated calf-leather copy of Goethe's *The Sorrows of Young Werther*. First English translation. Immaculate condition. And a book, as it happened, for which Stark had long held a standing order from a wealthy magistrate. "Well . . ." he said. "Well . . . I fear you will not find the price agreeable, lad, but these are hard times, you know."

"Hard times," the student agreed. "That's so . . ."

Stark tried hard not to grimace: it was too easy, almost unethical. He swallowed, set the books on the counter, and made a show of examining them yet again. But he could not even bear to look at the prize Goethe. He buried it, along with his guilt, under the three science books.

"I can offer no more than one shilling," he said through his teeth. He had not raised his eyes.

"For which one?"

Stark coughed. "For all of them."

He heard a silence, through which he imagined the student must have balked. But when he managed to look up he saw the boy only nodding distractedly. "I see, I see . . ." the boy said, glancing this way and that, as though he had something far more important on his mind.

Stark now shifted warily. There was nothing in the boy's manner to suggest that he was a thief—and Stark usually trusted his instincts on such things—but stolen goods were a bane of his trade, and such items appeared most frequently in the hands of starving students. *"One shilling,"* he repeated, as though to remind the boy of the miserable stakes, and inviting him to withdraw. "That's all I can offer."

"That will have to do, then, I suppose," the student said with a most peculiar smile.

Stark's eyes lowered. "I'll . . . I'll need to take your details, of course," he said, genuinely confounded. "In the register, you understand."

"Of course," the boy agreed, and readily accepted the proffered pen.

He bent over and scribbled his address—student lodgings in Howe Street—and when Stark handed him the money from the cash drawer he pocketed it without even a glance. And then he just stood on the other side of the counter, lingering there, his eyes making a furtive sweep of the rows of shelves, as though he had some great shameful secret to disclose and was just waiting for the proper moment.

Stark waited uncomfortably, his hands on the counter.

Finally the boy leaned forward, making one last check of the surroundings, and spoke under his breath.

"The young lady . . ." he said.

Stark stared at him.

"The young lady . . ." he said again. "The one who works here . . ."

Stark was silent.

"Might . . . " the boy whispered tightly, "might she be in today?"

For a while Stark remained completely unresponsive. He did not even blink. Only his hands moved, wandering furtively around the four books and drawing them possessively across the counter.

"I regret," the book dealer said eventually, "that the lady to whom you refer is unavailable at this time."

The student, hearing the clank and hiss of the printing press from the cellar, and sensing her proximity, felt bold enough to pursue his query.

"Might she be in later, perhaps?" he asked. "At some point . . . when I may return?"

Stark looked at the boy and saw all the familiar signs: lonely, underfed, no doubt steeped in debt, and hunting for a single spark to brighten the dour Edinburgh winter. It was impossible not to pity him, but simultaneously Stark felt duty-bound to be curt, for the boy's long-term good.

"I wouldn't return, lad, if I were you," he said firmly. "I wouldn't ask again."

He stared at the boy unwaveringly, to convey the gravity of his advice, and observed the young face slowly cloud.

"I'd look elsewhere if I were you," Stark affirmed tonelessly. "There's no point wasting your time."

The boy considered for a few moments and cleared his throat. "She is . . . with another?" he whispered fatalistically, as though it were something he had long imagined.

Stark held the books to his chest. "She is . . . unavailable."

The boy looked away, looked back, and then nodded defeatedly. "I see," he said, digesting his despair. "I see." He lingered there for another two or three moments, feeling his heart shrivel like a burning blossom, and nodded without raising his eyes. Then he turned, most abruptly, and headed for the door in a daze.

Stark felt his own heart swell.

"Lad," he said, before the boy had gone completely. *"Lad . . ."*

The student turned at the doorway, his face ghostly white, and Stark made a show of examining the books again, as though he had just spotted something.

"Er, this book . . . this one," he said, holding up the Goethe. "I fear I might have undervalued it." He looked at it again. "Aye," he said, appreciating that he could ill afford it, but feeling an overpowering desire to mollify the boy's despair. "I owe you at least another shilling."

He promptly reached for the cash drawer, withdrew the money, and looked up—but the boy had already disappeared.

Alone and strangely despondent, Stark replaced the coin in the drawer and sighed.

He had dealt with edgy suitors before and no doubt he would deal with them again. He knew that in Edinburgh, as in any other city, there is little more attractive to the lonely university student than the maiden in the local bookstore. And when the maiden is one such as Evelyn—blushing, vulnerable, and evasive—she becomes all the more appealing to such harried and desperate young men.

Sorting the new acquisitions absently, he reflected that perhaps he too might once have been the victim of her inadvertent charms, and in his own queer way similarly smitten. Stark came from an ever-dwindling family line that had developed a disdain for human intimacy and an inordinate compensating affection for the animal kingdom. It was a public display of concern for some imprisoned birds, two years earlier, that had first brought Evelyn to his attention and through which he had felt an agreeable kindling in his own stoic and cynical heart. He tried not to think about it.

He was about to head downstairs, to see how she was proceeding with the printing, when he noticed a bald man with shiny ears browsing in a desultory manner near the door. Stark was briefly suspicious—the customer, with his back turned, held his hat in his hands like an open bag—but it did not take him long to recognize, even from such an unhelpful angle, the singular bearing of Inspector Carus Groves: a man to whom he had once lent, on request, some books on the history of crime fighting.

The Inspector, finally turning, and ascertaining that he had been identified, now shifted on his feet and approached the counter, nodding. "Mr. Stark," he said.

"Inspector," Stark acknowledged coolly.

"Have some books by Dickens, do you?"

"Charles Dickens?"

"Aye."

"Of course, Inspector. But you won't find them in the History section." Not by nature an acerbic man, Stark had never forgiven Groves for returning the borrowed volumes soiled with spilled ink.

Groves nodded and quickly sought a digression. "Making books down there?" he said, cocking an ear to the sound of the press.

"Some pamphlets for the Faculty of Medicine. You would like one, perhaps?"

Groves ignored him. He looked from left to right, just as the student had done, and lowered his voice in a like manner. "You have a lass working for you here, do you not?"

"I . . . do," Stark admitted, momentarily entertaining the unappetizing notion that the aging Inspector had himself developed an affection for his assistant.

"By the name of Evelyn Todd," Groves said in a hushed tone, as though speaking of a demon.

Stark nodded.

"She is on the premises now?"

"That is so, Inspector. But out of earshot, I assure you, so you may speak plainly."

Groves listened to the huffing and cranking of the press, and when he spoke again it was only fractionally louder. "May I ask what it is that she does here?"

"She assists with printing, as now. And she serves customers."

"Ah?" Groves looked suspicious. "How so?"

Stark shrugged. "She accepts payments. She makes payments. She directs customers to the right shelf."

"Aye?" Groves made a show of looking doubtful. "Good at that, is she?"

"The best I have ever known," Stark replied truthfully: Evelyn had a truly extraordinary memory and in seconds could locate any required text from within the store.

"Friendly, is she?"

"Within limits."

"Aye?"

"This is a bookstore, Inspector. I think she finds no purpose in idle chatter."

Groves considered, listening to the subterranean press, then lowered his voice some more. "But might she have formed a special relationship with any customer, to your knowledge?"

Stark did not shift his eyes. "I do not believe she has much interest in special relationships, Inspector."

"You have not seen her in the company of others?"

"If you mean in circumstances other than strictly professional, the answer is no."

Groves considered a few more moments and then leaned closer. "And you yourself, Mr. Stark—might I ask how you get along with the lass?"

Stark recognized the insinuation and resented it. "I find her punctual, reliable, courteous, and efficient. I pay her accordingly."

Groves nodded. "Pay her well, do you?"

"In line with her performance."

The press squealed and puffed.

"How many days does she work here, then?"

"Most days during semesters."

"There is no fixed schedule?"

"It depends on my other commitments."

"You never leave the premises?"

"Frequently."

"Ah?"

"I must occasionally leave to examine collections. Books that are too many, or too valuable, to be carted down here."

"And so the store is sometimes in her jurisdiction alone?"

"That is the way of it. But I trust her like a daughter."

"Yet you cannot know who she speaks to while you are absent? Or what she does?"

"I have no doubt she shelves books when she is not at the counter."

"A full-time duty, is it?"

"Have a look around you, Inspector. You will nowhere find a more ordered bookstore." Indeed, Evelyn's efforts in regard to maintenance were practically obsessive: the shelves spotlessly clean, the spines immaculately even, the books filed with extraordinary precision. She even had the shrewdness to arrange at eye level those titles most likely to arouse interest in relation to current events, and recently had brought forward a stack of Bibles, some books on insanity, the memoirs of Colonel Horace Munnoch, and—most curiously, though Stark had not questioned it—a few titles of French philosophy.

Groves nodded. "Has she ever said any unusual things to you?"

"No more than any other person."

"She has never lost her temper?"

"No." Stark coughed. "Why would she do that?"

"And what of her activities beyond this store?"

"I know Miss Todd only professionally."

"She has never given you any indication of her interests?"

"I don't believe there is much to ask about, Inspector."

"And you have no reason to suspect that anything has changed in recent days? She shows no sign of being nervous?"

"I would think it unnatural if she were not somehow affected by recent events. We all have been. May I ask what this is about, Inspector?"

But at this stage the printing press stopped and Groves, on the verge of responding, paused to listen awhile, clearly unnerved. But there was no sign of anyone from the stairs, and eventually he drew back and changed the subject.

"The press you have down there." He raised his voice in a more businesslike manner. "Fast, is it?"

"The Koenig? It can handle a thousand impressions an hour."

"Prints books, I suppose?"

"It's only good for news sheets and pamphlets, I'm afraid. I have a Columbian for better-quality work, but that is appreciably slower." Stark frowned. "May I ask why you make such an inquiry, Inspector? Have you something you'd like to see in print?"

But Groves looked suddenly caught out. "Aye," he said ambiguously, and planted his hat on his head. "Well . . . good day to you, then, Mr. Stark. Your cooperation is welcome as always."

"Good day to you, Inspector."

On his way out, watched by the book dealer, Groves stopped to resume his perfunctory browsing, tugging his lip as though trying to ascertain if there were any other titles of interest, shaking his head to register some sort of disapproval, and finally turning and striding swiftly out the door.

In his wake, satisfied that he was alone and the Inspector was not about to return, Stark stood trying to fathom the reason for the visit and what on earth the investigation might have to do with his assistant. It was true, he had to admit, that Evelyn was a mysterious one—a bottle tightly stoppered—and capable of flashes of ill temper if prodded about her past, but at the same time he could not conceive of her becoming embroiled in any sort of sinister activity. He was the one in Edinburgh who knew her best, and he had seen too much pleasure in her face at the sight of a mere pigeon waddling in the street, or a passing tram horse, to believe her capable of genuine malice.

On his way down the narrow stairway, however, he was surprised to discern some sobbing and was further alarmed, emerging into the gloomy cellar, to discover some of the printed pamphlets scattered across the floor. Evelyn, near the rear of the press, was buckled over in tears.

"Whatever is the matter?" he asked, concerned.

Evelyn looked up at him, misty-eyed. "I am the very devil, aren't I?"

Stark frowned. "I don't understand," he said, fearing she might have overheard the conversation above.

"I was not concentrating," she said, gesturing to the printing press. "I should have been watching . . . but I was distracted!"

Stark looked at the press—a personally modified steam-operated monster with brass cylinders and hissing pistons—and went over to the loading tray to investigate. Examining the paper feeder he saw that one of the foolscap sheets had jammed in the uppermost frisket.

"It's all right," he told her.

"I was remiss," she said.

"No, it's all right."

"I was remiss," she insisted. "If there is damage I want you to deduct it from my pay!"

"There's nothing to worry about, Evelyn. This is hardly damage at all—it's easily fixed."

"You say that to be kind!"

"No, Evelyn, please don't punish yourself." He dislodged the jammed paper and held it up. "There? You see?"

"But the damage—"

"It's nothing. Evelyn. I'll have it repaired in no time."

"I'll pay for it!"

"You'll do no such thing," he said firmly, wiping his fingers, and briefly considered some manner of jocular comment, of the type he frequently employed to lighten her spirits. But glancing at her now he thought she looked unusually ghostly and thin, even by her standards, and his brow creased.

"Are you . . . are you feeling unwell?" he asked delicately.

She immediately diverted his attention to a page, still wet with ink, that she held in her gloved hand. "It's one of the pamphlets on the nervous system," she explained tearfully. "One that I had just printed. I got to reading it as I was feeding some sheets in, and I lost concentration. The words, they . . ."

"They disturbed you?" Stark knew it took little to upset her.

Evelyn nodded. "It compares the brain to an electrical circuit . . . and it says that when too much energy is generated—when there is too much thought—there can be an overload."

"It's merely an analogy," Stark told her.

"But do you think it might be true?" she asked, strangely earnest. "As others have also implied? That . . . that dreams can materialize in force? That anger has a physical energy?"

"Who suggested this?" Stark asked, figuring it was most likely someone in one of the lectures she attended.

"It was a . . . a professor. I overheard him."

"Professor McKnight?" he asked. It was to this professor that she had lately attributed some of her most interesting theories. She had become obsessed with the man and sometimes even mistakenly addressed Stark himself by the name.

She nodded sheepishly.

"Is that what worries you?"

She nodded again.

He considered a moment, thinking that this Professor McKnight, whoever he was, had filled her mind with many troubling notions and should be ashamed of himself. "Have you been unsettled by all the bloodshed?" he asked quietly. "Does it worry you?"

She wiped a tear from her cheek. "I fear," she said, "that I have a terrible hell inside me."

She spoke as though to imply that she was partly responsible for the atrocities. But looking at her now, frail and vulnerable, like an ill-treated dog or a cowering kitten, Stark saw only a history of suffering as plain as the pages of any book. And suddenly feeling an overpowering affection such as he usually experienced only for wounded animals, he stepped forward, extended a finger, and tickled her gently under the chin.

"Dear little creature . . ." he murmured.

Her lower lip quivered in a strangely bestial manner and finally settled.

Chapter XVII

THE PRONOUNCED SENSITIVITY of Groves's smell ("The Perfumed Letter"), his touch ("The Walls of Braille"), and his sight ("The Cricket's Footprints") had in frequent instances been the difference between arrest and the evasion of justice. But of all his senses it was his hearing that was most celebrated in his diaries and memoirs, and before bed each night he duly cleaned and polished his ears like a soldier's rifles. He could hear a sparrow alighting on eaves, he claimed, or the stifled panting of a thief behind a hastily sealed door, or even—as now—the rubber-soled boot slap of a fellow officer pounding through the nocturnal streets to fetch him in an emergency.

He did not even bother to wake up. He pushed himself deliriously out of bed, performed his ablutions in a daze, dressed mechanically, drained a glass of cold tea, and by the time Pringle arrived he was already brushed, combed, freshly soaped, and ready for action.

"What is it?" he asked, opening the door before his assistant was able to apply a frantic knock.

Pringle looked astonished, no doubt by the Inspector's uncanny prescience. "It's . . . it's the Todd woman," he said, catching his breath.

Groves frowned. "What of her?"

"I think," Pringle said, still with some difficulty, "that it's best you find out for yourself, sir."

Groves grunted, vaguely irritated by the dramatics but relieved to have the chance to assess the new development free from distortion. He locked the door behind him quietly, mindful of not waking his sisters, and took a bracing look at the fading stars. "Let's be on our way, then," he said, careful to betray not a hint of emotion, and with great energy he took off up Leith Walk with Pringle fighting to keep pace beside him, drawn by some overpowering instinct to Candlemaker Row.

✠

Thoughts of the insidious Evelyn Todd had barely had a chance to leave his mind from the previous day. It had begun as early as his arrival at Central Office, with a telegram from the Head Constable of the Monaghan police:

> CI GROVES EDINBURGH CITY POLICE
> E TODD POSTULANT DISMISSED ST LOUIS
> CONVENT 1878 STRANGE TENDENCIES
> SUMMARY ARREST 1881 ASSAULT OF SUITOR
> NO CHARGES SENDING LETTERS HC CURRAN

Groves was just coming to terms with this when a constable entered with a report, gleaned from a meticulous examination of police records, of her further criminal activity. Two years previously, when she was residing in a lodging house in Bell's Wynd, she had been arrested for releasing the parrots of the caged-bird seller in St. Giles Street. According to her own testimony she had been strolling through the area on a Saturday afternoon when, spying the rows of cramped and listless birds, she had been overcome with the urge to free them from captivity. She could not properly recall what had happened next, but the bird seller—a hunchbacked crone of sixty, a fixture of the area—claimed the young woman had methodically unlatched every single door and shaken each cage in "an animal frenzy" and "could not be beaten off for the love of God," until all her prize birds—"parrots of the rainbow's spectrum"—had been dispersed into the smoky skies.

Tried before the Police Court, Evelyn had presented a picture of genuine remorse, fully accountable for her indiscretion and willing and eager to compensate the victim. It was noted that her act of avian emancipation had accomplished little, in any event, as for days afterward the frozen cobbles had been littered with parrots and the city's cats had returned home with colored bundles. The notoriously lenient Bailie Ryan, taking into account Evelyn's disposition and circumstances and observing that she had not been motivated by notions of personal gain, had ordered her to pay two pounds in damages to the bird seller and a five-shilling caution for future conduct or suffer five days' imprisonment. Evelyn herself had then claimed she would voluntarily contribute another five shillings to the St. Mary's poor box, further appealing to the Bailie.

Tracking down the arresting constable, Groves was unsurprised to learn that Arthur Stark had been in the public gallery that day and afterward was seen introducing himself to Evelyn, her criminal act thus leading directly to her employment in the bookstore.

Baffled by her contradictions, in any case, Groves decided he could no longer avoid a visit to Dr. Stellmach, the Wax Man's source on criminal behavior, to take at least a token academic reading of her mental state. Arriving at noon at the doctor's cluttered terrace house on Regent Road, he found his host a most curious little figure, beetle-browed, poorly shaved, and gifted with a startling Beethoven-like coiffure that Groves, for all his fatigue and confusion, could not help staring at enviously. The two men sat in a parlor sprayed with the spidery shadows of thick lace curtains.

"This lady you speak of," Stellmach asked, "would you know the background?"

Groves tore his gaze from the man's hairline. "She is an orphan. Her mother was a prostitute."

"A prostitute." Stellmach clicked his tongue meaningfully. "What became of her?"

"The mother? She died of cholera."

"The father?"

"He's . . . ." Groves thought the better of mentioning his suspicions, ". . . unknown."

Stellmach nodded somberly. "There exists a degenerative streak in those born to the prostitutes. A taint of the nerves."

"Aye," Groves agreed, pleased with the word *taint*.

"The taint, it works through the system like an infection. The daughter you speak of, is she a prostitute herself?"

"Not that I am aware of."

"Is she celibate?"

"That," Groves said uncomfortably, "is not for me to say."

"Does she have the aspects of a maiden?"

"Her aspects are . . . contrary. She was a nun at one stage."

There was an upstairs noise at this point—a woman in heels—and Stellmach rose to ease the door shut before returning to his seat, where he coughed and went on, in a strangely furtive tone. "A nun, you say? Does she have any particular friends?"

"Particular?"

"The nuns, they are known to have what are called 'particular friends.'"

Groves was not sure what he meant, but noted that the man spoke with some relish. "She is no longer a nun," he said.

"You are sure she has no particular friends?"

"I . . . I am aware of no friends."

Stellmach looked disappointed. "Is she pale?"

"Very much so."

"Tired-looking? Dark circles under the eyes?"

"Aye."

"And she wears the tight clothes, heavily laced?"

Groves had always imagined they were tight, and he nodded vaguely.

"Does she have obstructed menses?"

"Good Lord, man," Groves said, trying to imagine himself asking such a question, "what does that have to do with it?"

But at this Stellmach sighed wearily, well acquainted with such skepticism. "It is all part of the modern malady," he explained, leaning back and fingering his suspenders, "which I have written about in great detail. The woman raised on cheap romances and lurid gossip. The heavy drinking of coffee, sugar, and spiced breads. The constricting clothes. The unhealthy contrast of heat and cold in the northern cities. The breathing of foul air and dust. This is the combination which brings about the disequilibrium of the nervous system. With the imbalance comes the upsets of the gastrointestinal tract, the disrupted menses, the volatile disposition, the frailty, the distemper. This is the foundation of the woman's mental instability, combined in many cases with the degenerative taint and the inherited moral degeneracy." His eyes flared. "May I proceed with my questions?"

Groves could not but admit that the doctor had spoken with some authority. It was strangely exciting, in fact, to have Evelyn stripped of her enamel coating and her malfunctioning clockwork innards exposed. "Aye," he said. "Go on."

Stellmach stroked his chin. "Does the lady show symptoms of seizure? Grand movements?"

"She is flighty at times."

"But no convulsions? Blackouts? Hallucinations?"

"Not while I have been present."

"Where does she work, if she has no husband?"

"She works for a bookseller."

"And before this?"

"She washed dishes. She was a match dipper."

"A match dipper?" Stellmach tilted his head suggestively.

"Aye. Is this important?"

"Match dippers breathe the fumes of the phosphor and suffer hallucinations, Inspector. The lady, does she have any medical conditions? Does she take laudanum? Morphine?"

"Not that I'm aware . . ."

"Does she visit a doctor?"

"I've not asked."

Stellmach looked displeased. "These are things you will need to establish, Inspector. It is not easy to reach the accurate conclusions without all the proper information."

But Groves disliked the implication that he had been less than thorough in his investigation. "In case you don't know," he said testily, "the Lord Provost himself has declared this a case unlike any ever seen in this city. I personally have been occupied with all manner of leads and I am here only because it is my duty to investigate every possibility. You came highly recommended to me."

"By Chief Inspector Smith?" Stellmach asked with obvious affection, to the further irritation of Groves.

"By him, aye," Groves said, and inhaled. "Listen, man—can I rely on you to hold a secret?"

"It is an oath of the profession."

"It is my suspicion," the Inspector stated, "that the lady I speak of is not just tainted, and not just unstable, but capable of the most ferocious strength, the most violent acts, and that is what I am here to discover."

Stellmach considered. "You say she is generally delicate, that is so?"

"Most often she gives that appearance, as I have already said."

There was a further indication of movement above, and in response Stellmach leaned forward in his chair. "This can be deceptive, Inspector," he whispered, as though terrified that an incriminating word might escape the room. "A mask, you see. The fairer sex, they have mastered the stealth of hiding strength. The woman, she throws around her the veils of delicacy and virtue, when in fact she is the incarnate predator. She fans herself in the heat and she will not step over a puddle in the wet, but she has a tolerance for discomfort that far exceeds the man. She puts on the air of innocence when in fact her mind churns constantly with schemes. But the powers she harnesses she does not apply to noble pursuits. The energy the man feeds into creativity and manufacture, the woman channels into discord and destruction. She is the great deceiver."

Chilled, Groves wondered if Stellmach had chosen the last words knowingly.

"But this is something that the woman herself, sometimes she is not aware," the doctor went on. "This is the performance that the society has her play and which she struggles to maintain night after night, and she tries to nail down her instincts, she deprives herself of her illicit nature, and she becomes agitated and unruly. In many cases there is no telling of what the woman in the state of hysteria is capable. Have you ever visited an asylum, Inspector?"

"I have been to a madhouse."

"Then you will know that the madwoman, she claws and fights like the cornered beast, like no man is capable, and the doctor who attends to her puts his life in danger."

Here Stellmach unbuttoned his sleeve—rapidly, as though fearing he might be caught—and exposed a remarkably hairy forearm, decorated with livid tooth marks. "I was an intern, Inspector, and stronger in those days than I am now . . . but the woman, she was like a wolf, and she could not be fought off."

Groves recalled the words of the priest—that the monsignor had been torn apart "as if by wolves"—and those of the caged-bird seller—that Evelyn "could not be beaten off"—and he felt strangely queasy. He watched Stellmach refasten his cuff.

"Then you believe the lady I have mentioned," he asked, "for all her delicacy, might have been able to kill like a savage beast?"

There was another noise—the creak of someone coming down the stairs—and Stellmach, visibly ill at ease, answered in a hastening tone, "I would need to examine her and measure her skull, for there are many physical traits of the born killer, but many times the real indications are buried deep, and the examination would need to be very detailed."

"But you would not discount it?"

"Her madness could be so great that she is capable of transformation."

"Transformation?"

"I am most serious."

"What sort of transformation?"

Stellmach spoke earnestly. "The great powers of women, the hidden powers, have been known for centuries and recorded in detail, but not in the medical texts, and you must know where to look." He snapped up a pen and hunted frantically for a piece of paper. "May I write for you a list of books?"

"Books?" Groves tightened instinctively.

"The hidden history of hysteria, Inspector, which the other doctors ignore. It would be very good for you to visit the library and examine the evidence with your own eyes and tremble at the powers woman has unleashed over thousands of years, and which, under many names—"

But here he stopped, and froze as if caught in some crime, because the door knob had turned and a woman thrust her head into the room, I took it to be his frau, and she asked in a barking tone if he was ready to escort her to Jenners for Christmas shopping, and he smiled and begged her indulgence, saying he would only be another minute or two, and with great haste he scribbled out a scrawl of titles on a blank sheet, before ushering me out the door like I was a drunken sailor.

The listed books had daunting names, many in noxious Latin, and Groves had little intention of tracking them down until he returned to

Central Office and was apprised of the reports, still surfacing from the Old Town in general and in particular from the Cowgate, of a monstrous figure glimpsed in the mist and shadows of the previous night. Descriptions were characterized only by a confounding lack of consistency: batlike, reptilian-skinned, scaled, silky black, beetroot red, bovine-eared, elegantly attired, man, ghoul, beast, apparition. Further, the wave of sightings seemed to unleash a tide of previously unmentioned encounters and memories: an ogrelike creature seen galloping in the Pentland Hills, an inhuman creature pursued by dogs near St. Bernard's Well, a ghost of formidable size inhabiting the mock Warlock Weir's House at the summer's International Exhibition (though claims of the last were easily attributable to canny publicity on the part of the organizing committee).

Moreover, he was informed that, as the investigation into Ainslie's business dealings had unearthed a ganglion of fraud, debt, and shady associations, Sheriff Fleming had made an approach to Seth Hogarth seeking more information, only to discover that the great tragedian was in St. Heriot's Hospital after tripping over a floorboard and plunging into the orchestra pit. The very idea that this might have been a cunningly contrived murder attempt, deliberately conceived to ensure the actor's silence, now troubled Groves deeply (as indeed did the Sheriff's investigation itself, which embarrassed him with its thoroughness). He declared his own intention to file a comprehensive report, and headed with a sense of escape to the library.

Though in truth he had little need for spectacles, the sensitive nature of his visit made him suddenly inclined to secrecy and, convinced his was a visage known all over Edinburgh, he procured a thick pair of lenses and a worsted jacket with an upturned collar, and made the brief journey to the Signet Library stumbling over runnels and buffeting hushed onlookers awaiting a verdict outside the Justiciary Court. Sweeping up to the top of the triumphal staircase, he was immediately intimidated by the deep ranks of books, the coffered dome, the pompous portraits and unforgiving silence, and he retreated cravenly to a corner, deposited himself in a leather-bound chair, and through his absurd glasses tried to make sense of the procedures without having to call for assistance. Ascertaining that a sheaf catalogue system was in place, and with Dr. Stellmach's scribbled list concealed in one hand, he was eventually able to locate the desired books—most of them grouped closely together—and he was on his way out the front door when he was informed that he was not permitted to leave the premises with such valuable items. Here he could have invoked his position or even his redoubtable fame by disclosing his true identity, but he prudently elected to sidle over to one of the substantial reading desks, arrange his miniature ziggurat of musty-smelling titles, and remove his pad and pencil to jot notes.

He read as a majestic shaft of sunlight, thickly populated with motes of dancing dust, swept across him like the beam of a slowly rotated lamp. The books were in scarred leather bindings and loaded with exacting typescripts and incomprehensible words. There was *Anatomy of Melancholy, Discourse of the Damned Art of Witchcraft, The Kingdom of Darkness,* the *Compendium Maleficarium* (three volumes), *Saducismus Triumphatus,* and the only title he was halfway acquainted with, the Scottish favorite *Satan's Invisible World Discovered* by the Reverend Sinclair, former professor of philosophy and mathematics at the University of Edinburgh. He struggled gamely at first, intending with great ambition to read every page before the sunlight faded, but he was soon frustrated, Stellmach's point eluding him, until some of the woodcuts slowly began to snare his attention and he incrementally became absorbed. These were books concerned with the folklore and perfidy of witches from the darkest ages to the most recent century, with frequent mentions of Edinburgh that invariably quickened his heart. He read of sabbats, orgies, seductions, shape changing, curses, spells, invocations, and nightmares and illicit dreams visited upon virtuous men. He read of Satan's propensity for capturing the minds of mournful maidens and leading them down the paths of iniquity. Of women who made stews of boiled children, walked on their backs, spoke in arcane languages, thrashed about, vomited strange objects, gushed blood from their orifices, and visited upon their enemies the most appalling species of violence. Of the Scottish witches Agnes Simpson, who raised fierce tempests; Isobel Grierson, who turned herself into a cat (the book did not suggest of which variety); and Isobel Gowdie, who soared through the skies and suckled Satan in 1662.

This was what Stellmach had directed him to, the madness of women in an awesome record of degeneracy and diabolism, now all but buried under the quilt of the Enlightenment and the silk of superstition. And the more Groves read, the more he was transfixed.

He learned of women who raise mists and flames to muddle the senses and affect pious demeanors to camouflage their nefarious intentions. He read of the symptoms of possession—debased imaginations, phenomenal strength, an emaciated appearance, and the ability to speak literary and grammatical Latin. He found repeated mentions of incubi, the insatiable demons frequently summoned by witches to quench their lusts and do their bidding, and who sometimes appear as men, sometimes as satyrs, and sometimes as beasts and illusions. He examined the dreadful family tree of demons, including Aerial Demons, who assume bodies made of the dense air of hell and stalk the earth searching for victims; Water Demons, who live softly with women until their anger is inexplicably and irreversibly aroused; and Lucifugous Demons, who walk only at night and kill strangers with some breath or touch. And with an accelerating pulse he read of *metamorphosis,* the theory accepted by Thomas Aquinas and sanctioned by Augustine, in which the devil forms an image in the mind of the witch and from this immaterial state knits a second body to correspond to that projection, indistinguishable from a real being.

By the time he was finished he had a notebook bursting with arcana: everything from the location of the *stigmata diaboli* (the devil's marks, most often buried in the privy regions), the demons' fear of salt, a list of prayers to be used as talismans, and numerous notes reminding him to check any future murder scenes for drips of wax (the devil was said to keep a lighted candle up his excretory passage). He left the library with his mind swarming with appalling images, convinced that Edinburgh itself had been a veritable seminary for witches and devil worshippers, and seriously contemplating whether he might be justified in extracting a confession from Evelyn with glowing irons and rawhide whips.

When he reached home some yellowish urchins were skipping rope outside his very door:

> Is she ugly, is she pretty,
> Is she the witch of the cobble-stoned city?

The childish voices, resisting the charm of the first bedtime prayers he had muttered in fifty years, whirled and weaved around visions of orgiastic sabbats and ritualistic attacks, trawled through his dreams, and were still with him now, huffing and clanking away like Arthur Stark's printing press, as he crossed graveyard-quiet Princes Street past stirring market gardeners and edgy piemen, with his head still throbbing and his heart pounding in his throat. He was heading directly for the Old Town, where he had Evelyn under constant surveillance and where his assiduous sentinels, making no secret of their presence, had reported mysterious shadows at her windows and unusual noises from inside her room (the men had been able to prove nothing, though, for knocking on her door had found her alone, ruffled as though having been disturbed from sleep, and staring at a single candle fluttering on her table). Her neighbors, too, agreed that she was an odd one, keeping unnatural hours, often departing for walks in the middle of the night, and harboring an uncommon affinity for homeless animals. None of this constituted damning evidence, of course, but neither did it dampen Groves's suspicion that he was dealing with an unbalanced woman who inevitably would spill secrets of a dark and diabolical nature.

But presently climbing Candlemaker Row he found Pringle, to his surprise, calling him back and redirecting him into the Cowgate and, from there, to the nearby mortuary, a building that already featured regularly in his nightmares.

He shuddered with a now familiar mixture of dread and anticipation. Clearly another body had been found, and the implications of that alone were staggering. All the defiant humor the city had generated—at the University they were speculating that the killer might simply be boosting his shares in the Edinburgh Cemetery Company—could not conceal a darkness that bore talons and a fog that tasted of fear. And Pringle's evasiveness suggested a new form of victim or a new manner of death: perhaps the body had been mutilated in a style more gruesome than could be accurately recounted. But that it was the work of Evelyn the witch—or Evelyn the devil's spawn, or Evelyn's own incubus—he knew in his very marrow.

"It's her, isn't it?" he muttered to Pringle as they passed a red-eyed cat.

But Pringle for some reason seemed amazed. "Aye . . ." he agreed in a whisper.

And when they opened the green-painted mortuary doors Groves braced himself.

The caretaker was in the middle of the sawdusted floor surrounded by bell jars and bloated organs, inspecting the body of a fully naked woman laid prostrate on the central slab. When he heard the two policemen approach he turned and retreated deferentially, saying, "Not a scratch anywhere, gentlemen. This was no murder. The death certificate has been signed."

"I had Professor Whitty called to the scene of death," Pringle explained to Groves. "He was the nearest residing doctor."

But Groves was barely listening. He was staring at the white spotless body with racing eyes, unable to organize his senses but suspecting some unaccountable horror.

"Who . . . who is this?" he asked hoarsely.

"Sir?" Pringle said, looking at him curiously. "Did you not say you knew it was her?"

Groves squinted, confused, but then the realization cleaved him like a sword.

His eyes darted back and forth between the corpse's chopped hair, the dainty ridges of the spine, the cleft of the petite posterior, and the immaculate alabaster of the skin, and he felt helpless, confused, abandoned, and betrayed. Pringle was saying something to him, but the words seemed spoken in a separate room.

Surely, he thought, it could not end this way. But neither could he deny the terrible evidence before his eyes.

It was Evelyn Todd who lay before him on the ungodly mortuary slab.

"Where did you find her?" he said, barely audible.

Pringle looked at him. "In . . . in Belgrave Crescent, sir."

"Where Smeaton lay?"

"In precisely the same position, sir."

"There were no signs of attack?"

"None, sir, that are visible."

"Then how . . . how did she die?"

"They will drain her stomach, sir, but they believe she has poisoned herself."

Groves clamped his teeth together and felt a violent skirmish of emotions. There was disappointment: the murder spree might now be over, but there would be no triumphant conviction to be recorded in his diaries. There was an irrational resentment: in death the waif had taken her secrets with her, perhaps spitefully. There was a flicker of pity: perhaps he had misread the seriousness of her instability from the start, or underestimated the legitimacy of her grievances. There was even a modicum of doubt: perhaps she had nothing to do with the murders after all and now herself had become a victim of the terrible forces. But more than anything else there was a deeply troubling tremble of something dark and unspeakable, a shameful frisson he experienced when his eyes caressed her pale, bare-skinned body.

He felt enclosed in a tiny, airless space. Some distant voice was trying to tell him that this was not real, but it was a futile denial.

He locked his throat and, reclaiming his senses, decided he would need to examine her for the *stigmata diaboli,* to at least establish her credentials as a witch. He turned to solicit assistance but discovered that Pringle had left his side to confer with the caretaker on some procedural matter, the two men muttering monklike in the darkness behind him. Left alone, he inhaled, sealed the disinfectant-heavy air in his lungs, and, not breathing, levered his fingers under the cold shoulders and thighs and diligently rolled her onto her back. The skin felt supple and the limbs yielding: there was not a sign of rigor mortis or lividity. Her face looked remarkably composed, in fact, and invested with a greater luster now than she had exhibited in life.

His eyes skipped her nether regions on a first visual sweep, but he could not avoid it for long: it was in the meager tufts that the marks were most often concealed. Exhaling, he tried to imagine his fingers prodding and peeling in those parts, but even as speculation it was too much to bear, and with his loins in turmoil he stared at her angelic face with a brand of apology.

Though it seemed to him . . . looking at her now . . . that her lips were unnaturally vibrant for one deceased . . . almost stained red, in fact, as though she had been feasting on blood . . . and her cheeks, too, had acquired an oddly whoreish rouge.

He glanced around at the others, as though seeking an explanation, but the two men were even deeper in shadow and engaged in some increasingly cryptic conversation. He turned back, extended his hand tentatively to her mouth, and ran his fingertips across her rubied lips, startled to find that they were not only moist but that, underneath, her teeth were glistening with saliva.

Indeed, when he leaned forward a fraction he saw that her canines were unnaturally long and sharpened like fangs . . . bestial fangs, tiger fangs . . . and his pulse at once began hammering in his ears.

Simultaneously he noticed something in her mouth, something hidden there . . . a rolled-up page marked with Latin characters. . . .

And now, with all the signs indicating that something was seriously amiss, he for the first time experienced a premonition of danger, the sense of being lured into a trap. But his movements were dictated by some deeper consciousness.

He inserted his fingers into her mouth.

Her body in response seemed to quiver.

He blinked. He thought at first it was an illusion, a trick of the fluttering light. He hesitated, hearing only the thunder of his heart, and then he noticed it again. A ripple of muscles through her torso, a spasm, as though a creature were buried inside her. It could not possibly be normal.

He watched it all, oddly paralyzed. He could not even blink. He had a strange conviction that Pringle and the caretaker had already fled the room. His own mind told him to withdraw as well, to pull out immediately, but his hand felt immersed in glue. He could not turn. He could not move.

He watched helplessly as her eyelids fluttered like bee wings and peeled back on yellow irises.

He tried to call for help, but his throat was jammed. He tried to squirm and thrash, but her mouth was a sucking void.

Her pupils contracted to slits.

He had a moment to register a feeling of mortality as piercing as any blade.

And then she clamped her saber teeth around his fingers, crunched through the bones, and rose up from the slab like a succubus as blood jetted from his ravaged hand. She enveloped him in her bony limbs and squeezed him like a monstrous octopus.

He screamed and squirted as her godless sucking mouth descended over his head.

And Acting Chief Inspector Carus Groves, fifty-seven years old, spasmed and wailed and fell in a tangle of soiled sheets from his Leith Walk bed, imploring the Lord God to save him from such frightful dreams as in the lurid chambers of his mind the skipping song echoed incessantly:

> Is she ugly, is she pretty,
> Is she the witch of the cobble-stoned city?

Chapter XVIII

McKnight reassured himself of the book's weight in the side pocket of his jacket: a light volume, missal-size, almost concealable between two flattened palms, all the better to be carried with ease by the roaming pastor. Hundreds of years old, gilt-edged and decorated with gold leaf, it had been a component of his library for so long that he could not even remember purchasing it and had discovered it the previous day quite by accident. It now constituted another key in the complex procedure of unlocking the fortress of Evelyn's mind.

"Have you been here previously?" he asked her.

"I come here . . . sometimes."

"It is a place," the Professor admitted, "of paradoxical privacy."

They were in the Crypt of the Poets, the public house not far from Candlemaker Row where James Ainslie had once stalked for prey. It was an insalubrious establishment, glorying not in its blackened friezes, beer-soaked mats, and choking air but in the great spectrum of its patronage—quarreling students, cinder gatherers, horse soldiers in scarlet tunics, pricey courtesans in their finery—and the omnipresent thrum of its clashing conversations, fiddle music, and shouted orders, resilient even in a time of fear. This, together with its fabled gloom (the gas had long been cut off, and the place was illuminated by candles in ginger-beer bottles), meant that a company could repair to a rear table and engage in a game of whist, hatch a seditious plot, or indeed garotte one another without the turn of a single head or the presumption of an uninvited ear. McKnight, Canavan, and Evelyn now occupied a horseshoe-shaped booth beneath a begrimed portrait of Thomas Campbell, some ragged sandwiches and a barely touched bottle of port on the table between them, and the thick swirls of the Professor's pipe smoke further enshrouding them in their own contracted universe.

"I appreciate your attendance here tonight," McKnight told her, "and I assure you that, whatever happens, it is not my direct intention to hurt or disturb you. May I ask, to begin with, if you have experienced any nightmares since our last meeting?"

"None that involved murder."

"And we could not have failed to notice that our streets have simultaneously been bereft of corpses. So you will concede that no harm can be done by prying a little deeper?"

"I care not for my own welfare," Evelyn replied, "but submit myself in the hope of being some assistance to others."

Canavan, sitting directly opposite her and staring at her in fascination, now interjected with a translation: "She will be as honest as it's possible to be."

And when Evelyn, for her part, glanced the Irishman's way and nodded gratefully, McKnight had the unaccountable sense that the two had spoken together since their meeting in her little room. He was not inclined to verify the suspicion by asking them directly, but saw all the indications of an infinitely logical but nonetheless disturbing affection.

"I wish to talk about desire," he announced bluntly, and noticed Evelyn's gaze drop self-consciously to the table. "And the way in which people go about feeding their desires."

She was silent.

"Evelyn," McKnight went on, "you have spoken with some disdain, I believe, about romances . . . works of fiction . . . . books of fantasy and the imagination."

Evelyn nodded stiffly. "Others find satisfaction in them."

"And you cannot imagine what sort of satisfaction this is?"

"They find . . . refuge in them."

"Refuge from reality? From the harsh and the mundane?"

She nodded, but clearly was suspicious of his purpose.

"So a man who reads a seven-seas adventure is feeding a desire to travel, even in his imagination, on the seven seas?"

"That is quite possible."

"He might settle on this vicarious voyage because he is in reality fearful of the water, perhaps? Or he is restricted from a life on the seas by his commitments on the land? In any case, you will agree that his selection of the book defines in some way his desires?"

"I suppose that might be the case."

McKnight nodded. "It is important here that I specify books, because a man's broader choices can be narrowed by status and conditions and other factors beyond his influence. But books are by their nature so accessible and affordable, and in range so vast, that no one who regularly selects them could be said not to be leaving in the aggregate an expression of his deepest yearnings."

"Not," Canavan interrupted, "the only expression, I'd hope."

"Of course not. But certainly the *via regia* to some inner being—some craving of the hungry mind. In your case, Evelyn, I refer of course to some of the books I found on your shelf, and I trust you will not think it improper if I name them?"

"Of . . . of course not," she replied with some trepidation, because she did not wish to be guided into some sort of trap.

McKnight nourished his memory with an intake of smoke. "There was Plato's *Republic*," he said. "Grant's *The Literature and Curiosities of Dreams*. Schopenhauer's *The World as Will and Idea*. Leibniz's *Monadology*. And of course Hume's *Treatise of Human Nature*."

"They were not my own books," Evelyn reminded him.

"No—on loan from the venerable Arthur Stark. So it might be said that they represent but a fraction of similarly themed books you have devoured."

Evelyn looked unsure if she should be proud or ashamed.

"I seek not to cast doubt on your choices, Evelyn," McKnight assured her, sending out a cloudy veil. "For these are all meritable works, and indeed they are all residents of my own library."

"I have not yet read *Monadology*," she clarified.

"But you will undoubtedly get there," McKnight said, "and it is an effort to be admired."

"Very much so," Canavan added.

"You are compelled to read these texts not by the need to obtain a degree, and it must be said that many of my own students have found some of them difficult to the point of indigestible. I admit to struggling myself on occasion. And yet you, Evelyn, have selected them to read solely in your hours of leisure. It is, you have to admit, unusual."

"I care not for the usual," Evelyn said.

McKnight nodded. "I can barely attack you without attacking myself, of course. For I too was drawn to philosophy by a yearning for answers that other studies had failed to yield. I was impelled by a need to confront my demons and lay waste to delusions. I could not rest until I had located my true identity, which still eludes me."

Evelyn nodded, surprised—even disconcerted—by this admission.

"And as a tangent of this quest I have naturally made it my task to keep abreast of all the developments in psychology, and in fact in all things to do with the mind. You've heard, of course, of the surgeon James Esdaile?"

"The mesmerist?"

"Aye. His book *Mesmerism in India* is one of the titles I observed on your shelf. What do you know of him?"

She delivered a faltering answer, partly directed to Canavan, as though in explanation. "He was a Scottish surgeon in India . . . in the 1840s . . . who used an advanced form of mesmerism to remove tumors, ingrown toenails, teeth, even limbs . . . without the need for chloroform."

"Chloroform having been discovered at roughly the same time," McKnight added patriotically, "by another Scot. And mesmerism itself, for that matter, being later refined by yet another. Tell me, Evelyn, what do you know of James Braid, formerly of the University?"

Evelyn forced herself to answer. "Braid wrote *Neurypnology; or the Rationale of Nervous Sleep*."

"And his teachings, in a nutshell?"

"Braid believed that in a certain state of sleep the higher faculties of the mind are dethroned from their supremacy . . . and surrender to the power of the imagination . . . which is capable of being directed and controlled by outside forces."

"Most authoritatively put," McKnight said, genuinely impressed. "Braid called his advanced form of mesmerism *hypnotism*. Might you ever have seen a hypnotist at work, Evelyn?"

"I have seen Professor Herrmann perform at Albert Hall," she admitted.

"Aye? And what marvels did you witness?"

"He . . . convinced a young man that he was a jumping gazelle."

McKnight chortled at the thought. "And other tricks?"

"He temporarily erased from a young lady's mind the letter *g*. She could not even pronounce the word *dog*. And an older lady wrote a letter in the name of Cornelius Agrippa."

"And may I ask if you found this entertaining?"

"I was not there for entertainment."

"Of course not—that would be decadent. You were there, were you not, to acquaint yourself with the hidden powers of the mind?"

Evelyn's eyes shifted.

"Even the earliest mesmerists," McKnight went on, "reported that in the altered state patients would frequently exhibit greater strength and powers of perception than they did in full consciousness. In some cases it extended to a sort of communion of minds: the patient humming aloud a tune the mesmerist was playing only in his head. Rarely had it become so apparent that man is jacketed by his own expectations of his mental capabilities and that some of his greatest strengths can be summoned only by deliberately circumventing the conscious plane. All of which suggests a magnificent and terrifying subterranean world where all sorts of beauties and terrors hibernate."

He was watching Evelyn closely, but she did not lift her eyes.

"Many of these terrors lie in the form of hidden memories, it seems, and we are only beginning to explore this faculty in man. It is said that every single event in a man's life is stored somewhere in the cerebrum, able to be retrieved with the right impetus. There are numerous instances, indeed, of hypnotized patients retrieving episodes, entire dialogues, in minute detail, that they believed they had forgotten completely. Clearly the cryptic memory is infinitely larger than the conscious one. So in removing the tumors there with surgical skill, the hypnotist has assumed the role of the modern exorcist, with far more comprehensive results."

Still observing Evelyn carefully, and noting in particular how she had stirred at the mention of the word *exorcist*, McKnight now reached into his pocket and extracted the missal-size book, depositing it on the table between them and watching her face slowly drain of color.

"Do you recognize it, Evelyn?"

She said nothing.

"A standard procedural guide for the Roman Catholic cleric. Mine is an exceptionally seasoned edition, true, but is it possible you chanced across other, fresher editions in the library of your convent?"

She was completely silent. But she was staring at the book fixedly.

"The *Rituale Romanum*," McKnight said. "'The Roman Ritual.' Covering every major Church order from Baptism to the Last Rites. And in the rear, *De Exorcizandis*—the Rite of Exorcism. Would you object if I now read a passage?"

She seemed to have drawn inward, as though conferring with some interior being for an appropriate response. But McKnight did not hesitate. He gathered up the red silk cord, flipped the book open at the chosen page, slipped on his spectacles, and in a dispassionate voice read that which he had already memorized.

"'*Exi ergo transgressor. Exi seductor, plene omni dolo et fallacia, virtutis inimice, innocentium persecutor . . .*'"

He raised his eyes to Evelyn again, slowly folded the book, and translated the words in little more than a whisper. "'Go out, therefore, thou transgressor. Go out, thou seducer, full of deceit and guile, enemy of virtue, *persecutor of innocence . . .*'"

He noticed Evelyn's chin starting to quiver and Canavan shifting sympathetically beside him, but he would not be thwarted. He spoke softly but steadily.

"'Persecutor of Innocence,' Evelyn—the same words that were left with the body of Professor Smeaton."

She glared at the book as though to render it to cinders.

"The same words you identified in your dream."

Her eyes narrowed.

"Evelyn . . ." he said. "It is my belief that the killer who scratched the message on the wall was making an explicit reference to the Rite of Exorcism."

She shook protestingly.

"It is my belief that the killer is a devil who is now asking to be exorcised. And it is my belief that this devil resides deep in the mind of a fine and reputable young lady who releases him only in her dreams . . . and who for years has tried to bury this terrible suspicion while seeking to understand it through the reading of academic texts."

She glanced at Canavan, as though to ask how he could possibly allow this terrible accusation to go unchallenged.

"A lady who wants desperately to bring an end to the bloodshed . . . and who is appealing to be hypnotized so that the past can be uncaged and the parrots set free."

She turned her watery eyes on McKnight, her lips trembling. "You . . . you accuse me of *murder*?" she asked hoarsely.

Canavan said from the side, "We accuse you of nothing, Evelyn."

"Of nothing but a singularly powerful imagination," McKnight clarified.

But to Evelyn it seemed that this was even worse. "You're *lying*," she said, with surprising vehemence.

McKnight was persistent. "Would it surprise you to learn, Evelyn, that I have been in contact with a former inmate of your orphanage? A fine young lass, now married to one of the University's librarians. She remembers you as a headstrong little girl who frequently led the other girls on nonsensical flights of the imagination. She—"

"Who is this?" Evelyn had clenched her fists.

"Her name is not important, Evelyn. She—"

"Who? Tell me who."

"She particularly remembers what she called the Incident of the Chalk. Apparently you had rendered a majestic, dragonlike creature on the wall of—"

"You lie! This person does not exist!"

"She is as real as I am."

"She does not exist! Tell me her name!"

"I cannot tell you her name."

"Because you think that I will kill her? Because you think that I will strike her down in my dreams, is that it?"

"On the contrary, Evelyn. The lass I speak of has done you no harm. Whereas the men who have died must have wrought very serious damage on your imag—"

But she did not allow him to repeat the forbidden word.

"Why do you hurt me?" she cried abruptly, springing to her feet, unsettling the table and overturning the bottle of port. "Why do you persecute me?"

"Evelyn—"

"What do you mean to do to me!" she cried as disturbed smoke waved and twisted around her. *"Do you think that you are . . . are . . ."*

"Are what, Evelyn?" McKnight asked earnestly.

But sensing the sudden attention of nearby patrons, Evelyn could stand it no more. Tears erupted from her eyes and she reddened and wavered and, before Canavan could reach her, spun around and bolted for the exit, weaving and ducking through the crowd and hurdling puddles of gin.

Canavan shot one reproving glance at the Professor and promptly took off after her. The smoke slowly settled.

McKnight sat alone as chatter and song, briefly repelled, flooded back in to reclaim the empty space. He sighed, mopped up the spilled port, emptied his pipe, gathered up his cane and the *Rituale Romanum,* and went to the counter to pay.

Awaiting his turn, he reflected that the evening had run very much as he had expected but for the multiplying indications of Canavan's deepening affection for the lass, which of course were linked inextricably to his own uncompromising manner. As far as the investigation went this was not essentially a hindrance, and might indeed prove useful in orchestrating another meeting. But he was worried about the welfare of his friend, as he might worry about any friend who had taken leave of his senses. In Evelyn the Irishman no doubt saw an invitation to unlock his considerable reservoirs of pity, and a cross he could happily bear. In Canavan's bleached eyes and considerate words, Evelyn in turn probably saw the incarnation of all her yearnings. But rather than finding a correcting balance there, McKnight perceived only peril.

On his way out of the place he overheard some revelers, deep in some musty corner, engaged in a spirited performance of the latest pantomime song from the Theatre Royal.

If I ever cease to love,
If I ever cease to love,
May the camels have mumps,
On top of their humps,
If I ever cease to love.

✠

Leaning on his cane, the Professor waited outside in the cold and the rising mist until Canavan returned, breathless and steaming, to his side.

"She's back in her room. And won't be seen. I think I heard her sobbing."

"She will recover swiftly," McKnight assured him, setting off at once, "and summon us again."

"This is a very dangerous business."

"There are always dangers."

"And I'm not certain you know her well enough—I mean know her *heart*—to be making such drastic diagnoses."

"A surgeon on the battlefield has little time for poetry."

They entered the largely deserted Grassmarket with mist gathering at their heels.

"There are dangers to others," Canavan argued, "if her imagination is as powerful as you say. The more you stir her up, the more vengeful she could become."

"There is little evidence of that. There have been no murders since our first meeting."

"And what of yourself, then? If you move too close to the devil you speak of, isn't it likely he might rear up and smite you with his claw?"

"She does not feel that level of animosity toward me."

"She's crying now, and is quite probably resentful."

"She will not carry that resentment into her dreams."

"And this," Canavan noted, "is exactly the place where the shortcoming of your theory is exposed. Because the devil you speak of is not a product of her dreams. People have seen him while Evelyn was wide awake. You must have heard of the monstrous shape seen in the night streets?"

"Mass delusion invoked by a climate of fear."

"Aye? And how then do you dismiss my own report? For I've seen the beast as well." And when McKnight frowned derisively: "Aye—last night, from the George IV Bridge. I saw the creature, and I assure you it was no dream."

McKnight sighed. "You saw the creature directly, I suppose? In all its glory?"

"I glimpsed it," Canavan admitted, "as it was turning a corner. But there was no question of what I saw."

"It was an illusion," McKnight insisted as they passed the Corn Exchange.

"No, it was *fundamentally real*," Canavan said. "I had just met Evelyn, and I was speaking to her when we both saw it."

McKnight blinked. "Oh, you were with Evelyn, you say?"

"Aye."

"You claim you were with her and she was wide awake?"

"And she herself referred to the beast as the lamplighter."

McKnight snorted. "And you did not see fit to mention this earlier?"

"I was biding my time. In her interests alone."

"This is very convenient."

"I stand by my claim."

McKnight thought about it and shook his head. "But it's preposterous, don't you see? You claim you saw the beast while Evelyn was fully conscious?"

"I did."

"And yet we already know that the beast walks only in her dreams."

"I know what I saw," Canavan said. "And I'm surprised that you of all people would call anything preposterous."

McKnight actually stopped in his tracks, close to the site of former executions. "You yourself were dreaming," he decided. "That's the explanation."

"I assure you I was very much awake."

"Then the dream was just very vivid."

"It was no dream," Canavan countered.

"The devil cannot exist outside her dreams."

"His impact certainly has."

There was a distant scream of terror.

"No." McKnight glanced back into the mist-flooded Grassmarket. "The metaphysics are complex, true . . . ."

"I doubt the devil obeys the rules of your metaphysics."

"But don't you see?" McKnight said as they distractedly heard another squeal. "To accept what you say would be to overturn all that I have been attempting to establish. It would throw the whole world into disorder."

"A world you yourself have created," Canavan reminded him, "and jacketed with your own expectations."

"No . . ." McKnight shook his head and decided to risk chastising his friend. "You must be wary, in your current condition, lest your thoughts become muddled."

"And what's my current condition?"

McKnight exhaled. "I have no wish to offend you," he said, "and it is assuredly none of my business. However, I cannot help but feel that—"

But he did not get a chance to finish, because both men heard it simultaneously: a dissonant blare like the seventh trumpet of Revelation.

✠

In those last moments McKnight experienced an odd sense of culpability, as though he had summoned the creature with the incantation of his own skepticism. He turned in unison with Canavan and looked up at the blossoming clouds of mist, rooted in place, feeling curiously insignificant and listening helplessly as the accumulating sounds—a monstrous huffing, the rattle of hooves like a runaway draft horse, and an immense rustle of silk and leather—echoed around the facades of the square and advanced upon them with an onrush of displaced air and the heat of a hellish breath.

I have challenged the Beast, McKnight thought fatalistically, *and he has come to claim me.*

Then the mist rolled back like proscenium curtains and, with time to glimpse a single apocalyptic figure bearing down upon them, Canavan lunged forward to push his friend to safety.

But the Beast did not attack the two men; did not even appear to notice them. It surged past in a blur, shrouded and incompletely glimpsed, and headed urgently for its lair, dragging behind it great waves of fog, embers, heated air, and slaughterhouse stench. Left in a vacuum, without the chance for a single heartbeat or inhalation, McKnight and Canavan watched in astonishment as it hunched and hobbled past the Bow Foot Well and descended without hesitation into the Cowgate.

They spared just enough time to glance at one another blankly—resignation from McKnight, who did not even stop to retrieve his fallen cane—and then they tore themselves out of stultification and launched into pursuit.

Other onlookers had recoiled or been bowled over, the Beast's path marked in gasps and awestruck faces. At the foot of the slum the Irishman paused, with the Professor bringing up the rear, and watched as the great dragon trundled down the slope, cleaving the darkness and fusty air, bundling aside skinners and match sellers, ruffling the flames of open fires in a tide of squeals and sucked breaths. Trailing the night, the air, the very frontiers of credibility, it lurched under the arch of the George IV Bridge and like some oversize insect scuttled into a fissure-sized wynd.

Canavan pounded down the greasy cobbles and at the intersection saw the Beast scrunching and sliding down the narrow alley. McKnight joined him, breathing raggedly, and both men watched the ungodly spectacle in fascination, the creature, some twenty yards away, bowing and contorting itself into a dark orifice in the wall.

"*Murderer!*" McKnight shouted impulsively as they plunged into the alley. "*Persecutor!*"

They were just five yards away when the Beast raised its magisterial head and stared back at them, its face illuminated by some deviant glow.

For Canavan it was recognition. For McKnight it was what he had been seeking all his life. For both men it represented eons of fear.

The Beast rumbled, jetted vapor, folded itself into the shape of a wood louse, and squeezed into the hole with sounds of creaking bones and rustling fabric. There was a gush of sulfur and pestilence, the distant rumor of clanking chains and tortured wails, and a blast of furnacelike heat. A descending gate thundered, the dragon slid downward, and with a grumble of unearthly pain it disappeared safely into its abode.

Canavan stopped outside the misshapen doorway, his throat locked against the fetid odors and his face burning with the heat. There was just sufficient light to discern a portcullis gate.

"Where does it lead?" he asked McKnight, and stepped warily into the gloom to rattle the bars. But the gate was as impregnable as anything in Edinburgh Castle, and the Beast was well and truly hidden in its subterranean world.

Both men retreated from the wynd and fell gasping into the Cowgate, the squalid underworld that suddenly represented all the security a man could possibly require. They stood wordlessly amid the swirling smoke and mist, between the scattered cinders and pools of fish oil, battling to dislodge, if only for a moment, the imprint of the face that had glared at them, but finding an afterimage of such stark relief that a century of storms would scarce erase it.

Chapter XIX

IT WAS A MISSION, and I felt righteous, but in fact he felt deeply and unutterably scared—mortified—and the perspiration froze on his face and his heart was thumping like a lunatic in a cell. He was flanked by Pringle and a plainclothes constable and together they were heading for Candlemaker Row, Groves repeatedly clearing his throat and fighting for composure, for manly power, indignation—for anything that might take the place of fear.

"You know what the good Piper McNab used to say?" he muttered, to belie his nerves.

"What did he say?" Pringle asked.

"That a cornered dog has one instant in which it decides to become either a tiger or a hare. One instant. And do you know the most merciful thing the aggressor can do? In that instant?"

"What's that, sir?"

"Make the decision easy for the dog, one way or the other. For it is the moment of decision that is terrible, not the decision itself."

"Aye," Pringle managed.

"You see my point?" Groves persisted. "We must not allow her the option of defiance. We must remove that moment from her completely. It is why I have called the two of you to be at my side."

"Aye . . ."

They arrived at her tenement under darkness and swiftly moving clouds. At a gesture from Groves they made first for the laundry, but it was vacant. They turned and headed purposefully for the dogleg flights of stairs, and with each creaking step Groves felt his innards clench and his hands tremble helplessly. His disquiet was such that had he been alone he might have reconsidered. He might have retreated. The powers facing him were potentially enormous. But the real reason he had brought the other two along was to commit himself to action; to make prevarication too humiliating to be a ready option. He was going to confront the Todd woman and shake loose the truth. Or at least exert such an atmosphere of intimidation that she would be propelled into incriminating action and guided into one of his still-assembling traps. But it was all so very delicate.

"You have your truncheons ready?" he asked when they arrived at her eerily grooved door. "Very well. Then let us not waste another word. Let us do our duty. Let us not hesitate or be repelled in any way. Let us perform our duty, in the name of God." He fondled his silver buttons, trying to summon a wave of determination. But all day his head had been reeling.

The morning again had been marked by numerous reports of an abominable creature roving the benighted streets. In one particularly disturbing testimony, a Marchmont widow—seventy but steely of face and constitution—claimed that the beast had pursued her through the back streets and vennels and almost snatched her at her gate. Making it inside, with a clump of her hair missing, she had sealed the door and cowered in her bedroom as the creature—she claimed it was Satan himself—rattled the bars of her fence for close to an hour before departing. In the morning she burst into Central Office demanding that she be locked in one of the holding cells for her own safety, and relented only with Groves's assurance that she would receive a police escort home and be guarded day and night. Her name was Hettie Lessels, and she was the erstwhile matron of the Fountainbridge Institute for Destitute Girls.

"He's come to take me!" the woman cried, hysterical and barely comprehensible.

"Who is this, you say?" Groves asked. "The devil?"

"Aye, the de'il—she's sent him for me!"

"Who?"

"The wean, don't ye know!"

"You speak of Evelyn Todd? A lass from your orphanage?"

"Aye—the wean! We thought she was dead! But she's come back to claim me!"

Pasted with powder and damp with perspiration, she was hunched in a corner of the Chief Constable's Office and kept glancing at the window, as though fearing she might be taken at any moment.

"You're making no sense, woman," Groves said, though he had a terrible feeling she was making perfect sense. "Who is it that is after you? Is it Evelyn Todd or the devil?"

"The two! The same!"

"And why should either want to claim you?"

The widow was sobbing. "I had no direct part in it!"

"Part in what?" Groves asked, pulse racing. "Tell me, woman—for your own good!"

Her hand slid over her mouth.

"Do you want to swing from the gallows? Is that it?"

Her grief gave way to resentment. "Ask him! If ye must know!"

"Who? The devil?"

"Ask Lindsay! It was he who was at the head of the matter!"

"Who?"

"Abraham Lindsay! The orphanage governor!"

"Abraham Lindsay?" Groves recognized the name. "He's still alive?"

"Aye! He's the one! I had no direct part in it, I tell ye! No direct part!"

Abraham Lindsay, founder of the Fountainbridge Institute for Destitute Girls, was well known to the police, especially at the West Port Station, where Groves had once been stationed. A severe-looking man of great rectitude, he had been for several years in the 1860s the subject of some incongruous scandalmongering, generally related to the demise of his second wife in childbirth. Veronica Lindsay had been a celebrated beauty and free spirit, at least thirty years her husband's junior, and the unlikely union had been more or less forced upon her by a strictly conservative father seeking to "correct her inclinations." But unsavory rumors continued to plague her marriage, culminating in 1865 in the premature arrival of a firstborn child with skin the color of Ceylonese tea. Due to the unexpected nature of the birth and the fact that it was Christmas, Lindsay had been forced to perform the midwifery himself, and the next day, with vacant eyes and impassive voice, he informed the police of the terrible tragedy: the demise of both mother and child in labor. Under the circumstances this was entirely plausible, and none of the subsequent suspicions could ever be validated. The Indian manservant of a neighboring property denied any knowledge of Veronica Lindsay; her father, a member of the Faculty of Advocates, had no interest in pursuing the matter; and Abraham Lindsay himself was considered a man of impeccable character. And so wife and child were laid to rest at Drumgate Cemetery with a headstone inscription of either piercing grief or shameless duplicity (*"Sweet hallowed ground, I'll long revere thee . . ."*).

Lindsay's subsequent demeanor was similarly difficult to interpret. As flinty as he had been, he became adamantine. As menacing as he had been to his charges, he became positively hostile. His religious convictions, once admitting some chink of clemency, now became declarations of war. The Fountainbridge Institute formed a carapace around him, into which no stranger dared venture and through which no secrets were allowed to seep. Since the day of the building's destructive inferno he had retreated even farther into obscurity, with most happy to think of him as deceased.

But, as Groves discovered later that day, the fossilized remains still breathed, a heart still pumped, and bile still spilled from the parched lips. The old man was seated in an archaeological chair in a dust-filled villa shuttered with yellow blinds, not far from Queensberry House and the eternal Crags. He looked sapped, coarse-hided and shriveled, his flame of life reduced to a barely distinguishable gleam, his eyes as white as the ice accumulating on Duddingston Loch. And he proved as cryptic and unhelpful as the matron Hettie Lessels.

"I have done unspeakable things," he wheezed as behind him a clock marked time in curiously protracted seconds, "and I have had unspeakable things done to me."

"A lass by the name of Evelyn Todd resided in your orphanage, did she not?" Groves asked, ill at ease in the heavy air, which reeked of dust and rotting flesh.

"That much is certain."

"And she was discharged at some stage to the care of some relations?"

"She was discharged."

"Did you have anything to do with it?"

"I . . . arranged it," Lindsay said. He spoke as though testifying before a judge, though in a higher court than any that could be called terrestrial.

"Did you know her mother?"

"The girl had no mother."

Groves sniffed emphatically. "She was the daughter," he stated clearly, also as though making an official statement, "of Isabella Todd, a notorious prostitute."

Lindsay did not speak or move his eyes, and Groves was not even sure if they were capable of sight. "The girl had no parents," the old man said defiantly.

"Then who did you discharge her to?"

Lindsay moistened his lips. "To the care of some people."

"To a society? To the Mirror Society, is that it?"

Whether Lindsay could actually see or not, he now turned his eyes and stared at Groves frostily.

The man could not hide everything from me, he was awed by my knowledge, and for all his years, he quivered before me like a feeble adolescent.

"It was a society formed," Lindsay said, "with the most divine intentions."

"And who was part of it?"

Lindsay looked away. "Few who remain alive."

"Colonel Munnoch?"

No response.

"Professor Smeaton? James Ainslie?"

"Ainslie," Lindsay said, "was not one of us."

Groves frowned. "Then pray tell, sir, what was his part?"

Lindsay shook his head slightly.

"And the lighthouse keeper Colin Shanks? The widow Hettie Lessels?"

Lindsay's brow creased. "Mrs. Lessels?" he asked, curious. "Has she also been taken?"

"I met the woman this morning. She has not been taken."

The old man grunted. "Then it is only a matter of time."

Groves shifted on his feet. "You still have not answered my question, sir. About the members of the Society."

"It will serve no purpose for you to know. Justice will be administered by a greater power."

Groves felt his hackles rise, partly at the man's continuing recalcitrance and partly at the suggestion that the resolution of the case was beyond his capacities. "And what power is this, that it has been elevated above the country's courts and forces of law enforcement?"

"I speak of the Lord God, Inspector."

"It is God, now? And not the devil?"

Lindsay spoke solemnly. "The Lord has the devil as his executioner, and unleashes him to deliver justice on notorious sinners."

"And what sins are these, sir, that they are beyond the laws of normal men?"

Nothing.

"What did you do to her? To Evelyn Todd?"

Lindsay looked briefly as though he were about to say something, but thought the better of it.

"I said what did you do to her?" Groves repeated, more loudly. "What on earth did you do that you warrant such punishment?"

Lindsay's knotted hands slid around the arms of his chair. "Do you know . . . do you know what he said to me? So many years ago?"

"Who?" Groves asked, his brow bent. "Do I know what *who* said?"

But Lindsay was looking dreamily at the amber blinds. "I hear his words most distinctly, and I have lived with them every day."

"Explain yourself."

The old man recited the words with fatalistic relish: "'I shall hibernate, draw nourishment, and when I return, though it be an eternity, it will be with great vengeance and no mercy.'"

"Who said this?"

But Lindsay, ignoring him, had not finished. "'In punishing me unjustly you have just awakened me. But you can never eliminate me . . . for in shattering the mirror you only create a thousand new reflections.'"

The man was grinning at the recitation of these words, which he pronounced like a prayer, and I judged him the maddest of the mad lot I had met in this terrible investigation, he had drawn himself through years of ill health with the mad aim of being properly punished, by a severe hand, before his demise.

Groves hissed his impatience. "Who said this to you?"

Lindsay chuckled feebly, enjoying his own evasiveness. "She said it. The lamb."

"You said it was a man."

"They were his words. But I did not say he pronounced them."

"Then who? Who said them? The devil?"

Lindsay drew air through his papery nostrils. "You might ask her, Inspector. And pray she is not dreaming."

"Ask Evelyn?"

No answer.

"You speak of Evelyn Todd, is that it?"

"Have you seen her?" Lindsay asked suddenly. "Have you met her? What does she look like? Is she beautiful?"

But now it was Groves who did not answer.

Lindsay nodded delightedly. "The others thought she had died, you know. On the seas. They thought she had perished. But I knew better. She was too strong to die. I was the one who chose her, you see, and I was the one who first lashed her. There was a creature she drew in chalk. . . ." He lapsed into silence, remembering.

"This is madness," Groves decided, though in truth he desired most of all to be away, for with each passing moment he felt more in the presence of some contagion, some being truly beyond human jurisdiction. Each of Lindsay's hints seemed calculated to urge him closer to a revelation that he could barely contemplate, but this was something he wanted to extract from Evelyn herself, and indeed it was a scene he had written countless times in his head. "I shall come back," he warned, "and I shall bring the entire constabulary with me, if that is what it takes to make you talk."

Lindsay shook his head. "I will not be leaving the city, Inspector. Though I will certainly advise the others to take that course."

"What others? The Mirror Society?"

But again Lindsay did not respond, and Groves posted a constable outside to check for any movement. If the Society was to be drawn together one last time he wanted to know immediately: it could prove most illuminating. He returned promptly to Central Office, fetched a package of letters freshly delivered from Ireland, summoned Pringle, and now stood in the gloomy passage outside Evelyn's corrugated door, recalling with distaste the she-devil of his unmentionable dream, battling whole armies of nerves, and raising a tight first to deliver the Fearsome Knock of Inspector Groves.

RAT-TATTA-TATTA-TAT.

✠

Canavan was as pleased as he was awed. For all its surrealism, the Beast was too real, too temporal, to be denied, and this must surely exonerate Evelyn, even in the eyes of the skeptical McKnight. Because she surely could not have been dreaming, or even sleeping, so soon after leaving the Crypt of the Poets in such an agitated state. So the Beast did not live entirely in her imagination, as the Professor believed. The Beast was not harbored exclusively in her dreams. It was alive in Edinburgh, and an entity in its own right.

He claimed this not as a victory for himself or for theology, or even as a certainty. Science might still have an answer. Philosophy, too, though it would require McKnight to seriously reorganize his theories. It was no victory at all, in fact, because their adversary was incarnate, with a dwelling place all its own, and to defeat it would require a truly biblical confrontation.

When he arrived at McKnight's cottage it was with a lingering quiver in his skin, but no one who had so recently looked into the eyes of the Beast could expect less. He was confident he would find the Professor similarly shaken—the pallor of his face after stumbling out of the Cowgate was that of a man who had stared into the Abyss—and indeed Canavan prepared himself to be as magnanimous as possible in victory. It was the least he could do for a friend who might well be shattered.

He was surprised and a little alarmed, then, to find McKnight exuding an atmosphere of grim satisfaction. Ushering Canavan to the kitchen, he chuckled repeatedly and fatalistically under his breath, for all the world as though he had made a discovery that was everything he had always suspected and everything he had always feared.

"Time to eat," he said first, and directed his guest to a table where he laid out a most generous meal but absentmindedly jumbled the order of courses, so that mutton was followed by soup, fruit by fresh bread, and the singing brass kettle ignored entirely. He paced around the room distractedly and with great energy, his own plate steaming but untouched.

"I'd be obliged if you'd join me," Canavan said at one point.

"Hmm? Very well," McKnight responded, though he seemed to have misunderstood, for he disappeared for a moment and returned from his library with two black books, which he placed on the table in front of his still-dining friend.

"Recognize this volume?" he asked.

Canavan swallowed. "Your Douai Bible. The one I had at Drumgate."

"Are you quite certain?"

Canavan dried his fingers and reached across to flip the book over and examine the spine. There was clear scuffing where the book had hit the watchtower floor.

"Entirely," he said.

McKnight smiled. "Then what about this one?" He placed beside the first an identical black book, scarred and scuffed in precisely the same places.

Canavan shrugged. "Another Bible."

"This is the Bible I lifted from Evelyn's shelf," the Professor explained. "The same as my volume in every aspect."

Canavan conceded the point but saw little relevance. "I'm sure it's a popular edition," he noted, "and prone to being damaged in the same way."

McKnight turned each book to the Gospel According to St. John, Chapter Eight.

"Take a look," he urged, and—a little uneasily now—Canavan did so, reaching over his unfinished meal and fingering the ragged ends of the torn-out pages as McKnight watched expectantly.

"Identical," he agreed.

"Indistinguishable," McKnight contended.

Canavan shrugged again. "At a cursory examination."

But the Professor would not have it. "The sliver of page left in the binding of each book is precisely the same. Down to the minutest visible fiber."

"You've examined it with a microscope, I suppose."

"I have." McKnight smiled.

Canavan felt an unsettling in his stomach. "Such is not impossible," he argued valiantly, "in two books that have been cut, so to speak, from the very same cloth. And torn, perhaps, by the very same person."

"By the very same devil."

Canavan remembered the face in the Cowgate wynd. "Possibly . . ." he said.

"The two books are exactly the same," McKnight said, closing them together and putting one atop the other. "Identical in every respect. They are not just similar. They are the *same*. There is only one book. Not two. Only one."

Canavan sighed, staring at the two books pointedly, as though to reiterate the evidence of his eyes.

McKnight smiled sympathetically. "Do you remember," he asked, "the wynd into which we chased the Beast?"

Canavan coughed. "Of course."

"Shand's Wynd. I noticed the name on the way out. Have you heard of it before?"

Canavan thought about it. "No . . ."

"Would it surprise you to learn that, having scoured every survey map of the area in great detail, I can find no evidence of any such wynd? Any close, any street—anything with that name?"

Canavan was defensive. "Not all maps are complete. And most quickly become obsolete."

"So you believe its omission proves nothing?"

"I believe it proves little."

"And the Bibles?"

"Even less so."

McKnight picked up an apple. "Then follow me," he said, and turned for the library.

✠

He knocked again.

In his pocket he had two letters. The first was from Head Constable Curran of the Monaghan Police, detailing some of Evelyn Todd's previous brushes with the law. An incident involving a man who had escorted her home to her lodgings, only to be violently repulsed—"with animal force"—when he made some intimate advances. An unproven allegation that she had smuggled out the harried wolfhounds of a well-known lord. A childhood charge of stoning the stained-glass windows of the local church. As well, there was Curran's full report of his visit to the St. Louis Convent and his interview with Mother Genevieve Berthollet. Very much like the clergymen Groves had recently encountered, the nun proved initially hesitant, but under pressure seemed relieved to divulge the incriminating details. Evelyn Todd, she claimed, had been a challenging girl, for the most part superior to her sisters in industry, humility, and commitment, but prone to erratic and inexplicable outbursts that were all the starker in contrast to her natural bearing. In the blink of an eye she could switch from piety to tormented grief, and occasionally to the most virulent invective. The last, though infrequent, seemed triggered chiefly in moments of the deepest devotion and was sometimes accompanied by paroxysmal blackouts. Her subsequent acts of contrition were sincere and self-punishing, and for a long time her behavior was tolerated and rebuked with only prayer.

But then the Mother Superior discovered an unsolicited "examination of conscience," copied many times over in Evelyn's own hand. Groves presently had a copy in his possession.

An impure attraction draws my heart to him and removes it from God. I delight in the prospect of being part of his Empire. It flatters me to think that he elects to be inside me, and protects me from those who might harm me. I know he wishes me no harm, and I remember that he was once an Angel, and his only misconstrued sin was Pride. There are moments when I cannot tolerate the harsh words raised against him, and in these moments I feel great difficulty in reconciling my Being between the Adversaries. I must choose to give my heart to the Redeemer, and divide my mind between my powers of reason and the Will of the Other. I wonder however if my Temple is large enough for all these inhabitants. It seems increasingly likely that a forced eviction will be required, but I am alone, as I always have been, and I fear I must act with my own secret armaments.

Curran had appended a note:

When confronted by Mother Berthollet, Miss Todd claimed to have no recollection of writing this letter, though she did not deny it was in her hand, and in a state of delirium later, she recanted, and she claimed that the one she spoke of in the letter was not some secret lover, as had been supposed, for such confessions are not uncommon—but the Lord Lucifer himself.

And now Groves knocked again, insistently, and in time with his heart.

RAT-TATTA-TATTA-TAT.

But there was still no response. He looked suspiciously at his companions, grateful for the opportunity to vacillate and wondering if he had done just enough to withdraw without losing face. He knocked just one more time, to be certain. Nothing.

He was about to turn when Pringle produced a stock of skeleton keys and, as the Inspector watched in alarm, methodically turned them out one after another and inserted them into the simple barrel lock. Groves was on the verge of delivering some note of protest, disguised as a warning, when the younger man released the bolt and pushed the door back on the awful gloom.

All three men stood tensed, half expecting some batlike monstrosity to spring out. The constable lit his lantern and directed the beam into the tiny room. Nothing. Groves summoned the courage to crane his head forward investigatively, but it was not bitten off. Pringle stepped all the way in, but was not swooped upon. The others, following his example, squeezed in behind him.

The room was meticulously neat and well dusted, its books primly lining the shelves, its utensils arranged like a surgeon's blades. The only anomalies were a certain scorched-air smell, like that of lightning on a humid breeze, and the insistent scuttle of a rat in the roof. Pringle found a match and applied it to a slush lamp. Further brightened, the room could barely have appeared less threatening.

"She's not home," Groves breathed, as relieved as he was disappointed.

"Where could she be, sir?" Pringle asked.

"Who can say?" Groves tried to imagine her engaged in some sinister activity: stewing a potion in a vat, dancing at a sabbat, conspiring with her incubus. But the simple truth was she was just not there, and he resolved to make the most of the opportunity.

"You two go back downstairs," he ordered. "And if she returns, hold her up at once, and one of you head up to warn me."

Left alone, he stood in place for perhaps two minutes, slowly turning his head, listening to the rat gnaw at the ceiling, and trying to read the place with his nerve ends, his preternatural senses. But in truth it was difficult to perceive anything beyond the heat of his own blood.

He started with her bed linen, turning back the obsessively boiled sheets and hunting under the pillow for talismans, locks of hair, amulets. He searched around the floor for droplets of wax. He checked her eating area for signs of an unnatural appetite: baby livers, cat entrails, predigested hair. He examined the walls and ceilings for some sign of an aperture, a secret door, through which a visitor might enter. He picked up a rag doll and examined it for signs of voodoo manipulations. And finally, and with great reluctance, he turned his attention to the unavoidable centerpiece of the room, the bookshelves and their range of intimidating texts.

He could find no familiar titles, and his lips pursed in disdain. He ran a fingertip along the embossed spines, hoping to find something damning: a grimoire, a book of magic, a missal bound in wolfskin. A few of the volumes were marked with prices and stamped by Arthur Stark, and he wondered if she had stolen them. He inspected her damaged Holy Bible, and he levered from the end of the shelf a thin, untitled notebook like those purchased by students. Flipping it open, he found meticulous transcripts of speeches from the University, including a lecture attributed to Professor Hamilton, whom he remembered as having something to do with philosophy.

"Gentlemen, I want you to look at me now and ask yourselves if I exist. I want you to consider the possibility that I might be no more than a shadow, or something else of completely immaterial value. Not, I hasten to add, because I regard myself as a ghost, or indeed a shadow. In fact, I would be recognized as human in any number of venerable faculties . . ."

His nose recoiled, as though having inhaled some toxin, and he was about to slide the book back into place when he noticed the sliver of another book, hidden flat against the back of the shelf. Curious, he pushed aside the other titles and worked it from its hiding place into the light.

It was a ledger book, in appearance much like the one in which he recorded his own memoirs. He opened it distastefully.

He found numerous diagrams inside, most seemingly aborted or even scrubbed out with a sense of shame: grotesqueries such as resided in the margins of Gothic prayer books, gargoyles, strange birds, winged mammals, and increasingly bizarre hybrids. Repeatedly there were the hazy beginnings of a dragonlike creature—a head, or a sketchy outline, or a set of claws—but never more, as though she would not permit the beast to escape fully from her imagination. There were attempts at stories and poetry, all quickly abandoned, the handwriting invariably exhibiting an initial confidence but quickly fading to wavering lines and ultimately dissolution. Halfway through the book a page had been ripped out, and he remembered that the message *Ce Grand Trompeur* had been inscribed on similar paper. Chilled, he was about to snap the book shut when a soiled and folded page fell loose. He plucked it from the floor and unfurled it with instinctive trepidation.

The handwriting was vaguely innocent and the ink much faded, so he could not be certain when it was written, but he had little doubt as to the author's identity. He read the text with mounting revulsion.

> *I swallowed a worm. I dropped it into my mouth, let it wrap around my tongue like a vine, then flipped it down my throat and let it creep and coil in my guts like a snake in a pit.*
>
> *I ate a fly. I lured it through my lips and let it crash frantically around my mouth, then crushed it against my palate with the tip of my tongue, squeezed out its tiny pellets, rolled its legs like whiskers, drowned its carcass in saliva, and sent it on a swift journey to the pit with the screaming worm.*
>
> *I ate a spider. I held it struggling in my pincers and then I snapped off its head with my two front teeth. I bit into its sac and tasted joyfully of its acrid cream, then ground its limbs to sugary fragments and digested the lot like some divine Turkish sweetmeat.*
>
> *I ate a rat. I began with the tail—*

But Groves could read no more. He could barely credit it, but it was as though he himself were tasting those vile creatures, as though they were churning and seething in his own stomach. Feeling a burst of sweat on his forehead, he shoved the letter back into the book, and the book into the shelf, and was so busy wiping his brow that he did not hear the door creak open behind him.

It was the shivering lamp flame that alerted him. And of course his own celebrated senses.

He wheeled around to find a chimney sweep standing at the open door, staring in at him. A shock that was compounded seconds later with the realization that it was not a sweep at all, but Evelyn.

✠

Stepping into the library Canavan was seized with dread, for everything about McKnight's manner suggested a true revelation—a final surrender to the Apocalypse.

Shelving his lamp, the Professor gestured to the bookcase facing them. "Observe the titles," he said, and Canavan did so: *The Republic, The Literature and Curiosities of Dreams, The World as Will and Idea,* and three volumes of *A Treatise of Human Nature*—some of the very books in Evelyn's possession.

"I've not moved them an inch in months," McKnight said. "They appear before you conspicuously identical to their order on Evelyn's own shelves."

Canavan could not apprehend the meaning of it, and he shook his head indifferently.

"Have a look at one of them," the Professor urged, and he selected one of the *Human Nature* volumes, pressing it into his friend's hands.

The Irishman fanned through the pages absently. It was an imperfect edition. There were gaps on certain pages, the print haphazard and the ink frequently faded.

"Purchased at a discount, I hope," he said.

The Professor smirked, retrieving the book and replacing it on the shelf. "Then try this one." He handed to Canavan his *Rituale Romanum.* "From a more distant shelf, and not in Evelyn's visible collection. Open it," he suggested, "at the marked page."

Canavan turned to the Rite of Exorcism, finding a woodcut of cowled monks gathered around a possessed man, a winged serpent fleeing through a window. The text was a mixture of vibrant red and black inks.

"Try the previous pages," McKnight said. "The Last Rites. The Rite of Marriage . . ."

When Canavan turned to these pages he noticed what appeared to be more serious printing errors, though here in even greater abundance: whole pages blank or decorated with just a few strings of blurred sentences. He still could not comprehend it, though he was beginning to feel uneasy.

"I found it in the very depths of the labyrinth," McKnight said. "In a bookcase I barely knew existed. Where there are whole books—entire shelves—filled with blank pages, isolated phrases, disappearing words. The diagrams remain in good shape, generally, but the text . . ." He smiled. "Mine is a library from which even the words have drained."

Canavan shook his head protestingly. He turned the *Rituale Romanum* over and over in his hands, hoping to find some button, some note, that might reveal its secret.

McKnight finally pried the book from his grasp, but only to replace it with another.

"Leibniz's *Monadology,*" he said quietly. "The book, you'll recall, that Evelyn claimed she has not yet read . . ."

Canavan had little doubt what he would find, and indeed the book seemed to sigh with shame when he opened it. The pages shimmered, practically sparkled at him with their immaculate whiteness. First page, tenth page, hundredth page. All completely devoid of text. The words had never been read by Evelyn, and it was as though they had never existed.

✠

In the elongated silence Groves found himself grappling for the wisdom of the good Piper McNab, but instead of inspiration he found only a savage irony. Because rather than feeling like the aggressor, he felt like the one who had an instant to decide if he was a tiger or a hare.

"What . . . what do we have here?" he asked, a stupid response, but all the words he had rehearsed for this moment had evaporated behind uncertainty as to which of the two Evelyns he now faced, or indeed what powers she had at her disposal. "Where have you been?"

She tugged the door shut and stepped sideways into the corner of the room, where the light was weakest. She did not look at him directly.

"I . . . I have been walking," she replied, in a voice pitched somewhere between self-reproach and umbrage. "And what are *you* doing here?"

"Aye?" Groves raised his head, as though he had no right to be asked. "I am here," he said, drawing himself to his full, defensive height, "with stout constables, who are posted outside." But he spoke optimistically, because he could not be certain that she had not already accounted for Pringle and the plainclothes policeman.

She gave no indication either way. She removed her cap, and what there was of her hair fell free. "Has there been more tragedy?" she asked quietly.

"Tragedy?" He felt rooted to the floor. "And why . . . why do you ask? Have you dreamed of some tragedy?"

"I have dreamed of nothing."

"Aye?" He made an effort to hold his gaze on her, but the nightmare image of her glistening fangs returned to him insistently, and he tasted bile in his mouth. He tried to distract himself with visions of his forthcoming diary notes: *There was no telling what powers of darkness she had at her call, but I had as many powers of my own. . . .*

"But you are surely not here," Evelyn added, "to wish me well."

"Is that right?" He drew courage from the genuine note of regret. "You make it sound like you have been expecting me, lass."

"I fear," she said, "that you have sniffed my blood."

"I am a predator, is that it?"

"I . . . I did not say that."

"Then I target you unfairly? Or are you confessing to me?"

She dropped her cap on the table and seemed to drag the darkness around her. She was barely a couple of arm's lengths away, but she seemed at the other end of a stadium. "I am no longer sure of anything," she said.

With further effort Groves managed to roll on his heels. "I came here simply to clarify some matters," he said. "I did not expect you to be absent."

Nothing.

"Can you explain why you were out, woman? And why you are dressed in that manner?" He had always disliked sweeps—the only thing blacker than their faces was their souls—and on Evelyn the effect was especially disagreeable.

"When I walk . . . at night," she said, "it is better not to be a woman."

"It is a grand thing," he returned, finding fortitude in scorn, "that a woman is ashamed of her sex."

"I'm not ashamed. . . ."

"Aye?"

"I'm simply wary of strangers."

"Then why do you roam the streets at all?"

"I have already answered this to others."

He frowned. "What others?"

She seemed protective.

"What others, I say?"

She did not deign to respond.

He saw an explicit reflection of the Wax Man in her—the same aspect of superiority—and he experienced a surge of resentment, which gave him extra strength. "You play the innocent lamb, don't you," he said, "but in secret you are quite deranged."

Her gaze remained lowered.

"Aye, lass," Groves said, his lips trembling, "you can hide behind what you call your dreams, but I cannot be fooled. If you have secrets to spill, they will come out."

She seemed resigned. "It is what everyone tells me."

It seemed a further suggestion that there were other investigators involved. "Who?" he demanded again. "Who tells you this?"

She hesitated.

"I asked a question, woman."

"My . . . my visitors."

"What visitors are these?" He wondered if she meant the Sheriff or the Procurator Fiscal, or even the Wax Man himself. The notion that these men already knew all about Evelyn and her potential powers, and had preceded him with an interrogation, was terrible in its implications.

"Mr. Canavan," she answered, "and the Professor."

"Professor? What professor?"

She hesitated. "Thomas McKnight, Professor of Logic and Metaphysics at the University of Edinburgh."

Groves could recall no such man from his visit to the University and was suddenly convinced she was lying. To provoke him, perhaps; to make him *jealous*.

"He has questioned you, I suppose, this professor?"

"He believes I harbor hidden memories."

"That's what he believes, is it?"

"He believes he can make me divulge my secrets."

"Aye?" Groves snorted. "Well, there are many ways to divulge a woman's secrets."

He took a tentative step forward—little more than an inch—but to his relief she did not rise up defensively.

"Do you know who I have spoken to, woman?"

No answer.

"Does the name Hettie Lessels mean anything to you?"

She averted her head, but the recognition was clear enough.

"Hettie Lessels," Groves repeated with relish. "The woman remembers you, all right. And Abraham Lindsay?"

She looked further stung by the name.

"That's right." Groves inched even closer, surprised by his own boldness, but then she had given no indication that she was about to turn on him. "Do you know what they said? What they said about you?"

She was barely audible. "What did they say?"

Groves twisted the truth adventurously. "That you despise them for what they did to you and that you are hunting them down for their sins. Aye."

She did not deny it.

He slid a trembling hand into his greatcoat pocket and withdrew the examination of conscience, thrusting it at her like a cutlass. "You remember writing this, do you, woman?"

She kept her hands clasped in front of her, not wanting to accept the evidence. He tossed it at her and it spiraled to the floor like a loose feather.

"From your convent? Your letter to the devil? Do you not remember that?"

She stared at the settling sheet.

He risked stepping so close that he was practically breathing on her. "You have some pact with him, is that it? He does your bidding because of this pact?"

She backed away.

"You employ him for revenge, is that it?"

"No . . ." She pressed against the wall as though for protection.

"When will it end, woman? What will it take?"

"You have no evidence. . . ."

"Aye?" Looking down on her cowed form Groves could barely tolerate his own excitement. "What do you call the testimony of my witnesses? Abraham Lindsay and the widow Lessels. What do you call that?"

"They have not—"

"*What?*"

"They have not spoken. . . ."

"They have not spoken, have they? And yet I have heard them with my own ears."

"They have not spoken!" she insisted.

"And how could that be?" he asked, nearly spitting on her. "Why do you think I might lie?"

"They would not make statements—"

"Aye? And why is that?"

"Because they would not want to damn themselves," she said finally, forcing it out, and sagged with the effort, so that he had to thrust his hand out to prevent her from collapsing. He squeezed her forearm, almost crushing her delicate bone, and drawing her to her feet he noticed that her sleeve had fallen back on her wrist, the whiteness of the skin there startling in contrast to her sooty hands, and—he could not be sure, for he had his back to the lamp—there seemed the remnant of something there, a *wound,* and he met her eyes for the first time. She regained her senses just enough to squirm free, dragging her sleeve over her hand and staring at him challengingly now, daring him to say something, to divulge this terrible secret, and he found himself suddenly enervated, staring back into her eyes and seeing the Wax Man's terrible spark, and he felt himself falling into her, being *absorbed* by her, and the blood surged in his head and his tongue struggled to conduct words, but he was oddly paralyzed . . .

The door burst open.

He was still staring at her, transfixed, when Evelyn finally broke the contact. Emerging from the spell, Groves turned to see a breathless Pringle looking at them in wonder, and he felt curiously ashamed.

"What is it?" he snapped.

"Mr. . . . Mr. Lindsay, sir," Pringle said, still coming to terms with Evelyn's presence, and not sure if he should go on.

"What about him?"

"He's made a move, sir. By cab. You asked to be informed. . . ."

Groves took an inordinate length of time to digest the news. "Aye," he said eventually, as though he had expected nothing less. "So I did."

And in truth he welcomed the excuse to escape, for his head was still pulsing and his lungs felt uncomfortably parched: Evelyn left too little oxygen in her proximity for another to breathe. But he had breached her defenses and weakened her for the next assault, he assured himself of that, and he would most certainly return to finish the battle.

"Let's . . . let's be off, then," he said, and headed away at once—

leaving Pringle to spare one last glance at the downcast Evelyn before
pursuing the Inspector down the stairs.

✠

Canavan stared at the pages incredulously. "All the books . . ." he whispered. "All incomplete?"

"Most are missing a few pages, and at the very least a few words."

"Which . . . which books are most intact?"

"*The Science of Nervous Sleep.* Braid's *Neurypnology.* Teste's *Practical Man-
ual of Animal Magnetism.* Anything related to hypnotism and its associated subjects. Evelyn clearly has been reading extensively on the matter
in recent days."

"But why?" Canavan asked, already dreading the answer.

"So that we might be prepared," the Professor answered, and chortled
mirthlessly. "Don't you see? Here in this library we have all the answers.
The reason Shand's Wynd appears on no map. The reason we were able
to face the Beast while we believed Evelyn could not be asleep. The reason we seem to have been specifically summoned. Even the reason my
true identity has always eluded me. Here, in this murky library, lie all the
answers."

Canavan stared at him, awed but still needing to be convinced.

McKnight duly produced the apple. "Tell me what you see."

Canavan shook his head. "An . . . an apple."

"But as a symbol? What do you see?"

Canavan struggled. "The forbidden fruit . . ."

"A true theologian's answer." McKnight smiled. "The apple with
which the serpent tempted Eve. The symbol of all we were never meant
to have but which we grasped anyway through temerity and imperti-
nent curiosity. The icon of the unknowable, and lines which should not
be crossed." He raised the fruit and regarded it contemplatively. "But it
is also, is it not, the symbol of Isaac Newton's universal gravitation and
the immutable laws of science. Of everything we have learned and
believe we have mastered—the single most important symbol of the
Enlightenment. A truly significant irony, is it not? For though it has
taken us many eons, we can now measure with great accuracy the speed
with which an apple might have fallen from the forbidden tree in the
Garden of Eden."

He lifted the red and green orb to the space between them. He fanned out his fingers until it was held by only his thumb and forefinger, then paused and released his hold entirely.

The apple, without any visible means of support, hung in midair, completely unmoving.

Canavan stared at it in astonishment.

"I believe we have an important duty to perform," the Professor said, and the apple finally dropped.

✠

That Evelyn had so easily slipped past him was a source of great embarrassment to Pringle, but oddly Groves did not seem in the mood to chasten him. Instead, the Inspector had his eyes set and his mouth sealed, and for a while seemed absorbed in his own musings, or working his way through the aftereffects of some serious shock.

"The news arrived while you were upstairs, sir," Pringle explained hopefully as they rattled down Castle Terrace in a westbound cab. "Mr. Lindsay dispatched a messenger to the home of Hettie Lessels, summoning her to a meeting at a certain address in Atholl Crescent Lane."

"Atholl Crescent Lane . . ." Groves finally muttered, still staring ahead blankly. "The Mirror Society."

"Beg your pardon, sir?"

But Groves did not answer. "So we head there now?"

"That's right, sir. It was agreed that the widow Lessels should proceed as instructed to the meeting, secretly accompanied by her police escort. At about the same time Mr. Lindsay left his own premises. They would be there by now, I should think."

"Together again . . ." Groves said, nodding somberly.

"I'm sorry, sir?"

But Groves fell silent.

Outside, a torrential blast of rain was lashing the streets and surging in the gutters; sheets of lightning flashed around the Castle ramparts. They swung into Rutland Street with the cab wheels sluicing through gurgling streams, and swept past the square to the corner of Atholl Crescent Lane. Here they were greeted by a lantern-bearing constable in a streaming waterproof.

"They're inside, sir," the man said, leaning into the cab. "Some sort of meeting."

"How many?" Groves asked.

"Three, far as we can tell. Lessels, the one called Lindsay, and some-one else."

Groves and Pringle looked down the winding lane, where three cabs were stationed in close proximity to a house with a glowing lamp case over its door. The cabdrivers were inside their vehicles, out of the rain, clearly instructed to hug the building closely.

"Did you get a look at the third person?" Groves asked.

The constable shrugged. "Couldn't make him out too well, sir."

Groves eased himself out of the cab, straightened his back, and strolled as casually as possible down the lane, the cabmen all the time watching him suspiciously. Approaching the house with the radiant lamp, he judged himself most fortunate, for he was well acquainted with the couple that resided in the opposing residence—a clock maker and his wife who owed him favors ("The Hour of Judgment")—and would cer-tainly be admitted without hesitation. He rapped confidently on the door.

Inside he quickly explained his requirements, whereupon he was cor-dially led to an upstairs storeroom filled with dismantled timepieces and directed to a window affording a splendid vantage point. Conceal-ing himself behind the musty drapes, he first surveyed the cabs to ensure that he could not be seen, then looked into the brightly lit upper-level room across the lane, where he discerned three figures seated around a table, their features difficult to distinguish through the cascading rain.

"Who owns the place?" Groves asked the retreating clock maker.

"Henry Proudfoot, the solicitor. He rents it out."

"The upper floor?"

"The upper floor's been a club room for as long as I can remember."

"Used often?"

"Very rarely."

Groves strained his eyes but could only make out a harried-looking woman, who would have to be Hettie Lessels, and a white-haired figure that was presumably Abraham Lindsay. The third party—a larger, smartly attired man—was clearly agitated, rising and walking around the room throwing up his arms, to which Lindsay appeared to have no response.

Groves stood watching for endless minutes, his only company a black cat that curled around his legs persistently. He was convinced that he would recognize the third figure if he could steal a clear glimpse, but the rain continued pelting unabated, and he challenged himself not to lose patience. He assured himself that his strategy was sound. He was accelerating toward the triumphant moment when the whole city, the entire Lothian region, would bow before him in gratitude.

Twenty minutes elapsed and the cat finally withdrew in frustration.

Another fifteen minutes and finally it looked as though Hettie Lessels had risen and was dabbing her cheeks. The distinguished-looking man was drawing on a coat. Even Abraham Lindsay seemed to have roused himself.

Wasting no time, Groves hastened down the stairs, slipped into the lane, and watched as the first cabman guided his vehicle as close as possible to the front door. There was a flash of light from inside the house and Groves glimpsed the Lessels woman almost leaping from the hallway into the open vehicle, which bounced with the sudden application of weight. The cab took off without delay and, as though executing a military maneuver, the second one immediately drew up in its place. The front door creaked open again.

Groves stepped forward.

The rain had eased, but a steamlike mist was curling off the cobbles.

The distinguished-looking gentleman—an immense and florid figure in a spotless Chesterfield overcoat—bustled out the door and was in the process of stepping into the cab when his eyes alighted on the watching Inspector.

Groves frowned, squinted, and his lips parted in surprise.

The other man seemed momentarily seized by indecision, unable to decide if he should glare or skulk, and he froze fatally.

Suspended in this awkward moment, grasping for a reaction and wreathed in mist, the two men only belatedly became aware of an advancing cacophony of hooves, a blast of withering air, and a hiss like that of a wounded buffalo.

Their heads swung around, their eyes struggled to focus, but it was all too late.

They had a mere second to register a great demonic juggernaut bursting from the fog and hurtling down the lane toward them.

No reflex could possibly be adequate.

In one continuous and strangely balletic movement the great crimson-skinned Beast swept past Groves, drove between the cab and the door, collected the distinguished-looking man in its talons, ripped out his gullet like chicken gizzards, tossed aside the body like a little girl's doll, and careered up the dark lane before vanishing in a whorl of silk and steam.

His heart smashing in his ears, Groves watched the horses rear up and the cabs peel away to reveal the Right Honorable Henry Bolan, Lord Provost of Edinburgh, flopping around like a dying sturgeon in the garish light of a bracketed lamp sprayed red with his own blood, as outside McKnight's cottage Canavan watched the stars melt from the sky, and in her little room in Candlemaker Row Evelyn awoke screaming.

Chapter XX

DEEP IN THE GULF of Princes Street Gardens, Canavan held out his hand and felt a snowflake land and melt on his palm, the cool water draining through his fingers. He kicked at a ridge of black leaves and heard them squelch and scatter. His eyes swept from the colored lights of the street—red tobacconists' lanterns, blue pharmacy lamps, illuminated Christmas baubles—and across the deep-set gardens to the arabesque of shining windows in the Old Town skyline. He saw flitting shadows and flapping washing. He smelled the tang of reeking chimneys. He heard lusty shouts and songs. He hunted for a single false note, a simple lapse in this meticulous reconstruction. But the overlay was so immaculately rendered and aligned that it was practically undetectable.

He passed a bandstand where two vagrants huddled shivering in the cold. Were they real, or a demonic illusion? The train quitting Waverley Station and puffing eastward—made of atoms or dreams? The intonations of organ music from one of the High Street kirks—real sounds, or echoes reverberating in some vast cerebral chamber? The whole of

Edinburgh itself—a genuine city, or a projection of a young lady's unconscious?

McKnight had always been on a headlong rush to the truth, and Canavan had always said that intuitive knowledge was the path to God . . . so why did he now find the truth so hard to accept? Everything pointed to it unwaveringly. The titles in McKnight's library, the twin Bibles, their encounters with the Beast when they assumed Evelyn could not possibly be dreaming . . .

It was too painful to believe, because it robbed him of a personal destiny, the one indulgence he had sought from God. Because it meant that he had not chosen martyrdom but had it assigned to him. Moreover, if he answered not to the Lord but to a tormented young woman, then what did it mean to feel pity for her? To love her? To sacrifice his life for her? What did it mean to have no identity?

He watched his misted breath rise like chimney smoke into the darkness. He felt a cruel gust of wind sting at his cheeks. He could even taste mustard lingering from McKnight's generous dinner. Never at any stage had he felt more alive. And yet he had never at any stage existed.

"This whole library," McKnight had said, gesturing around him, "the shelves and everything on them . . . all of this is simply a projection, a metaphor for her mind, her memory. This entire cottage is just a fantasy. The streets we walk in are immaculate re-creations of real streets. The air we breathe is the abstraction of dreams." He was looking at Canavan directly, and, sensing the potential impact of the revelation, he put out a hand both to steady his companion and to draw him closer to the truth. "And you and I," he whispered, "the two of us . . . I fear that we, too, are just figments of a truly extraordinary imagination."

At some indeterminate point, he said, in the darkness of concealed memories, Evelyn's mind had been so violently assaulted, so deprived of natural outlets, that it had swollen internally, feasting on reason, knowledge, and all the senses of recognition, and assembled entire refracted cities and populations of archetypes more nuanced than living creatures. It had objectified its own aspects and assigned voices and faces to them, and harbored and nurtured them, and furnished them with lives, memories, and characteristics . . . and all this in the shadow world of the imagination, cut off from temporality, in a separate consciousness as vast as Edinburgh and as deep as hell.

"The Beast himself comes from the underworld, from some subterranean realm we have only glimpsed, but at least he has the supernatural power to burst into reality, to scratch messages on walls, tear pages from Bibles, and strike men down in the street. We, I regret to say, have no such power. But then we were never conceived for such a purpose. . . ."

He himself was a composite figure, he claimed, a mixture of living lecturers and dead philosophers. Physically, who was to say? A miasma of appealing elements glued together by an extraordinarily disciplined memory. His history? A fabrication that even all her energy could not prevent from fading behind him. His wife? A mirage. His students? Mirror images of real young men. His purpose? *Well . . .*

"I am the archetype of logic," he announced, "and the frontal lobes are my home. I am the personification of intelligence in the same way the devil is the face of evil. You, on the other hand, I gather, come from an even more tender organ. . . ."

And Canavan, his own heart pounding sickeningly—he could actually hear it (surely it could not be a dream?)—heard himself say, as though from a great distance, "And who am I?"

To which McKnight, with a familiar look of mock admonishment, slapped him on the arm and said affectionately, "My boy, I fear you would think me blasphemous to say it."

Intuition leads us to God. And not wanting to accept that which he had always suspected, Canavan had fled the cottage to find the skies yawning in revelation.

For it was a responsibility too great to contemplate and a loss too overpowering to bear. The communion he had felt with Evelyn had been more deeply felt than anything he had ever experienced, and it had the potential to become more than that: a material union. But the consummation could never be, because there was only one spirit, one God, and he was already part of Her.

"All deities reside in the human breast," McKnight had reminded him later in front of the hearth.

His face in his hands, Canavan had spared the time to nod in recognition. "William Blake . . ." he said hoarsely.

But McKnight only grunted. "Is that where she found it?" he asked, genuinely disappointed. "Pity. I thought it was one of my own."

Snowflakes now swirled around Canavan like a blizzard of frag-
mented Eucharists. *Ecce Agnus Dei, ecce qui tollit peccata mundi.* As much
as he had always known that he was not destined to live on earth for
eternity, he now balked at the idea of separation from the world he so
dearly loved. This when McKnight, at the other extreme, seemed quite
happy to have all his questions answered, his doubts leveled, and all his
debts reduced to illusions. Canavan was the one who was supposed to be
more disposed to martyrdom, and yet it was he who now, with a great
sense of shame, wondered if the chalice could possibly be passed from
him.

Bent over on a park bench with the snow gathering on the nape of his
neck, he tried to imagine the magnitude of what was to come. It was the
Professor's belief that Evelyn had constructed a genuine hellish underworld that they would need to breach through the agency of hypnotism.
Here they would work to exhume her deeply buried past, present it to
her, and in so doing allow her to hurdle and vanquish it. But what if even
that did not work? What then?

"What would be required in that instance, I fear," McKnight said
solemnly, "is almost too grand to contemplate."

"And if we *do* succeed? Will we dissolve even in her imagination?"

"Our world will only collapse if we do *not* save her."

"But there's no *world* to collapse," Canavan pointed out. "It has no substance greater than dreams."

"And who is to say that any world is made of more?" McKnight said,
and chortled. "Be grateful, lad, that we are at least constructs of a truly
superior imagination—one with a continuity that is beyond practical
measure—and that we have been able to experience an existence as rich
as any living being. Be happy that we are not true creatures of fiction,
leading cramped and cluttered lives and perishing with the last page of
a disposable book. She has given us independent thoughts, this God of
ours, and hopes, and aspirations, and we have acted of our own accord,
and we have been permitted to stumble, to make mistakes, to question
Her in person, and now even to offer our own lives to Her. *And all of our
own volition.*"

The Professor was exhilarated: he had become the subject of one of his
own lectures. What did it mean to exist in the imagination? Was it any
inferior to reality, simply because the imagination inevitably has to sur-

render to reality? Does reality in turn not have to surrender to the imagination? And which truly has sovereignty? The questions were generating whole networks of further questions right before his eyes, but rather than feeling lost in some futile maze, McKnight found philosophy the key to existence—his own existence—and as tangible and relevant as any experiment in the Faculty of Medicine.

Canavan now raised his head and watched a squirrel scamper across the powdered grass. He felt the windows of the city stare down on him. He felt the oppressive weight of destiny. He looked at the Castle, glowing with light on its implacable rock, and sensed the city's atmosphere of burgeoning tension, the expanding ripples of tightly woven whispers: *Did you hear . . . ? The Lord Provost . . . Torn apart in the street . . . No one knows . . . No one understands . . . The devil walks among us . . .*

Then, lowering his gaze with a sigh, he saw a familiar figure wrapped in coat and gloves negotiating the park's winding paths, looking one way and the other, and, spotting him, pause for verification before coming briskly forward.

"I suspected I might find you here," McKnight said, drawing up at his side. "Are you ready?"

"I'm not sure my presence is necessary."

"On the contrary, your presence is essential. Without you beside me she will never be accessible. She will see me as pitiless logic, working not entirely in her own interests, and the barriers will be insurmountable. With you offering support, however . . ."

Canavan shook his head. "This is . . . *absurd.*"

"This is our duty."

"I've never avoided a duty."

"Then why do you question it now?"

Canavan struggled. "Because I need a say in the matter . . . I need to feel that I have exerted . . . *free will.*"

"And this free will . . . this would give you the feeling that you truly existed?"

"It is the very basis of existence."

McKnight sighed. "Then perhaps," he said, with an aspect of dismay, "it is best that you do not come after all."

And then Canavan experienced it: an overpowering sense of shame and thwarted responsibility. And he understood that he had always had free will. He had as much as any man. The forces that directed his actions had simply been filtered through another mind, but they burned on him with the heat of a concentrated sunbeam.

"*No*," he said, and exhaled fatalistically. "No . . ."

McKnight waited patiently, with a creeping smile, and eventually he put out his hand to assist his friend to his feet.

Canavan accepted the offer, and the two men were finally as one.

It was midnight when they headed for Candlemaker Row, the time when the lamplighters normally began their second nightly circuit, selectively snuffing out those lamps considered not integral to public safety. But in a hasty muster the Town Council had relieved the leeries of this duty until further notice, because the city's mounting fear had now been consummated with historic audacity—the murder of the Lord Provost—and the darkness had become more palpable and threatening, even, than the specter of increased expenditure.

✠

Clutching a chipped cup of coffee, which he had accepted absently, the liquid long since tepid and untouched by his lips, Groves stood at the window of Hettie Lessels's Marchmont villa, staring over the railed fence that she claimed the Beast had rattled and into the street where a lamp blazed boldly beyond the midnight curfew. The window was frosted with condensation, there was a rim of dust on the sill, and the sash was cracked from overuse. It was odd that a man could notice such insignificant details—become fixated on them—when by rights he should have been in a state of insensibility.

He heard the door of the adjoining room creak open and turned to see the Sheriff—a dour man called Fleming—emerge with the Sheriff-clerk. They had come to Lessels's home to conduct a precognition, not under oath, wasting no time after the murder of the city's most eminent citizen. But to their frustration they had found the woman virtually impossible to take seriously. It was not that her sentences lacked meaning. They just seemed demented.

"Preposterous," Fleming now sniffed. He went to the kitchen sink and washed his hands like a surgeon performing postoperative ablutions.

"Do you want me to have her taken away, sir?" asked the clerk.

"Not yet." Fleming sighed. "We're not leaving until we get some sense out of her."

"More coffee, then, sir?"

"Aye. We could do with some of that." Fleming dried his hands and looked across the room at Groves. "Has she said anything to you? Anything that made the slightest bit of sense?"

And now Groves, questioned directly, was forced to find refuge, like so many others before him, in the security of ambiguity. "It has been a case," he said carefully, "of little sense from the start."

It was a case, he wrote later, *that the Sheriff himself could scarce credit, and though there was no message left at the scene of Bolan's murder, as there had been in the past, what I had seen with my own two eyes was message enough, and now I was ready for anything.* For all the new developments, indeed, Groves felt remarkably serene. No one had said anything directly, but the death of the Lord Provost would lead inevitably to that which he had always feared: the Procurator Fiscal assuming complete command of the case and, ultimately, the forced reappointment of the Wax Man. The Prime Minister would write letters; perhaps the Queen herself would register interest. The pressure applied to Central Office through the frigid Yuletide season would heat the rooms more efficiently than any furnace.

All of which might have been cause for concern, except that Groves had moved to an elevated plane. Having been with the investigation from the start, he was confident he was still the one who knew it most intimately, whatever intrigue might have been conducted beyond his knowledge and influence. Further, while Pringle and a couple of constables had glimpsed an indistinguishable shape bolting down Atholl Crescent Lane, he was the only one who had seen the Beast's face directly, and from a distance that left little doubt as to its identity. So he had been accorded a special status far beyond anything he would dare explain, and Fleming's manifest incredulity only made that clearer. It was his fate to be there at the end, he was suddenly and irrationally convinced of it, and the machinations whirling around him seemed as insignificant as the buzzing of jungle insects.

"Have you met this Todd lass she speaks of?" Fleming asked.

"I have."

"And what was your impression?"

"A troubled woman," Groves admitted.

"But diabolical?"

Groves smiled enigmatically.

Fleming looked at the stove, where the coffeepot was beginning to bubble, and sighed heartily. "It will need to be a powerful brew," he said to the Sheriff-clerk. "This could well take all night."

✠

The lamps fluttered, the whispers spun, and in her little room on Candlemaker Row, Evelyn unfastened the muslin sealing her window and, craning her head, looked down into the starkly lit street, where at least two sentinels were visible, staring up at her tenement.

She withdrew, feeling a wave of revulsion on top of the nausea she already experienced since the Lord Provost's murder in the nightmare she knew was real. Since the departure of Inspector Groves and the unpleasant gleam she had discerned in his eyes.

She had not slept. She doubted she would ever sleep again. She knew they would be coming after her now. They had been planted outside for days, occasionally even knocking on her door to verify her presence. Soon they would find no option but to come and claim her. They would not know what they were doing, but they would need to do something. She was resigned to it. She *wanted* it. There was an enormous congestion in her heart, and a great turmoil in her head.

She heard the rat resuming its busy scratching in the roof and she rose stiffly, filling a glass with buttermilk and setting it on her tiny table. She lit a candle and fixed it in the middle of a saucer, then returned to her little bed and sat primly on its edge, staring into the candle flame until the brightness filled every corner of her vision. It was something she did occasionally, when she needed to block out all distractions, but she did it now with a particular urgency, drawn to the process by a need beyond her conscious understanding. Was she escaping? Or driving herself deep into danger? She knew only that the answer lay in the brightness of revelation.

She stared at the mesmerizing flame.

Her head was radiant with light and she felt herself plunging when, as on previous evenings when she had attempted the procedure, she heard a pounding on the door.

The brightness faded rudely.

Another knock, and she heard a voice. "Evelyn . . ."

She swallowed her despair.

"Evelyn . . . will you open the door?"

It was too late.

"Evelyn . . ."

She pushed herself from the bed and paused, her hand on the latch.

"Evelyn . . . I believe you have been expecting us."

She frowned, puzzled by the familiarity of the voice, and opened the door, not sure why she was surprised.

Professor McKnight smiled at her from the hall, his hat in his hands, and behind him Canavan looked at her with his customary warmth. "May we come in, Evelyn?" the latter asked, in little more than a whisper, and of course she could not refuse.

Chapter XXI

THEY ARE HALFWAY to Kumasi when they stop to rest on a fallen cottonwood trunk amid trees the size of Big Ben. They are gasping from heat and exertion: the humidity is unforgiving, and the path has become progressively more entangled with cordlike creepers and shrouds of leathery leaves. Corporal Ainslie is the fittest of the three—always alert, always scheming; never pays to turn your back on Ainslie—and it is now the canny Scotsman who recovers first, after a ration of water and biscuit, and as though personally challenged by the environment to announce his origins or to herald his conquering of it, he lodges his Highland pipes against his shoulder, applies the blowpipe to his freshly moistened lips, and begins sounding off some experimental bass drones before launching into a spirited strathspey.

It is a music unlike anything the jungle has previously heard. It hums through the ribbed trunks, unsettles columns of industrious ants, and vibrates through the rigginglike mass of corkscrew creepers to the vast canopies of leaves. Here sparrow-size parrots pause in their chattering to listen to the wheezing of this unfamiliar beast, and, cocking their heads, they eye with some trepidation a white stalker-man, far below, being assailed by some monstrous arachnid, while his two companions look on with no visible concern. The parrots, too, eventually determine no reason for alarm, and return with renewed vigor to their discordant song, raising the pitch to account for the pervasive new intonations.

But when Ainslie stops, a good five minutes later, it is most abruptly, as though he has been struck by a spear. The parrots tilt their heads. The pipes whine to silence. Ainslie's companions turn to look at him in surprise and follow his gaze to the far end of the fallen tree, where a native boy is staring at them.

There is no sound at all but for the drip of sweating leaves, the gurgle of rising sap, and the disquiet of the birds shifting in the branches.

The boy is perched on his haunches and is completely naked. As young as he is, he seems as old as eternity. He smiles at Ainslie with glimmering black eyes.

"Pray continue," he says.

✠

"From the start, madam," Fleming said impatiently. Lessels was anchored in an oxhide armchair in a room that stank of starch and vinegar. She was forever declaring her innocence and bursting into tears.

"I was only there to assist, I tell ye."

"You've said as much, madam. Now——"

"I attended to the lass, and that was all."

"Aye, you have said that a dozen times. Now please take us to the beginning. How did you first meet the Lord Provost?"

Lessels shook her head. "He was no Lord Provost back then. It were twenty years ago or more."

Groves, having been invited to take part in an unofficial capacity, now interrupted. "At that stage," he suggested, "Henry Bolan would have been only a medical doctor."

"Aye," Lessels agreed, "a doctor. But to me, he was just another face in the Mirror Society."

"The what?" Fleming asked.

"The Mirror Society," Groves answered, as though in a dream. "The official name of the club that convened tonight in Atholl Crescent Lane. The previous victims were all members, and as of tonight there are only two remaining."

He was focused on Lessels, who refused to look up at him as he spoke.

"Munnoch and Smeaton were part of it. A society dedicated to rigid principles and the suppression of dangerous ideas . . ."

"The Mirror Society," Fleming said dubiously.

"But that," Groves said to Lessels, "is not really where the story begins, is it? There was another point, wasn't there?"

Her face seemed to tense.

"Involving some devilish scheme . . ."

In the subsequent silence Lessels at last seemed to gulp the first morsel of responsibility. She glanced up at Groves with a guilty expression.

"Aye," she agreed at last. "I suppose that is true."

"Go on, madam," Fleming ordered as the Sheriff-clerk prepared his pen.

"I suppose it begins with Ainslie . . ."

✠

"Your unconscious is a delicate device," McKnight said, "and you can be assured that we will treat it respectfully. We will gingerly remove it, Evelyn, with your full cooperation, and we will blow away its dust, scrape out its rust and algae, and return it to its case as a polished and newly oiled mechanism. It is what I believe you have called us to do."

He was holding a burning candle fifteen inches from her face and repeatedly drawing his thumb and forefinger from the bridge of her nose to the flame.

"You will remain masterful," he said, "and clear-minded and cognizant. You will surrender because it is your own command, and with the absolute certainty that it is only temporary, and you are in any case surrendering only to yourself. We are bound by your instruction to do you no harm."

Canavan was half sitting on the corner table, having fully accepted his purpose by now: a presence, a foil, the personification of reassurance.

He watched in fascination as Evelyn began to respond to the Professor's mesmeric passes. Her limbs by degrees seemed to lighten, her right arm in particular rising as though by some independent impulse. Her eyelids fluttered a moment and were still.

"You are beginning to see dark spots at the periphery of your vision," McKnight told her. "A warmth invades and floods through you. All your sinews are loose, your muscles are pliant. You glory in your security and contentment. You have never been more relaxed, and yet you are entirely in control. This universe is completely your own."

It was imperative to overcome Evelyn's barricades, and to do so her defenses had to be breached from within. That McKnight had reached this point, especially after the inflammatory tone of his previous questions, might have been deemed a significant achievement. Except that it was a path down which Evelyn had always been guiding them.

After nearly twenty minutes of flourishes and deeply intoned words she was frozen, her senses subjugated but alert, and still awaiting a question. The Professor now handed to Canavan the candle, much of which had dissolved into a puddle of wax, and instructed him to hold it steadily as a continuing focus for Evelyn's eyes. He stretched, worked the blood back into his limbs, and refreshed himself with a few sips of buttermilk.

"Tastes sour," Evelyn said dreamily from the chair, and McKnight glanced at Canavan with a smile of satisfaction.

✠

Lieutenant Colonel Hammersmith of the 4th West Indian Regiment has been hallucinating, stricken by a most implacable species of fever. None of the usual remedies has proved in the least bit effective. He has been moved from the stockade near Kotoko to the cruising HMS *Cobra* at Accra, where it is hoped the sea air might restore him. But after two weeks he is deemed close to death, and in desperation one sergeant, one bluejacket, and Corporal Ainslie of the Royal Rifle Corps have been dispatched through fifty miles of hostile jungle to Kumasi. Here, in the Ashanti capital, King Kwaku Dua I is rumored to employ powerful native restoratives stewed from acanthema petals and the wings of monarch butterflies. It is said that no Ashanti has died from fever in living memory.

But when the three Britons fall into Kumasi after days of sapping heat and relentless downpours, they are barely alive. The King receives them in a Moorish palace decorated with skulls and clots of flesh. From his golden stool he booms with laughter when he is informed of Hammersmith's plight and offers a gourd filled with a stinking paste that might, in fact, be a miraculous remedy but looks like something less. He sends them back through the jungle to the pounding of the death drum.

Two days later only Ainslie is alive. The Ashanti gourd is completely empty, the supposedly magical restorative consumed in vain by his two companions. Resting half-delirious amid candlestick trees not far from where he first played the pipes, the Scotsman is approached by two saintly natives in saffron robes. He assumes they are tribesmen of the Fanti, who inhabit the surrounding rain forest and have fought alongside the British in numerous engagements.

They offer him sweet water, which almost instantly clears his head, and escort him to a platform high in the ribbing of a vast, umbrellalike tree— a magical haven festooned with flaglike cloth and populated by chattering monkeys. A fetish priest with ornate scalp tattoos and ageless eyes, chewing continuously on amber leaves, welcomes him and communicates to him with hand signals, the native Twi, and fractured English.

That thing, you make music with it?

"If you mean the pipes, I am the one," Ainslie agrees, ill at ease in the lofty cabin.

My master, he like to hear this music again.

"Again?" Ainslie asks, confused. "Your master has heard me before?"

Some days ago my master, he met you.

"At Kumasi?"

In the jungle he met you, at that place you have come from.

Ainslie blinks, thinking about it. "The boy? The boy is this master of yours?"

The priest agrees, and Ainslie feels strangely chilled. "I will gladly play for your master," he manages, "but I have little time to spare."

Play now, and my master, he will hear the music echo.

Ainslie is further puzzled by this, and asks the fetish priest to repeat himself several times to make sure he has understood.

"Where . . . where is this master of yours?" he asks, frowning.

My master, you can see him here, the fetish priest replies, and gestures to his eyes.

✠

"Your days at the orphanage, Evelyn . . . what do you see?"

"A parcel . . . tightly bound."

"But I seek to invoke specific memories, Evelyn."

Nothing.

"Do you recall the Incident of the Chalk?"

Nothing.

"Do you remember anything at all to do with chalk?"

Evelyn's face was completely unmoving, as though she had not even heard the question.

McKnight breathed out. "It is important that you transport yourself back to those days, Evelyn. There must be atmospheres, episodes, incidents, and emotions that we can attempt to unlock."

No response.

"Do you not remember enthralling the other girls with your fantasies? Do you not remember those bitterly cold nights when the only warmth was generated through the power of your imagination?"

Total blankness.

"This is disappointing, Evelyn. I believe you agreed to this process with the understanding that you would hold nothing back. That there would be no barriers. I will not insist, nor will I drag anything from you forcibly, but I remind you that we cannot succeed without your full cooperation. If you understand me now, I'd like you to respond with a single nod."

There was a long pause, but at last she did so.

McKnight cleared his throat. "Do you remember the chalk?" he asked again.

Nothing.

"Do you remember the girls there?"

Nothing.

"Your friends? The governor? The ones who came to claim you?"

No answer.

McKnight sighed. "This is most disheartening, Evelyn."

✠

"I never met him directly," Hettie Lessels insisted. She had a moistened rag she was using as a handkerchief and she was unfurling and twisting it incessantly. "He did all his dealings with Lindsay and Smeaton, not me. He did not want to be known, and he was a cagey one, that much was plain. He did his business and then he was gone."

"And what business was this?" Fleming asked.

"They . . . they would not tell the likes of me."

"They must have told you something."

"Nothing."

"Come now, madam."

Groves, feeling uniquely authoritative, interjected again. "No one is holding you accountable," he said. "And Mr. Ainslie is already dead. So please, you may proceed, and hold nothing back. It will all come out eventually."

She looked up at him with an air of struggling remorse. And in truth she wanted so desperately to purge herself, to lay herself bare, whatever the consequences.

"What did they tell you about Ainslie?" Groves went on. "It is clear that you know more than you have said."

Lessels hesitated, overcoming a final surge of resistance. "Only that . . ."

"Aye?"

She squeezed her rag. "Only that he came back from Africa with . . ."

"With what?"

"With a way of snaring the de'il himself," Lessels said, and quivered at the memory.

✠

The Reverend Smeaton and Colonel Munnoch, sitting in the parlor of the latter's Moray Place abode, observe the visitor with disapproval: a cock-sure type, irreverent, insubordinate—his military discharge has been noted—and done up in a burgundy frock coat like a brothel proprietor, he represents in many ways everything they most despise. But he may nevertheless serve a purpose.

"Lieutenant Colonel Hammersmith made a complete recovery," Ainslie says. In his hand he has a glass of fine scotch that he is swilling appreciatively, having always had a fondness for whisky. "I made it back to the coast and fed him a mixture of grass and berries in the guise of an Ashanti restorative, the one we had been sent to find, but it was only a pretense. In point of fact, his health was restored by a far greater power, as a form of payment—a pact, if you will—for my performance with the pipes."

"And what sort of payment was this," Colonel Munnoch observes, stroking his mustache, "when you were out on your heels not one year later?"

"It drew me certain privileges, for a time. But very soon the army had nothing to offer me. I had developed more ambitious plans, you see, of a more personal nature."

"You headed back into the jungle?"

"And I played the pipes some more."

"For the fetish priest you speak of?"

"For the lodger in his mind. The one who walks in his dreams."

"The wee fellow—the naked imp you saw on the tree trunk?"

Ainslie raises his glass and takes a sip, as though to fortify himself. "That was one of his incarnations, aye."

Smeaton sniffs, vaguely unsettled. "And how, sir, are we to accept that you would even recognize the one you indicate? Are you a churchgoer, by any chance?"

"A man does not need a bank account to recognize a financial institution."

Colonel Munnoch grunts at the man's impertinence. "So he appeared to you in person, you claim, when this fetish priest dreamed?"

"Several times."

"And what . . . what was he like?"

Ainslie stares into the whisky. "A rather agreeable fellow, I would have to say. A weary old soul, worn out by past revelries. In other circumstances I believe we might have got along famously."

Smeaton and Munnoch glance at each other, unhappy with this sympathetic assessment. "And what did the Lord of Lies say to you?" the Colonel inquires pointedly.

Ainslie smirks and stares at the two men steadily. "He said that he was tired of residing in the old man's imagination. And that he was hunting for a room with a more interesting view."

✠

Canavan cleared his throat. "Try the third person."

McKnight glanced at him at first doubtfully, but then remembered her habit of objectifying herself in her dreams, and looking back at Evelyn, he decided that it could do no harm.

He stared again into her eyes. "There is a little girl, much like you, Evelyn," he said. "She is in the orphanage. Do you recognize her?"

Blankness.

"I believe she is holding something. A piece of chalk. Do you see it?"

Evelyn's eyes narrowed almost imperceptibly.

"You see the girl, Evelyn? The girl? Do you see her?"

Nothing.

"I know you see her, Evelyn. What is she doing?"

Evelyn trembled.

"Does she cry? Does she sing? Does she remember anything?"

Evelyn gulped and her pupils contracted as though at a burst of light.

"She remembers something?" McKnight said hopefully. "What is it, Evelyn? What does she remember?"

"She remembers Leerie," Evelyn said.

✠

"Think of it, gentlemen," Ainslie says, enjoying the righteous gleam on their faces and rueing the time he has wasted in not returning to Scotland earlier. "The devil. Lured into an empty vessel. Trapped inside and completely at your mercy. I leave it to your own imaginations as to what you might do with him."

✠

"I never liked him."

"You have said that, madam," Fleming said impatiently.

"He was a swindler, he saw only ways of making gain. And if that meant practicing his craft on the very de'il, then so be it, he could not be stopped."

"Aye . . ."

"There was a lass, she played his wife. A comely type, a lady friend from the theater. The type a man might grieve over and do everything to save. They painted her up to look ill."

"To look ill? Why?"

"As part of the pact."

"With the devil?"

"Aye—with the de'il. The de'il was supposed to cure her, but did not know he was being duped."

"Because she was not in fact ill?"

"Ye do not have to believe me."

Groves interjected. "I believe you."

But Fleming had a more cutting tone. "And what was this mysterious woman's name, madam?"

"I canna remember her name."

Fleming nodded skeptically. "Aye."

"I never met her at all."

"Aye."

"She stayed at the lodge for a time, and when she played her part she was gone."

"What lodge was this?" Groves asked, fascinated.

"A hunting lodge of Colonel Munnoch's. It had not been used for many a year. On the Old Dalkeith Road, next to Drumgate Cemetery . . ."

✠

When it becomes clear that the deal will be settled and that he will be receiving a substantial fee, Ainslie produces a formidable cigar and strikes a match on the fireplace: an ostentatious gesture that sets Smeaton's teeth on edge.

"We'll need a house," Ainslie says, issuing smoke. "A fair house, not bare of furnishings."

"It can be arranged," Munnoch assures him.

"I'll need to return to the Gold Coast to fetch the priest. The man trusts me, and he must never be allowed to suspect anything. I cannot make this warning more emphatically."

"We appreciate the gravity of the situation."

"I will escort him to the house, which I will introduce as my ancestral home, and allow him to memorize the rooms in necessary detail."

"That can be arranged," Munnoch says, but his stomach clenches at the prospect of such a man setting foot on his estate. "How long will all this take?"

"I believe it will take some days for the house to appear in his dreams, and even longer before his lodger walks in its halls. To facilitate this, the priest will need to be offered some safe and peaceful accommodation . . . some place conducive to rest and dreams."

Munnoch's throat tightens. "That, too, can be arranged."

"The lodger may appear at any time. In order to make the transition as smooth as possible, he will tailor a form specifically to appeal to his new host. I don't believe that we personally will be in any danger, but I think we should do our best to avoid laying eyes on him."

The two men nod uneasily.

"When the . . . transaction is complete," Ainslie says, smiling ambiguously, "I will require the second half of my payment promptly, in pounds sterling. I will never speak of this matter again, and I expect you never to tip your hat to me if you cross me in the street."

"That can most assuredly be arranged," Munnoch says.

Ainslie smirks. "And we'll need a host, of course. A young and healthy specimen is in order—a child, perhaps, who I can pass off as my own. It is expected to be an indefinite lodging."

Munnoch now looks at Smeaton, who thinks at once of his friend Abraham Lindsay.

"That also can be arranged," Smeaton adds quietly.

✠

"She is in a carriage . . . she is traveling somewhere . . . and she is *exhilarated*."

"Where is she going, Evelyn? Can you see?"

Evelyn shook her head.

"And there are no distinguishing signs at all? Buildings? Hills?"

"Her eyes are covered."

"But where is she taken, Evelyn? Can you tell us that?"

"A large house. She has never seen such comfort."

"And is she treated well there, this little girl? She has done nothing wrong, after all."

Evelyn looked upset. *"No,"* she spat. "She is . . . *imprisoned*."

McKnight nodded sympathetically. "As she was at the orphanage? A parcel, tightly bound?"

"No . . ."

"She is not, Evelyn?"

"The bed is most comfortable and she is fed well."

"Aye? Then how is she imprisoned, Evelyn?"

"She is restricted."

"Restricted, Evelyn? By whom?"

"The Great Deceiver."

"Mr. Ainslie? But why does he restrict her, Evelyn? Is it punishment?"

"He does not want her to see things."

"He does not want her imagination to take flight, is that it?"

"No," Evelyn answered firmly. "He does not want her to see beyond the limits of the house."

"Why is this, Evelyn?"

She struggled but could not answer.

"Does he not want her to know where she is?"

"Not her . . ." she answered hoarsely.

"Excuse me, Evelyn?"

"Not her," she repeated, slightly louder.

"Then from whom is he withholding the location of the house?"

"From Leerie," she replied.

✠

Fleming regarded Hettie Lessels with disbelief. "Let me see if I understand you," he said. "You say that this African fellow, this witch doctor . . . he had the devil himself living in his mind."

"Aye," said the widow.

"Hibernating there, safe and sound."

"Aye."

"That this is the way the devil has always lived, hidden in the mind of some chosen host. Somebody with a brilliantly developed imagination. An artist, a writer . . ."

"Aye . . . it was what the others believed."

"And he can walk the earth, the devil, but only while his host is asleep."

"His greatest power, they said. To cast a shadow from the world of dreams."

"So if this witch doctor dreamed of the jungle, then the devil walked through that jungle, in whatever shape he desired. And if the witch doctor dreamed of some far-distant city, then the devil walked in that city."

"And if it was a real city, and pictured well enough from memory," Lessels said, "then he could not only walk its streets but speak to its people, and do exactly as he liked."

Fleming nodded in mock understanding. "Only he had become weary of this witch doctor's imagination."

"Aye."

"It wasn't spacious or fresh enough for him."

"Aye."

"He was hunting for fresh lodgings."

"Aye."

"And so a little girl was selected for him."

"Aye," Lessels said. "The wean."

Fleming looked at her for a moment, as though waiting for her to admit it was all a jest. But she did no such thing, and so he threw up his hands in disdain. "Preposterous," he said, turning away.

"Go on . . ." breathed Inspector Groves.

✠

For Abraham Lindsay there is never any question as to the selection. The little one so fanciful and disobedient, so fetching in her way, and so much like his departed wife.

In the role of her lost father Ainslie removes her from the orphanage to Colonel Munnoch's hastily refitted hunting lodge, mindful that she record in her mind no room or landscape that might later form the geography of her dreams. He introduces her first to the actress playing his sickly wife and then to the African fetish priest. The regal black man, so long the devil's landlord—and as such the beneficiary of untold pleasures and gratuities—is nearing the end of a prolonged and gifted life, and quite happy to have his apartment vacated. He wanders around the hunting lodge, absorbing its every chamber into his memory. He is introduced to the young girl, whom he knows only as the daughter, the one whose mind has been offered in payment for the wife's cure.

He delights in contemplating the infinite pleasures that await her and the adventures that in turn will occupy her tenant.

He is presented with a sheaf of her drawings in which an avuncular lamplighter appears repeatedly. It is immediately apparent what shape his lodger will assume when he appears to the girl. And when he meets Ainslie's seriously ill wife, he strokes her hair warmly and assures her in his broken words that her complete recovery is imminent. His lodger, he says, has never been late with a payment.

After his departure it takes several days for the hunting lodge to appear in his dreams, but when it does his tenant is packed and ready to move.

"It's me, Eve," he says affectionately. "It's Leerie . . ."

In the sepulchral bedroom he speaks to the girl for close to an hour, relishing her company, charming her with his wit, indulging her with sweet words, and by the time he departs he is deeply and irreversibly printed on her memory and imagination.

In the ensuing days Ainslie repeatedly asks Evelyn if she has dreamed of the lamplighter. When she admits, almost inadvertently, that she has, they know the transaction is complete, the bait taken, and Ainslie discreetly withdraws as the Mirror Society springs into righteous action.

✠

Evelyn had been proceeding well to this point, but now she froze, staring fixedly at the candle flame, which in response seemed to flare and flutter under the intensity of her gaze.

"What is it, Evelyn?" McKnight asked, bending forward. "What do you see?"

Her eyes widened.

"Where have they taken her?"

Nothing.

"What are they doing to her?"

Her lips buckled. "I see the little girl . . ."

"Aye?"

"I see her in a closed room . . ."

"In the house? The big house that you mentioned?"

"In the cellar . . ."

"They have locked the little girl in the cellar?"

Evelyn swallowed.

"Are they starving her, Evelyn?"

"There is . . . much food."

"Are they beating her?"

"No . . ." Evelyn shook her head, as though considering the reality to be much worse.

"What are they doing to her, then?"

No answer.

"You must tell us, Evelyn. We still might be able to save her. What are they doing to her?"

Evelyn looked as though she could not believe it. "They are . . ."

"Aye?"

"They are *indoctrinating* her."

✠

"I attended to all her needs," Lessels said, twisting the rag on her knee, "and I saw that she was never without. Dr. Bolan examined her nearly every day. I never hated her. None of us hated her. But she was so hard to control. . . ."

Groves nodded in personal understanding. "She snarled at you?"

"She spat and she kicked, and would not obey."

"And how did you reprimand her?"

"I was not there to reprimand her."

"Then what were you doing to her all this time?"

"It was not me, I tell ye. I was doing nothing to her. I was only—"

"Yes, yes," Fleming interjected, exasperated. "You've made that plain, madam. But what of the others? What do you claim they were doing to her?"

"They were . . . reading things to her. To him. The one in her mind."

"What things?"

"The Bible . . . catechism . . . it never stopped."

"They were reading Scripture to her, is that it?"

"Scripture, and other things."

Fleming shook his head. "Why, by God?"

"They were trying to tame him. Convert him. But he could not be converted."

"The devil could not be converted?"

"Aye, the de'il."

Fleming sighed incredulously.

"We never touched her," Lessels insisted. "Not to begin with."

"To begin with?" Groves queried, but the woman lowered her gaze.

✠

It is an onslaught: psalms, prayers, missives, adjuration. It is a military engagement conducted on the battlefield of a little girl's mind. And in truth, though they have begun with the ambitious intention of returning Lucifer, as a shining seraph, to God's court, they quickly have no aim but to kill him.

Leerie himself is furious at the apostasy and buries himself deeply in Evelyn's imagination, into the depths of a rapidly expanding and meticulously constructed hell. He throws out hooks and barbs, constructs a stockade, then a fortress, and readies himself for Armageddon. To have been lured into such a trap only proves that he has become too complacent. But now alert to their game, he will not be evicted, and he will never be killed.

His assailants are astounded by his resilience. They paint Evelyn's consciousness—her very soul—with Scripture, and still the lodger will not wilt. They bombard him with fire and brimstone and he will not budge. They judge him and call him to account for his crimes, but he accepts no verdict. The invective inevitably turns on Evelyn herself.

"Do ye protect him, child?" Smeaton screams, his lips white with froth. "Are ye in collusion with him?"

They are careful never to be in the room when the girl is asleep. For when she dreams Leerie sometimes is released into the cellar, shrieking his displeasure and hammering on the walls with the intensity of regimental drums. Sometimes he materializes in Evelyn's former bedroom. On the staircase. In Drumgate Cemetery, which she has glimpsed though the broken shutter. And once even in the dormitory of the Fountainbridge Institute for Destitute Girls.

He is no longer the Bearer of Light, however, for the onslaught is beginning to transform him. And since the hunting lodge is no longer adequate as a holding place, a new prison must be found.

✠

"She was a cunning one," Lessels observed. "It was hard not to think she was in league with him."

"With the devil?"

"She would pretend to be awake—her eyes would be open—and then in a snap she would fall down and start dreaming, and he would appear. It was lucky we escaped sometimes. Lucky we got out of the room."

"Did you see him yourself?" Groves asked curiously, still with the afterimage of his own encounter fresh in his eyes.

"Aye." But she could barely tolerate the memory.

"And it was the same beast that chased you home last night?"

"Oh, no . . ." She looked up, pale. "'Tis much worse now."

"But still nothing human?"

"A man . . . a bat, with wolf teeth . . . he began that way, and got worse."

"Then how did you contain him?"

"It was no longer safe at the lodge. But Colonel Munnoch, he had a small island north of the firth, and on the island was a lighthouse."

✠

They strip the hunting lodge, lay upturned nails and broken glass on the cellar floor, and ultimately incinerate the place, along with the Fountainbridge Institute for Destitute Girls. They secrete Evelyn in a sloop, secure a black felt bag over her head, and transfer her by night to the isle of Inchcaid. When she protests, she is thrashed. When she squirms and screams, Dr. Bolan administers chloroform.

They come upon the lighthouse at dawn, a pillar of olive sandstone rising out of the fog. They lock Evelyn in the windowless provision room with surplus supplies of cotton wick, coal, castor oil, and oatmeal. She has no sense of the outside world but for the thunder of the waves and the massed shrieks of kittiwakes and gannets. The Mirror Society visits regularly to continue the onslaught, but what has been envisaged as a brief skirmish, and a rapid suppression of the Adversary, has developed into a full-scale war.

There are two permanent lighthouse keepers, whose families live in Arbroath with vegetable gardens and poultry. One, Colin Shanks, is a heartless brute who joins in the battle simply to relieve the boredom. The other, Billy Connor, is a reformed drunkard of faltering spirits. One day, alarmed at what they are doing to the wee girl, Connor sneaks a look at the dreaming Evelyn from the sealed door of the kitchen above. He sees a bedraggled, bloodless urchin curled up in the protecting arms of a winged demon.

✠

"I never went to the lighthouse until . . ." Lessels could not bring herself to say it, as much as she found it necessary.

"Until what, madam?"

She shifted focus. "We had little time for Papists, all of us, but the wean, she had worn us down. Dr. Bolan, he got the idea that we should call in a Roman priest, a specialist in such things. It was something none of us would have thought of, but seeing as we had no choice . . ."

"An exorcist," Groves said, almost delightedly.

Lessels looked up at him.

"Monsignor Dell'Aquila, of Italy," Groves added, when the name returned to him in a flash.

"Aye, he . . . he was the one," she agreed. "Three weeks he was at the lighthouse, they say—I was not there, I saw none of it—and in all that time he did no good. He only made it worse."

"What was this man's purpose, you claim?" Fleming asked, confused.

"To smite the de'il with his potions and smoke," Lessels said, and shook her head disdainfully. "To wear him down with his fine Latin words. But the one inside her would not be done so easily. He laughed at the priest through her. He said he was no ordinary foe."

"And the priest retreated," Groves said.

"Aye."

"And the girl? What of her?"

Lessels gulped and fidgeted and tore at her handkerchief. "We never set out to hate her," she insisted weakly.

Monsignor Dell'Aquila dries his brow, feeling immeasurably old. He has battled demons in Sicily, Prussia, and Egypt, and chased them through the Alps of Austria. He has had his faith challenged and his soul shaken by unimaginable powers. He is now in a vibrating Scottish lighthouse at the request of some coldhearted Calvinists, and he feels saddled with the entire credibility of his creed.

He looks ruefully at the ragged little girl, who is held down with cords and netting and kept awake with smelling salts, and wonders if the torment she has endured is possible to justify. But the equanimity she continues to exude is positively sinister, making a mockery of pity. And her eyes have darkened so much it is impossible to read her mind.

He sighs despondently and returns to a *Rituale Romanum* blotted with his own sweat.

"Exi ergo transgressor. Exi seductor, plene omni dolo et fallacia, virtutis inimice, innocentium persecutor. . . ."

But his voice, initially forceful, has become despairing, because he knows this is a battle that will never be won with mere words. A more drastic statement—an insuperable talisman—is required. Because he has faced many demons before, but never one with the power of Leerie.

✠

They never set out to hate her. For personal reasons Abraham Lindsay in particular has never liked her, but even he recognizes this is partly irrational. They have selected her fully realizing that she will be confused and possibly traumatized, and suffer emotional consequences that might prove incurable. They are not even certain how much she will be harmed physically. But the stakes are of a magnitude that makes such considerations insignificant.

They never set out to hate her. Their enmity is directed solely at the one she houses. But the longer it goes on without success, the more difficult it becomes to distinguish the tenant from the host.

When she is racked with anguish, it is difficult not to interpret guilt.

When she is resistant, and screams invective, it is impossible not to see her as his agent.

When she is quiet, it can only be a sign of complicity.

They never set out to hurt her. But by the time the exorcist retires, defeated, they have squandered months and a small fortune on the engagement. They have wrought so much damage on her that it is impossible to believe she might ever salvage a worthwhile life. They are riddled with doubts about their own accountability and are terrified of their own fates. But they cannot surrender. They are condemned to victory.

When they think of Evelyn now they experience only revulsion and shame. They can barely begin to contemplate the terrible ordeal they have visited upon her. They have flayed from her a personality and replaced it with something hideously mutilated. And all the time Leerie has offered not a hint that he is weakening.

The girl is beyond hope—she is the manifestation of their own self-loathing—and any action becomes justifiable.

They never set out to hurt her.

But desperation has given them no option.

✠

"A lighthouse? What do you see?"

Evelyn was shivering violently, and Canavan looked away, savaged by pity.

"They have removed the little girl to a lighthouse, is that it?" McKnight tried again. "What are they doing there? Continuing the torment?"

Her lips staggered forward and withdrew.

"It is perfectly well that you protect her, Evelyn," McKnight whispered. "In fact, it is decent and honorable. But please share with us your vision, so that all of us can be enlightened. It is not too late to save the little girl. You must tell us what you see."

"There are . . ."

"There are what, Evelyn? We only want to save her."

"There are waves."

"You hear the waves? Booming against the rocks?"

"The little girl . . ."

"Aye?"

"She is in a boat . . . and there are waves."

"In her mind, Evelyn? Is she manufacturing a rescue?"

Evelyn shook her head decisively. "She is being saved."

"Saved, Evelyn?"

"Rescued . . ."

"Rescued? From what, Evelyn? What has happened at the lighthouse?"

"Waves as high as houses . . . the girl is so scared . . . it is so dark . . . and the boat is so frail. . . ."

✠

The boat is barely adequate and the seas unexpectedly hostile, but Billy Connor will not be daunted. He has seen enough of what they are doing to know that he can no longer live with inaction. He has no illusions about the audacity of his deed, but he is empowered by an enormous redemptive spirit. He is a good man, a true Christian, and he will not tolerate those devils acting in the name of God.

He has rowed out to Inchcaid in progressively more agitated seas. His brother and sister-in-law, fine people, are waiting ashore for his return. They are muttering prayers for him, though he mutters none himself, for he reckons the girl has heard enough of prayers.

He has entered the lighthouse furtively, an hour before dawn, and broken into the storeroom hardly breathing, his shoes wrapped in cloth. He has swaddled the vacant and unprotesting girl in thick blankets, hugged her close to his chest, and bundled her out of the storeroom and down to the landing jetty, a daring operation unthinkable ten years earlier, when he was rarely sober. The only keeper present is Colin Shanks, and from the light room above he has been too preoccupied with the lenses to notice anything through the great dashes of spray. The storm is like a gift from God.

But now a massive swell lifts and sucks them from the island. Billy tries to angle the oars, to find leverage in the water, but they are entirely at the sea's mercy. The rain is sweeping over him in great horizontal drifts, soaking his pullover and dripping from his uniform cap. He knows that in the lighthouse library there is a plaque for six builders drowned in similar conditions, and if he is washed overboard now, there will be no one to rescue them.

Two waves collide in an explosion of froth, gathering the little boat up and hurling it toward shore. When the swell subsides Connor has the briefest moment to glance at the girl, to see her hopeful eyes gleaming above the blankets.

"I will not let ye down, lassie," he breathes, the first kind words she has heard in weeks.

He works the oars ruthlessly. The lighthouse beam scythes through the mist and rain. A ship's horn bellows in the distance. The little boat rises and plunges with the mountainous waves, and in no time they spy the flickering lamps of shore.

"Not long now," Billy Connor says. "I won't let ye down. We'll find a new home for ye, I promise ye that."

But his words are hardly uttered before a brutal wave crashes over the gunwale and sweeps him into the abyss.

✠

"No one could have survived," Lessels said, as though still to deny the possibility. "They found the keeper's cap washed ashore . . . and the boat, it was all in flinders. No one could have survived it. We said our prayers for her, and we observed a silence for her soul . . . for we did not set out to hate her."

"But not all of you believed she was dead," Groves stated authoritatively. "There was Abraham Lindsay . . ."

"Aye. Lindsay said he knew her best—that she had a power in her from the start, and now the power of the Beast. He reckoned she would not die so easily, and he reminded us no body had been found."

"You chose not to agree with him?"

"Aye . . ."

"Because you could not live with the idea that she was still alive?"

She looked caught out.

"Because of what you had done to her? On top of everything else?"

Guilty silence.

"And what," Fleming interjected, "is this thing that you are meant to have done to her, madam? It is a serious allegation that is being made against you, and it is best that we hear it now, for your own welfare."

Her face reddened and she tried to build the courage to confess.

✠

The boat is overturned. She clings to the wood. There is no sign of the keeper, and the lighthouse is a distant obelisk. She rises and plunges. She is half submerged in the freezing water and for seconds the shock is so great she might well be dead.

Before tonight she has known the sea as only a distant abstraction. Something she has read about in books, glimpsed from a great distance, and heard thundering against the lighthouse walls.

You will not die, lassie.

Another massive wave bears down on her. She closes her eyes as the water smacks her like a punishing fist. She loses her grip. The boat is torn away. She is swallowed completely by the sea.

Her mouth is full of brine, her wounds are stung by salt, her whole body is immersed in bubbles and blackness. But beneath the surface there is remarkable solitude. The lighthouse beam briefly carves through a rolling wave and lights up the ghostly figure of the insensible Billy Connor, drifting into the deep as though hauled by a rope.

You will not die, lassie.

She does not know where the energy comes from, but suddenly she must do something. She begins to move her limbs, to kick and thrash, at first protestingly, but soon as a means of propelling her way to the surface.

You will not die . . .

She bursts into the air coughing and gulping. She is swept by a wave into the faintly brightening sky and spots the glimmer of shore lights. She has never swum before and has no idea from where the explicit memories flood.

She strokes through the water like Robinson Crusoe.

✠

McKnight breathed a sigh of relief. "The girl is saved, Evelyn?"

"The girl is alive," Evelyn confirmed, and seemed to marvel.

"The keeper's family, they find her?"

"The keeper . . ." She nodded and frowned, concerned about the brave man's fate.

"And they—the keeper's family—they take her away somewhere, do they not?"

She nodded.

"It is no longer safe in these parts, they know that. But they have family . . . in Ireland."

She nodded again.

"And the girl is well cared for there. She recovers and grows."

Evelyn seemed close to tears.

"Everything is well," McKnight said. "Except that she can never really forget, can she? As much as she might try to put it all behind her, there is a force inside the girl that will not allow her to forget."

The whole of Evelyn's lower face now started to quiver.

"Because something terrible happened to her in that lighthouse. Beyond the realm of words. Something happened to the little girl, did it not?"

She stared into the fluttering flame and again her pupils contracted.

Canavan now put aside the candle. "*Evelyn* . . ." he whispered, unable to stand it any longer, and stepped forward protectively. "Evelyn," he said again, to assure her of his presence.

But McKnight, close to revelation, would not be hindered. "What happened?" he asked, stalling the Irishman. "What did they do to her? Tell me what you see, Evelyn—tear it loose and set it free!"

Evelyn struggled to force the words out, needing the release but resisting the complete exorcism.

"They . . ."

"They what, Evelyn, *what*?"

"They—" Her face was suddenly sucked of blood.

"Tell us, Evelyn, tell us now!"

The memory coalesced and seared her mind. "They—"

But no words were adequate. McKnight and Canavan watched in terrible silence as she methodically turned out her wrists in explanation.

"Dear God," Canavan breathed, staring at the stigmata.

✠

"What did you do to her?" Groves demanded.

"It was not just me," Lessels insisted. "It was all of us."

"What did you do?"

"The priest was gone, but it was his idea, I tell ye. A last resort. He said we must brand the suffering of the Redeemer on her mind, and so onto the Evil One. The Papists, they have always been fond of the cross. . . ."

"What, woman?"

"It was a last attempt to save her, you understand. To save them both. We would not have done it otherwise." She put her hand over her mouth. "And we knew . . . we would need to share it. If we were to be damned, we would be damned together."

"What did you do?"

Lessels sobbed. "The keeper held her down . . . it was the priest's idea . . ."

"Tell us, woman!"

"There were the four men . . . and I had the spear . . . and the keeper had the whip . . . oh dear God have pity on me . . ."

"It's too late for that now, woman!" Groves said hysterically. "Say it!"

"One of the men held her to the boards, and the others took turns with the hammer, and . . . and . . ."

"What? *What?*"

Hettie Lessels looked up with eyes both beseeching and angry, for she had not expected to be driven so far. But she shook off the urge to bite down her words, even at this late stage, and, bursting into tears, she made the terrible admission.

✠

"They *crucified* her, didn't they, Evelyn!"

McKnight was leaning forward, still managing to restrain Canavan.

"They crucified her!" The Professor was breathing the words with indignation. "The little girl, they *crucified* her in that lighthouse!"

Evelyn started to shake violently.

"They were trying to kill the devil inside her! So they crucified the little girl! They crucified *you*! Admit it, Evelyn! *Admit it!*"

"For God's sake!" Canavan said, and surged forward.

But McKnight was surprisingly strong. *"No,"* he said, staring at Evelyn. "You must acknowledge his presence, Evelyn, and you must set him free! You must do it, Evelyn!"

She started to convulse.

"There is no shame, Evelyn! You must not deny him! It's imperative that you set him free!"

"No," she said.

"You must!"

"I can't . . ." she said defiantly, and tears stained with blood dribbled from her eyes.

"Evelyn!" said Canavan, no longer able to bear it, and pushing aside McKnight he swooped in to embrace her with genuine sympathy as the candle flame fluttered and died.

Chapter XXII

Pringle had defined himself through his comprehensive obedience to his immediate superiors. Scrupulously avoiding questions as to the Wax Man's unorthodox methods, he had been content to learn and observe while assiduously warding off the contagion of the man's weaknesses. Assigned to Inspector Groves, he initially had been relieved, figuring that the man's notoriously pedantic procedures might better suit his own sensibilities and allow him to pass a month or two untouched by the merest breath of scandal. But now, nearly two weeks after the murder of Professor Smeaton in Belgrave Crescent, he was beginning to suspect that the mounting pressure had squeezed Groves's imagination in unnatural directions.

It was an extraordinary case by any measure. Four men killed, an unlawful exhumation, the city on edge, an accelerating sense of mystery, the enigma of Groves's methods (the notion, frequently promulgated by the Inspector himself, that there were complications beyond any understanding save his own)—all this meant that, for a while at least, Pringle had felt on the periphery of a greatness unlike anything he had experienced with the Wax Man. The gruesome death of the Lord Provost had now magnified the importance of the case to previously unimaginable dimensions and left them with another two potential victims—Abraham Lindsay and Hettie Lessels—but still no one whom the law would accept as a murderer, or even a firm suspect. Groves had been summoned to several meetings with the Sheriff, the Procurator Fiscal, and the Lord Advocate, resolving little. The introduction of the devil, the very invocation of the name, was regarded as outlandish to the most proper and studied men, and his indictment as manifestly ridiculous. In lieu of a more satisfying resolution, they committed themselves to more official examinations with a view to prosecution. The revelations about the activities of the Mirror Society, gleaned through Lessels's preliminary statement, were themselves subject to further scrutiny, in particular the testimony relating to the crucifixion of the young Evelyn Todd. But the eminent gentlemen were uneasy even here, averse to posthumously soiling the name of the Right Honorable Henry Bolan, to whom many were deeply indebted. And while the victim of this alleged outrage loomed large over these discussions, with her criminal record duly noted, they were unsure if they should regard her with pity or contempt—certainly they could not conceive of her as a monstrous murderer—and here they sought some clue from Inspector Groves, who was becoming increasingly inscrutable.

"I have seen things," he said, "which make nothing unquestionable."

And indeed he had worn a deathly pallor ever since witnessing the ruthless slaughter of Henry Bolan, so that none of the men felt inclined to question him further or make an issue of his failure properly to identify the killer.

The Inspector's eyes were still glazed, and he bore about him the aspect of a fanatic when he confided his suspicions to Pringle sometime later. "She will not allow it," he whispered confidently. "She will have Abraham Lindsay done away with tonight. Before it is too late."

It was a prediction later given weight, as it happened, by the orphanage governor himself. "It was my final exhortation," the old man wheezed, his eyes shining with sickly satisfaction. "I told them to run. But our Lord Provost was too bound to his burgh. He wanted to strike down the girl and do away with her once and for all. But there is no point to that." He did not even deign to look up at the Sheriff, Groves, and Pringle, not expecting them to understand. "If you kill her, I told him, he will flood out of her in her final moments and he will brand himself on your very soul."

Fleming was still exasperated. "Stop this gibberish, man. This sort of talk will stand in no court."

But Lindsay was staring into more distant realms. "No," he said. "It is as it should be. I will not run from him. I will not hide."

He did not explain how he expected to be punished, or indeed where, but later in the day, in full view of the watching Groves, he emerged from his crumbling residence and hobbled to the cabstand near Queen Mary's Bath. Here he dispatched one vehicle with a message and secured another to take him to his final destination. He was dressed in a thick greatcoat, black frock coat, and silken top hat, armored against the cold but not against damnation.

Groves elected to follow the first cab, which as he expected wound through the labyrinth of streets to Candlemaker Row, where Pringle was posted. They intercepted the messenger on his way up the stairs, and here read Lindsay's spidery note.

Awaiting dissolution in the house of the Great Deceiver.
Abraham Lindsay

"What does it mean, sir?" Pringle asked.

"It means we have one last chance," Groves breathed. "Before the Wax Man takes control and draws a blanket over his bairn."

"His bairn, sir?"

But Groves did not respond. He instructed the messenger to deliver the letter without a further word and withdrew to the shadows at the bottom of the stairs.

✠

Aeneas and Psyche had been there, so too Ulysses and the mighty Hercules. Saint Paul and Saint Anthony had visited, at least in their imaginations, and Christ Himself was said to have been harrowed there between His death and resurrection. For McKnight and Canavan, then, preparing for this most mythological of odysseys, a trail of legendary precedents lent gravity to their every word and gesture. But beyond what they had heard and smelled through its gates in Shand's Wynd, and the sight of the medieval Beast itself—signs that were hardly encouraging—they could not be certain what they should expect to find there.

"All aspects of hell," the Professor observed, "have been in a state of continual evolution."

It was a place whose boundaries had been repeatedly expanded and contracted, its topography raised and flattened, its population variously rampant, magnified, rounded up, imprisoned, and finally dispatched on a sort of demonic diaspora. From the classical Hades of the Greeks to Ezekiel's fire pits, Isaiah's abyss, John's Apocalypse, Saint Thomas Aquinas's elaborate prison, Dante's carefully segmented levels, Bosch's chaos, Milton's majesties, and ultimately the cerebral hells of psychology, it had been at all times subject to mutating theology, pervasive dogma, the feverish torment of poets, the boundaries of language, and all the prevailing perceptions of evil, shame, and discomfort. Likewise the face of Satan. First assuming his satyric features when the Church demonized the cult of Pan, he later acquired elements of the Dragon of Revelation, Job's Leviathan, the Greek harpy, and every cunning and repulsive characteristic that could be imagined from flared eyebrows to dripping orifices, until—with the coming of the Enlightenment—he evolved into the immaterial form of abstract concepts and insuperable instincts.

"And now I fear we have no option but to meet him personally," McKnight said. "Or at least the monstrous form that indoctrination has stitched for him."

Mere hypnotism had proved inadequate. The purging of hidden memories had revealed that they were dealing not just with a tormented unconscious but the very devil himself. This was no metaphor, but an ageless entity in his own right, the Prince of Darkness born as the Bearer of Light. In establishing this at last, and forcing Evelyn to acknowledge his tenancy, they had successfully levered open the gates of hell, but releasing the ruthlessly persecuted prisoner inside would require more than just spells.

"Sooner or later," McKnight noted, with incongruous enthusiasm, "all true heroes must go to Hades."

For Canavan, too, an undeniable sense of determination intoxicated him beyond the realm of doubts. This was an exertion of will he found impossible to view as anything less than independent. And it occurred to him with satisfaction that Evelyn herself had never, in their presence, given any direct indication that they were less than real. So if their God accepted their existence, then who were they to argue?

Arriving with McKnight at Clancy's Maritime and Hunting Goods Emporium in Leith, there to stock up on weapons and provisions for the coming expedition, the Irishman was again given cause to question the nature of a reality that could be so effortlessly simulated down to such annoying obstacles as the Professor's temporary loss of his wallet (he had slipped it into an irregular breast pocket after cashing in some more of his books) and an emporium proprietor unwilling to open his downstairs store on a Sunday without a substantial bribe.

"If I'm to go to hell," said the flustered Mr. Clancy, "then you will need to make damnation worth it."

"I shall put in a good word for you," McKnight assured him ironically, "and secure a suite with a commanding view."

The two visitors then roamed across the unlit shop floor—Clancy was nervously sweeping the doorstep outside—trying to ascertain just what items were required for the unknown depths.

"Evelyn has certainly been exposed to the Bible, and the dogma of various churches," McKnight observed. "But is she familiar with Alberic? Dante?"

"I don't know," Canavan replied. "Are we . . . ?"

"We know only this much for certain," McKnight predicted grimly, surveying a rack of alpenstocks and cord ladders. "Whatever has been driven into her unconscious, with all the powers of her maligned imagination, has had twenty years to fester, coagulate, and build impenetrable barriers to reason. We can most certainly expect to find tempests there, and tangled woods, and baking gridirons, and clanking chains. These are present in the most serene of minds, so we should have no reason to be surprised, and even less to go unprepared."

It was into the dungeons of this underworld that an unsuspecting Leerie had been ruthlessly flattened by the Mirror Society, while in the realms of reality he had found his movements inhibited by a form conducive only to nightmares.

"An agreeable tenant, too, I've no doubt," McKnight said, "given the proper circumstances."

ANTHONY O'NEILL

"He is, and always will be, the Prince of Darkness," Canavan reminded him.

"We all have demons in our minds," the Professor argued, selecting a coil of stout rope. "It's just a matter of how we integrate them. Some, of course, are allowed to become undisciplined and inflict damage on their hosts. But it's difficult to imagine Lucifer himself, with all his age and wisdom, would be such an ingrate. Look no farther than the tribesman he previously inhabited. A man of enormous tranquillity, from Evelyn's own account."

"It's as if you admire him."

"If God truly created man in his own image," McKnight said, "then it's equally true that man created the devil in his own."

"No man is born evil."

"Nor, you'll recall, was Lucifer."

Canavan snorted.

"Nor, indeed," McKnight observed charitably as he examined the soles of some watertight boots, "were the members of the Mirror Society. But their ambitions—their very quest for purity—made them obsessive and irrational. Their extremism made them the servants of their enemies, and with the abandonment of all their credibility they became fanatics, justifying anything in the name of survival."

Canavan sighed, too distracted to find words as anything more than decorative now, and he listened to the Professor as he might to a bishop from outside a crowded cathedral.

"The devil, very much like the Mirror Society, must have spent years pondering what was to become of him. If the pitiless march of science meant that he would be transformed permanently into some lifeless symbol. So imagine his dismay when, having decided to take refuge in Evelyn's bounteous imagination, he found the fabulous vistas and fauna of her dreams shrivel and disappear, to be replaced by a reality reproduced with mathematical exactitude. Imagine him there, mutated by the Mirror Society and scalded by Evelyn's corrosive guilt, desperately nurturing in his host the need to return to Edinburgh before it is too late. Imagine him compelling her to roam the streets at night and print every facet of the city on her memory, so that through her dreams he might burst into reality and consummate his indignation. Imagine him realizing that each murder will have to be effected with unnatural speed—

because their very gruesomeness will rip her from sleep—planning all the attacks in advance, and planting cryptic messages, and through all the mayhem summoning us, as he always intended, to mount a fearless expedition to save him." McKnight smiled. "Imagine that . . . ."

"And if we don't succeed even now?"

"We have to succeed." The Professor took up a spring-loaded rifle. "We were born for this moment."

"For martyrdom?"

"It need not look so bleak. I cannot see her abandoning us entirely. Indeed, if you'll forgive me, I'd say it defies all logic." He handed to Canavan a percussion revolver.

"Is this really necessary?"

"It might be difficult, lad, but you know it's right."

"I've no doubt it's right," the Irishman replied. "But I pray we're equal to the task. To the Adversary."

"The Adversary himself is not the problem. It's the traps laid in our path, and the demons that do not recognize us, which will be our bane."

Canavan looked at the gun and sighed. "I've never used one," he admitted.

"It's an action to which one quickly adapts."

"You've fired one yourself?"

"Of course not." McKnight smirked. "I've no idea what I'm talking about. But I've never let that obstruct me."

Armored in hunting jackets and moleskin trousers, festooned with ammunition and supplies, they headed briskly into the deepening darkness and by the time they reached the Cowgate, having made one last detour to Candlemaker Row, they were marching in formation. They parted a pack of snarling dogs, crunched over leaves of rotting cabbage, waved away clouds of fish-oil smoke, and entered Shand's Wynd without a flicker of hesitation. Kindled with purpose, they sidled down the alley's dark depths to the newly opened orifice in the wall and for one last time paused to marvel at the intricacy of Evelyn's composition: the gurgle of a broken soil pipe, the odors of disturbed ash buckets, the very trickle of snowflakes melting in midair over the gateway to hell.

⌖

Standing near the tenement entrance, Pringle was alarmed by the notion that the Inspector had deliberately retreated to allow a murder attempt to proceed according to his own sinister expectations. Abraham Lindsay's message would prove compelling evidence if reinforced with an attack, after all, and would almost certainly secure the arrest warrant Groves had long sought. As to how Evelyn might try to effect the punishment—through the mind devil, as the Lessels woman had indicated, or through some other means—Pringle felt not sufficiently informed to speculate. But he was deeply troubled by the multiplying signals that Groves was taking the case far too personally—something the Wax Man never did—and that his fascination with the Evelyn woman was verging on the vengeful.

He was staring at the Inspector pensively, trying to come to terms with his feelings, when they heard the creak of a stair above. Groves slid deeper into the darkness.

Moments later Evelyn swept past them as though sleepwalking. Her face was blank, her eyes fixed ahead, and in her hands she held a felt purse just ample enough to conceal a weapon. She glided into the street.

Having received Lindsay's message, it seemed she was to make the move herself. Or direct it personally. It could not have been more perfect, and Groves's excitement was conspicuous.

The two men fell in behind her, one eager, the other irresolute, and at a wary distance they followed her down Candlemaker Row and into the drizzling snow.

Chapter XXIII

FOR ALL THEIR RESOLVE, their righteousness, and even McKnight's insurmountable confidence in the outcome, they could not help but tremble at the magnitude of the undertaking. With the portcullis gate reduced to flinders, they peered into the no longer impregnable realms with a sense of dread, and McKnight was cautionary.

"Hell is a place without comfort or justice, where all reason is transient, and we can rely on few certainties except the threat of challenge."

Notwithstanding his words, however, their first faltering penetration was into a chamber little different from any in the Edinburgh catacombs: a low-vaulted cellar with Italianate arches, needlelike stalactites, and centuries of piled brick dust. They angled their lantern beams around but found no evidence of recent habitation, or any sign of recent passage at all but for some scoring around a doorway in the rear wall, the surrounding bricks blackened as though by some great heat. Lowering their heads they entered into a similarly sized and empty chamber, and then another, and finally a fourth, in the rear of which there was not one doorway but five. Breathing the stale air, they shone their beams at each individually, judging none especially promising, and not sure which to select.

Hell is a surfeit of choices.

They chose the middle one for no reason, and passed into a seemingly endless series of subdivided chambers and progressively narrower corridors, heading lower with each new door, striking their heads against projections and shuffling onward with cramped backs and sore legs and not convinced they were heading into any hell but that of futility.

So when they encountered an impassable wall they were, if anything, relieved. They rested, their backs to the cool brick, and indulged in a few sips of water before returning through the string of vaults to the crossroads.

"What do you think?" McKnight asked, eyeing the four remaining doorways.

"It's not a region I know especially well."

McKnight smiled. "It's always best to follow your heart."

Canavan chose the leftmost door, for no particular reason, but their initial hope quickly surrendered to further despair as they negotiated another endless series of airless cellars and sloping passages carpeted with fragments of stone.

Hell is monotony; the complete absence of promise.

By mutual consent they paused to recuperate on a ruptured platform, and here Canavan felt an intrusive breeze on his cheek and smelled a rogue waft of incense. Briefly departing McKnight's side, he ventured into an adjoining gallery and was soon calling the Professor to join him.

He was directing his lantern beam into a deep pit, where a marble staircase swept down into what looked like the vestibule of a Romanesque cathedral.

✠

On her initial return to her city of birth Evelyn had wasted little time before reacquainting herself with the route out of town and up the Old Dalkeith Road to the lodge where she had first met Leerie. She had never seen the building from the outside, or any length of the road leading up to it, but the journey was imprinted on her remaining senses more deeply than an instinct. She only had to sublimate her eyesight to be drawn to the place by wood smoke and foxgloves, by creaking branches and twittering hedge sparrows, by the play of shadows and contesting breezes.

Even now ferocious gusts and snowflakes could not overwhelm the
memories. She was a girl again, naive enough to be trusting, and on the
road to liberation. She was barely aware of the streets she negotiated in
her relentless march: Bristo Street, Chapel Street, Nicolson Street, Lut-
ton Place, Dalkeith Road. At Newington Terrace a man in a flapping
scarf stepped out to caution her.

"It's no' safe, lass, out in the streets at this hour. There's all manner
of evil about."

But she barely noticed him. Her eyes were dimmed, focused internally, and she forged on, thinking of the wise Professor and the com-
passionate Irishman, dressed as though to hunt tigers, who had
materialized in her room to advise her that she would need to mount an
expedition of her own.

"What am I supposed to do with it?" she asked hoarsely when the Professor pressed a weapon into her hand.

"I believe you will know what to do," McKnight said, "when the time
arrives."

She looked for assurance to Canavan, who nodded obligingly. "You
may trust us," he whispered tenderly, "just as surely as we trust you."

And then, in a blink—a correction of the vision or the emergence
from a reverie—they were gone, so quickly she had questioned if they
were ever actually there. But if not, then where had she procured the
weapon? Had she been storing it in her room for just such a moment?

She shivered and marched on, drawn as though by a current, and inside
her mind the odyssey continued.

✠

It was groin-vaulted and narrow, on its floors a pattern of geometric marble, in its walls a succession of clerestory windows depicting a haloed
Christ in a series of beatific scenes. Emanating from some indeterminate
source, radiant light sprayed the two of them with shafts of muted vio-
let, emerald, and rose—an incongruously peaceful gallery, undisturbed
by the faintest sound or suggestion of discomfort.

Hell is deception.

As they continued downward a cauldronlike heat introduced itself in
waves, the air slowly thickened with stinging smoke, and the walls trembled with cathedral-organ bleats. The vaults became ribbed in the
Gothic style, the lancet windows more flamboyantly decorated with jew-

els and hallucinatory designs, and Christ's blood sprayed over them in infinite gradations of red. The stained-glass skies became gradually more oppressive and the Redeemer's tormentors more sinister, until it was difficult to distinguish a Roman centurion from a cackling demon and impossible to separate oppression from victory. Serpents and gargoyles started to emerge in bas-reliefs and statuary, coiling with increasing confidence around pillars and weeping saints. The gallery itself, to this point uniform in all but style, became warped and unpredictable—the steps fractured and irregular, the windows blossoming into distorted shards stained with appalling visions—and soon it began to turn obscenely, dipping and escalating and looping in on itself in odd permutations, so that McKnight and Canavan had to forsake the stairs and walk first on the side walls, stepping over the windows, and then hobble over the Gothic ribs themselves. And finally there was no recognizable church at all, the path dissolving into something like a jungle track swathed in unyielding vines and creepers carved as though by French stonemasons. Mounted overhead on intricate scaffolding, an immense palpitating heart, wrapped tight in thorns, was swarming with agile gargoyles methodically clawing away its membranes and replacing them with panes of stained glass. Great lines of blood leaked through the cracks and splattered in dollops on the path.

"If you can't go through," said McKnight, "you circumvent."

They toiled along a precarious path ringing the jungle, ripping pockets and sleeves on the bluestone spurs. Departing the oppressive forest through a doorway of hammer-rigged stone, they entered a doom-laden court where ranks and ranks of faces glowered at them from figures part magistrate, part constable, part field marshal, and part bishop. They moved at a God-fearing pace, never certain when they would be challenged, accosted, or even obliterated by a punitive verdict. But the deeper they traveled the more the judges mutated into massive centipede forms with eyes multiplying into glimmering discs and gowns that became carapaces held in place by cobwebs. But no gavel was struck, no judgment delivered, and no punishment executed.

"They do not even recognize us," the Professor marveled, and they descended into Pandemonium.

✠

They watched Evelyn stagger and almost swoon—she might have lost her footing on a drift of snow, or perhaps it was something else—and

Pringle had to resist the urge to spring to her assistance. They had drawn steadily closer since leaving Candlemaker Row, for it was quickly apparent that she had no intention of looking around, and now that she had passed Peffermill Road they were in a sparsely populated region bare of streetlamps, and they could ill afford to lose her in the dark and the storm.

They waited patiently, not uttering a word, until she collected her senses, straightened, and forced herself on.

"She returns to her maker," Groves said, warming the air with a snarl. "Piper McNab put it best. 'The statue answers first to the sculptor' . . ."

He cared not if Pringle had understood him. He could not remember the last time he had enjoyed an uninterrupted sleep or a substantial meal, repelling the twin demons of fatigue and hunger with an overriding sense of predestination. He was convinced that these were his last hours at the head of the investigation and that the night would furnish him with a resolution. But he no longer dared to dream ahead to the words he might immortalize in his nightly gospel, or indeed the biblical flourish with which he might tie it all in a knot, because all his hard work and confidence had yet to avail him of a conviction.

His head was guttering like a faulty lamp. He was unable to think obliquely, engage in any complex speculation, or see into any future more distant than his immediate steps. He focused instead on Evelyn, his nemesis, his salvation, the Wax Man's unacknowledged spawn, and he tracked her into the wooded areas with the single-mindedness of a foxhound.

✠

For McKnight and Canavan it was a suspicion verified by the very act of recognition: that at some stage Evelyn must have been exposed to the flamboyant Old Testament artwork of John Martin.

The city represented the worst excesses of Babylon, Rome, and Nineveh, an immense row of palaces and ziggurats under a sky of undulating sackcloth and spearing lightning bolts. In the portico of the largest temple they glimpsed a Dionysian orgy amid golden calves and burning braziers. The swirl of fabrics was Mesopotamian, Greek, and Roman: a blur of biblical decadence. There were lawless squeals and laughter, shuddering tambourines and braying animals.

In the shadow of the temple buttresses—constructed either to hold the building in place or keep it at bay, it was difficult to determine—McKnight and Canavan now perceived a horde of protesting supplicants with eyes of stained glass and knees bare and bloody from incessant praying. Repulsing the horror of the debauchery with all their energy, they bowed, wept, fired volleys of castigation, and beseeched the storm clouds to coalesce and smite the unholy Gomorrah. From within the temple came a sudden cannon blast, and a great projectile of claws, gizzards, and marinated flesh scattered across the marble floor in front of the supplicants, who now dispensed with their invective and rose up to fight for the morsels like hungry gulls, stuffing them into their mouths and swallowing them without a single chew—feasting on their own indignation.

McKnight and Canavan threaded their way through the madness without being noticed by a single eye. They heard a high priest exhorting his congregation to don the breastplate of righteousness, to stand resilient to the great corruption, and to fight to the death, if necessary, with the monstrous heathens. The priest himself had blistered flesh, a missing eye, and a mouth unable to contain lines of drool and speckled froth, but no one seemed to care, so profound was the fervor.

The clouds enmeshed and pelted McKnight and Canavan with a rain of frogs and beetles as they hustled through the fantastically gilded doors of the great temple, immediately coming in sight of a veritable circus of depravity: men in silk and scarlet gobbling pigs' trotters and grapes and hallucinogenic spices, women with reverse digestive systems wolfing food with their anuses, rhinoceroses fornicating with antelopes, peacocks with hyenas, horse-size locusts hovering overhead with wings thrumming like chariots heading into battle, and everywhere shameless parasites sucking blood from any titillated organ or barest inch of exposed flesh. This was the realm of perversity, Bacchanalianism, profligacy, wantonness, and extravagant furnishings: the cannibalistic terminus of affluence without self-discipline. The supplicants were here mocked in processions of withering virulence and boiled in great cauldrons of stinking fat, the revelers likewise drawing succor from their enemies, engorged on their own derision—this hell a place of unchecked extremes and improper balances.

Cloaked in impunity, the Professor and the Irishman ventured through a flock of flesh-eating birds and located a descending stairway behind a raised altar awash with discarded bones, drifts of cinnamon, and all the fruits of despair. They took one last look at the circus as an enemy incendiary pierced the purple awnings and exploded in a cloud of frankincense and myrrh.

"The Last Battle," McKnight said.

"No," Canavan corrected sadly. "A meaningless skirmish."

To this point they had discharged not one bullet or raised a blade in self-defense, and they were fully aware of their good fortune, and equally aware that it could not possibly last.

⬧

She tilted into the wind, undaunted by any gust. The snow thrashed at her face, but she would not be repelled. She knew every dip and rise, every sweep and curve, though she gave no thought to her destination, the man she was due to meet there, or indeed the weapon in her purse.

She moved into an area of open fields, billowing grey grasses like witches' hair, copses of yew trees flailing at the sky, and whistling winds unhindered by hedges, fences, or habitation. But rather than seeing any of this she was deeply engrossed in sporadic and incomprehensible visions of two men pitting their lives against great obstacles to save her. It was deeply absurd and yet strangely comforting.

Ahead on the left Drumgate Cemetery came in sight, perched awkwardly on its hill. And beyond it, glowering over a substantial forecourt overgrown with weeds and thistle, lay the gutted hulk of Colonel Munnoch's hunting lodge—the house, as she knew it better, of Mr. James Ainslie, the home of the Great Deceiver, and her introduction to hell.

⬧

The skies flashed and grumbled and marshaled their redoubtable energies. But the new path was more a gentle gradient through a terrain of almost lunar desolation: parched earth, smoking craters, distant mountains like the peaks in a child's drawings.

But as they progressed they noticed leafless white trees crowded with strangely familiar, harpylike creatures glaring at them with red eyes. The harpies scratched their naked haunches, stroked their drooping breasts, and hissed and clicked their tongues, communicating in some alien code.

"Have your gun ready," McKnight warned, but Canavan already had drawn his revolver, sensing they would no longer travel unnoticed.

They were in sight of a glowing cleft in a looming cliff face when there was a bansheelike battle cry, and a flock of the creatures launched from the trees and took to the air with a frightful flapping, merging overhead and spearing down at them with raucous shrieks.

The first assailant had no sooner laid a claw on Canavan than he wheeled around and aimed the revolver at its head. But his finger froze on the trigger when he noticed, with a shudder of horror, that the face of the creature—the face of all the harpies—was that of Evelyn.

There is no hell quite like self-loathing.

Appalled, Canavan could not bring himself to fire. But McKnight had no hesitation.

"It's not her, lad!" he cried, thrusting the rifle into the harpy's mouth. "It's only what she sees in herself!" He squeezed the trigger and the head exploded in chunks of flesh and pus.

Two more harpies, sensing the Irishman's hesitation, wrapped themselves around him and dragged him to the ground, dislodging his gun. It took all McKnight's strength to reach through the wings, pry one loose, and cleave its head with a well-aimed machete. The other he shot at point-blank range, and was sprayed with a backwash of oily blood and writhing tissue. Trembling with disgust, Canavan himself dispatched a fourth assailant with his retrieved revolver.

The remaining harpies hovered above them warily, snarling and spitting but strangely unwilling to attack. Pointing their firearms threateningly and backing through clouds of gun smoke, McKnight and Canavan, dripping with effluent and entrails, made it through the fissure and rolled a boulder across the entrance, having one last glimpse of a hundred disfigured Evelyn faces staring at them delightedly.

They turned to find themselves in a cavernous nest of harpies.

✠

From a distance, with her black dress bellied by the wind, she looked crowlike and sinister. She drifted into the forecourt and halted in front of the lodge, staring fixedly at the blackened unicorn rebus in the facade as though emerging from a dream, and behind her Groves and Pringle for the first time thought it prudent to conceal themselves behind a withered hedge.

The old building's doors were missing, its windows like gaping wounds, the roof a mixture of fallen arches and surviving beams. But there was light glowing dimly from somewhere within.

"Abraham Lindsay . . ." Pringle whispered, but Groves said nothing.

They watched Evelyn fondle her purse, as though to reassure herself of the weapon's presence, and then raise her head and march, not without hesitation, into the building's impious maw.

Pringle moved at once to follow her but was surprised to find his forearm clasped tightly.

"No," Groves breathed through clenched teeth, and Pringle looked back at him with dismay.

A vile grin was tugging at the Inspector's lips, and his eyes were set like glaciers.

✠

The legion of harpies slept and snored, clinging to the roof upside down amid huge stalactites. The cavern was choking with superheated air and sulfurous fumes of lava. Bridging the chasm below was a single nail-studded arch barely the breadth of a hand.

"I have a feeling," McKnight said tightly, "that we are not welcome here."

"Perhaps we should reconsider," Canavan whispered. "The damage . . . it might already be too late."

"That's not you talking," McKnight assured him, "but the voice of self-destruction."

They forced themselves onto the bridge, dizzied by the bending waves of heat and blooming gases, and almost immediately mosquitoes the size of stag beetles materialized to alight on their faces. Brushed off, the insects wheeled around and attacked with even greater ferocity. The two men fought frantically for balance as the disturbed harpies jostled and squealed in their sleep.

Their bodies dripping with perspiration and their thick-soled boots repeatedly pierced by wicked barbs, McKnight and Canavan soldiered across the bridge, batting continuously at the mosquitoes, gasping at the scorching air, and fighting the attraction of the glowing swirls of lava. They were halfway across when an eerie silence alerted them to the fact that the harpies had awoken.

They no longer had time for diligence. Without turning they pounded down the last length of bridge, balanced by momentum alone, and it was only the immensity of Evelyn's self-hatred that allowed them to escape, the thousand pursuing harpies colliding and tangling in midair, rendered

useless by numbers and haste, and watching in vain as the Professor and
Canavan slipped breathlessly through a door into the land of malfunctioning mechanisms.

✠

The building had no right to exude ashen odors, the fire that had ravaged
it having burned out nearly two decades earlier. But Evelyn's nose now
curled at even older fragrances, even deeper permeances. The smells
invaded her memory and generated a storm of long-dormant associations:
the frills on her pillowcases; the kindly eyes of the regal black man; the
sight of Lindsay and three strange men entering the room to seize her and
bind her limbs. The wind hummed through the mutilated walls, snow
dribbled in shafts between ceiling beams, and through holes in the
charred floor she caught sight of the cellar where she had first been
imprisoned. She blinked and almost blacked out, gulped for air, clutched
a banister for support, and whimpered helplessly.

She heard a voice, far away—a man calling to her. He sounded imploring, guiding her through the darkness to the light.

"I'm here. . . ."

She thought it was the lamplighter.

"I'm here. . . ."

She thought it was the devil.

"I do not fear you. . . ."

The voice, very real, was coming from a room at the top of the stairs.

✠

Great roaring thunderbolts and sizzling ropes of electricity forced them
to dodge and duck. Their firearms were useless here.

They continued down a winding wrought-iron staircase panting
from exertion, their clothes stained black with sweat and shredded by
talons. The skies fell away to reveal a dangerously overworked anatomy
of groaning ratchet wheels, huge revolving cogs, squealing ventilators,
spindles, regulators, hissing belts, and pistons oiled with blood. Brass
cylinders swelled and shot jets of steam, cog teeth issued showers of
sparks, gears vomited clots of grease, and horns blared incessantly in
protest and alarm. The whole structure looked as though it might
explode at any second.

But as they descended deeper, white-painted masonry appeared to
cloak the hideous machinery, and they heard waves boom, seabirds caw,

and the walls shudder like instruments of percussion. They entered a room filled with glittering panes of glass, dazzling reflectors, and polished lenses, and perceived that they had descended into some great cerebral lighthouse. They clambered down a stout brass ladder into a bedroom area set with two modest cots, a kitchen where pork chops were heating on a skillet, a storeroom filled with lenses and paraffin, and finally they came to a crudely fashioned door of nail-studded wood armored with steel plates. The door was set solidly into the floor, secured there with clamps and sturdy bolts, and resisted easy access.

Hunched over, his eyes squeezed shut and his neck tendons like bowstrings, Canavan hauled at the brass ring with all his might until he achieved some submission of wood and metal. The door popped loose and yawned back with a puff of distasteful mist on what should have been the provision room but instead was a bottomless void of infinite terror and blackness.

They craned their heads over the emptiness but as hard as they tried could make out no walls, no floor, nothing but a few sparkles like a far-distant constellation. They inhaled the ancient air and discerned eerie sounds: inconsolable breezes, sobs and whispers, and even, far below, a plaintive skirl of music.

"Bagpipes . . ." Canavan marveled.

Straining their ears, they listened some more: "Amazing Grace," no less, but played in a painfully discordant manner that elicited no emotion other than despair.

Canavan grimaced, but McKnight nodded resignedly. "I always suspected hell would be a place of poorly performed music," he said.

✠

Pringle tasted the bile of disaffection and experienced the great hollowness of betrayal. He had manfully suppressed his doubts about Inspector Groves, wanting so dearly to believe in him, to surrender without question to a superior in exactitude, deductive powers, and moral fiber. But standing beside the man now, watching the dilapidated lodge and feeling the lingering burn of the Inspector's fingers on his forearm, his final resistance melted and all his willing delusions crumbled.

Evelyn had entered the house to inflict some sort of revenge on Abraham Lindsay, who had set himself up there to facilitate the punishment— that much was clear. But rather than impeding her, as it clearly was their duty to do, Groves now intended to remain outside and wait patiently for the evil to be fully perpetrated. Because he valued conviction more than human life; because he wanted to catch Evelyn after the crime rather than thwart her before it. And to Pringle this was simply unconscionable. And certainly beyond any impropriety that the Wax Man might sanction in the name of expediting justice.

Unchecked, Pringle's previously stifled suspicions about Groves's questionable motives and methods were writ large. And the man's repeated and presumptuous assessments of character, how could they be given any credibility? A dozen times he had quoted the late Piper McNab with hushed reverence—the man's name uttered as though he were a robed prophet or uncanonized saint—and a dozen times Pringle had tried to convince himself that Groves was speaking in jest. Because Pringle thought everyone in Edinburgh knew that McNab had been an incorrigible old lecher whose regular street performances were just a code to alert the city's bohemians to another after-hours orgy in the windowless upper rooms of a Rose Street bar. The rascally piper, who uttered nary a word that was not facetious, presided over the saturnalia like a bony Bacchus, playing his wicked strathspeys and toward the end of the evening hoisting his kilt and inviting the pink-cheeked lassies to play a tune on his own little blowpipe.

How could Groves ever have believed in such a man? Trusted him? Stood beside him?

Without the status to exert his own will or the courage to disobey, Pringle could only burn in silence, his frustration rising from him in clouds of steam.

✠

Swinging from the extremity of the cord ladder, Canavan finally struck something: a curved ridge, deeply scored. Landing here, he was able to secure the end of the rope with a piton and hold it steady as McKnight slid down with the depleted provisions.

The glow from the lighthouse storeroom above barely penetrated the darkness. The only suggestion of a deeper world was the wall at their backs and the sparkles that still peppered the blackness like celestial bodies. And still the bagpipes droned on.

"He's calling us," McKnight decided. "Leerie . . ."

"Guiding us," Canavan agreed, awed.

And indeed they found it difficult not to warm to the appeal, the cry of one so long lost, entombed in darkness and begging as much as Evelyn to be free.

They hammered pitons into the wall and took step after step, then slid down a curved surface coated with fungus. By the time they had landed at the floor of the massive chamber they were grazed and thirsty and covered in adhesive grime. Their lanterns had given out entirely. They looked up to see the square of doorway an impossible distance above and the cord ladder hanging from it like a forlorn tongue. They emptied their canteens and dispensed with their weapons.

They trudged with great uncertainty across the undulating floor, never sure when they would stumble over a ridge or be swallowed by a pit. The surface was at times so hot that their shoe soles smoldered, and in places so covered in writhing creatures that they could barely take a step without crunching some scampering form. The sounds merged with that of their own sawing breaths and returned to them in the echoes of an eternal whispering gallery, strangely musical now, as though joined in some incomprehensible hymn.

Halting, they felt a breath of incongruously cool air and the sensation of moisture, and perceived the nearby rustle of water, which at first they had mistaken for another echo. It was a river, flowing swiftly by the sound of it, but invisible to their eyes save for the faint phosphorescence accompanying the churning of the currents.

"The Styx?" breathed McKnight, and Canavan dropped to a crouch and extended a hand, dipping his fingers into the current.

"Freezing," he said.

McKnight nodded. "The Frigid River."

They listened in vain for the sound of a ferryman and even jangled some coins hopefully, but they heard nothing until, making their way down the banks, they noticed a change in the tenor of the current—more agitated now—and they discerned, amid the great luminous swirls, huge blocks or boulders laid across the river like stepping-stones.

"Of course," McKnight said. "Even Leerie needs to get out."

"But he has wings," Canavan noted.

"Then he has laid them down in a nightmare, specifically for our access."

The stones were the great marble remains of a church altar, and

McKnight and Canavan now hopped warily from one to another, fight-ing to maintain a foothold and not slip into the fabled waters. When they reached the other side they looked up with gloom-adjusted eyes and saw that what from afar had looked like stars were in fact highly reflec-tive jewels set into the adamantine walls of a massive citadel. It was a structure so dark, so hostile to light, that it stood out even against the blackness, and they were soon able to descry lofty towers and spires thrusting into the heavens. But approaching the great plated walls they found no doorway, no aperture, no hint of an entrance or a window, and no inkling of how even the music might have escaped. Leerie had been sealed in a seemingly impregnable fortress.

"We might need to climb," McKnight said, looking doubtfully at the bejeweled walls.

But Canavan now retreated a few steps, and was quiet a few moments, mustering his powers. And when he spoke it was in a determined whisper.

"Lift up your heads, o ye gates . . . and be ye lifted up, ye everlasting doors . . . and the King of Glory shall come in. . . ."

In immediate response to the sacred command the walls of the great castle shook, there was a cascade of glittering dust, and two of the mas-sive blocks separated just enough to reveal a narrow and brilliantly lit passage into the chambers within.

McKnight turned in wonder and saw in Joseph Canavan a bleeding and strangely luminous longhaired figure in tattered clothes resembling robes.

✠

The stairs were delineated with snow, and the steps creaked in protest as she ascended. She looked up through the broken corbels and the charred oaken beams, her hand gliding over the jagged banister, her head all the time feeling on the verge of collapse.

Remembering Ainslie's stuttering ascent when he had carried her up to Leerie, on stairs that were at that time immaculate, she arrived on the landing and turned to what had been her bedroom, and from where lamp glow now emanated just as it had twenty years earlier.

She shuffled tightly toward the door . . . and arrived there unblink-ing . . . and peered with great dread into the room.

There was an old man inside, staring back at her.

He was folded into an austere little chair in the middle of the room, underlit by a low-burning lamp. He looked surprised, even alarmed, to see her.

"Who . . . who is it?" he whispered, as though he had been expecting someone else.

She stared at him wordlessly.

He blinked and squinted, and finally seemed to understand. "Evelyn?" he said with awe.

And though she did not answer, the old man decided it made perfect sense, and squinting some more he ascertained that it was indeed his former charge—fully mature now, and bearing an even greater resemblance to his departed wife—and he eased back in his chair, delighted that she had honored him with a personal visit and overwhelmed by the prospect that she would effect his punishment with her own hands, in full command of her senses.

"It is I, child," he whispered, smiling in welcome.

Her eyes widened in recognition.

"It's Lindsay."

✠

He was what incalculable generations had made him, the personification of ultimate evil. He had the eyes of a crocodile, the ears of a boar, the horns of a steer, the teeth of a tiger, the rings of a pirate, the nostrils of a savage, the beard of a dilettante, the hide of a bull, the shaggy flanks of a stag, the hooves of a goat, the wings of a bat, the talons of an eagle, the tail of a scorpion, the exaggerated physique of a colossus, and the robes of a pharaoh. He was ensconced in an ornate throne of bonelike forms in the center of a majestic candelabra-lit chamber of impossibly intricate carvings and fantastically ornamented crystal pillars, the whole palace of a type that had rarely existed on earth, for if there is one thing that is constant about evil, it is that it has always had more money than sense.

Spotting his visitors he discarded his pipes like a toy and swept down the crimson-carpeted steps to welcome them, bowing deeply before McKnight and kissing Canavan on both cheeks with puckered equine lips. Rising to his full height, he looked down on them, smiling, and relinquished two decades of despair.

"It really has been too long," he said sincerely, for all the world like an old soldier greeting battle-scarred comrades at a reunion.

✠

The walls had sagged, and the roof was in places open, exposing the spars, but of all the rooms in the lodge this one had survived in perhaps the best condition, and she knew every inch of it in memories more deeply branded than any stigmata. She moved forward, swaying uncontrollably, her eyes fixed on the decayed, shivering figure watching her from beneath the still-severe brow.

"You must administer His wrath, child," the old man croaked, commanding even in contrition. He watched approvingly as Evelyn pulled apart the drawstrings of her purse, and he closed his eyes in preparation for oblivion. "Come and soothe away my bitter pain," he whispered, "for I am weary of the struggle."

Evelyn stood over the wrinkled form and slowly removed the weapon, her movements dictated as though by some higher force.

✠

Individually they could not have done it, but united their power was beyond measure. Using a thorn-wood staff and a candelabrum as large as a scepter, they levered back the already parted blocks so that there was just sufficient room for Leerie to squeeze through.

The whole edifice shook as though in an earthquake, there were showers of plaster and gold dust from the vaulted ceiling, and great cracks snaked up the walls and enmeshed in splintering webs. The very foundations were beginning to crumble.

Leerie looked back and regarded his collapsing castle with a hint of regret.

"Will you miss it?" Canavan asked.

The lamplighter considered. "Once I'm relieved of this form," he decided confidently, "and free to walk outside her nightmares, it will not take me long to secure a new asylum."

"Another part of the world? Another immense imagination?"

The lamplighter smiled, as though he already had a destination in mind. "I would like to stay in Edinburgh and look over Eve awhile," he replied. "Though I think this time a simple seedy imagination will suffice."

A chandelier exploded at his hooves.

"There are moments for fond memories and speculation," McKnight observed, "and there are times when it is best not to tarry. May I suggest that we make haste, gentlemen, before we are buried in rubble?"

He spoke not in reproach, however, but with genuine affection, and indeed for all of them there was a transcendent sense of accomplishment. As they departed the huge citadel, the walls of the old world collapsed behind them in great ungodly heaps of marble and plaster, and a new landscape opened up before them, illuminated as though by the sun, with horizons that were practically limitless.

✠

At least twenty minutes had passed without a cry, a whimper, or any perceivable sound at all, and Groves instructed a strangely peevish Pringle to cover the rear of the lodge while he circulated around the forecourt warily, suddenly fearing that she had committed her crime and then taken off into the skies, or disappeared into a pit, or vanished like the Beast into a knot of heated air.

But when at last he saw her, materializing dazedly through the doorway like a ghost, he actually yelped with excitement. "There!" he cried, to alert Pringle, and immediately he was springing on her and wrapping her up before she could spirit herself away, though in truth she was not in the least bit defensive or protesting.

"What have you done?" Groves breathed. He attempted to cuff her, but his own hands were shaking with excitement, and she was holding fast to something, her fist was closed around it, and he observed that she was no longer clutching her purse.

"Pin her arms, laddie!" he ordered when Pringle appeared, and, taking hold of her forearm, he tried with all his might to pry open her fingers.

She was astonishingly resistant, even in her stupefied state. He grunted and cursed but finally managed to uncurl her fist and disarm her of her terrible weapon, which fell into the tangled grass. But it was so small he almost lost sight of it. He foraged around and snatched it up and found it almost breaking apart in his hand. He stared at it, frowning in disbelief.

A blunted stick of white chalk.

He looked at Evelyn, then at Pringle, and then at the lodge.

"Hold . . . hold her tight," he breathed, and, gulping, he plunged into the darkness.

He ascended the staircase at a reckless speed, possessed of an urgent need for discovery. He needed, in truth, a corpse—a man with his throat slit, his chest blown open, his head lolling and spilling streams of blood. And yet in all the time Evelyn had been inside he had heard not a gunshot, not a gurgle or even an impulsive squeal—nothing. And the only thing he heard even now, as he rounded the landing, was an insane cackle that turned his dreams to vapor.

He arrived at the open doorway and stood there for a full minute, gasping, trying to make sense of it all.

Abraham Lindsay, former governor of the Fountainbridge Institute for Destitute Girls, was seated beside his dying lamp, laughing with the euphoria of a punishment greater, even, than death. *Existence.*

Groves looked around the room with astonishment and despair.

The floor and the blackened walls—all the available surfaces—were festooned with figures meticulously rendered in chalk. Fire-breathing dragons, monstrous butterflies, fantastic griffins, capering fairies, frowning goblins, mischievous trolls, bearded wizards, and grinning lamplighters . . . and all of them turned in on Abraham Lindsay, surrounding him, closing in on him, *daring* him to imprison them again and feel the sting of their vengeance.

Epilogue

IT WAS A MOMENT to savor. Facing a polished doorknob set in a paneled door, Professor Thomas McKnight—snugly attired in tweed, with a cherry-wood pipe in his mouth and a substantial meal in his stomach—drew on a pair of luxurious suede gloves, flexed his fingers delightedly, extended his hand slowly, and—with the utmost diligence, so as not to blemish the brass with a single stain—took hold of the gleaming knob and swiveled his hand with clockwork precision. The oiled bolt withdrew with a ready click, his heart quickened and his nerves fluttered, and he simply stood there, breathing the warmed air, before pressing back the door on his newly renovated and lavishly appointed abode.

It was beyond the limits of his wildest dreams. A cavernous library greater than anything in London, the Vatican, or historical Alexandria. Glassed cabinets, polished mahogany bookcases, and sturdy oaken shelves swept ten storys high and half a mile deep, complete with spiral staircases, ladders on greased rails, and carpeted balconies that trailed into infinity. There were reading carrels, escritoires, cozy armchairs, blazing hearths, silent clocks, drinking fountains, innumerable writing utensils, reams of blank notepaper, a row of magnifying glasses . . . even a pipe rack. And all of it illuminated with more lamp cabinets and gas mantels than there were stars in the firmament. He might never leave.

He exhaled heartily, surveying both the gold-embossed spines already arranged on the shelves and the crates spilling over with folios, quartos, octavos, and priceless manuscripts waiting to be catalogued. He barely knew where to begin. But as the appointed curator he had a lifetime, and he doubted his excitement would ever wane.

His only regret was the absence of Canavan, with whom he might have shared his sense of satisfaction, his great triumph. But he consoled himself with the thought that Evelyn had installed his friend in a place of even greater magnitude, and even more beauty, than this majestic repository of knowledge.

✠

On a Boxing Day of cerulean skies and thundering church bells, Evelyn Todd roamed the streets and alleys of the Old Town, as she had done every Sunday, to feed the city's strays with chopped meat provided by Arthur Stark.

It was difficult to explain, but this morning, despite the fact that she was still under nominal investigation—though clearly the Sheriff and Procurator Fiscal gave little credence to Inspector Groves's increasingly flaccid accusations—she felt unusually content, giddily so. She moved not furtively or sheepishly but with true assurance. The dogs, which had previously accepted her proffered morsels and quickly recoiled, now lingered at her side and sniffed her repeatedly, as though to verify that this was in fact the same person. The reliant strays had always gladdened her heart, but to this point she had felt shielded from any expression of pleasure by some antiseptic force. Now she dropped to her haunches, genuinely welcoming of the attention, and in response the dogs circulated around her with ears flat and tails dancing. She put out her hand and scratched the neck of a tousled mongrel, which tilted its head gratefully.

Emerging from a workhouse door nearby, a broad-shouldered man ambled up the wynd and, seeing her thus encircled, smiled and tipped his hat. Their eyes locked, however briefly. Then one of the strays peeled off to follow him, and when it brushed his leg he briefly lowered a hand to ruffle its head before turning into the festive street and making off into the sunshine.

Evelyn rose and looked after him as the dog trotted back to her side. There had been a shared communication, she was sure of it, and she found herself hoping that the stranger would reappear and explain himself or flash another smile. But a minute passed, the dogs nudged at her, and she squatted down again to resume her ministrations, dismissing the hope as a fleeting absurdity. There had been no recognition, she assured herself, and in any case she had no time for such frivolity.

But in the back of her mind, in some steadily brightening recess, she could not help wondering if she might one day find a man onto whom she could project the divine qualities of the one wrapped in the warm petals of her heart.

✠

39. Higher authorities than I have their own opinions, and it is not for the likes of me to question them, and though they had retired the case, and were happy to think of the murders as unsolved, I continued to follow Evelyn Todd the Wax Woman of my own accord, and when she slept, I began to notice an old man lurking in the street outside her building, a lamplighter, who once even had the cheek to wink at me, as if we were well acquainted.

40. I followed this bold leerie, with his deceptively friendly features, but he disappeared before I managed to track him to his home, and neither did I see him again in any of the lamplighter assemblies, so that my suspicions grew, and have since been consolidated.

41. Strolling in the vicinity of Queen Street Gardens last February, Evelyn Todd was recognized by the former matron Hettie Lessels, who others have decided is mad, and this unfortunate woman, briefly taking leave of her senses, issued a cry of alarm and tried to attack the former foundling, and scratch her to the ground, only to fail due to the swift intervention of the man whose description closely matches the lamplighter I have already mentioned, and who whisked Miss Todd to safety before vanishing without a trace.

42. This incident was noted by several witnesses, and I saw it myself at the very same time, in a dream of remarkable clarity.

43. I believe that this lamplighter has been Miss Todd's protector, her guardian angel, and that he was embroiled deeply in the sinister goings-on that for some weeks beset the Modern Athens, and I will follow him to Hades if necessary to solve this terrible mystery.

44. Be sober, be vigilant, said the saintly Piper McNab through the Epistle of Saint Peter, because our adversary the devil, as a roaring lion, walketh about, and as a humble servant of the Lord I can do no better than to repeat this admonition, for the lesson of this whole bloody episode is that while we are all carved in the image of God, we can never be certain where the Evil One might lurketh.

The Lamplighter

My tea is nearly ready
    and the sun has left the sky;
It's time to take the window
    to see Leerie going by;
For every night at tea-time
    and before you take your seat,
With lantern and with ladder
    he comes posting up the street.

Now Tom would be a driver
    and Maria go to sea,
And my papa's a banker
    and as rich as he can be;
But I, when I am stronger
    and can choose what I'm to do,
O Leerie, I'll go round at night,
    and light the lamps with you!

For we are very lucky,
    with a lamp before the door,
And Leerie stops to light it
    as he lights so many more;
And O! before you hurry by
    with ladder and with light,
O Leerie, see a little child
    and nod to him tonight!

ROBERT LOUIS STEVENSON,
A Child's Garden of Verses, 1885

Acknowledgments

Of the innumerable writers whose works on Edinburgh I consulted I am particularly indebted to Robert Louis Stevenson, James McLevy, James McGowan, J. W. McLaren, Alisdair MacGregor, Charles McKean, E. F. Catford, George Baird, J. M. Barrie, Thomas Speedy, Sandy Mullay, and David Masson. For matters of the mind I tip my hat to Ernest Geller, Seth Pringle-Patterson, Robert C. Solomon, James Hillman, Jacques Maritain, Mario Praz, Philip J. Davis, Walter E. Houghton, George Frederick Drinka, Alan Gould, Henri F. Ellenberger, Robert Van de Castle, and Peter O'Connor. For diabolical substance I bow deferentially before Rossell Hope Robbins, Alice K. Turner, R. Love Thompson, Piero Camporesi, Alan E. Bernstein, and Sir Walter Scott. And for miscellaneous subjects I thank Molly Weir, Mary Peckham Magray, Catriona Clear, R. W. Munro, J. A. R. Stevenson, and Bella Bathurst.

In Edinburgh I was graciously assisted by Patricia and Donald Watt, Eddie McMillan of the Lothian and Borders Police, Ann Nix and the good people at the Edinburgh Room of the Central Library and the National Library of Scotland, and Pam McNicol of the Edinburgh City Archives. I further wish to acknowledge the gracious help of Carl Harrison-Ford, Jean Curthoys, Linda Funnell, Mark Gibson, Doctors A. Chin and J. G. Kendler, Guy Carvalho, and T. C. Macleod. And for obvious reasons Rose Creswell, Kim Witherspoon, David Forrer, Mark Lucas, Annette Hughes, Sadie Chrestman, Shona Martyn, Joan Deitch, Emma Kelso, John McGhee, Tegan Murray, and my astute editors Colin Harrison, Flora Rees, and Rod Morrison.

About the Author

Anthony O'Neill is the son of an Irish policeman and an Australian stenographer. He lives in Melbourne.

CPSIA information can be obtained
at www.ICGtesting.com
Printed in the USA
LVHW041656251021
701495LV00013B/576